Thunder of Silence

To Martha:
Enjoy this journey
Vicki Diane Westling

Vicki Diane Westling

authorHOUSE®

AuthorHouse™
1663 Liberty Drive
Bloomington, IN 47403
www.authorhouse.com
Phone: 1-800-839-8640

First published by AuthorHouse   8/10/2009

ISBN: 978-1-4490-0590-0 (e)
ISBN: 978-1-4490-0588-7 (sc)
ISBN: 978-1-4490-0589-4 (hc)

Library of Congress Control Number: 2009906878

Printed in the United States of America
Bloomington, Indiana

This book is printed on acid-free paper.

Thunder of Silence is dedicated to my sister Jan whose unwavering support, encouragement and love kept me going during times when I was ready to quit. You are my idol and best friend.

And to my husband, Richard, whose patience and understanding throughout this process has been more than any wife should reasonably expect. You are my heart and my soul.

To Jan and Richard, thank you, I will forever be in your debt.

PART I

... Practicality and dreams are not synonymous,
as we grow older we learn such.
Dreams become secrets
not meant to be kept
and practicality becomes a burden
with responsibilities to be met

Chapter One

Thaddeus Flanders was a man closing in on seventy who had lived his life outwardly as an honorable husband, uncle and friend. Now he was facing the sobering knowledge of his imminent mortality and the thunder of all that had been hidden inside of him was about to break the silence of his saintly façade.

Now as he sat on his front porch smoking his pipe and whittling a piece of cherry wood, his mind raced back some two decades earlier to a time he had tried to forget but which remained instead folded into the crevices of his memory ready to spring forward when he least wanted it to. How could so many things have gone so terribly wrong, he wondered. He remembered that day as if it were yesterday; he could see the images in his mind, smell the cigar smoke and hear the voices … … …

……… He was once again sitting in the smoke filled boardroom of the St. Lawrence Railroad Company. "Excuse me Mr. Flanders, we just received this here wire and I was told to get it to you right away," the clerk whispered as he handed Thaddeus the piece of paper. It was a telegram from Matthew. It seemed that Matthew was in St. Louis and once again he had found an opportunity to get himself into trouble, he needed cash and he needed a lot of it fast. He had bailed Matthew out of more scrapes and had given him more money than he ever told Martha about, and he knew he would do it again. Each time he would hand over whatever it was that Matthew needed, but he was never quite sure if it was out of guilt or shame. Now, again Matthew was calling and he would respond. What had he done now? He was annoyed by Matthew's lack of personal responsibility. Although the message sounded a bit contrived, it did appear that there might be a serious problem. His feelings of guilt and sense of responsibility for Matthew once again surfaced. There were so many complications. He was in Chicago and Matthew in St. Louis; the timing was typical

3

Matthew...at his convenience and the rest of the world be damned. It was Friday afternoon and the banks had already closed. Swearing under his breath he rose as discreetly as possible and quietly excused himself from the meeting. He took the telegram into an adjacent room to contemplate what he would do. He took a chair by the window, and as he lit his pipe and inhaled he could feel the tingling and almost burning sensation of the smoke traveling down his throat and into his lungs. He closed his eyes as he considered his options only to be once again interrupted. This time it seemed that his friend Herbert Bernstein had left a message asking him to share dinner with him that evening. Unlike Matthew, Herbert's timing was impeccable, as usual. Once again he was grateful for Herbert. But, gratitude would in time turn to regret and heartache. He remembered breathing a sigh of relief and saying out loud, Thank God for Herbert. How many times since that day, he wondered had he wished that he had never responded to either one of them? He could still see every detail of the small room, just as if he were looking into his own drawing room today. The smell of the dampness, and the cold air was all about him. The memories lingered. He remembered the note he wrote to Herb advising him that he must decline dinner, but could meet him for a quick drink at the Railroad Station at 5:30. He added that he would be grateful if Herb had his usual emergency fund. He would explain the situation to Herbert and borrow the cash until the banks opened. This would be the last time, he told himself, he would tell Matthew how he really felt about his philandering and he would make sure that Matthew knew this was the end of the line. Damn, Matthew. Goddamn Matthew! He knew then, as well as now the person whom he was really damning was himself for his own weakness and failure. And, he knew that it was that very weakness to succumb to the forbidden with which Matthew was possessed.

Trying to shake loose the memory, he stood up and shook his head as if to remove the haunting thoughts from a lifetime ago, at least for now. He must turn his attention to a problem that he could do something about. But, the memories, the smells, the racing of his pulse and the fear were as real today as they were then. Now, sitting here waiting for Daphnia to return from her picnic how he wished that dreadful night had never happened. Where is she, anyway? He called into the house, "Martha, when is Daphnia coming home? I didn't want her to go out today, why did you let her go?"

Thaddeus and Martha had been married for close to fifty years. Their lives together were rich and full. Over the years they had buried a son, a brother, her mother and father as well as his own, Thaddeus' brother, Joshua and his wife Sarah; Matthew was their son. Daphnia was Matthew's daughter.

Daphnia was barely four years old when she came to live with them on their large farm just outside of Lansing, Michigan. With its rolling hills and crisp, clean air there was an abundance of laughter at Sunshine Acres once Daphnia moved in. Until then, they had pretty much gone on with their lives as if they were living in a vacuum. Martha still mourned the loss of their only son, and Thaddeus was kept busy with the railroad. But now Daphnia was all grown up and about to be the trigger that could release a flood of heartache and long held secrets.

"Mart, Mart, when is she coming back? It is getting late, Mart, can you hear me?" he called into the house.

"Good Lord, Thaddeus, you are going to wake the dead. What on earth is bothering you? What has gotten you so upset?" the round little woman asked as she hurried toward the front door. "You know perfectly well that Daphnia and young William have gone on a picnic, they are meeting up with some friends over near Peterson Creek, what has got you so worked up?"

"I am not worked up, Martha! I just have some things to talk with Daphnia about and I wish she would get on back here so I could get this out of the way. Herb and Melissa want her to come to Huron

City for a while, and I'm just not all that anxious to let her go. This time won't be like any of the others. I won't be there to keep things in check, and she won't be coming back right away, if at all. This time I won't be able to stop them, this time she will be at their mercy and the mercy of that town that they love so much. I wish to God we had had this talk long ago, where did the time go, Mart, have we been so wrong all these years? Damn Melissa, by God Martha I wish I could damn her straight to hell, but I just can't, you should have seen her. I swear she looks just like innocence all wrapped up in a woman's smile. Where the hell is Daphnia, why did you let her go today, why doesn't he bring her back?"

"Now, Thaddeus, get hold of yourself, it will all work out. You know Daphnia, she makes up her own mind, lessen she gets into one of those spells of hers and lets her mind wander off into Lord knows where, but she'll come around, she'll do the right thing, you'll see. Now, lie back on that pillow and shut your eyes, supper won't be ready for awhile yet. Try to remember what it was like to be young and out on a picnic on a crisp clear summer day like today. And Thaddeus, stop all of this crazy talk about Melissa, I don't want to hear no more! Try to remember the good times, the sweet times, the times you and me used to have, do you think you can do that, Thaddeus? Do you think you can clear your mind of all this nonsense and remember the goodness of being young?"

"Mart, remembering is not a problem for me, at least not yet. I just wish you had told her not to be out late this evening; I wanted to see her when I got in. Didn't you tell her that I was coming home today? I thought that since she knew I was coming in from Huron City that she would be eager to hear anything I had to say about Melissa." Then pulling on her hand he pleaded, "Martha, stay out here and sit with me awhile."

She sat down on the other end of the porch swing and patted her lap, "Here, now, you put that stuff down and rest your head in my lap. You can tell me all about Huron City and what's going on with Herbert and Ruth, I don't much care about what's happening to Melissa, any woman who would give up a baby as sweet as Daphnia out of pure selfishness don't need to take up any room in my heart or my mind either for that matter. Tell me about Herbert and Ruth. It has been so long since I seen them, and we used to have such good times. How long have you and Herbert been friends anyway? Almost fifty years I expect. How are things in Huron City?"

He laid his head in her lap but he didn't feel like talking, at least not about Huron City. He was thinking of earlier times that she hadn't any idea about. With Martha gently massaging his temples he drifted off to sleep as his thoughts of Daphnia soon disappeared giving way to a peaceful rest. She would be home soon, and besides Martha was right, Daphnia and young William were just enjoying the luxuries of being young on a beautiful summer day. And, if there was anyone with whom he could trust Daphnia's well being it was William Johnston. The two had practically grown up together. The Johnston's lived the next farm over, albeit a tenement farm, but they were good people who worked hard. His father had some problems with the liquor and the women in town, but his mother didn't seem to notice. William was a fine young man. Thaddeus smiled as he remembered picnics on warm sunny days such as today, and he envied the two young lovers. He took in a deep breath and sank into a peaceful slumber there in the soft lap of Martha.

"Come on Daphnia. Daphnia, come on, get up, put your shoes on they're waiting for us," William Johnston urged as he gently shook her shoulder. "Get up, get your shoes, let's go. Where are you shoes anyway?" he asked almost absentmindedly.

She heard him, but she didn't want to wake up. What was he talking about? Shoes! It's always shoes. Why do I go back there? She thought as she shielded her face from the sun with her hand and looked up into the laughing green eyes of William. "I just need a little time, William. You go on ahead without me, I'll catch up."

He sat down on the blanket, and cupping her face in his hands he kissed her gently. They had spent many hours together over the years, and he knew her better than she knew herself, and she knew him equally as well. With the changing of the seasons he had watched her grow into someone to be reckoned with. But lately her independence had become more pronounced and it seemed that she was anxious to be alone, it was as though she were wrapped in her own private thoughts and dreams more frequently than usual. He felt confused and shut out, and he wanted to ask questions, he wanted to talk about their future, he wanted to tell her about the colonel, he wanted to tell her that he loved her. He needed to find a way to break the silence and shake up her contentment with him, but he just didn't know how. He just never seemed to be able to find the right time to ask her the one question he wanted so desperately to ask. He could not give her up, he could not let her go, and he could not ask her to leave all that she had to marry him, a person of no wealth, no land and nothing by which to provide for her. Now as he looked into her eyes, he felt a peculiarity about their relationship. For the first time in all their years together he could feel the hair on the back of his neck stand out. For a brief second he questioned just who was waiting for whom. And now this business with the colonel made his future even more up in the air; he felt his confidence in their relationship and in himself begin to shake.

"Daphnia, hey look, maybe we should talk about some things, about us, maybe we should talk about things, I don't want to just leave you here alone. I mean, maybe we should talk. Do you want to talk, Daphnia?"

"What do you want to talk about William? Is everything okay? I'm safe here, it isn't as though I haven't napped right here on this very spot hundreds of times before. Are you sure you are feeling alright, you're acting a little strange today, is there something on your mind that can't wait until later? Go ahead, I'll be fine."

"I'm not acting strange. I am a little tense maybe, but honestly, Daphnia you have a way … fine, I'll go but I still don't like leaving you here alone. I just, well I just, I'll make an excuse for you to the others. I'll tell them you are wrapped up in your own private world, off on your own, exploring God only knows what." He stood up all the while looking down at her and almost gave way to his desire to hold her, but he couldn't bring himself to move.

"Well, go ahead, William, don't worry about me. And, William, please don't be mad with me I guess I am in the mood to just be alone for a while. Do you mind terribly?"

"Okay, Daffy Girl, if that is the way you want it. Lie back and rest, you can stay here all alone if that is what suits you. I'll tell the others that you are staying here among the heather and primroses, I'll tell them that you are wrapped snuggly in your day dreams and are taking a trip on the sunbeams to a place that only you can know."

She smiled as she watched him walk away. As much as she enjoyed his company, she was happy that he left her so that she could be quiet and think, she had too many thoughts all swirling around in her head, and she didn't know what to do with them. Lately she was disturbed by fresh memories and haunted by old nightmares. There was something missing that she was unable to pinpoint about her life. She felt as if there was something buried deep in her subconscious and until she finds it she can't move forward. She knew that until this internal mystery was solved and her haunting memories were pieced together she could not concentrate on William or anything else.

She needed to sort out what was real and what was not. Were her dreams just dreams or could there be something in her past, some memory that was trying to surface, could it be the answer she was searching for? Closing her eyes and kicking her shoes off the blanket, she allowed herself to drift into a peaceful sleep. Peace was not to be long lasting during this nap. Once again she felt herself in between lifetimes. It was as if something or someone was pulling her and she could not resist. She could hear her mother's voice calling … … …

… … … *"Daphnia, get your shoes dear or you'll miss the train. Daphnia, hurry up, where are your shoes?"*

"What train, Mother? Where are we going? It is still dark outside, Mother. Why are we going in the dark?"

Although it was a warm and sunny June afternoon in the year 1904, she was reliving a much earlier time… … … The year was 1884, and Daphnia was just four years old, it was cold and damp outside and in her heart she knew that her Mother was sending her away.

"Where are we going, Mother?"

"You are going on a train ride to Lansing, Dear."

"Just me, Mother? Aren't you coming with me?"

"No, Daphnia, I am not coming with you. You are going to see your Great Uncle Thaddeus and Great Aunt Martha. You will be living on a farm with ducks and cows and all sorts of animals. Now, hurry, dear, please hurry."

"A farm? Where is Lansing? Who are Uncle Thaddeus and Aunt Martha?

"Oh, Daphnia, please don't ask so many questions. Now please go find your shoes."

"But, Mother, I don't want to go. I don't want to leave you and Aunt Ella I don't know Thaddeus and Martha.

"You must go, Daphnia, Thaddeus and Martha are waiting for you. You will like them Daphnia; they are wonderful people. They have wanted to spend some time with you for a while now and they will love you very much. Your Uncle Thaddeus is on the Railroad Commission for the St. Lawrence Railway out of Lansing. You might get to ride with the engineer and blow the whistle. Oh, hurry, Daphnia, please hurry. You will miss the train. Now, go find your shoes, Daphnia, hurry, dear."

Daphnia knew just where her shoes were. Knowing that there was no need to argue with her Mother when she was in a hurry she gave up and ran down the hallway and through the kitchen to the back steps. There they were, just where she had left them. She sat down and put on the little shoes. With her chest puffed out and a big smile on her face she walked back into the parlor showing off the scuffed brown shoes. Her moment of pride faded as she saw the familiar look of anger and disapproval on her Mother's face. She felt shame and sadness and looked away from her Mother's piercing glare... ... ...

Awakening with a chill, she sat up and shook her head trying to remember what she had just dreamed and why she felt haunted by fleeting dreams and memories that she did not understand.

She thought of her mother and could see her in her mind just as clearly as she could see the blades of grass before her.

***

Melissa Flanders was neither tall nor short. She was of slight build with raven black hair, which she braided into a bun and pinned to the back of her head. She was a pretty woman with large violet eyes that looked almost iridescent; her skin was like ivory and it was flawless. Her lips were full and soft and the color of the tiny tea roses outside of the kitchen window. While others often told her how very beautiful she was, Melissa did not think of herself as pretty, and she rarely smiled. But, when she did it was as if the entire room would light up. Her laugh was like music and she could charm the most worthy opponent into submission.

***

Daphnia could remember her Mother laughing only once. It was during the last Christmas holiday they shared as a real family. Daphnia's father had come home on Christmas Eve with a little monkey dressed up like a band leader with cymbals tied to its hands. The monkey danced around and banged the cymbals; it was wonderful.

Two days later her father left and took the little monkey with him. He left her a doll with a china face, but he didn't say goodbye. When she awoke, and the house was quiet, it was as though the whole thing had been a dream. Melissa was again sad and disapproving of any noise, laughter or questions. Daphnia learned to play alone. She had make-believe conversations with her dolls and at least one invisible friend, but she saved her questions for when the doctor or Aunt Ella had time to talk with her.

Thinking of her Aunt Ella brought a smile to her face and she once again lay back on the pillows and drifted off to sleep. The dream came back exactly where she had left it earlier... ... ...

… … … "Please don't be unhappy, Mother," she pleaded as she stood in the foyer and looked up into Melissa's eyes and tear-stained face. Daphnia needed to hear a word of praise for finding her shoes. But, even at the age of four, she knew her Mother would not have any kind words for her this morning. She realized that in her eagerness to show her Mother how grown up she was she had only added to her disappointment and unhappiness.

"Oh, Daphnia, not those shoes. Where are your Sunday shoes?"

Daphnia had put on her favorite shoes. They were brown with scuffed toes and they had laces - not buckles. She had a hard time with buttons and buckles. She didn't understand how her Mother could fasten all of those buttons every day, the buttonhook was too hard for her and she couldn't pull it through with the button still in place. Daphnia loved the little brown shoes. They were warm and her toes stayed snug and dry.

"Please, Mother, please, these are my favorites. Besides I can't find the other ones."

"Just hurry, Daphnia, please just hurry."

Melissa had begun to sob as she often did during times of stress and with this Daphnia knew that she would be wearing the little brown shoes on her trip. Daphnia grabbed her coat and while her Mother was nervously tying on her own bonnet, Daphnia pulled on her stocking cap with one hand while trying to fasten her coat with the other. She was sure the mittens were in the pockets somewhere.

Walking out into the cold winter morning she was startled by the horseman and carriage waiting at their gate. She was not used to riding to the station, and she had never ridden in a carriage like this. Her mother had said there was not enough money for such things as carriage rides.

She stood looking at the carriage not sure of how to get inside of it. With one swoop of his arm, the carriage driver scooped Daphnia up and sat her down firmly inside the carriage on the seat facing forward; her mother stepped in behind her and sat down next to her. Daphnia smiled as she saw her Aunt Ella sitting on the other seat of the carriage facing them. As Daphnia started to squirm down from her seat to go over to that of the kind and gentlewoman, she felt the wheels begin to move tossing her off balance. As her mother reached to grab hold of her, Daphnia saw her Mother was sobbing.

"Why are you crying Mother? What is wrong?"

"Don't worry about it, dear, you just think about the wonderful time you are going to be having very soon." As Melissa patted Daphnia's hand she looked down at the little face and the innocent eyes of a little girl who loved her and one she wanted so desperately to love, but couldn't. Melissa put her arm around Daphnia and held her close.

The Carriage moved forward and Daphnia could hear the clip clop of the horse's hooves hitting the bricks. There was a slight mist in the air, and she could see the treetops gently swaying. As she looked through the window of the carriage, she played a silent game with the bare branches; to her they looked like great hands with long crooked fingers sticking out in all directions. The sun was rising in the east and there were streaks of pink and yellow starting to spread across the sky. She was restless. She had so many questions. As she sat quietly, she thought they would never get to the train station, the horses obviously didn't know any of the shortcuts. Leaning against the warm firm body of her mother she could smell the sweet scent of lavender, and as she laid her head next to her mother's side she could hear her steady breathing. Melissa pulled her close and held her in her arms gently rocking her and singing a lullaby, and she thought this the most wonderful feeling she had ever known and silently prayed for it not to end, as she slipped off into a quiet peaceful slumber.

As William approached the blanket he could see that Daphnia had fallen asleep. The sun was beginning its downward slide, and there was a chill creeping in the air. He lay down next to her and pulled her into his arms. He loved her very much, his heart was crying out to ask the question, but he couldn't do it. There were things that he must do first. He must make a name for himself; he wouldn't live on her money or that of her Great Uncle Thaddeus. He needed to prove that he was somebody, and someone worthy of loving her. He pulled her closer to him and breathed in the smell of her hair and ran his fingers across her neck. He knew it would be some time before he could hold her this close again; he needed to tell her that he was leaving, but not just yet.

Awakened by William's kisses, her dreams of her days as a child with her Mother faded. He was all she wanted for the rest of her life, he was good and kind and had shared a part of her very soul. William Johnston was a man of order. He stood just six feet tall but carried himself with such pride that others often thought him much taller. The scent of him was that of the land and woods around him. She snuggled under his chin and breathed deeply.

"We better get back, Daphnia, come on let's get a move on, get your shoes, let's go." Pushing her away from him he stood and started to pick up the remains from their picnic.

"What's the rush, William? It is so beautiful here. Don't you want me, William?" Whispering about his face and neck teasing him she ran her hands about his chest and shoulders.

"You know I want you and I love you. But, there are things I need to do later. Besides, if I don't get you home, Mr. Flanders won't let me hear the end of it. You know how upset he gets when you miss supper. Now, come on, I need to get you home. C'mon now, let's get movin'."

"Okay, but you'll be sorry." Gathering her things she started for the buggy while William followed behind her with the basket, blanket and pillows. He placed the things in the back of the buggy, unhitched the horse from the tree, and got onto the seat next to Daphnia. Taking in a breath of air, and looking to the western sky with the sun setting, he knew he had to tell her his plans. He could wait no longer.

"Daphnia, there is something that I need to tell you," he said as calmly as possible. Then, taking the reigns in his hands and making a clicking noise for the horse to begin his steady trot toward home, he steadied himself focusing his eyes on the road ahead of them, he wanted to say what he had to say in the same manner in which he had rehearsed it so many times over the past few days.

"You sound so serious, William, what is it?"

"Daphnia, last month I talked to Colonel Jackson of the 94th Infantry out of Detroit. He made me get to thinking about our future, I mean, well I mean my future and yours too if it turns out that way, but it, well Daphnia, things have to be right."

"Right? What do you mean things have to be right? William, what is it that is wrong?"

"Everything is wrong, Daphnia. I have to get away from here to make them right, and, well, anyway I have been doing a lot of thinking lately, and Daphnia, I have enlisted in the US Calvary. I could have gone years ago, but with Pop not doing so good, and all the younger ones at home, well it just wouldn't have been right. But now the colonel has told me that I can finish my schooling and in the meantime I can work right along side of the medics and doctors. I know I am a lot older than the others who are enlisting, but with things the way they are here, well, this is a good time for me to go in. Things are growing up fast out west, they need men like me, and I need them right now. If everything works out like the colonel said, I can be a real honest to goodness doctor. Daphnia, do you understand what that means?"

"William, you can be a doctor here. You know that Papa Tad will help you. You don't have to go away. You can do it right here."

"I can't live off of what your Uncle wants to dole out to me. I need to make my own way. I need to do what is best for me and for you. This will be a good opportunity for me. I can finish my education and get some experience doctoring all at the same time. Not only will I get to finish school but with my experience I will be able to doctor people, no more animals. I can help people, Daphnia; do you know what that means? I love animals, but I have always wanted to be a real doctor, a doctor for people. Please say that you understand. You do understand, don't you?"

15

"Don't keep asking me if I understand! Yes, I understand. I understand that you want to get away. If that is the case, then just say so."

"It has nothing to do with wanting to get away for the sake of getting away, Daphnia. This is the best way for me to do what I need to do to become a doctor on my own. I need to do this. Now is the time. My folks can barely keep food enough on the table for them and the little ones that are still at home. Even with my job at the dry goods store in town, and what I get from mending a broken bone here and there, and helping out Ole' Doc Logan, times are tough. It is about time I made something of myself for me and for you. I can't go on this way just watching while others see their dreams come true and me stuck here. If I stay my life will be spent watching someone else doing the doctoring, and me just barely able to sew up a cut or put a poultice on an infected foot. I just can't keep living this way just standing by to help the farmers around here with their cows, and horses. Besides, Daffy Girl, I don't want to be an animal doctor. I want to work with people." He was staring straight ahead at the road and watching the ears of the horse bob up and down. He would ride along quietly for a while; he would give her time to think about what he said. He wanted her to understand.

She understood all right, listening to him had put the present on hold! She was forced back in time without warning and without dreaming. She was wide-awake! It was as if a sheath of coldness had fallen over her and she felt paralyzed sitting next to him. She could hardly breathe. His words were like thunder roaring above the other voices pounding through her head. Daphnia closed her eyes and tried to shut out the all too familiar voices, but she could not. While she heard William, she was also hearing the voice of the soldier and her mother crying, she felt as if in a trance, she wanted to scream for all of them to stop, just stop …. if he would just stop and let her catch her breath; closing her eyes she could see the vestibule … … …

> … … … *"What is it, Mother? What is it? Please, please Mother, what is it?" She had been awakened by the sound of someone knocking at the door and she heard voices, a man's voice along with her mother's, it sounded like her father. It*

must be her father; she could hear her mother talking and she sounded excited. Getting out of bed she quietly crept across the hardwood floor and peeked out into the lighted vestibule. But, that was not her father. This man was wearing a uniform of some kind, and he was talking quietly now to her mother who was crying and sobbing and asking the man why. But the man didn't answer; he just walked out the door and closed it behind him... ... ...

Back on the wide porch at Sunshine Acres Thaddeus was sleeping soundly. Martha slipped a pillow beneath his head and made her way quietly out to her rose garden. She sat on the small stone alter and talked to the grave of her mother about everything and nothing.

Thaddeus turned on the pillow and was at once again dreaming the same dream he had dreamed over and over for the past twenty years. The dream started the way it always had ... ...

... ... He was once again in Chicago at the train station waiting for his friend, Herbert Bernstein.

Herbert had received the message, thank God. Thaddeus could see him waving and jumping as he walked through the crowd.

"Herb, it is good to see you, I wasn't expecting to hear from you today, what a nice surprise. How are things, how is Ruth and . . ."

"Everything is fine, Thaddeus, all is well at home. Why are you going to St. Louis and why did you ask about the emergency fund? You know I always keep it close at hand. Is there something wrong? You haven't squandered Martha's fortune already have you?

"No, her fortune is safe, thank you very much. It might surprise you to know that we have never touched one dime of her inheritance, life has been good to me and I long ago paid back every cent that her father loaned me. But, having said that, it is Friday, and dare I say that Matthew has gotten caught up in a mess again. I need several thousand dollars in cash in a hurry. I have to get the cash to St. Louis by morning. How much do you have on you?"

"I can float you a loan until Monday anyway. As a matter of fact, I am glad that you are going to St. Louis – I can use the company. Seems that a problem has come up with the family estate, and it is up to me to settle it. I hate St. Louis, Thaddeus! Every time I step off the train and walk up that path to the "Old House" it seems like I am nineteen again standing toe to toe with my father arguing for the right to live my life, make my own decisions and to see her get what she deserves. I hate it, Thaddeus, I tell you I hate it all and the misery it brings to me. Why can't Mekelstein handle things, he has the signed Power of Attorney, he can talk through my man in Huron City, but no that will never do, I have to make the trip. I swear, Thaddeus, I just don't understand why I can't break away. My old man might be six feet under but his bones reach out to me from the grave and he keeps pulling me back, sucking every breath out of my body. It is like I start to suffocate just thinking about him. This is the last time, I'm telling you! I'm not coming back. I'm sorry, I'm rambling, oh hell, never mind, let's just get there and get done with it."

The ride to St. Louis was uneventful. Matthew was not at the station, which was of no surprise to Thaddeus. The two friends took a taxi to the Fairmont, Herbert gave Thaddeus an envelope of cash, and the two agreed to meet later... ... ...

And then the sound of a gunshot... ... ...

Thaddeus awakened with a start. Once again, he tried to shake the recurring dream and the memories it brought. The memories seemed to flow in and out like the smoke from his pipe – it was as if they had their own mind and the will to force him into submission. He walked across the porch and looked out over the yard and fields. He could see Martha moving about the headstones in her garden. She was stooping, picking up weeds, talking and every now and then she would almost look as if she weren't alone. How very innocent she is, he thought, as the waves of guilt from an earlier life of lies and indiscretions flooded over him.

Martha was the epitome of trust and honesty. Her rose garden was her sanctuary. Along with the others, it was the graves of her mother, father and infant son that she visited. Walking among the flowers she hummed quietly and stopped to pull a weed or smell one of the sweet blossoms. Her stone bench practically had an indentation where she had sat for so many hours, crying and talking to God, her mother, the flowers as well as the many birds, rabbits and squirrels that visited there. This was the place she found peace, where order was returned to her thoughts and fears were erased. But, supper had to be on the table soon, and surely Thaddeus was calmer by now.

Watching her walk from the garden and wipe her eyes, he knew that she had been crying. He held out his hand to her as she came up the steps.

As she approached the porch she could see that he seemed out of sorts. "Thaddeus, are you okay? Your heart's racing, are you okay?"

"I'm fine, I think I'll just lie back down for a minute. Don't worry about me I'll be fine. I have just been back and forth between here and Chicago, Detroit, and Huron City so much lately, I don't seem to barely get my shoes off before I have to put them back on and get on another train or go to another meeting. Whew, I better take a little walk myself, gotta get the cobwebs out. Those kids should be back here soon, it looks like a little dust cloud coming this way."

William continued to let the horse amble down the road half paying attention and half dreaming about what was to become of them once he became a real doctor. He was unaware that Daphnia was not listening to his dreams. He was trying to tell her of the wonders of the California coastline, at least according to what the colonel had assured him what the coastline would look like. But, Daphnia wasn't hearing him, she, for the first time was wide-awake reliving a memory long ago suppressed … and she couldn't shake herself out of it. She remembered it as if it were yesterday . . . it was playing in her mind as clearly as the fields and the road before her … … …

> … … … *She could feel the hardwood floor beneath her bare feet as she ran across the room to her mother who had collapsed onto the floor with her nightgown flowing about her and her hair hanging down over her thin shoulders. She was crying so hard that Daphnia could hardly hold onto her without she herself falling over. Melissa was holding a piece of paper in her hands but Daphnia was sure that it could not be very important since it was almost torn to shreds and her mother was using it to wipe away her tears.*
>
> *"What is it, Mother?"*
>
> *"It is your father, Daphnia, he has met with a tragedy and he is dead. He has been shot, murdered in a dark alley outside of St. Louis. It shouldn't have been that bad, he might have lived, but by the time they found him the only doctor around was one who hadn't had much experience working with people and he couldn't save him. They have buried him in St. Louis. He is already buried. They buried him back there in St Louis; I guess they felt they couldn't wait to contact his folks or me. He's dead, dead and buried already because of no doctor. Just imagine, a doctor that doesn't know how to take care of people because his only experience has been taking care of animals. I never. How can he be a doctor if he only works on horses and cows?"*
>
> *Daphnia could see her mother get up from the floor and go back to her own bed leaving Daphnia standing there and not understanding any of what had just happened.*

She remembered standing there in the vestibule where Melissa had left her for as long as she could and then she sat on the floor sobbing. Even at her young age of just a little more than four years, she knew that dead meant something very bad. Even though she did not understand the full scope of the word nor what it would mean to her in the weeks, months and years to come, she knew it made her sad. She fell asleep in the silent house curled up in front of the door... ... ...

The memory of that night was crystal clear to her now. It was as if she had been watching herself from the corner of the room.

There was no more laughter in the little house after that night. The next morning Melissa took to her bed and left Daphnia under the charge of her aunt. Daphnia's life was one of near silence, her only companions were her dolls and her Aunt Ella until the morning she boarded the train for Lansing.

"Well, what do you think, Daphnia? Do you think I am worth waiting for? Daphnia, Daffy, I've just asked you to . . . Daphnia, are you okay?" William realized he might as well have been talking to himself. Daphnia was sitting against the corner of the seat now, and it looked as if she was staring right through him. He had never known her not to say anything. After years of trying to get the courage to ask her to marry him, he finally did it and she looked as if she were in shock. "Daphnia, are you okay? You are so still and so quiet. What are you staring at? Why are you crying, is it because you are happy? Daphnia, talk to me. Daphnia, say something!" Taking her into his arms, he brushed away her tears. " I didn't mean to upset you. I have been trying to talk to you about this for days now, but I just never found the right time. You must understand, Daphnia, tell me you understand. Tell me yes, Daphnia, please answer me. Please forgive me for waiting to tell you, for not asking you sooner, but please understand that I must go. Daphnia, please say yes, please say you will marry me."

"Oh, William, yes I'll marry you. Of course, I'll marry you, I love you William Johnston. Don't worry about leaving. I do understand, honestly I do. I know you want to go away and see the world. I know how important it is that you become a doctor. We will tell Papa Tad and Aunt Martha tonight and I will be ready to leave with you as soon as you want me to. It won't take me long, I promise. We can get married right away; it doesn't have to be a big wedding, just your folks and mine. How soon do we have to leave? When do you need to report to the Colonel? It will be fine, I promise."

"Daphnia, I am going alone. I can't ask you to leave your home and go away with me to God only knows where. Not now, not yet. I have to go alone. We will get married when I return next spring. I can't ask you to go just now, your Uncle would kill me, besides I have to go through a lot of training first. I love you, I want you, we will get married, and we will be together, but not just yet."

"You're not asking me to go with you? But, I thought you wanted... well, I guess I was just thinking... well if that's what you think, William."

"I do want you to marry me, and I do want you to be with me, but not just yet. I have to do this on my own, I will be back in the spring and that will give you time to make all the proper plans for a proper wedding. Please try to understand."

"Okay, William, I'll wait for you." Her mind was racing, her thoughts were everywhere, and she was glad that he didn't want her to come right away, she needed some time, too. But, for a year! A year without him would break her heart; she felt the tears start to slide down her cheeks.

"Oh, my Daffy Girl. What am I to do with you? I love you, I want you to be my wife. If I ever hear of someone else taking my place I promise to return post haste and shoot him at dawn."

"You know there will never be anyone for me but you, William Johnston! You know that I love you.

Squeezing her tightly to him he breathed in the smell of her hair then releasing her, he slapped the reigns against the horses' rump and pulled the buggy back onto the road. They talked about their plans for the future and promised to write each other every day. Inside their hearts were breaking, while they laughed and sang as they trotted past fence posts, and farms through the rolling countryside and under the archway of Sunshine Acres declaring their entrance into the "Home of Thaddeus, Martha and Daphnia Flanders."

The happiness and freedom they felt would be short lived. Their lives would be forever changed by the events of this day, but not because of William Johnston's decision to join the US Calvary or of Daphnia's memories and nightmares. The next bend in the roads they were to take would take them to places not in their dreams of the past or the future they had come to believe in.

Chapter Two

William and Daphnia could see the broad porch of the great white house as they rode past the pastures on either side of the well-traveled dirt road.

Sitting on the front porch swing smoking his pipe Thaddeus breathed a sigh of relief as the buggy pulled up. "Good evening, children," he said with a wink to William and a smile for Daphnia, "did you have a good day?" He could hardly keep from running down the pathway. When Daphnia approached him, he took her into his arms and held her close to him. He needed to talk to her. "Come inside William?" he asked politely hoping the young man would decline so that he could spend some time alone with Daphnia. He had been waiting for the right time to talk with her about Huron City and Melissa, and he and Martha had decided that the time to have the long overdue discussion was this evening. He didn't want to wait any longer for fear of losing his nerve and resolve to keep his promise. He knew that once Daphnia heard what he had to tell her, she would, for the first time in her life, be in total control of the next step each of them would take.

"Thanks for the invitation, Mr. Flanders," William said politely, "but I think I had better get moving toward home before it gets too late. But, sir, before I leave, I have asked Daphnia to marry me and I am hoping that you and Mrs. Flanders will give us your blessings." Taking Daphnia's hand and pressing it to his lips, "Daphnia, I will be leaving for Detroit tomorrow. The colonel is expecting me. From there I don't know where I will be or what will happen, but I will write, I promise. I love you, Daphnia. Mr. Flanders, we are planning to marry next spring, will that suit you, sir?"

"This is no shock young man, I have been expecting this for some time. How, and I don't mean to seem insensitive, just how do you plan to care for Daphnia? What are your long term plans for settling down?"

"Don't worry, Mr. Flanders, I realize that I don't have the means right now to care for her the way she has been brought up, but I will someday, I promise. I will continue my medical training while in the

Army, and it will be a decent and honorable life, we will do fine, we love each other, Sir, we're getting married in the spring. Daphnia, I love you, I'll write; I promise."

Daphnia felt as if her heart was being torn out of her body. She pulled him to her and kissed his mouth passionately as if she would never kiss him again. The tears ran down her cheeks, and she sobbed against him. "I love you, William."

"Don't cry, Daffy Girl. I'll be back. Now don't you take up with any rounders that might come passing through. Remember you promised that you would always be my precious Daffy Girl." Taking her hands from around him, he moved away from her. Then he turned to shake the hand of Thaddeus. "Mr. Flanders, I hope we will have your approval and your blessing."

"Well, this is not what I intended, don't you think you should come into the house and maybe let's have a drink of brandy and talk about this? I think I need some answers before any approvals or blessings are handed out.

"I wish I could join you, Sir, but I must be heading back home. Daphnia will fill in all of the details, and I do hope that you will approve." With a brisk turn, he walked around the front of the wagon and climbed back onto the seat. With two clicks of his tongue and a quick slap of the reigns to the broad hindquarters of the great horse, the buggy moved forward and down the dirt road and through the archway.

Wiping away her tears Daphnia watched until he was out of sight. Then taking the arm of her Papa Tad they walked down the stone lined path and up the steps of the big white house. She could hear her Aunt Martha inside. She knew the little woman was busy preparing supper. She smiled as she walked close with her Papa Tad and thought of her Aunt and how much in love they were, their type of love was what she had dreamed of having with William Johnston.

⁘⸺⸱⸺⸱⸺⸺⁘

Her life with these two wonderful people had been filled with love and happiness. She often wondered how she had come to be so very lucky to have lived in their home and grown up with their love surrounding and protecting her. While others thought Thaddeus to be stern and solemn and her aunt to be quiet and reserved, they were just the opposite.

Martha was a round woman, soft and warm. Thaddeus often said that if Martha ever got tired of walking she could just sit down and roll the rest of the way. She barely stood five feet tall and was almost as big around. Her cheeks were full of color and rarely still, for it seemed to Daphnia that her Aunt Martha was talking, singing or laughing her every waking moment. Her eyes were small but bright and shone with the color of the sky. She wore her hair pinned up on top of her head in a tiny little knot. Daphnia often wondered why she even bothered putting the turtle shell combs on the sides of the little bun in the morning, for by the end of the day they would barely hold her hair back and there would be little strands of white flying all about her face. Aunt Martha's hair was snow white and had been for as long as Daphnia could remember. When Daphnia was small, she would sit on the stool next to the wood stove placed in the middle of the cozy kitchen and watch Aunt Martha move about with what looked like a great white spider's web floating around her face and neck. She loved Aunt Martha. There was never a more loving or giving person anywhere, of this Daphnia was certain.

⁎⁎⁎⁎⁎

Stopping at the top of the stairs, Thaddeus turned Daphnia toward him. "Now, listen my girl, I need to talk with you about some serious business. And, I'm not speaking of your young beau or you getting married. I need to talk to you about Melissa! I received some news a few weeks ago, and I think it is time we talked. You know that I correspond and see my dear friend, Herbert Bernstein, in Huron City on a regular basis. Well, a while back I got a letter from him and decided that I should make a trip to see him, I saw Melissa too. We are going to have to make some decisions, and when I say "we" I mean you, your Aunt Martha and me."

"What kind of decisions? What's happened to Mother, Papa? What is it that has happened to require such a serious discussion?"

"Well, Daphnia, the long and the short of it is whether or not you want to take a leave from Lansing and spend some time in Huron City, maybe you should get to know Melissa, she is very ill. I know that you have only seen her a few times over the past twenty years, but let me tell you what I have learned. I'm not sure what decision you'll make. But, I do know that you will agonize a great deal about what is the right thing to do. When you talked about going to spend some time with Melissa several years ago, I was against it. I thought you were too vulnerable and much too young. Maybe I was too stubborn and too selfish, I wanted to keep you here where I knew you were safe and where I could protect you from life's meanness. Well, maybe I was wrong. Maybe I should have let you go then and get it out of your system, but I didn't, and now here it is, that damn gray wet city calling for me to send you back and I won't be able to talk you out of it this time. I'm not saying you have to go or that you even should go, I just want you to be able to make up your own mind. And, Daphnia, whatever you decide I will be here for you and with you."

"It sounds like you have already decided for me. I haven't thought of going to Huron City in a long time now. As for Mother, well she hasn't bothered to ask for me before, are you saying that she is asking for me now? Why? After all of these years, what has made her decide that she wants to get to know me now? Or is it that she needs me to take care of her now that her health is failing and Aunt Ella isn't as able to care for things the way I'm sure she once did. How on earth can anything having to do with Mother make me change my plans? I might be willing to go for a brief visit, but a visit isn't forever. Anyway, she has not felt any obligation to get to know me, why should I feel obligated to spend time with her now? Besides, William just asked me to marry him, and I said yes. I have an obligation to the school and to my students who will be expecting me to be here when they come back in September. I have a wedding to plan and I am not convinced that Mother would want to be any part of that. So tell me, Papa what do you know that you aren't saying?"

"My dear, I don't even know where to begin with that one. Let's just say that when it comes to Melissa I don't believe for one minute that you have any obligations whatsoever to that woman, nor do I believe you should change your life just to please her now. But, I want to let you know what is going on so you can be free to do what you believe to be the right thing."

Thaddeus turned and stared off into nowhere and continued talking as if Daphnia wasn't there, he was looking off as if to a distant place and holding his pipe in his right hand like he was practicing a sermon or something. She had seen this look before when he was about to deliver a speech or unpopular news at one of his meetings of the Railroad Board Members. She was frightened and excited at the same time. Taking his hand in hers she looked up into his face.

"What are you talking about, Papa Tad? What decisions? If you have known something for a few weeks, why have you waited for so long to talk with me about it? Of course, there is a sense of obligation I am her daughter, Melissa is my mother, of course I care, but what could possibly have happened that would cause me to change my plans now? She hasn't needed me, nor wanted me for the all of these years. Why now?"

Remaining calm and sounding indifferent and uncaring was almost impossible. Her hands were shaking, her heart was beating faster than she thought possible and running through her head were the words *"she wants me, she needs me, she loves me"*. Daphnia had waited for this moment for so long it was hard for her to keep her balance now that the time had finally come and her mother was asking for her. She felt elation, fright and confusion all at the same time.

Thaddeus tried to believe that what Daphnia was saying was a reflection of her true feelings, but he knew in his heart that she was just putting on a front for him. With a strong pull on his pipe, he held the smoke in his throat and let the burning of the tobacco linger for as long as he could. Then, releasing the smoke up and into the crisp evening air, he said a silent prayer for strength as he turned toward Daphnia. "Well, she needs you now, dear, she told me herself that she needs you now."

Taking her into his arms he held her tightly then pulling away from her he slipped his hand around hers and they walked into the house and into the large kitchen where the smell of Aunt Martha's cooking filled the room.

"How long before supper, Mart? I am starved. Maybe I could just have some cold milk with one of those dumplings, for now. Daphnia care to join me or are you still filled with butterflies and stardust after your afternoon with the serious William Johnston? Mart, did you know that our darling here has just become engaged to marry Mr. Johnston?"

"That's it Papa, but there is more. William told me that he has joined the Army and will be leaving for Detroit tomorrow and then to the gold coast of California. It is so sudden. I will miss him terribly and I don't know what I will do without him. I don't think I have had a chance to really think about it yet, but I know that it is what he wants. And, that on top of your news about Mother and a trip to Huron City myself … Mother wants me to come to visit, Aunt Martha, did you know that? Please excuse me for a moment, please; I need to catch my breath. I don't know if I am going to cry or not feel anything … too much has happened all at once and the only thing I know for sure is that next spring I will be the wife of Dr. William Johnston." Giving her uncle a squeeze, she left the kitchen and walked out onto the back porch where she gave way to the long overdue sobs that she had so tightly held within for so long. She stood looking over the pasture and the hills in the distance sobbing quietly turning only when she heard the door open and the footsteps of her aunt.

"Now, now dear, it will be okay, you will see, you go ahead and cry on my shoulder, let's sit down right here on these steps and you just cry for as long as you like. Your Papa Tad has been an absolute bear all afternoon. He is so wound up about Melissa that he can't think straight. And none of that matters anyway, after all we have a wedding to plan. Did you and young William set the date? Spring is a very busy time around here and I will need to call the preacher, let's see, maybe I can get that sweet Mrs. Lutz to play the organ, and how do you feel about carrying roses from my garden. I will start pruning and trimming now so they will be just right for you, we will have the beautiful red ones and yellow and the pinks are especially nice, I can mix in some of the whites and even one or two of the lilac sprigs if we set the time just right. What do you think, dear, do you want red, pink, yellow, or lavender accents? Oh, I have been waiting for this for so long, aren't you excited? Now stop that crying and put Melissa out of your mind, she has never done one thing for you, don't you go changing your whole life just for her now. I won't let you, do you hear me, you and your Uncle Thaddeus can talk all you want about honor and duty, but you owe her nothing, do you understand, you owe her nothing! Now, this time is for you and William, tell me right this minute everything, don't leave out a thing. Did you set the date?"

"Oh, Aunt Martha. No, we didn't set the date, we barely had time to even get through the asking and agreeing part, but we will soon. It is just all so mixed up, everything has happened all of a sudden. I don't know what got into me running out like that. Can we just sit here for a few minutes? I need to think all of this through. You didn't have to come out here; it's getting chilly. Can we just sit quietly?"

"Of course we can, honey, we'll sit here for as long as you like. Are you sure that he's leaving tomorrow, honey? Now, don't you be upset. It will work out. When will he be coming back? What about his Mama and those little ones still at home? With his Pappy living the way he does, no telling what will happen now without William around. I guess they'll get by. Does he plan to be in Detroit long? Did you say he's going to California? Lord, I never been out there, don't reckon I would want to, it being so far from here and all. Are you sure he's not wanting you to go out there with him? Tell me he's not, is he? Oh, I hope not, not now, not with this thing with Melissa. I just hate it when you are away, even to go into the schoolhouse, and when you and Thaddeus are both gone, well, me, Lord only knows how I manage. I spend my whole time walking from the cellar to the garden, to the kitchen. I make half a dozen trips a day back and forth up and down those stairs and out to the roses. Just listen to me rambling on, just nerves I guess, I better go back inside, you stay out here and just relax, catch your breath so to speak, like you said. Do you want to go out into the garden and talk with Mother? She always listens to me. No I guess not. I have told her all sorts of things, like that thing with Melissa and Matthew, and even them Boston stories that I heard about, but . . . oh my, I am so sorry, I didn't mean to, please forgive me, I am just so worried I am rambling on like water rushing over them rocks and rapids of old Casey Creek."

"What Boston stories, what thing with Mother and Father, Aunt Martha? What stories? Papa said there was something happening in Huron City, he said that things were not going well, what does it have to do with Boston?"

"Your Papa will talk with you about it dear, now don't you worry. Let's just sit here. Look at those stars, aren't they just the brightest you've ever seen?"

Thaddeus looked out at the two women sitting on the back porch steps. What was it about women that baffled him so? He was furious at himself for not giving Daphnia time to settle back into the house before he unloaded his frustrations upon her. He would say no more about Huron City or Melissa this evening.

Stroking Daphnia's hair, Martha thought of how much her life had been changed with Daphnia's arrival some nineteen plus years ago. To Martha, Daphnia was the little girl she had never been able to have, she loved her as though she were her own.

"You know when you came to us, Daphnia, it was just over nineteen years ago. When Melissa wired that she was sending you to live with us, it was one of the happiest days of my life. Finally I would have my little girl. Well, just let me tell you. I was like a new mother duck just fussin' and busying about. I sewed lace and ribbons on everything that I thought you would touch. Thaddeus carved animals, small furniture, a dollhouse and puppets from maple, oak, and cherry wood. Do you remember that baby doll of cloth you had? Well I had the best time cutting and sewing that doll, and then filling it with salt so it would be more natural. I stitched it a face with a smile and laughing blue eyes. Thaddeus made a rocking horse and a table with four chairs just the right size for a little girl. We just couldn't do enough to make our home and this here farm into a safe and warm haven for you. We got so much joy out of watching you chase the ducks and trying to ride on our big old Golden Retriever. It didn't matter what you did, honey, we just reveled in your happiness. Of course we were both well into what they call middle-aged by then, but it made no difference to us, we was just like two kids in a candy store loving and caring for you."

"I remember those times, Aunt Martha, they are as special to me as they are to you. I just don't understand why she ever sent me away."

"It don't matter now, she did what she did for whatever reason, Daphnia. As far as we were concerned, you were our little girl and that is the way it was. You didn't seem to miss her, and your rarely asked about her growing up."

"What about my father, didn't I ever ask about him?"

"Not so much. I was always a little worried about you not asking, but Thaddeus seemed to think it was because you were so young. The only time I can remember you asking about your father was when you asked what the word dead meant. Other than that, you never brought him up and neither did we. You visited Melissa in Huron City a couple of times, but it didn't seem to affect you any."

Sitting on the back porch and looking at Daphnia now, Martha thought of how she and Thaddeus had taken Daphnia in to raise without hesitation. She thought of their lives and the lives of Daphnia, Melissa and Matthew. She thought of how their lives had all become entangled through silence, secrets, mystery, deceit and triumphs. She thought of the burden that would now be forced upon Daphnia, a burden that she should not have to carry. She thought of the deceitful and beautiful Melissa, and the charismatic Matthew. One could see a resemblance between Daphnia and Melissa, if they didn't know no better. They both had high cheekbones, impeccable posture and a gift for lighting up the world with their smiles. But Daphnia's independence and self-assuredness was the undeniably bloodline of Matthew.

Daphnia's hair was light brown and hung down her back and shoulders and about her face like waves of golden wheat in the summer time and turning to a softer chestnut tone in the fall; she was careful to pin it up on top of her head for school and formal events. Her hazel eyes were large and almost danced when she was excited, and her skin was flawless. She was taller than Melissa as well, and others would just say that her height and coloring came from her father's side of the family. While not a great beauty, Daphnia was certainly pleasant to look at. She had grown up to be rounded in all of the right places. Although those who did not know her would think she was stuck-up and standoffish, but in fact she was just the opposite. Daphnia had a huge capacity for love; she was compassionate, kind, and generous. She was honest almost to a fault and she viewed one's duty to family and country as paramount, Martha could not figure out in two lifetimes where these latter traits came from, surely not from Matthew, so they had to come from her mother's side of the family, but that seemed almost impossible.

Thaddeus and Martha gave Daphnia everything she wanted and needed, to include responsibilities and chores. They instilled the importance of values and charitable ethics in her daily life. She went to church on Sundays and volunteered at the children's home one weekend a month from the time she turned eleven. Schooling was taken seriously. Daphnia attended Finishing School in Boston for two semesters and then private tutoring at Mrs. Bergeron's Teaching College in Lansing. But, teaching wasn't her first choice for a career. Daphnia had worked two summers with the Lansing Daily News. Martha had tried to keep her from doing this, but could never persuade Thaddeus that Daphnia's experience with the paper would one day come back to haunt them. Martha "had a feeling," as she would say, about the paper business and Daphnia's involvement. But, Martha did not prevail and Daphnia and Thaddeus won out. Daphnia loved working at the paper. Daphnia shared her dream of becoming a newspaperwoman with Martha long before the opportunity of summer work came along. When Thaddeus told her of the teaching position that was opening up in the little school, and that he thought that would be the best for her, Martha encouraged her, and Daphnia agreed to accept the position, and dismissed the notion of working for the newspaper.

Now as Martha sat on the back porch thinking of how Daphnia had changed their lives, she couldn't help but wonder if they had done the right thing. There were too many secrets, too much water over the dam and now in their golden years, they might just lose the one person whom they had come to rely on for bringing sunshine and laughter into their home. Martha had never liked secrets, and she knew from the time that Daphnia arrived to live with them that some day without warning Melissa would come forth and claim what she believed to be rightfully hers "for all of her pain and suffering" and turn their lives upside down.

"Come on dear, let's go in, it is getting cool out here and your Papa Tad will be wanting his supper." Martha stood up and went to the door and held it for Daphnia.

"You go ahead Aunt Martha, I will be in shortly. I just need to sit for a while longer."

"Whatever you say, Daphnia, but you need to know that no amount of sitting and thinking on these steps will solve your problems tonight. You are your father's child and no matter what I think or what your Papa Tad thinks, your final decision will be so because that is what you really want, and that pains me. I don't mind saying so; my heart will hurt from now until the next decade and beyond, if I live that long, for what you are about to do. That young William Johnston be damned. Melissa has called and any child wants their mama to want them no matter what kind of alley cat she has been to them. You want your mama to want you, and now that she has crooked her little finger and smiled and whined some, you will go and there ain't nothing that me nor anyone else can say to make you do differently. Now, I'm going in afore I catch my death you can come or you can stay, but you need to know that I love you no matter what, but I will see Melissa Flanders in hell before I give you my blessings to run to her side now." Martha stomped her way back into the house and into the warm kitchen where peace would not be found this evening.

"Well, you two talk everything out? Do you think we can have some supper now, or is it every man for himself?" Thaddeus asked Martha from where he sat by the wood stove whittling on a piece of wood from the top of his boot.

"Good Lord, Thaddeus, one would think you were half starved to death and that we had left you in here to fend for yourself. And, just how bad would that have been, you can slice a piece of ham or eat another one of those dumplings. Now, I want that child to come in here and I mean right now." Opening the door and speaking louder than what Daphnia or Thaddeus were used to Martha shouted with no lack of anger and frustration toward the young woman she had left sitting on the steps, "Daphnia, come on in here now, you will catch a cold out there and I mean come in here now and I don't want to hear any more about it."

Martha put supper on the table and the three sat down.

Thaddeus wasn't sure whether to eat in silence or to speak, but finally gave way to the need for some normalcy. "So, tell me more about this proposal from young William, Daphnia. What is this about him going away to join the Army in, where, California?"

"I guess William feels like he has to get away, Papa. He feels trapped here with no opportunity to become a doctor, there are no schools around here and the two years he had down in Chicago just aren't enough. You know what it is like with his father, and their house is so small. The Colonel has promised him that he will be able to complete his education while working with the Army Doctors, it is a good thing for him; he'll be back before we know it. I don't know what I am going to do without him. I will miss him terribly. I will be lost. Please, can we not talk about this right now? What is happening in Huron City? What is it that is so important that you must talk with me about? Exactly what is it that is going on with Mother? You mentioned Uncle Herbert, is there a problem with him too?"

"Yes and no. Melissa is not well, but then that is nothing new. She hasn't been well for years. Herb is in need of some help at the paper, and he hasn't forgotten how helpful you were a couple of years back when you visited. He also remembers your interest in the newspaper business. Melissa has asked for you, and Herb has agreed to help make life easier and more comfortable for you by giving you a job at the Gazette. He has also said that should you not want to live at Melissa's house, you are welcome to stay in the apartment over the newspaper office."

"Is Mother wanting me to come for a visit this summer, or is she thinking of me staying longer? Is Uncle Herbert prepared for something so open ended?"

"Yes, as a matter of fact he is. He has offered to let you live above the office for as long as you want. While it is a small apartment, he has fixed it up quite handsomely. Melissa asked that I talk to you about coming to stay for a while. She didn't specify a period of time, nor did she refer to your coming as a visit. I think she is hoping you will stay for at least several weeks and possibly months. And, with William going away, it might be good for you to take this time without any distractions."

"Are you suggesting that I go?"

"Well, I am suggesting that you give it some thought. I have a letter here from Melissa for you, she is asking for you, Daphnia. Lord only knows why she is asking now, but she is. You don't have to go, it is up to you. I don't want you to go, no! I want you to stay right here and tell Melissa Flanders to die in that bed where she has sentenced herself for the past nineteen years. She is selfish, and she has never cared for anyone but herself. Now she has come up with this idea and she thinks everyone should just stop the earth from spinning until she is able to

35

satisfy her own greed. No! I am not suggesting that you go to her. I am simply trying to find a way to rid my conscience of some of the guilt that I have chosen to hold onto for far too long. Melissa has made a request, nothing more."

"But she's asking for me!"

"Yes, Daphnia, she is asking for you to come for a while, for a visit."

"Aunt Martha, what do you think? It isn't as if my summer is without plans, I do have some obligations."

"Daphnia, Thaddeus, excuse me, please."

"Mart, where are you going?"

"What does it matter? You two will sit here and discuss this to death, and then do exactly what you want to do anyway. My feelings and my opinion won't matter. Melissa is a spiteful and selfish woman who only thinks of herself, never gives one thought to what anybody else might want or feel. She deserves to die right there in that dark house wrapped up in her misery – it is all she has ever agreed with anyways. If you let Daphnia leave this house to go there she won't never come back, not to live anyhow. I'm sorry, Daphnia, I know you want and even need for her to love you, but she ain't worth it honey, she ain't worth a hair on your head, I gotta get outta here. Excuse me, please."

Martha ran from the house as quickly as she could. She grabbed her shawl as she went past the hall tree, and wrapping it around her she went out the door and over to the stand of birch trees and her rose garden. She thought of the consequences of the past and how they were catching up with them now. She felt anxious. Her heart was racing, and she thought she might faint. She knew she had to settle down. She went over to the little bench and sat upon its worn seat. As she looked over her roses her mind wandered back to not so long ago when she and Thaddeus received the letter from Melissa stating her need for Daphnia to come to Huron City ... ...

... ... Martha argued as much as she had ever dared with her beloved Thaddeus. She had played and replayed the conversation over and over in her mind too many times to count.

"...No, Thaddeus, No! I will not allow her to go back there. How dare Herbert throw in that temptation of Daphnia being able to work in the newspaper office just to get her there out of his

own selfishness and all under the guise of needing Daphnia to help take care of Melissa? Melissa never wanted that child; she always resented Daphnia and blamed her for the loss of Matthew. Melissa was jealous from day one of Daphnia and the fuss Matthew made over his own baby girl. Why even when he left and joined up with those lumberjacks, Melissa blamed that on Daphnia and her only a child of three. No! I am telling you Thaddeus I won't let her go. I won't lose her to that woman. Melissa is and always was selfish. How could a woman turn away a baby as sweet and loving as Daphnia was? No, Thaddeus, Melissa is as selfish today as she was then, she doesn't see how what she says and does can destroy another human being, she never has and she never will see that what happened was her own fault."

"Now, now, Mart, you don't know Melissa very well. As a matter of fact, you never really did get to know her. We have to let Daphnia make this decision; we have to tell her the truth, Mart. We have to give her a chance. As for Melissa, well, maybe she did love Daphnia, and maybe she loves her today; at least in her own way. But, this isn't all about Melissa we have to consider Herbert, too. We don't know how Melissa may feel today. Maybe she has softened."

"Oh, Thaddeus, you know as well as I that Melissa couldn't love a bastard child today any more than she could then. She could never forgive Matthew for bringing home a child by another woman for her to raise before he was killed so what makes you think she has forgiven him now? How dare she call for Daphnia to come to that dirty wet city. I can't believe that Herbert would be the bearer of this news on Melissa's behalf only, he is in this for what's in it for him! I just have one question, how did someone as sweet and generous as Daphnia ever get born into the middle of the four most selfish human beings ever to take a breath of God's fresh air?"

Sitting on the stone bench and looking out at the lights of the big house, Martha wondered just what all the arguing and grief she and Thaddeus had suffered was about anyway. They were just as guilty as anyone else. They had kept secrets that they had no right to keep and now all of the lies each of them had lived with were coming around to claim their due.

She could have told Daphnia about her mother years ago, but she chose not to. She had promised Thaddeus that she would let him do the telling when the time came, and she had kept that promise. But it haunted her still, and now more than ever. She and Thaddeus had not spoken of the subject of Daphnia's birth Mother since the incident at the well some twenty-three years ago. It had not been an easy winter for any of them, but when Matthew rode up in his fancy buggy with his shiny black horse tied to the back and with the little bundle in his arms Martha was overjoyed. She had lost a second baby during her first trimester of pregnancy just months earlier and seeing Daphnia in Matthew's arms was just what she needed. As Matthew told them of the circumstances of Daphnia's birth four months earlier to the Widow Humphreys, Martha immediately bonded with the infant and nothing about how she was born or to whom mattered.

Thaddeus, on the other hand, felt somewhat different. He was aware of Matthew's activities and his tawdry affair in Boston that had brought its share of shame to the Flanders Family. It was just one more thing that he would have to keep secret. He listened only half heartedly while Matthew told his story of Grace, their love and what he knew of her past. Gossip soon followed, and Thaddeus would often times try to match up the stories from the busy ladies and those told to him by Matthew. Rarely were there enough similarities between tales to make any sense out of either version. With each story sounding more exaggerated than the last he prayed that Herbert would never hear them, even though he knew for a fact that most of what was said was not true. His bigger problem was to keep Herbert from knowing anything at all about Matthew and Grace Humphreys. He had made a point of telling Martha that she must never speak of Grace to Herbert or to Ruth, that Matthew had brought shame to the Flanders, but there was no need of bringing an innocent woman into the ring of slander and mudslinging that would surely take place. While this caused Martha to wonder why talking about Grace with Herbert or Ruth could cause a problem, she nevertheless agreed to obey his wish.

As time passed, she heard the gossip. In the beginning she made it her business to listen as much as she could to the women without being too obvious. In time, and keeping with her need for tangible information, she realized that there was too much gossip and not enough facts. Once Matthew took Daphnia and left for Huron City, the rumors began to hurt her and she was afraid for Daphnia, she began to stay closer to home and soon stayed away from the meetings and gatherings with the loose-tongued women.

What she eventually pieced together was that Grace was originally from somewhere down near Charleston, but she had left there after being disowned by her father for marrying a man from Georgia with few social graces. Stories had it Malcolm Humphreys had earned his fortune through the black marketing of slaves before the war ended only to steal them back from their new owners and transport them north to Canada. Some believed his own mother was a slave herself and sold by the very man who took pleasure in her at night until Malcolm Humphreys was weaned from her teat and able to be raised without the nourishment she provided. It is said that once Malcolm died, Grace had tried to return to Charleston to be with her family only to find that her father had moved the family up to St. Louis soon after she left with Malcolm. He had left a letter for her with the Town Postmaster should she should ever come looking for them. The letter stated that she was not welcome and should go about her life away from them. She should not try to trace them, and if she should happen to find them she should not speak to them since she had only brought them shame. The letter went on to state that she was the cause of her own Mother's death. After reading the letter, Grace, dejected and alone, moved back to Boston where she made her living doing sewing for others.

Martha went over the varying stories and gossip now, piece by piece in her mind. Although she never pursued nor participated in the rumors she had always wondered about them. None of the stories could be substantiated although Matthew had given some merit to those about Grace's heritage and how she ended up so far away from her home. The rumors that Grace was the daughter of a wealthy lawyer in St. Louis who had disowned her for her love of Malcolm made their way from the little hamlet back to the church on the outskirts of Lansing and were confirmed by Matthew and Thaddeus. Martha felt some compassion for Grace, and she was certain that the rumors and gossip that Grace endured for her affair with the handsome Matthew Flanders had taken their toll. Matthew portrayed Grace as a gentle and compassionate woman of integrity and honor. He shared with Thaddeus and Martha his guilt for causing her pain. He told of how she held her head high and tried to ignore the whispers and sneers of the ladies who would cover their mouths and turn their backs when she approached them, but he knew it broke her heart. He felt that it was because of her past life with Malcolm that she stayed to herself in a modest house just outside of Boston.

Martha had heard that Matthew was not the only visitor to the Widow Humphreys, however. It was with great satisfaction that one of the local women made sure Martha knew about the other visitor to Grace, a man the opposite of Matthew, a small man, darker and certainly not attractive who would steal into Grace's house under the darkness of night and leave the same way when Matthew was not around. He was a bigger mystery than his stature allowed. Many persons would swear to seeing the small man although few had actually done so, and no one had ever spoken to him. Some believed he was just an imaginary figure who was added to the many rumors for the spice of it and with the hopes to get the over confident Matthew riled. Others claimed it was a slave coming back to pay back a debt to Malcolm, yet others had their own version of what the man did in the small cottage; how else could a widow woman live on the mere pittance Grace's sewing brought in?

While Martha never put much stock in gossip, she did know that Matthew would never allow anyone else to share the bed with Grace once he had found his way there. He was a man who commanded ownership of all he came in contact with. Like it or not! If there was such a man, likely he was a doctor or servant of some sort, Martha was sure of that. Martha knew Matthew all to well. She knew the truth about Matthew regardless of the gossip. Matthew Flanders was the envy of all the men in the area and the secret desire of all the women. When he walked into a room all eyes turned toward him, even those who hated him could not deny his presence. He was tall, over six feet two inches, his shoulders were broad and his waist narrow, his sandy blond hair was thick with soft waves which he combed straight back leaving his bronze face fully exposed. His teeth were wide and white and perfectly straight behind a broad smile. The light that danced in his hazel eyes was of both delight and sorrow; Matthew was filled with mysteries.

Thaddeus had tried to quell any concern Martha had. He tried to explain the relationship between Matthew and Grace and Matthew and Melissa in a way that she could accept, if not understand. He had to be careful, but he also had to answer as many of her questions as he could without divulging more than he absolutely had to. He told her that Matthew had met the Widow Humphreys in the spring of 1879 while Melissa and he were in Boston so Melissa could sit with her dying Mother. Of course when Melissa could no longer deal with the shame of the gossip and talk through the generosity of the all too kind and helpful busybodies in the area, she became anxious to leave regardless of her mother's failing health. It was only due to her daughterly obligation that she remained. Once the older woman passed away, Melissa wasted no time packing her things and cleaning up the business of her estate. Once things were under control, Melissa packed her own personal belongings, left a note for Matthew and boarded a train back to Huron City. She made it clear in her note that she did not want Matthew to return with her, she asked that he leave her alone.

It was only after several months of Melissa's own suffering and Matthew's letters pleading with her to forgive him and to allow him to return to her and their home in Huron City that she gave in. For a while things went well for them, they looked like the perfect couple and Melissa managed to once again walk with pride on the arm of her husband. This time was pure agony for Matthew, however. He missed the companionship and the deep sense of belonging he had known in Boston. His thoughts frequently returned to his memories of Grace and the goodness of her love. He stayed awake nights wide eyed and praying to once again lie next to her with her head upon his shoulder. He longed to talk through his dreams and plans with her just once more. He made promises to God that if he would just answer this one prayer and let him be with her just once more that he would live the rest of his life with the beautiful but oh so shallow and selfish Melissa. It was these thoughts that kept Matthew up walking the floors at night and reading until the lamps would run dry of oil. Matthew felt he was loosing his mind. If he didn't see Grace soon and taste the sweetness of her he would never know peace again. Finally, after the longest six months and most miserable Christmas of his life, he knew he had to leave. He had to find a way to go back to Boston where he could again be himself and be truly happy and with the one woman he had ever really loved.

It was after supper on February 8th. Melissa had invited a few ladies over to visit and Matthew, trying to keep out of the way, was sitting quietly in the next room when he heard the gossip that the Widow was expecting "a child to be born any day now, and her not married." Matthew almost jumped with glee. He knew the child had to be his own. He didn't have time to listen to another word, nor to put up with Melissa's whining and crying all night. Matthew packed his things and left a note for Melissa.

As Thaddeus was telling what Matthew had told him to Martha, he walked about and made it a point of looking out into the distance; he didn't want to look into her eyes. He told her of the note that Matthew said he left for Melissa asking her to forgive him and to understand that he was going to be a father, and he had to go and be with the mother of his child.

Martha sat and listened to Thaddeus tell the story of such a wasted life. She didn't interrupt and she didn't need nor want to know anything more than what he wanted to tell her.

Thaddeus continued to tell of what Matthew had shared with him. He told Martha of how happy Matthew was and how desperate he felt when he arrived at the door of Grace's cottage two days later.

When Matthew entered the cottage he barely saw the face of the doctor nor did he take any notice of the ladies from the church that had come to help out. He rushed to the side of Grace and buried his face against her neck. He lifted her face close to his and told her things would be all right. He knew that things were not going well for her and that she was having a hard time bringing this child into the world. He gently released her back to her pillows and sat quietly by her side until she once again slept.

As Thaddeus told the story of Matthew holding onto the woman he loved who was giving birth to his child a tear escaped from the corner of his eye, and he had to stop and regain his composure. His mind wanted to take him back to an earlier time when he too held onto the woman he loved as she believed him when he told her it would be okay, only to bury her after all. Like Thaddeus, Matthew was frightened. He asked questions of the doctor and became the additional hand they needed to boil water, make coffee; bring in clean towels and cool cloths. It was almost dawn before the doctor finally told Matthew that Grace might not pull through. Just after sunrise, the church ladies were sent home to be with their own families, and the doctor and Matthew sat by the fire in silence. Grace slept most of the morning and awakened in the early afternoon again with a new resolve to deliver this child and raise it with Matthew. The next eighteen hours were difficult, but finally Daphnia was born as the sun was peaking into the small kitchen shooting streaks of light across the hardwood floor. The birthing process took its toll on Grace. Matthew was informed that she would need lots of rest and the baby would need a nanny of her own for a while. Grace was simply not strong enough to care for the small infant.

There were those who reveled in the drama of it all, but there were those who were relieved to see Matthew return to the small hamlet and do right by Grace, Grace herself was ecstatic. Seeing him hold their child and take care of her brought her happiness and strength. Although she tried to get well and made attempts to hide her pain and weakness, she knew that she would not be the one to raise her beautiful little girl. She made promises to Matthew that she would get well soon, but she did not. Grace never got out of bed again after the birth of Daphnia. On March 18th, 1880, just five weeks after Daphnia was born Grace Humphreys passed away in Matthew's arms.

Matthew was lost without Grace. He waited until spring and then boarded up the little cottage and put some of Grace's precious belongings into safekeeping. He sent a telegram to Melissa that he and young daphnia would be coming to live in Lansing where he would live and work. He tried again to explain to her what he had been through and told her that if she felt she could accept them both he would return home to her in Huron City. He believed Melissa would forgive him and accept Daphnia once she had been given enough time to think and get over her hurt pride; besides, if she loved him, surely she could love his child. He felt he could convince her in time that there was no reason to be angry. Anger got in the way of things, he thought, and Daphnia needed a mother and he needed a wife. He could not come to terms with the idea of it being a sin to love two very different women, and he did love Melissa. He would stay in Lansing and grieve Grace's death where he felt comfortable and where he could spend time with his precious baby girl. He knew he would go back to Melissa eventually, but in the meantime, he would enjoy a slower pace and allow the healing process to begin.

❦

Sitting on her stone bench, Martha remembered the conversation just as clearly as if it happened ten minutes ago. She thought of these things. She remembered talking with Matthew and how he had told her once that Sunshine Acres was a grand place if one liked cows, horses, cornfields and peaceful evenings, but this was not the life for him. He had always been a free spirit. He needed excitement and entertainment. He told her that since his return, she seemed distant from him, and his Uncle Thaddeus frequently would stop talking in mid sentence and walk away. Things just weren't quite right this time. Matthew found that their discussions would always end with them never seeming to understand what he had done, nor could they accept the fact that he didn't feel bad about it.

It was shortly after this conversation that Matthew tied his horse to the back of the buckboard and told them he was leaving and returning to Huron City to be with Melissa. Despite their protests and pleas for him to stay, he told them that he couldn't. He tried once again to explain to them why he made the decisions that he made and why he was leaving now. They tried to reassure him that they loved him and they loved Daphnia. They told him he always had a home with them then they hugged and kissed him and the baby and wished them well. Turning toward each other as Matthew rode out of sight, Thaddeus and Martha cried.

Martha knew that surely Melissa had done her own share of crying. The shame of it all was almost more than she could stand. She had written to Martha and to Matthew telling him to stay in Lansing with his bastard child. She begged him not to return to Huron City telling him that she did not ever want to see either of them. She asked her cousin, Eloise Barnes, the same cousin who had introduced her to Matthew in the first place, to move in with her. Of course Matthew did not listen to Melissa nor did he believe for one minute that she didn't love him. He did what he wanted, he returned to Huron City as if nothing had ever happened with his pockets filled with maple syrup candies and bottles of lavender toilette water. He returned to a woman who wanted him but not his child.

Melissa was not mean spirited just selfish. She tried to love the child if for no other reason than the fact that Daphnia reminded her so much of Matthew with just a hint of his arrogance, and all of his charismatic soul. Martha knew, however, that Melissa would find that Daphnia's resemblance to Matthew would not be enough to satisfy her and she would eventually send Daphnia away.

Now, with the darkness all about her Martha sat in her beloved rose garden and relived every moment of their lives with Daphnia; Matthew and his ways that made even the worst of his enemies make an abrupt about face and love him as much as they despised him a moment earlier. She thought of the argument she and Thaddeus had over Melissa's selfish request, but she knew that all of the crying and wringing of hands now was futile. Gathering her thoughts, she had finally stopped sobbing. She stood and looked about her garden. There was little light from the moon, and unless one knew exactly where they were going, they might have some difficulty making it out of the sanctuary that Thaddeus had built for her. She looked about and tried to regain her focus, not just visually but mentally as well. She heard Daphnia talking softly to Thaddeus; they must have moved from the kitchen and out to the porch she reasoned. Standing still for a moment she wiped her eyes and tried to listen.

"Please start from the beginning, Papa. I am already confused and not sure of just exactly what it is that you are afraid to tell me."

"Okay, my dear, but there is a lot to tell, and I am not easy with doing the telling." Steadying himself Thaddeus took a deep draw on his pipe. "Herbert's letter was brief and to the point, Melissa is seriously ill and she has asked for you to come and spend her last days with her in Huron City. I didn't want to just take his word, I guess, so I visited him. That's where I have been over the past week. I wanted to assess the situation for myself. Herbert is right, Melissa is gravely ill and the doctor does not expect her to get well. When I came back today I talked things over with Mart, and we agreed that you need to make up your own mind about whether to go or to stay here."

"Well of course I must go, what kind of a daughter would I be if I decided to put my stubbornness and anger above my duty to my mother. Isn't going to Huron City the right thing to do?"

"I have to be honest with you, Daphnia, right or wrong doesn't have a lot to do with it. I don't believe that if you go, you will come back to us. I want you to know that up front. I don't believe this will be just a short visit. This has to be your decision, don't allow your dreams and your life to be swayed because of someone else's newly found emotion and need for self-serving gratification. And that is what it is Daphnia, someone whom you don't even know is pulling at your heartstrings and you need to think with your head now. You have a wonderful position at the school and the kids love you. There is William and your upcoming wedding. Daphnia, this place will all be yours someday, you don't have to go anywhere. Family is family, and we are as much your family as anyone you will come to know in Huron City. I am your father's only remaining blood relative; Mart and I are your only true family, Daphnia. And, you and William will have a family of your own someday, you will raise them right here where you grew up. Huron City is not a bad place, don't get me wrong, but it is a small town on the banks of Lake Huron, it is squeezed between the lake and the St. Clair River and there are forests to its west and north. Sure it is a beautiful place to be in the late spring and early summer, but the winters are cold and wet and there isn't much to offer a young family. I am not even sure if there is a school house … there is a lot to think about, Daphnia, the barest of necessities, the type of people who live there … they have to keep their doors and windows locked, Daphnia, they have fences around their yards, there is more than one tavern and outside of town there is a camp used by the lumberjacks and river men. It is a different way of life, there is the train depot because of the shipping ports – but it is different Daphnia, so very different from these rolling hills and clean air. There is so much to tell you, so much that I don't know how to tell you, and so very much that I don't want to ever have to tell you. Like I said before, it is your decision."

"What do you mean, Papa? What is it that you don't want to tell me?" She watched him stride across the porch and lean against the railing. It was long after twilight, and she could see what appeared to be fog rolling in ahead of them.

"Give me a minute or two here, please, Daphnia. I need to just stop for a minute."

Chapter Three

Thaddeus breathed in the cool air as the memories of the last few weeks washed over him. It seemed like a lifetime and only yesterday when he got off the train in Huron City. Herbert and Daniel Bernstein were waiting for him with their shiny automobile. As usual it was raining and the sky was a slate gray in the middle of the afternoon...
... ...

... ... "Good afternoon Herb." Thaddeus said as he took the small hand of his friend being careful not to shake it too vigorously.

Herbert Bernstein was a good man, a little odd by Thaddeus Flanders' way of doing things, but they had been friends for over fifty years, long before they left St. Louis with dreams of wealth and high rolling. Thaddeus was already working with the railroad on a limited basis and Herb had left his father's law practice and was working at the St. Louis Post. They were full of life and decided they owed it to themselves to kick it up a little. They were just two young men then traveling through Chicago around the great lakes, visiting as many of the start up towns and out of the way places they could. They had stopped in Huron City for a while, but didn't stay. They decided to go back down to Detroit and eventually they went on to Lansing. It was in Lansing that Herbert left Thaddeus and went back to Huron City. Herbert had found Huron City comfortable for him, and he made the decision to set up his business there on the waterfront.

Thaddeus on the other hand, needed hills, green grass, land, and stability. And, he did not care much for Huron City. He had met Martha Collins in Lansing and felt that with the railroad station being planned there, and the help offered by her father for the down payment on a piece of land with a house and some out buildings Lansing was where he wanted to settle. He loved Martha at first sight. He was head over heels in love with her although she was a few years younger than he. He knew that to take her away from her family would not be fair. So after promising Herbert they would keep in touch, he helped him get on his way back to Huron City. Thaddeus stayed in Lansing and married Martha. Their life together was good. Theirs was a beautiful farm, the land was fertile, and there were rolling hills and creeks and forests that became a part of his soul. He fell in love with the land and enjoyed making a living with his own two hands from the richness of the earth. Eventually he gave some acreage to his brother Joshua and his wife Sarah. So they too could have a small farm. Joshua was not like Thaddeus, however, keeping up with the doings in town was much more appealing to him. The three men would meet on occasion and talk about how Thaddeus needed the land as a confirmation of his self worth and all they needed was to walk down the streets with the music coming from the taverns and to feel the brisk air at their backs. Herbert, however, was more like Thaddeus than he would admit.

While Herb Bernstein felt alive just knowing that he was a part of the birth of a town with its waterfront, its timber and smallness right at the mouth of the St. Clair River, he was comforted by owning land himself, and shared with Thaddeus his sense of pride and respect for all that it was. Helping to establish the town was good for Herbert, he was confident that with the promise of the railway and shipping port, this was his dream come true. The memories of his family's shame could stay buried and he could start with a fresh slate. No one would know him or of him, he could be who he wanted to be, not the son of a tyrant who had ranted and bullied his way through life. He set up a small general store with some typesetting equipment and newspaper office in the back. He bought a piece of land on which he would build a house that would be one of the finest in the area. He opened up the attic of the store and fashioned a comfortable two-room apartment that was more than suitable for him to live until his house was built. Huron City would become his town, and his head for turning a dollar would not go unnoticed. Herbert Bernstein was a businessman, and he needed a business to which he could devote his talent and time. He had met the woman he would marry back in St. Louis and he declared his love for her through a telegram. She responded and they were married. He promised to build her the nicest house in the entire town, and he did.

Both men had realized their dreams and stayed in touch over the years visiting, traveling, and all the while silently wondering what the other person saw in their way of living, but respecting one another just the same. Two more different men were rarely found sharing stories, sipping whiskey, and smoking their pipes around a warm fire. But

Thaddeus Flanders and Herbert Bernstein truly enjoyed each other's company. They had a history so to speak, some of it painful. There were few secrets between them and each knew there were these things that they could never share. While there friendship was more than that of blood brothers they knew that there were secrets so powerful, and so heinous that if shared with the other could result in permanent estrangement, and neither of the two was willing to gamble on such a potential risk… … …

Standing on his front porch now, Thaddeus felt Daphnia's presence behind him. If he stood silently maybe she would go away, maybe she would leave him to his thoughts… his thoughts of his last visit to Huron City; his memories of that visit were as clear as the stars in the sky, and he knew they would set things into a motion that no one would be able to stop. Secrets! God, he hated secrets!

"You better go inside, Daphnia, there is starting to be a chill in the air," he said to her hoping that she would leave him to his thoughts.

"I guess I should go in and get a wrap, I'll be back. I see Aunt Martha is still sitting on her alter, maybe I will take her out a shawl."

Thaddeus watched the young woman leave the porch and he settled himself down on the swing and looked to the sky. Had it really been just a few days ago when he was in Huron City feeling his chest tighten as the silence of secrets turned to a raging storm inside of him.

… … … Stepping off the train almost one week ago he saw Herb and his son Daniel waving frantically; he feigned a brief grin. Extending his hand to his old friend he could feel his fingers trembling and upon releasing Herbert's hand, Thaddeus thought it seemed wet. He remembered looking at his old friend and turning to Daniel who extended his hand and shook it soundly. "Well, Daniel I believe you have grown into a fine young man. You are the image of your father, maybe a little better looking." Thaddeus winked at the younger man. "How are things at the paper, Herb? How's Ruth?"

"Good, Thaddeus, real good. The Gazette has grown into a solid newspaper. I have added a room to the store, put up a wall dividing the building with Ruth running the General Store and Post Office on her side of the wall and Daniel and me taking care of the newspaper business on the other. We put out a weekly every Saturday and between Daniel and me we do a damn good job, yes sir, we do a damn good job."

It seemed to take a complete lifetime before they finally arrived at the large yellow house on Pine Street and Ruth was standing on the front porch wiping her hands on a kitchen towel. When she saw them pull up, she ran out to meet them putting her arms around Thaddeus' neck and telling him how great it was to see him. "Oh, it is so good to see you Thaddeus, you are looking well." She took his hand into the both of hers and walked with him up to the house. "I have a fresh pot of coffee and I made some maple cookies just this morning. Once you get settled in you can come down to the parlor and we will visit, I do wish Martha could have seen her way fit to come along with you. It has been a while since she and I were able to just sit and gossip. So what brings you here anyway? I know that you have a lot of things going on with you holding such a powerful position with the railroad, but …my, oh, my, but you do remind me of someone from long ago, you are still as handsome as ever, Thaddeus Flanders, I do swear you are. Let me look at you. How have you been?"

"Now, now, Ruth, let the man get inside before you start pawing all over him and asking a lot of questions, you know you might be asking for more information than he might be ready to share," Herbert scolded the over-exuberant woman.

"I'm sorry, Thaddeus, I was just so surprised when Herbert said that you were coming for a visit. And, it is so good to see you." Ruth was annoyed and gave a disapproving look toward Herbert who had just cut her off again by motioning to Daniel to take Thaddeus' things upstairs.

"Just let me get freshened up a bit, Ruth, and I will be right down and I will be happy to answer your questions and fill you in on all the gossip, at least that gossip that I know of," he turned around to see Daniel with his satchel. Walking over and taking the satchel from the young man he said, "I'm an old friend, not a guest, and I expect to be treated like one young man, no need to carry my bag for me. I'll be back down directly." He nodded at the trio standing before him then turned and walked up the stairs and into the room they had made up for him. Once in the room, Thaddeus sat down on the bed and took out his pipe, lit it, and took in a few deep breaths before going to the satchel and taking out the baked goods that Martha had prepared for Ruth and Herbert. There was also a white handkerchief crocheted with purple and pink threads in a spring flower design around the edges, Martha was fond of any type of needle work, and this was especially pretty; she had made it for Ruth after she and Thaddeus had talked, and when it was decided that he would be taking a trip to see their very dear friends. He picked up the gifts and headed back downstairs; he hoped young Daniel would be kind enough to go out for the evening so that he could talk freely with Herb and Ruth.

Upon re-entering the parlor, he saw that his friend had taken care to ensure their privacy. Young Daniel was on his way out the door.

"Daniel won't be joining us for dinner Thaddeus; I hope you won't feel hurt. He had accepted an earlier invitation for dinner with a friend and then he has promised to do some work later for this week's edition. And, thankfully, Ruth has given up interfering for the moment and she has gone into the kitchen to put the finishing touches on dinner, its one of her specialties, interfering I mean. Have a seat. I hope you aren't disappointed that Daniel isn't joining us. And with a little luck, maybe we can find a way to escape Ruth's inquisitions as well."

"Of course I'm not disappointed, Herb. I do have to say that it might have been interesting to hear his viewpoint on the happenings here in the big city of Huron. But, I remember what it was like to be young and carefree, and the two of us spending our evenings spinning tales and sharing dreams. But in all honesty I was hoping that we would have some time to talk alone before I see Melissa and we have to deal with some sticky details. I'll catch up with Daniel before I leave so this worked out just fine. Once again you have taken care of everything – you are the master of neat and tidy, tying up all the loose ends, and being careful to see that things are in the expected order leaving no room for questions or second-guessing. You never change, do you?" Thaddeus could feel the sting of sarcasm in his voice but it was something that just came out without warning, he wanted to say something kinder to alleviate the tone but he didn't know what to say.

Herb, too, felt the jab. He had not heard such sarcasm from this friend in the past and he was caught off guard. Suddenly he was not comfortable at all with this evening and felt more than a little defensive; maybe a little diversion would be good after all.

Fingering the rim of his glass he mused as to why Thaddeus had ridden from the station without mentioning Daphnia or Melissa. What was this sarcasm all about? Was his old friend more than just tired? Trying to pretend not to notice and certainly not to take Thaddeus' comments to heart he stood and walked over to the hearth. Taking out his pipe he filled it with tobacco from the engraved humidor.

"By the way, Thaddeus, I have told you how sick Melissa is haven't I? She is having a rough time of it. You have spoken to Daphnia, haven't you? How did she take the news? How much does she know? Will she be coming for a visit soon?"

"To tell you the truth, Herbert, I haven't talked to Daphnia about any of this. I needed to see a few things for myself first. I just didn't want to get her all worked up before I had a grasp of what was truly going on. I know that Melissa is gravely ill, but I believe that is a poor excuse to get Daphnia here. She has a life all planned out for herself. Martha and I just aren't ready to send her to live here where she knows no one and where there is no …well, family."

"Where there is no family, Thaddeus? You are wrong and you know it.

"Herbert, you have to see this from my point of view. Martha and I are the only real family that Daphnia knows, why change all of that now?"

"Because it is the right thing to do, that's why! Time changes everything. People change, they grow older, Thaddeus, they grow more cynical and sometimes they even grow more sentimental. I know how you feel, believe me. This is a serious time and a serious thing that we need to do. You know that Ruth and I will do all we can to make her life here comfortable. Anything she needs from us we will be more than happy to give to her. It doesn't matter what you or I want. What matters is what is right. We are getting old, now. Life was different when we were young. Forty or fifty ago, hell, we would have been out there with Daniel and that young Tom Saunders making our voices heard and puffing out our chests like there was no tomorrow, and that is what we did, Thaddeus. We did some stuff, we said some things, we took action. By God, Thaddeus, back then we didn't stand on the

53

sidelines waiting, watching, listening for signs of danger, we lived, we laughed and now and then we loved."

"Those times are over, Herbert. Besides I don't need to go back forty or fifty years, I can stop at twenty! I wish like hell that I had stood on the sidelines back then, and by God, Herbert we are paying for it now. Don't the voices come back to you at two in the morning? Don't you see the mud and hear the rain pounding against the buildings and feel the water running down your collar? Do you wake up listening for the laughter at the bar as a sign telling you that no one heard, no one knows, and no one will ever know? Well, I do. I know what it is like to hold the mother of your child while she lays there begging you to make the pain go away and to promise her that everything will be okay. I know what it is like to bury a child and to see the heart of a mother break. I know what it is like to hold the woman you love while she lays there ....Goddamn it Herbert, I know and I don't need to know no more. So don't talk to me about getting old. Damn, you sound like Martha asking me if I have forgotten what it was like to be young. Not everything is about getting old, Goddamn it! Some things are about the memories of being young and having to revisit those times when everyone else has gone to sleep and there is nothing stirring but you and the bats flying around the treetops looking for mosquitoes. I just don't know why Melissa has come forward after all of this time. I just don't understand."

"Melissa is very ill, Thaddeus. For her to want to see Daphnia now is only reasonable. As for being old, I am not so old that I have forgotten about being young. But you need to remember too that even a very young man can sometimes feel very old, but let's not get into that right now. Let's deal with what is happening to Melissa and how comfortable we can make Daphnia during her visit. She can live with Melissa and Eloise, she can live here if she wants, or she can live in the apartment over the Gazette office, it will be her choice. I will work with her, she loves the excitement of writing the news and she has a real knack for words and numbers. She will be of tremendous help to me and to Daniel, it will be a good learning opportunity for her, and she will get to know Melissa. But, let's take things one at a time."

"Moving Daphnia here and having her learn a new career under your tutelage and direction is not taking things one at a time, Herbert.

I don't care about who or what decisions need to be made nor who is ill or how gravely. What I care about is Daphnia. Now how about you telling me just what exactly is going on? And, more importantly how about telling me what has happened that you are so desperate to use Melissa as the lure to get Daphnia here?"

"There is a lot going on, probably more than you will ever know or more than I could ever tell you. Let's just say that it is time for Daphnia to learn more about who she is and time to fulfill the promise to a dying woman. Melissa has been ill for sometime now and this sudden turn for the worse was not totally unexpected, but certainly her interest in seeing Daphnia came from her without prompting from me. I was as surprised at her request as I am sure you are. Melissa is a complicated woman and she has suffered greatly. I know that you never really thought too much about her, but it was painful and very difficult for Melissa to send that child away. But, she did it because she felt it was the right thing for Daphnia. After, Matthew, well Melissa was never quite right. You can't go on blaming her. If I had only known then of the pain and suffering she would endure, I mean things could have been different. Jesus, man why are you making this so difficult, you know what I am up against here, you know what I mean and what Melissa and Daphnia mean to me as well. Can't you put aside your own holier than thou attitude for just a little while and see that there are others in this world who can love and who do love? Can't you see that you and Martha, thank you very much for all you have been, are not the beginning and the end to Daphnia's life and bloodlines? Can't you find room for just a little compassion and understanding of what others might have endured and might be enduring today. Blood isn't everything, Thaddeus. Some people are family without ever sharing a name, bloodline, or eye color. Don't you ever stay up at night being tormented by your memories of things you did and cannot change but would change them if you could? Melissa is a good woman, Thaddeus! Don't blame her for this, her circumstances are merely a reasonable opportunity for Daphnia to learn the truth. We can't let this chance pass us by. Lord only knows how fate works, let's stop arguing. All of our questions won't be answered here tonight. These things will take time. Do you understand what I am telling you? Melissa needs this. Daphnia needs this. Maybe you and I need this, too. Do you understand what I am asking; do you hear what I am saying to you?"

"I know exactly what you are telling me Herb, but that doesn't change things. We have talked, you and I, for hours upon hours over the years about circumstances and events that have lead us to make the decisions we have made. But Melissa, Herb! I do have compassion for Melissa. I have seen her over the years, I have not been a stranger in her house."

"What do you mean, Thaddeus? Just how comfortable have you made yourself there?"

"Don't be ridiculous, Herbert. Jealousy is not becoming to you and I am insulted that you would imply that there has been …"

"I am sorry, Thaddeus, of course I know better, it's just that life has become more and more complicated. Go ahead. What were you saying?"

"I was saying that I have seen her change from a bright and spirited beauty to a woman filled with bitterness and envy. While I was not one of the men taken with her charms, I nevertheless can see why others were. I have talked at length with Melissa from time to time, and I believe that I have understood her, but I don't understand her now. Compassion, Herb? You ask if I have compassion, well I do. I am saddened by what has happened to her and I realize that she may have lost her ability to reason since the sickness has taken hold of her. But, this is beyond you Herbert. I am more than surprised at you; I am bewildered. What has happened to make this an opportune time? I know how you feel about Melissa, but even you have to admit that she is selfish and unyielding when it comes to getting her way."

"Thaddeus, Melissa took to her bed over six years ago. Six years ago, Thaddeus. She was just a young woman of thirty-seven. Since that time not even her cousin Eloise can coerce her to sit on the porch. The most she will do, or should I say would do, would be to just sit by the window in her rocking chair and stare out. She doesn't even do that anymore. When I used to see her she would talk a little, now and then she might even laugh lightly or softly hum a lullaby, but she doesn't do those things anymore. She lost all interest in everything some time back, and I don't know exactly why or even when. It happened, that's all I know."

"If that's the case, Herbert, and I believe you, then what is behind her sudden wanting Daphnia to return and help take care of her? It seems so strange. You do know that is what she is asking!" Thaddeus all but shouted at Herbert and pounded his fist against the arm of the chair causing Herbert to jump as though he had been struck.

Thaddeus stood and paced across the room. "Martha and I love that child. We took her in our home and raised her just as if she was our very own. It is breaking Martha's heart to have to see her leave. We have plans, and Daphnia has plans, and not one of them include her returning to this damn city to take care of a dying woman who never cared about her. Melissa has done nothing for Daphnia since she sent her to us. One would have thought Daphnia had dropped off the face of the earth until now. Now that this time has become so opportune!!!" Thaddeus was so angry that his knuckles were white and his teeth were clinched as he spoke.

Herb could hear the bitterness in Thaddeus' voice and he could see the rage in his face. Not wanting to intervene just yet, he felt it best to let his friend release this anger now rather than hold it inside of him. He sat quietly and stared out the window.

"You have no idea, Herb, what it is like, what it has been like raising Daphnia. She is a beautiful young woman with a wonderful life. She loves her home, her job and she has a young man with whom she is mightily in love. How can you or anyone else ask that she give all of that up? Martha and I are Daphnia's family. I am sorry, Herb, but that is how I feel. We are the ones who have loved her and watched her grow. We are the ones who have lived through the nightmares of her childhood and trials and temptations of her becoming a young woman. How can anyone ask that we give that up? And, we would be giving it up, Herb. We will be the losers here, not . . .well certainly not Melissa."

Calling on everything he had in him, Herbert finally rose and walked over to his friend. "Thaddeus, I love Daphnia too. I have made many sacrifices over the years, I have prostituted my integrity and my morals. I have done things and gone farther than anyone should be asked to do or to go. There are things that have happened that you are unaware of and may never fully know or understand. This situation with Melissa is an opportunity for everyone, and unfortunate one for you maybe, but nevertheless an opportunity for Daphnia. Melissa is dying, you and Martha have years ahead of you. I am older than you;

I don't have those years. It didn't seem to matter so much at one time, but now it does. My remaining years are fewer now and they continue to slip away. You can't keep Daphnia on that farm forever. You can't decide whom she can know and whom she can love, who is family and who is not. Families sometimes are like a patchwork quilt, not all of the pieces are alike but they are families just the same. Where does Melissa fit in, well I'll tell you. It is like this, Thaddeus, it is Melissa's turn to have some peace, to feel good, to make amends or whatever it is that she feels she must do. Now that is the truth of it. Melissa wrote to Daphnia on her own. It wasn't due to any prodding from me or anyone else that she has asked Daphnia to return to Huron City. Even you cannot deny a dying woman one of her last wishes. Even if that woman is Melissa Flanders, Thaddeus, you can't deny her that." Turning away from Thaddeus' glare, Herbert stopped speaking as he saw Ruth coming into the room, he wondered how much she had heard.

"I've got our supper on the table, now. You two come right along, don't dawdle, Herbert." Ruth looked at the two men and wished she had been just a few minutes sooner and a whole lot quieter. What was going on with all of this arguing and senseless talk between these two men? She knew they were talking of having Daphnia return to Huron City, but she was confused about why. Herbert had made several off the cuff comments over the past couple of weeks about needing help and Daphnia wanting to work with print, and how Melissa had been asking for her. He had presented the situation to her saying that Daphnia had a desire to become a newspaper woman and Melissa had asked Thaddeus to allow the girl to come back and help Eloise, but this seemed to strange. How did Herbert know so much about Daphnia? Maybe Thaddeus had visited Huron City and Herbert without coming to the house? Ruth was sure there was something going on and she didn't feel easy about it. What was this? Herb asked her just last week if she would mind if Daphnia came to Huron City for a visit. He mentioned that Daphnia might want to stay above the newspaper office, but wouldn't she want to stay with Melissa? Something was fishy here and Ruth knew it. Why was there so much seriousness? And, Herbert, he was acting very peculiar. She could see Thaddeus' temples working and she knew this meant he was in deep thought. She wished she had heard more of their conversation, but from what she heard it sure didn't seem like this was the idea of Thaddeus and Martha. Now it looked like Herbert was less than up front with her and that did not bode well with Ruth Bernstein.

"Come on to supper, Herbert!"

Moving toward the table Ruth tried to be coy and make light conversation, but she was too eager to learn more about what was going on. As she looked at Thaddeus she found herself staring. He looked so good to her, his jaw line, the way he held his head, the stirrings she was feeling were from the past, and oh so familiar. She tried not to draw attention to her staring, but just as she felt herself being drawn to an old memory Herbert's voice brought her back to the moment.

"Ruth, are you okay?"

"Of course I'm okay, Herbert. So, Thaddeus, Herbert tells me that Daphnia would like to come to Huron City for a visit. When might she be coming? Please tell her that she is invited to supper, we would just love that. Of course, I am sure she won't be able to stay long with her teaching and all. It has been just too long since I have seen her. I'll bet she is the image of that handsome and devilish papa of hers how is she anyway? She motioned for the two men to sit and she turned toward the kitchen. I just need to bring in the rest of the supper, you two sit, please."

As she went into the kitchen her mind raced. The truth of the matter was that she wasn't all that eager to prepare a meal for the illegitimate child of Matthew Flanders and that harlot Grace Humphreys; but God it was good to see Thaddeus, he brought back so many feelings she thought she had long forgotten.

She shook her head as if to clear her mind. What was wrong with her she wondered? Where were these thoughts coming from? They were a distraction to her; she needed to listen to the two men on the other side of the door, but she couldn't seem to shake Grace Humphreys and Matthew Flanders out of her mind. Although she had never met the widow, she had heard plenty. As for Matthew he was another story. The thought of him caused her face to flush bright red, partly due to guilt but mostly with memories of passion and hot summer nights... ... ...

… … …   Her mind went back to a time when Daniel was just a child and Herbert had become distant and spent more time with his newspaper office than he did with her. Their marriage had been arranged by her father after Herbert had done some fancy bookwork for him. Herbert had told the older man that he never thought much about love, but he was in need of a wife to warm his bed and cook his dinners up in Huron City. When her father introduced him to Ruth and her sister, neither of the young women were impressed, but that didn't stop Herbert. He sent a telegram informing her father of his intentions and stating that whichever daughter he thought would be most agreeable would be fine with him. Without so much as asking the girls their feelings, her father immediately accepted the proposal, made the decision and answered the telegram. It mattered not that Herbert was some seven years older than she, what mattered was that Ruth was not as attractive as her younger sister and this opportunity to marry was probably the last one she would ever have. The marriage was arranged, and the wedding took place in St. Louis in a small synagogue in the center of town. Ruth and Herbert were married, he promised to take care of her and she vowed to make him a loyal wife. Her promise was not as easy to keep as his. Once young Daniel was born their lives changed abruptly. She became lonely and depressed and he spent more and more time with work. In time her interest in him did not go beyond his ability to turn one dollar into two. After too many dinners left warming on the stove and her desire for him growing colder her life had become a disappointment. The two of them had nothing in common but young Daniel, any romance they once shared was gone within the first couple of months of marriage. It was bearable for Herbert; he didn't seem to mind at all. But an empty marriage and little or no conversation was more than Ruth could live with. Realizing how unhappy and bitter she was becoming, Herbert suggested that she return to St. Louis for a while and visit with her family. She didn't hesitate to accept his suggestion. She agreed to leave Herbert and Daniel for a while and to visit her sister in St. Louis. Herbert found a colored woman from down in the quarters to come in and care for Daniel and do the cooking and cleaning while she was away, and this suited Ruth fine. She delighted in the idea of spending time in St. Louis with the booming city and being free from a house without love.

It was in St. Louis where she met Matthew Flanders and had her thirst for romance and need for passion awakened and so delightfully satisfied. He was handsome, romantic, mysterious and a little on the dangerous side. He made her skin tingle and her stomach felt as if there were a thousand butterflies constantly fluttering inside. Maybe a part of the passion they shared was due to the fact that each had someone else waiting for them, she Herbert and he a special someone of whom there was talk, but never from him. Her sister told her that the woman's name was Melissa and that she was beautiful but dreadfully self absorbed.

Ruth had hoped that Matthew would see in her what he later saw in Melissa, but he didn't. He would tease her enough, but never returned her desire for a more long lasting relationship. He would remind her that she was married, had a child and was more than a few years older than he. This bothered Ruth, but she convinced herself that she loved him. She had allowed him to be with her and to fill the void left empty by Herbert. She went to sleep nights with her body and heart aching for more of him; but she knew that while she may be in love with him he did not share those same feelings for her. She prayed herself to sleep asking God to let Matthew return her love while devising a plan for telling Herbert that she would be leaving him. Her plans would not work out. When Matthew finally told her that he was completely and totally in love with Melissa, it broke her heart. They had gone to see a Minstrel Show, it was the spring of 1878 and Ruth could still smell the sweet fragrance of the Honeysuckle and Jasmine growing up the side of the brick wall near the town square. That was what she was leaning against so that Matthew could caress her backside with one hand while the other was having its way with her breast. Just as she was ready to succumb to his advances and beg him to join her in her room again tonight, he pulled away.

"I must tell you that I have finally made a decision. This has not been easy nor was it expected. But, Ruthie I am ready to settle down. I am in love. I am in love, Ruthie, I am in love with the most beautiful woman in the world. I am ready to make a commitment, I want to get married, I have finally found the woman of my dreams," he teased her with his kisses as he turned her chin up so that her eyes would meet his. He wrapped her in his arms and twirled her out again. "So, give me a kiss for luck, Ruthie, 'cause I'm going to ask her to marry me." He then took her back into his arms and kissed her passionately on her lips.

Ruth trembled in his arms and almost passed dead away from the taste of his kiss. When she pulled her mouth away from his he threw his head back and laughed like someone who had just won the golden cup at the County Fair. He spun her around, and without any knowledge of what he had just done to her, he laughed.

"Well, what's the matter, Ruth? You look like you have just had all the life drained right out of you. I have heard that my kisses can be intoxicating, but you look more than drunk, you look like you may faint. Here, come over here and let's sit down a minute."

He laughed loudly as he walked her over to the bench so proud of himself that he did not realize that it was not his kiss that had drained the blood away from her face, but the words he had just spoken.

"Why, Matthew, when did you decide all of this? I am so surprised and happy, I dreamed, but …."

"She's beautiful, Ruth, a little young, but she's all I'll ever need, all I'll ever want. She makes me happier than I have ever been in my life, you are wonderful, Ruthie, you have been just the diversion that I have needed – you keep me busy and don't put any demands on me, you have been great, truly. Thanks for understanding."

Ruth was in shock. She tried to back away as she realized that it was not her he was thinking of marrying. Scrambling to stand and trying to run at the same time she took hold of his arm to brace herself.

Matthew took her hand away and turned her toward him. "Listen to me Ruthie I didn't plan this. It was three weeks ago when I was back East. I swear to you it happened right out of the blue. I can't help myself, Ruthie. Are you okay? Let me tell you about her. She is everything I have ever dreamed of; she is the only girl for me. I know it. I'll be leaving tomorrow to return to Boston and ask for her hand in marriage. Her name is Melissa, isn't that the most beautiful name you ever heard, just think of it, Melissa Flanders, don't you like the sound of that?"

Ruth could hardly breathe, she felt faint. She could feel the tears burning as they ran down her cheeks. She wanted to scream at him and to tell him no, but the words she wanted to say stayed in her head, she couldn't speak.

"You don't look so well, Ruthie. I had better get you inside."

"Aren't you coming in tonight, Matthew?" she finally whispered.

"Can't tonight, ole' girl, I have a long train ride ahead of me, and I'm too wound up to sleep, I'd come up, but, you know, are you all right?" Throwing his head back and laughing right out loud, he grabbed her hand and spun her around and into his arms again only to wink at her and push her away when she threw her arms around his neck and pressed her body into his. The tears streamed down her face.

As they arrived at the Hotel Fairmont, Ruth was numb. She was waiting for him to say something to let her know that he had been only joking, he couldn't possibly mean that he had found someone else to fall in love with, not after this last ten weeks, not now, not when she had given so much. He was right; she didn't feel well.

They were standing at the front door of the hotel when he gave her backside a final squeeze and then skipped down the steps. She finally found her voice as he reached the last step and with a mixed cry and whisper she called to him, "Matthew, Matthew, when will I see you again?"

"I gotta go, Ruthie, got a lot of packing to do. The next time you see me will be if and when we run into each other in Boston. You take care, now. It has been good knowing you. Tell that husband of yours that you deserve better."

She saw him wink through her tears and blow her a kiss. He turned and almost danced down the street. She could hear him whistling for what seemed like an eternity before she finally left the steps and went up to her room and cried... ... ...

Yes, she remembered Matthew, when he moved to Huron City with Melissa he would walk right past her down the middle of town and never do more than wink and nod his head. He would come into the store and tease her with his flirtations, slight caresses and every now and then talk her into going into the backroom with him; but he never loved her. She was merely a diversion just as he had said back in St. Louis all of those years ago. It broke her heart every time she saw him. And as for Grace Humphreys, well she had heard plenty about her over the years when she and Herbert visited in Lansing.

As for what she thought of Melissa, she was nothing more than a pretty plaything who was selfish and lacked any true compassion or character. It wasn't long after Matthew's death before news of a secret benefactor somewhere surfaced only no one really knew much about him. It was someone of wealth and position who had set everything up between his out of state firm and the bank in Huron City, Ruth knew that Herbert was their liaison, but she never quite figured it out. She eventually surmised that since Herbert was one of the pillars of the city, and certainly one of an impeccable business reputation that it was just a natural fit, especially since Daphnia was the great niece of his best friend. And, besides everyone said that Melissa was so fragile. But Ruth believed different. She heard the rumors, certainly Melissa knew that everyone knew what she was doing and what Matthew had done and then him going off and getting himself killed and leaving her to raise his child conceived during a spring fling with the Widow Humphreys; of course Melissa couldn't love the child. It couldn't be Melissa wanting Daphnia to "come home" and Ruth was determined to find out who was behind this charade and why. But not tonight, she would let Herbert have his say and then she would begin her unweaving of the web that had been woven by someone who obviously had their own vested interest in seeing a reunion of Melissa and Daphnia, but who? She wondered these things almost to the point of distraction as she returned to the dining room with only a dishtowel in her hands.

<hr/>

"Well here she is. Ruth, we were beginning to think you had forgotten we were out here. Ruth makes the best Beef Stroganoff of anyone around Thaddeus. I have seen her put together a meal that one could feast upon for a week without anything more than a few potatoes, carrots and a shank of beef."

Ruth, realizing what Herbert had just said gulped and made a little squeaking sound as she cleared her throat. "Excuse me, gentlemen, but I must be losing my mind tonight, I have walked right out of the kitchen with nothing but this dishtowel in my hand."

Both men chuckled, but Herbert turned beet red. Ruth quickly returned to the kitchen for the night's main course. Upon once again entering the dining room, she placed the platter filled with beef, potatoes and rich brown gravy on the table. Herbert rose to pull out her chair, but it was too late, Ruth had sat down and looked as if she were trying to shrink beneath the table before he could get to her. "I am sorry,

Thaddeus, I will try not to be anymore of a distraction this evening, please enjoy your supper. Herbert, pass the rolls to Thaddeus, please."

"Not to worry, Ruth, we are all a little distracted these days. I can say this though, it seems Herbert might be right this looks just wonderful. I hope you didn't go out of your way here tonight just for me. I don't want to be a bother. And, I should warn you up front that I have not had much of an appetite since we received the wire from Herbert about Melissa. It has just about taken the spirit out of me, I swear. I am exhausted from thinking about it."

"I'll bet it's been more than exhausting for Martha, Thaddeus. Can you just believe how fate works? I don't know how to imagine what Martha must be going through with Melissa's request right at the same time that Daphnia has decided to stop teaching and change careers. And what an unlikely change it is too. Going from teaching in that little country schoolhouse to working in a real newspaper office, how will she do it? Didn't the Lansing Journal want to take her on as an apprentice some year's back? Herbert has always said that once that newsprint gets under one's fingernails it finds its way into their very blood. I guess that is what happened to little Daphnia. She must have gotten some of that newsprint on her and just could no longer resist the calling. Is that what happened, Thaddeus? Did she just come down stairs one day and spring her decision to throw her life as a respectable school teacher away and go chase some stories about cats getting stuck in trees or a goat in a well? Young people these days. But, then Daphnia is not really that young anymore, is she. Not so young as one would think a woman would be who still lived at home and still not married, or engaged, or, unless, I mean, well, I am sure you understand what I am trying to say. One would just expect that by the time a girl reaches a certain age they would be married, or at least settled down, unless, I mean, unless well, maybe she isn't interested in marriage?"

"Ruth! Please, of course Daphnia is interested in marriage. Did you forget something in the kitchen? Please excuse her, Thaddeus," Herbert shot Ruth a look filled with disgust as she rose from the table and returned to the kitchen.

"What is Ruth talking about, Herbert? What's going on here? Melissa is ill, isn't she? This isn't some game you are playing to manipulate . . ." Thaddeus saw the kitchen door move, but no one came through it. "Come on in, Ruth, you may as well listen in here at the table as out there in kitchen."

"I am not trying to eavesdrop Thaddeus Flanders, if that is what you are implying. I just got turned around a little. Here, I brought out more hot bread. I am sorry for my ramblings on earlier, Thaddeus. Sometimes I just don't know when to keep still."

Herb cleared his throat. "Now would be a good time for you to practice, Ruth. Thaddeus, Melissa is gravely ill. We all have our own demons, but feigning illness is not one of Melissa's. She needs and wants to see Daphnia. She is the only Mother Daphnia has ever really known. Regardless of our feelings about all that has happened, we are still walking around on two feet. Melissa is lying in that bed all day long seven days a week. She hasn't asked for much from life, I think we can honor this request."

"Honoring Melissa's request is not what is bothering me, Herb. It is this talk of Daphnia's love of the newspaper business. Have you heard something? I know you are friends with the people at the Journal, but Daphnia hasn't said anything to me about this."

"Why, I never!" Ruth jumped up from the table and putting her hands on her hips she huffed and stormed back into the kitchen and out the back door. She needed a breath of fresh air. What on earth was going on, she wondered.

The two men continued their conversation almost unaware of Ruth's outburst or the fact that she had actually left the house. "What I have heard is very little, Thaddeus. But, what I do know is that when Daphnia worked at the Journal she loved it and they loved her. I keep up with important information, and I am on top of this one. Daphnia is a grown woman. If she stays up there on that farm she will be a spinster schoolmarm with never any of her own dreams and capabilities realized. I can offer her that here in Huron City, unless, of course you are willing to tell her that her entire life has been a lie. What consequences would come of that? Besides, she has to do the right thing and return to help with Melissa." He tucked his dinner napkin inside the neck of his shirt. "Daphnia needs to make her own decisions. And, she can't make fair decisions unless she knows the options. Here in Huron City there are many opportunities. She can work right here at the Gazette, with Daniel and me she will learn from the best, we can teach her as much as she will learn anywhere. She will have us to look after her, and there are certainly eligible young men here that she may take a fancy to. You won't be losing her, Thaddeus, the trains run almost every week between here and Lansing. I won't tie her down, I promise. Besides, you and Martha can visit more often. Just give it a chance, Thaddeus. There is so much that ...."

The door between the two rooms swung open and Ruth once again entered, she looked tired and angry.

"Now Herbert, can't you see that this is all too much talk over supper? If Daphnia were to leave the farm, why it would break Martha's and Thaddeus' hearts. Thaddeus is already exhausted, he said so himself, and just look at him. I don't know when I have seen him look more gray and worn out. Why, I think Thaddeus that you have aged ten years since your visit here just last spring. What are you thinking about Herbert? You are rambling on like an old woman about Daphnia starting over, opportunities and beaus and such? The only eligible young man I know of who may have the slightest interest in someone of Daphnia's ..., well at her age and all, well the only one I can think of who isn't already spoken for is that Thomas Saunders that you and Daniel are so taken with. Besides she has lived on that farm for so long, it is in her blood. And there is nothing wrong with teaching school. It is an honorable profession for a young woman, and a safe one for sure. Why would she want to come here and work for our small town paper?"

"Now maybe you should stay out of this, Ruth," Herbert said between clinched teeth.

Ruth ignored him. She was determined not to be silenced or sent from the room this time. She continued, "Why, indeed? Why would she leave a home where she has been taken care of almost all of her life to move here to help take care of Melissa? Or, is she moving here to work? Why is she wanting to come here again, Thaddeus? I guess I have missed some of the facts somehow. She will have to work won't she? How else will she live? And, anyway, Herbert, with Melissa so ill, Daphnia probably won't be around for very long to make a dent in learning anything about the paper business, why would she stay here after Melissa passes. Of course, I must ask, why again, just why is she coming here at all? She has a home, a job and surely there are young men in Lansing that are suitable for someone with Daphnia's background. I heard that she has had a long and involved relationship for several years with a farmer boy. And besides, well you know, dear, besides, well she just won't have much time to get to know any young men, except for Daniel, that is, and my dear, well, I mean, after all any woman that would be good enough, that would be right, I mean, that Daniel would be interested in would have to be, well you know what I mean, Thaddeus, Daphnia is, Daphnia is, well, you know, dear, no offense Thaddeus, but Daphnia is more experienced than what Daniel may, I mean, than a younger, well, Thaddeus, Daphnia is just not Jewish."

Ruth knew she had gone too far. She caught her breath as she looked into Thaddeus' eyes, they were blazing. "I am sorry, Thaddeus, I didn't mean that to sound the way it did." She reached across the table to touch his hand only to knock over a water glass. "Here, here, let me get that, I am so sorry." Grabbing the end of her apron, Ruth began to wipe up the water and then without another word she got up and left the room.

Thaddeus was livid. Standing so he was sure to be heard he yelled in the direction of the closing door to the birdlike woman, "Don't worry, Ruth, I feel certain that Daphnia would not be interested in your Daniel. After all, she is a well-adjusted young woman of just over twenty-three, and Daniel must be well over thirty by now. And, the young farmer boy that you are referring to is a fine young man who is currently studying to become a doctor."

Sitting back down, Thaddeus was exhausted. "I do appreciate your words of encouragement, Herbert, thank you. Would you mind passing that stroganoff this way?" Thaddeus did not like this type of conversation, and he especially didn't like talking business and serious issues with women other than Martha, he could tell her anything. He did not understand the hidden meanings behind what most women said. He had begun to regret the fact that he had accepted Herbert's invitation to stay in his home. This would be a very long two days. He resolved to make the best of it and stay out of conversations with Ruth whenever possible.

"Now Thaddeus, Ruth sometimes talks when she should just serve the food and keep still. You and I know that the chances of Daphnia and Daniel becoming involved are far fetched at best. I am sure that

Ruth was just concerned because of Daniel's vulnerability. Things could happen, stranger things have, Lord knows. Let's not worry about the pettiness of a bitter woman tonight. We need to stay focused on the things that are important, like family. I am an old man Thaddeus, Melissa is dying; Daphnia needs to spend some time with us here in Huron City. Don't worry about Ruth; I will deal with her in time. Please don't be offended by her gossipy and unrealistic meanderings."

"No offense taken, Herb. Let's enjoy this supper and maybe you and I can take a walk around town later and you can show me all the changes since I was here last."

Leaning against the other side of the kitchen door, Ruth was intent on listening to the two men. So intent in fact that she bumped against the door causing it to swing open into the dining room with her stumbling through. She regained her composure and sat down at the table without looking at either of the men. She would eat her meal without comment. No questions came her way and the men talked around her as if they did not notice that she had re-entered the room much less joined them at the table. Silence was not what she would have preferred, but it gave her a chance to observe the two old friends and to listen to her husband's views on Daphnia, and his surprising compassion for Melissa. Why, to sit and listen to Herbert, one would think that he was rolling out the red carpet for Daphnia, and was eager to have her under foot. It was like he was going to be the mediator bringing these two estranged women together, but why. She almost forgot to chew when she heard him set in to telling Thaddeus about how Melissa had aged over the last few months. How did he know these things?

"It sounds like her health has gone down faster than what I originally thought, Herb. What happened to make her fail so quickly? How much has she been told about Daphnia's life today? What makes you think that having Daphnia come to Huron City now is the right thing to do for either of them? I don't feel at all good about this Herbert. There must be a better way to work through this need for family."

"Where do you want me to start, Thaddeus? Melissa has been bedridden almost completely for the last six months. I was over just last week and she barely recognized me. I sat with her for a while and read some to her, but I am not sure how much she actually heard. She has lost so much weight I don't believe she could stand if she wanted to, and she can barely speak above a whisper. She has gone down steadily this past year. She has some things that she needs to settle. How can I deny her that opportunity if there is anything in my power to help make it happen? Time takes away hurt and old hearts tend to become sentimental. We all get a little melancholy from time to time. You, Melissa and I, we're not a lot different, let's make things right, if we can, while there is still time. I know you are tired, but she is dying. I see changes in her from one Tuesday to the next; it is remarkable that she is still alive. God, she was so full of life, I can hear her laughter when I close my eyes, I can see her beautiful smile, I can't deny her a chance to laugh again, to smile again, to feel some happiness again if only for a short while."

With that, Ruth stood up and began to clear away the table. She thought just a short time ago that she wanted to know how Herbert knew so much, and now she wasn't so sure that was the right thing to wish for. He goes to see her every Tuesday! What for? Why? Every Tuesday, she wondered how long has this been going on. He reads to her? He has compassion? Why, he has never shown an ounce of compassion to her or to Daniel. And, he has never done one thing to convince her that he had enough feelings toward anything or anyone to ever be melancholy. As for sentiment, well she would swear that he didn't have a sentimental bone in his scrawny little body. She bustled out of the room in a huff.

"What does the doctor say, Herbert? You have surely talked to him about this. Does he feel that having Daphnia come to help out will do Melissa any real good?"

Walking back into the room to gather the rest of the dishes, Ruth couldn't believe what she had heard. Before she could stop herself, she practically yelled, "Help Out! Help out indeed." Then she accidentally let a piece of crystal slip from her hand as she moved to pick it up she again looked into the eyes of Thaddeus. Cold chills ran up and down her spine as she stood frozen in place holding his stare.

"Ruth, what is the matter with you? Come on Thaddeus maybe we should retire to the parlor. How about a glass of Sherry? Or would you prefer to take a walk around town before it gets too late?"

"No thanks to the sherry just now. Tell me, what has the doctor said?"

"The Doctor told me that there is no hope for Melissa ever getting better. Melissa said that she has some things she needs to discuss with Daphnia. I have kept her informed about Daphnia's life, her schooling, her teaching I even told her that I thought she was involved with a young man. Melissa cares about Daphnia. She needs to know some of the truths about her life."

"I think we should take that walk now, Herbert."

Herbert rose and walked over to get a light jacket from the hall closet. He suddenly realized that he may have said too much too soon to his old friend.

Ruth heard the door close behind them and she quickly went into the parlor and looked out the front window. She watched the two figures, one tall and muscular, and the other a full head shorter with his shoulders barely half the size of the taller man. Thaddeus' long smooth strides never wavered as he talked and waved his hands about. Herbert was all but running to keep up with him and would often run around and get in front of Thaddeus appearing is if he were trying to convince him of something. Oh, if Ruth could only be walking quietly behind the two determined men, she might find out what was, and what had been, happening between Melissa and Herbert -- especially on Tuesdays.

"Now, listen to me, Thaddeus. I know that you love Daphnia as if she were your own, but she isn't. You and Martha have raised that child at the own good graces of her own flesh and blood who felt that she needed both a mother and a father, and that she be able to grow up in an environment filled with love and happiness. You have to give credit where credit is due for that. This has not been easy for me, and I deserve some thanks for my sacrifices."

"That is true, Herbert. I do and have lived these past nineteen years giving credit where credit is due, and I have wondered just when it was going to be pay back time. Well, I guess today is the day, but let me tell you one thing, being grateful for these years is one thing, but I'll die and burn in hell before I'll give Melissa Flanders any credit for anything except selfishness and a lack of feelings. And, I detest this mockery and ruse that is taking place all for a woman who has never felt anything for anyone other than herself her entire life. And, now all she does is twist her little finger and another Flanders is forced to prostitute their entire reason for living just because of her. Goddamn her, Herbert, Goddamn her straight to hell and Matthew right along with her!"

"Now you don't mean that, Thaddeus. You better listen to yourself before you start damning people. You've done your share and remember, sometimes blood follows blood, even when we least expect it to."

"Well, let me tell you, Herbert, this is where the blood ends. You can't make me believe that Melissa is not doing this for her own selfish motives. She feels for herself and herself only."

"Melissa may be a lot of things, Thaddeus, but the one thing she is not is without feelings. I am not going to let you talk about her that way. You were not above having your selfish needs met from time to time when you were a young man, do I need to remind you of some of your selfish acts?"

"I don't need no reminding, Herbert. God knows I realize the depth of my sins. Matthew was and remains even with him six feet under the curse for my sins."

"We both have to live with the consequences of our actions, especially where Matthew is concerned, but regardless of what you think of Melissa I know that she is capable of loving. You can't go on carrying a grudge against her for something she did a long time ago. The decision she made was the right thing for Daphnia then, and it's the right thing for Daphnia now. Remember, Thaddeus she was young herself when she sent Daphnia to you and Martha. She had been through a lot of suffering in a few short years, more than you will know, and she is still suffering. But, Thaddeus, she isn't as selfish as you believe. She is kind and loving."

"And just how would you know about how much love she is capable of, Herbert? How about telling me about that? You say she knows how to love, well she has never shown it to Daphnia. Tell me about her love and compassion, Herbert. In the last four years, I have seen her three times and I have never seen her show anything but gratitude that Daphnia was out of her way. Daphnia was an inconvenience to her when Matthew brought her home and once he was gone, her shame was overwhelming and she felt that getting Daphnia out of her way would ease her own burden, but it hasn't. She has used Daphnia as a tool of manipulation and blackmail. She has never shown that child a thread of love or compassion. Just who has she been showing it to, Herbert?

Maybe she shows it to you on Tuesday afternoons!" Thaddeus stopped walking and looked down into the small brown eyes of Herbert.

Herbert was silent. He looked up at Thaddeus. "Yes she has shown me love and compassion every Tuesday for the last eighteen plus years. It is those Tuesday afternoons that have kept me sane. They have helped me to maintain a life of fullness and a semblance of happiness. She has kept me alive. Have you been blind all these years? Have you not even for one moment wondered why and how I was able to get information to you about her condition and keep you informed for Daphnia's as well as your own sake? Melissa does need Daphnia. What she did was the best thing for Daphnia. She has been ill a long time and she knew that she could not give to Daphnia what you and Martha could. No one could! You can't blame her or anyone else for that, Thaddeus, you can't. If you think that Melissa has been selfish well you haven't seen anything yet. I can be selfish, too. So if you are so sure that you have made no mistakes, if you have never acted out of pure selfishness, if you are so certain that your saintliness is all you want everyone to believe it is, then go ahead. Do as you always do, swear by your piousness and damn the rest of us to hell, Thaddeus, but this time you should know that you may be damning yourself as well."

Thaddeus wanted to stand still and make some sense of everything, but he couldn't. He slowed his gait so that Herbert could walk next to him, and he watched as the brown hat bobbed along with its brim tilting down toward the pavement. He had never heard Herbert speak this way before. He wasn't sure what to say or what to do. He wasn't a saint, far from it. As far as never acting out of pure selfishness, well he couldn't claim that either. He had been the selfish one, if truth were known. He had kept Daphnia away from Melissa and any other family because he was afraid of losing her. Their bond was more than what others thought. And while he often reflected upon their true connection with pride and satisfaction he also felt the pains of guilt. It wasn't so much that she was the child of Matthew and the widow Humphreys, but her resemblance to her own grandmother haunted him. And, he knew that by keeping Daphnia close to him kept a raging storm at bay. When he looked at her he saw into the eyes of an angel. Not an angel who lived only in a spiritual sense, but one who had walked the earth itself. One with whom he had shared an indiscretion so painful yet so delicious that it caused him ecstasy and pain to this day. Thaddeus's brother, Joshua was as worthless as Matthew. He drank too much, and worked too little. Matthew's mother was a saint. She never complained nor allowed anyone to criticize Joshua. Not even Thaddeus. She deserved a better life than the one she had been dealt. Once Joshua and Sara moved into the small house on the far side of Sunshine Acres, Thaddeus found himself incapable of resisting her. He fought with his demons and made every possible effort to stay true to Martha, but the allure of her was too great. In time, Joshua spent more and more time in town leaving the work that needed to be done for someone else, and that someone else was most often Thaddeus. Sarah died after giving birth to Matthew with Thaddeus the one holding her hand. He could close his eyes and see her smile, and he prayed that no one ever found out their secret, but Herbert had learned of it by pure accident. Once confirmed, the two never spoke of it again. But, Thaddeus knew full well that it was there, right in the back of Herbert's mouth ready to jump out at any moment, and he was terrified at the very thought of it.

They had arrived in front of the Gazette. The green shades were pulled down and it was dark inside. Herbert reached inside his coat and pulled out a key from his vest pocket. Quickly unlocking the door and raising the shade with almost one motion, they were inside and he was walking across the room to the lantern hung on the wall next to the door leading to the upstairs apartment. He lit the lantern and set it down on the counter. Even though there was electricity throughout the building, Herbert loved the smell of the oil lamps, and the ambiance they provided. He often worked late at night by the light of the lamp.

"Well, whaddya think? Have things changed much? We have added a second typesetter and there is another desk over there with all the latest news from the wire. Daniel now has his own office. He felt that once we were able to hire part-time help, you remember young Thomas Saunders his father runs the feed and grain down the street, he makes a good living, but has a couple of sons and with all of them working and drawing money from the same pot, it makes putting food on the family table pretty tough. So, Tom has come to work with us giving Daniel some time to stay inside more and not have to drum up the stories like he used do. He is down south right now, though, but we expect him back most any day now. Have I been rambling? I'm sorry, Thaddeus. I know how disturbing all of this has been for you. We've been friends a long time; let me show you around."

"Where's the apartment that you have in mind for Daphnia? She has been so accustomed to a house I just can't imagine her in an apartment. How safe is it here at night, there won't be anyone else in the building after the office is closed up. How will she get help if she needs it? Does Ruth still manage the store by herself, or does she think Daphnia will be working with her also?"

Thaddeus was tired, and he was worried. He had always protected Daphnia and now to think of her in this city living all alone over this small office with the ink, and papers, it looked like such disarray to Thaddeus. He was wishing he could sit down in the rocking chair on his front porch with a piece of whittling wood and sort everything out. As he was trying to make some sense out of the clutter he saw before him, he kept thinking about his conversation and the words that kept running through his mind: Herbert and Melissa! Herbert and Melissa every Tuesday afternoon for more than eighteen years! What would Ruth say? Oh, my God, does Ruth even know? Who would have thought it about Herbert? Although Herbert felt differently, Thaddeus did not think of himself as a pious man, but Herbert and Melissa!

"What does Ruth think about Melissa, Herbert?"

Herbert spun around so fast that he lost his balance and almost fell across young Daniel's desk for they were now in his office. " Well, what do you mean Thaddeus?"

"I mean just what does Ruth think about you going over to see Melissa every Tuesday afternoon for the past eighteen years getting a little love and compassion? That's what in the hell I mean! And, now you have found a way to make your whore happy while disrupting my family! You are playing with all of our emotions here not to mention how you are manipulating Daphnia's heart. So, I ask again, just what the hell does Ruth think about you and Melissa?"

Thaddeus was suddenly angrier than he could remember being in a long while. He moved forward and grabbed Herbert by his shirt collar and pulled his face close to his, thus lifting Herbert right off the floor. " Just what are your plans for our lives now, you Goddamned Hypocritical Bastard? Does this make us even?" He threw Herbert back against the desk and turned and walked out of the newspaper office and back to the two story yellow house on Pine Street.

Thaddeus entered the house leaving the front door standing open. He made four long strides across the foyer and onto the landing of the staircase. He practically ran up the stairs taking two steps at a time. He rushed into the guest bedroom and threw his things back into his valise and left the house in the same hurried fashion as he had just entered it without saying a word to Ruth. Just as he reached the front steps Herbert was coming up the walkway toward him.

"Don't say a word, Herbert. You can tell Ruth anything you want. I will tell Martha that I felt I was imposing on our friendship and that I needed to be alone where I could sort through everything. I will see Melissa tomorrow; I will stop by the newspaper office on my way back to the station. I'll be taking the first train out in the afternoon to Detroit then will catch a westbound out of there for Lansing."

Herbert said nothing, just nodded and walked up the stairs and into the house.

Ruth was standing in the middle of the parlor wiping her hands on her apron. "What was that all about, Herbert? As a matter of fact, what has this entire evening been about?"

"Thaddeus has decided that he needs to be alone to think through all that is happening. You know how he is, he needs privacy and a place where he can pace and carve those damned toys he has showered Daphnia with all of these years. Why, that girl must have enough wooden toys to fill a house and two barns by now. I'm going up to bed, Ruth, it has been a long day and I don't wish to be disturbed. Now I am tired. Good night!"

Going up the stairs drained his energy, he felt more tired than he had in a long while. With each step he took he heard again every angry word that had been spoken between he and his best friend this evening. He was grateful for the solitude and peace he would find as he opened the door to the sparsely decorated room. He and Ruth had not shared a bedroom since Daniel was just a toddler, and he had become accustomed to that arrangement, it suited him.

Ruth was left standing and wondering just what had happened. She was certain that she would never know what had gone on between her husband and his long time friend, but one thing she did know,

Thaddeus was upset, he had come there planning to stay with them, visit Melissa and talk to the owner of the lumber mill about moving the timber via rail, or so she thought. She turned and walked back into the kitchen and finished wiping down the sideboards and tables before going up to her own room.

When Daniel approached the house he was whistling and still exhilarated by the goings on down at the local pub where he had spent most of the evening drinking ale and laughing with the other patrons. He did not realize that everyone had gone up to bed and he entered the house without considering how much noise he should or should not make. When he saw there were no lamps lit and the parlor was empty he walked into the kitchen only to find it dark as well. He quietly walked up the stairs and noticed the light shining from beneath the door of his Father's room; he knocked softly. Herbert did not answer the door but the light went out and Daniel turned and went to his own room at the other end of the hallway.

Thaddeus walked all of Pine Street on both sides before turning onto Maple and entering the Hotel. Checking in he thanked the desk clerk and went up to his room, undressed and fell into bed where he slept in fits and starts. He dreamt of years ago when he was a young man doing what young men do only to be swept up in rolling thunder and fall again into the arms of sweet and forbidden love. He felt himself being tossed into the black sea of turmoil in St. Louis where blood mixed with the rain and sleet ran through the streets like a great rapid leaving him unable to swim against the current. Sleep was not his friend this night and it was with a certain amount of relief when the sounds and noises from the street below awakened him. When he stood he found his bedclothes wet from sweat and the bed covers were a tangled mess. He poured water into the washbasin and methodically washed up, shaved and dressed then went downstairs for breakfast. He was anxious about getting on with the reason for his visit. After eating, he paid his bill and walked out into the fresh new morning.

He thought of Herbert as he walked. They had been friends for longer than either of them could remember. While Thaddeus had been born in Chicago, he often frequented St. Louis, Herbert moved there with his father and mother from Charleston. Neither of them ever spoke much about their families as they were carousing and sowing their seeds wherever a fertile field lay. Thaddeus had not pried into Herbert's past nor Herbert into his. The two had bonded instantly and it seemed that Herbert had always been there when needed and vice versa. Their friendship had saved them many times, and they shared some deep secrets, it was such that was causing him so much turmoil now. It seemed that they were always getting each other out of some type of situation, and he knew that they would work this through as well. But, not right now. Right now he had to get over to see Melissa and find out exactly what was going on, he didn't want Daphnia hurt. And he didn't want her to leave her home for the whims and selfishness of someone she barely knew.

"He walked up to the small white house with its picket fence and pink and yellow flowers lining the walkway. He knocked softly on the front door, but loud enough to let someone know he was there. Although from what Herbert had told him, she would not pay the knocking any mind anyway.

After several minutes and just as he was turning to walk away, Eloise Barnes came to the door, "Come in Thaddeus. We've been expecting you. Won't you leave off your coat and hat? I'll let Melissa know that you are here. Would you care for some coffee, I believe there is some left from breakfast?"

"No thanks, I'll just speak to Melissa for a short while and then be on my way."

Eloise motioned for Thaddeus to go on in, she then turned and walked to the back of the house.

Melissa was lying in the big four-poster bed propped up against satin and lace pillows, she was beautiful even though she was frail and more delicate looking than he had imagined. Her dark eyes took up most of her face and her once pink cheeks were sunken in. Her hair was brushed down and softly curled around her shoulders, her skin was as pale as cotton and Thaddeus wondered if there was any blood in her veins for she looked as though one could almost see through her. Walking over to her bed he could not be angry with Melissa Flanders any longer. He took her small hand in his and held it gently as if it were made of fine crystal. He bent down and kissed her forehead lightly. She smelled as if she had just stepped from a garden of fresh lavender. "How are you Melissa?" he almost whispered.

Looking up from her pillows Melissa smiled. "I'm not too well."

"Don't talk if you are not up to it."

"It's okay, there are some things that I need to say. I am so happy that you came to see me. I have always respected you and Martha, and I thank you for coming today, it has been awhile."

"It has been a long time, hasn't it?"

"Yes it has. I suppose you are not too happy with me for asking that Daphnia come home for a short while, but I need to see her, Thaddeus."

"It doesn't matter if I am happy or not, Melissa. You didn't ask for my permission. I know you feel that this is the right thing for you, but are you sure this is the right thing to do for Daphnia?"

"No, I'm not sure. But the word from the doctor is that I won't be around much longer, and I would like to let her know why I sent her away. I know that some people might think that I am being selfish, but it wasn't that I didn't love her or want her, it was so complicated and I was so weak, even then."

"You were never someone that I thought of as weak, Melissa."

"Regardless, Thaddeus, I want her to hear it from me - I think she should know everything! Maybe I need to clear my conscience, but there have been too many lies, and I need to die knowing that I have done the right thing. It is time for truth and I need to be the one doing the telling."

Thaddeus could hear the strength and determination in her voice and her words. She was serious about this and he knew he was beaten. "Okay, Melissa, I will go along with this for now, you just calm down and take a sip of this water. Then you need to rest."

As she leaned against his arm and held her hand on his so she could take a drink of the water, she looked up into his face and tears filled her eyes and began their slow trek down her cheeks. "I know that you don't understand, you may call me selfish if you would like, but I am dying and I need to see her." Melissa closed her eyes and he laid her back against the pillows. "I'm sorry, Thaddeus. It's this sickness. The Doctors have told me that there is nothing they can do, it is a cancer of some sort and it seems to be throughout my body. Talking is difficult for me as is most everything else these days. Tell me, how is Daphnia? Is she beautiful, does she look as much like him as you do?"

As Thaddeus began to tell Melissa about Daphnia, her life, her teaching and of her beauty and strength, she drifted off to sleep. He sat for a while watching her and wondering of just how many hearts she had broken before Matthew came into her life. There was a spirit about her that made her almost irresistible, even now. Once again, he kissed her forehead and lingered there for longer than he had planned breathing in her fragrance. He blushed when he saw the shadow of Eloise fall upon the foot of the bed.

"So, Thaddeus, is she as you had expected?"

Walking over to the older woman, Thaddeus took her by the elbow and turned her toward the door. "Melissa is the same as she has always been. She can still charm anyone who comes near her and somehow make them forget what they had intended to say or do. Let's talk outside."

Walking arm in arm through the house and outside to the front porch, Eloise began to fidget with the ties to her apron; she was a little nervous around Thaddeus, he was so up front and determined. He had always made her just a little uneasy, it was like he could see right through her and she guarded every word she spoke when he was around.

"How sick is she really, Eloise?"

"She is dying," Eloise said without blinking an eye. "The doctor has given her less than six months, and I think he was being generous. She is set on seeing Daphnia and putting the record straight, Thaddeus, and I believe she will hold out until she does." Eloise knelt down to the ground and began pulling weeds from the garden now and digging in the soil as she spoke. "Melissa has not had an easy life. I know that you and the missus feel that she did wrong by Daphnia, and I guess that I would have to agree with you mostly. But, Melissa has suffered more than you will ever know. She loved that child the only way she knew how and if Matthew had not gone and gotten himself shot in some alley somewhere she would have raised Daphnia just as if she was her own. But he did get shot, and he did die, and she couldn't raise the child by herself, so she did what she thought was right for Daphnia and for herself. Why live with the pain and agony of knowing that you are raising some other woman's child by the only man you ever loved."

As she said this, Thaddeus pulled back and stood straight.

"Oh, I beg your pardon, Thaddeus, I didn't mean to ... well she has had to struggle just to exist and it wasn't her intention to short change the child at the same time? You and Martha are family, you could provide for Daphnia in a way that Melissa never could, why was it so wrong for her to send her to live with you?"

Eloise looked up at Thaddeus again, but before he could say anything, she continued, "Now don't go telling me about how she went about not sending cards, and gifts and such. She didn't have hardly enough to live on herself, and she knew about Herbert Bernstein keeping you informed as to what was happening here. Mr. Bernstein has been a good friend to Melissa and to me. He has always come through for her when she needed a little helping hand. He has seen to it that she receive the best of medical treatment and he has been a true friend to you and the missus and to that little girl in spite of the strangeness of it all."

"Why do you think that is so strange, Eloise? Herbert didn't have to interject himself into this, he chose to be the go between, and he suggested it even. Herbert and I go back a long way, long before Melissa and Matthew even met. So, what is it that is so strange?"

"Well, you know what I mean, I mean the way he carries on and such, why one would think that Herbert Bernstein was the long lost relative, not Melissa."

Looking up at Thaddeus she caught his eye then quickly turned away. "All I am saying is that he was a stranger to Melissa, that's all. He had no need to befriend her, but he did. He has seen to it that she has been well taken care of. Maybe you don't know just how bad off she is and has been. Well, let me tell you, Mister, Melissa was sick when Matthew went away that last time, and she knew it. She was already having problems that most men wouldn't know too much about, but maybe you would with farming animals and all. It seems that husband of hers had been around more than with just the widow. Melissa started having some serious bouts with all kinds of sicknesses the winter before he left and it didn't get no better come spring. She took to the bed after she sent Daphnia away and the doctors had one devil of a time getting her to where she could get up and about again. Part of it was her grief and sorrow for having him taken from her the way he was, but the other part was that she just pure out didn't feel good. She was never right after that first summer that Daphnia was gone, and if it weren't for Herbert

Bernstein bringing in that specialist from Chicago, I think she would have died long ago." She stopped talking and stood up. "Now, you are a powerful man, you have all the wherewithal to make this turn into anything you want it to be. So, I just want to know what you got to say about Daphnia coming back to see Melissa before she dies? Are you gonna let her or not?"

"I can't make Daphnia come back here if she doesn't want to, Eloise. I don't have any plans just yet as to how or what I will say to Daphnia, but I know this. I know that Melissa needs to clear her conscience, but at what price? Daphnia has a wonderful life, she is happy, why spoil all of that now to give a dying woman peace of mind? I will talk with Daphnia and I will let her make the decision. You tell Melissa when she awakens that I will let Daphnia make the choice of whether or not to come here, but as for setting the record straight, I am just not ready to give her that yet. I know my Daphnia, she is my blood, and I am just not ready for a stranger, and that is what Melissa is to Daphnia, to bring her pain and destroy her world as she knows it. I must go now, you take care of yourself." With that he turned and walked out of the yard across Oak Avenue right onto Maple and then left onto Pine Street where he stood looking at the newspaper office.

Thaddeus hated the dampness of this town that these people called a 'city'. He fastened his coat and with determination and a resolve to make amends with his old friend he opened the door to the Huron Gazette. There, sitting at his desk with his green visor shading his eyes and his fingers coated with ink, Herbert looked up and smiled.

"Good day, Thaddeus," he said as if there had been not one harsh word between them. "Come on over here and take a look at what just came off the wire, it looks like Henry Ford is really making some noise, looks like he is going to change the way he pays his people, by the hour, do you think that will start an uprising? What do you think of 'Ole Henry, Thaddeus?" he queried his friend.

"I think that is fine if that is what he wants to do, but I need to talk about the uprising that got started right here last night." Thaddeus pulled up a chair to the front of the desk. "You know that I don't like conflict of any kind, Herbert. And right up there next to conflict is hypocrisy and deceit. And, I'll be damned if you, my oldest and dearest friend are not tied up in all three of them. Just how involved with Melissa are you and where do you see Daphnia fitting in to your plan? I need to know the answers to these things if I am to talk to her about coming here anytime soon."

"Have you seen Melissa, Thaddeus?"

"Yes, I saw her today. I agree with what you told me last night, I think she is failing fast. If Daphnia is to see Melissa alive, it will have to be soon. But you haven't answered my questions, Herbert; tell me what is really going on here. Just what is it that is driving this desire of yours to manipulate Daphnia into coming here. You can't possibly be planning on doing or saying anything about St. Louis or Boston or any of the things that happened way too many years ago. You can't possibly be ready to say anything about what happened way back then are you? This isn't the time to break her heart and shake up her world, Herbert. Why take away her fantasy about Melissa and Matthew? Those dreams about her father are all she has to hold onto, don't destroy that Herbert."

"It is not my desire to destroy her dreams. I just want her to have a chance to learn the truth; the truth may give her happiness and a belonging that she has never really known. You want to talk about dreams Thaddeus? I can tell you about dreams. Dreams that keep me up at night wondering about right and wrong and whether or not doing the right thing is always right and when should we let the wrong things be? Dreams keep me up wondering just where I fit in this great universe of ours. Dreams, Thaddeus, dreams of my family, all of my family sitting around a dinner table holding hands and thanking God for one another. But, my family can never do that. The family I have dreamed about for all of my life doesn't exist. You have a family. You have a family that was handed to you. But you need to know that it was never yours by right, it was a stolen family, stolen from others by circumstances beyond their knowledge or control. We grew up together in St. Louis, but we grew apart there as well. There are pieces of me that were left behind all over this country, but my soul was lost in St. Louis, and I suspect that a part of yours was too. Now I don't expect you to understand something that you don't know anything about, but I do expect you to understand that if I can make a dying woman's wish come true, then I will do that. And, I'm not just thinking of Melissa, here, you and I both know there are others. I don't expect you to understand that, or to even understand me for that matter. Life is not always what we understand, things happen to us and to those we love, and sometimes we get by and sometimes we take matters into our own hands and make things happen. And, I don't really give a rat's ass whether or not you understand right now or even care!"

"I understand Melissa, and I might even understand you more than you know, but I just don't understand the timing of it all. Just what has happened, Herb? How did this allegiance of yours to Melissa develop into something so powerful? When did you decide to step up to the plate and make things happen? Who are you really thinking of, Herb?"

Herbert Bernstein did not know where to begin. He got up from behind his desk and began to pace the floor. He filled and refilled his pipe. Walked back and forth to the window and then finally sat down on one of the chairs usually used by the people waiting to see him where they would sit and read the Farmer's Almanac.

"I guess it is like this, Thaddeus, St. Louis, Boston, Chicago, when we were young and where we grew into know it all adults, those places and the things that happened were a long time ago, but not long enough to erase them from my mind's eye. I have been spending a lot of time up in Boston lately and it has brought back some painful memories of people, places and years lost to shadows and darkness. I feel as if I am in a storm with thunder and lightning all about me, but I don't hear anything. It is like silence and shadows drawing me into an abyss of secrets that come to me at night and eat away at me. Yes, what is happening today is the result of what happened a long time ago. How did I become so close to Melissa, when did I develop this "allegiance" you ask. Well I guess it started the day I arrived at the train station back in 1884. I was coming back from St. Louis when Melissa and Daphnia were waiting for the train. I remember it just like it was yesterday... ... ..."

"... ... ... As I stepped down from the train, I saw the two of them standing there. Melissa looked so proud and beautiful. She was standing so straight she almost looked like one of those mannequins in a store window. Daphnia was sobbing, and as I walked nearer I remember hearing her ask her mother why she had to go away. I tried not to listen, but I was taken in by the sight of the two of them, Melissa so emotionless and Daphnia overcome with it. A mother and her child in what one would expect to be a tearful parting on both sides was anything but. I had not slept in a while and was exhausted, and more than that I was physically and emotionally ill. I had stayed in St. Louis for a day or two after you left. There had been so much that happened in a short period of time and I needed to get away from my own demons. In spite of the fact that I was sick with pneumonia and needed to be home in bed, for some reason I couldn't take my eyes off the woman and her child. It was like a veil had been lifted, I knew them immediately. I had seen Melissa around, but before I took that trip to St. Louis I just never really had paid much attention I guess. Now, it was like I was seeing her for the first time. It was all I could do to keep from staring at her and the beautiful child. I thought of how foolish I had been not to notice before. Huron City is not that big, and I had waited on both of them at the store, and of course Miss Eloise had been in with Daphnia many times. I finally sat down on a bench nearby and watched them. I heard Melissa tell the child that her father was dead and that she herself was not well. I heard her tell the child that she was going to live with her Great Uncle Thaddeus and Great Aunt Martha on a farm in Lansing. I wanted to kick myself."

"When I saw Melissa that day I was no longer puzzled, but I was shaken to my soul. I felt like life was moving in slow motion and was ready to leave when I heard Melissa mention your name, I became frozen to the bench and felt my heart leap from my chest. It couldn't be, I thought. How could it be? I could not move. I sat there dazed for what seemed like an eternity going over our lives together. I was startled when I heard the train whistle blow and the sound of the steam coming from beneath the wheels. I watched Eloise and Daphnia get on the train and wave good-bye. Melissa came over and set down on the bench next to me. She was sobbing. She looked so fragile and alone. As you can well imagine, I was drawn to her, but not for the reasons one might expect. I had heard her mention an Uncle Thaddeus and Aunt Martha in Lansing; and she called the little girl Daphnia, it was too coincidental that I should actually meet her now at this time and place. I needed to know more. But, I swear to you it was not my intention to grow to feel about her as I do, but at that moment she needed consolation and I was there. I was shaken beyond description, but I was there nonetheless."

"You must understand, Herb. I couldn't tell you before then. I have regretted that, but I was afraid of what you would do if you knew the truth. By God, Herbert, you know what Matthew was to me, and how painfully things played out. How ironic that he was killed the way he was without ever really understanding why. I know it had to be done, I hated everything he stood for. It wasn't just you or me, it was the way he lived and those woodcutters he hung around with. They were like vultures just waiting for the right time and place, and the right amount of money to be sure that the job got done right."

"I did what I had to do, Thaddeus, truth or no truth. We should know by now that secrets always come out. But, I did more. I took Melissa home that day. I made her some tea and listened to her speak of her own childhood and her dreams of a family that had been taken away from her by a misguided man in a dark alley with a gun. She told me the story of how her beloved husband had been shot with no one seeing his killer. She told me of how there was no one around to call for a doctor. She made Matthew seem like a God among men, a perfect husband and an ideal father. Her heart was broken and she said that she no longer had a reason to live. Yes, Thaddeus, I consoled her, I held her that day and for the first time in my life I vowed to prove Ruth wrong, I would be compassionate, I would feel what others feel, I would care. I watched her as she slept, then leaving a note by her bed telling her where to get in touch with me should she ever need anything, I quietly crept out of her room. That is when I decided that I would protect her, I would be there for her whenever she needed or wanted me. She would want for nothing, I could be a silent benefactor so to speak and, yes, salve my conscience. I knew this would be an opportunity for me to try to make things right. That's when I confronted you! That is when Ruth and I made our visit to Sunshine Acres. I knew what you had kept from me and I wanted you to pay. But, I couldn't do to you what you had done to me. I took the higher road, Thaddeus. Something you seemed to have forgotten at the time. I knew it would be good for me to be the liaison between you and her and Daphnia. I knew that I would have to be careful and that there would be some difficult times, but I knew that I had to do this. I told myself that this would be my good deed, it was my way of paying back a debt."

"Herb, you must understand. We have talked about all of this so many times, and you know how sorry I am for everything. I was just waiting for the right time."

"The right time, Thaddeus? Just when did you think the right time would be. After I had been made a fool of for what? All I could think of when I visited you was how stupid I had been. During all of those trips and visits you and I had over the years, I really didn't connect any of it until you invited me for a drink and offered to relieve me of several thousand dollars during a trip to St. Louis. Of course I knew Matthew, I knew he was married to Melissa, I guess I even knew there was a child born out of wedlock, you and I had talked many hours about his escapades and yet, I was completely oblivious as to who Daphnia was and God help me, I had never given her or Melissa a second thought."

"The real anger set in, Thaddeus, when I realized that you knew the truth all along and had kept if from me. Had I seen you at that moment I believe I would have shot you dead and taken full pleasure in doing so. That night in St. Louis was the worst night of my life. Sitting in my room listening to the rain and sleet pour over the muddy streets of that God Forsaken town I was almost in a catatonic state. It was like an avalanche consuming me, suddenly all of the pieces fit perfectly. All I could think of was that Ruth was right, I was caught up in my own world without regard to how anyone who didn't directly impact that world felt or was feeling. My life had been shaken up that night, and God help me, I knew it would never be the same. I knew that I had to find a way to make things right, so I took it upon myself to avenge the wronged and make the world a better place for them. And that's what I did, Thaddeus. Rightfully or wrongfully, I made a decision that I have relived almost daily for nearly twenty years."

"But, Herbert, that was also long ago. Honestly, don't you think that we can ..." Thaddeus began.

"It was like yesterday, today and tomorrow to me, Thaddeus. I never get away from it. You ask when the allegiance began? It began that day at the train station in February 1884. In time, Melissa told me her version of Matthew and the widow, it was all I could do to listen to what she had to say. I could hear in her voice the bitterness she felt toward Grace. I found myself needing to listen regardless of how painful it was to me, I knew that I had to learn more. This may sound strange to you, but I understood - I understood her. I understood love and hate and envy and knowing how it felt to be deceived and betrayed and expected to just understand, bury it and move forward. There was a kinship that developed between us, she filled a void in my life and I obviously filled one in hers. Our time spent together seemed to make all that I had done and was doing seem respectable and right for some reason. When I had a chance to reflect on everything some days and weeks after we had begun our ... relationship, I felt it was fate that I was the piece of the equation that would connect all of the other pieces. I believed that then and I believe it now. Good God, Thaddeus, I had to make it work. I was so Goddamned sorry for what had happened. How was I to know who Melissa was and who she would become? How was I to know that one act of selfish drunkenness albeit wished for and dreamed about could turn into such a sad and tragic secret that would eat away at me every waking hour and keep me thrashing about with nightmares at night? Once I knew the truth, I knew that I had to make things right. And that is what I am still doing, I am still trying to make things right. Don't you see that? It is these damned secrets, Thaddeus, I have had to keep them and I can't forget them. They have eaten away at me all of these years. But, finally I have to put an end to them all. Daphnia has the right to live the rest of her life knowing the truth. And, you know what, she might not find it so bad. I have been silent too long, maybe I can never truly clear my conscience, but at least I can do what I can. At least I can keep a promise to a dying woman." He took a deep breath, rose from the chair and began pacing again. "Now it is time for things to be out in the open."

"Will keeping that promise help you, Herbert? Will it help Daphnia? And, what about Martha and me? What about William Johnston and all of the other lives you are about to disrupt with your plan?"

"Good God, Thaddeus, I didn't plan this. I don't know if I ever had a plan or even have a plan now, I wish to hell I did, but I don't. Plan or not, I do know that Melissa Flanders is not the hard hearted and unloving person that you think she is. I also know that I would walk over hot coals for her if she asked me to. Shit, man, this whole damn mess is like a bad dream and now it is time to wake up and fix it. You don't know Melissa the way I do."

Walking over to where Thaddeus sat, he leaned over the larger man's shoulder. "You can't know what caring for Melissa and her caring back has done for me, you are tall and muscled, you have self confidence and a presence that commands respect. Look at me, Thaddeus. What kind of presence do I command? I'm short, my hair is wiry and frayed, I'm Jewish trying to live in a Christian world in the midst of this town run by heathens most of the damn time. I try to go about my life quietly and peacefully minding my own business and being a good neighbor. Even with this business, the general store, a fine house on Pine Street and behaving respectably, everyday is still a struggle. You wouldn't know about any of this, Thaddeus, but she made me feel like I was everything every man could ever want to be. All the logical and illogical reasons for doing what I had done when I started seeing her soon dissipated and I found that seeing her was like a potion for me. I couldn't stop myself from sitting in her presence and watching her weave her dreams and share her innermost thoughts. Having her fall asleep with her head on my shoulder, holding her when she cried, hearing her tell me that she wouldn't know what she would do without me."

Herbert stopped talking long enough to tap his pipe against the palm of his hand; he put in fresh tobacco and lit it by striking a match against the table. He turned and looked at Thaddeus. "Do you know what it is like to have people laugh at you, make fun of you, talk about you not for who you are but for their idea of what they believe you must be like? Have you ever turned back the covers of your bed hoping for some physical response from your wife only to have her turn her back to you and suggest that you read for awhile before coming to bed so that you will be ready for sleep and won't lie there awake bothering her? Have you ever been made to feel that closeness and intimacy end once the marriage vows are over? Ruth and I haven't shared a marriage bed for many years, Thaddeus. Hell, we never had a real marriage bed again after those first few months and Ruth found that she was pregnant with Daniel. Now I am not saying that any of those things made it okay for me to develop a relationship with another woman, especially Melissa, but, by God, Thaddeus, it sure as hell helped. And, if you are asking me to apologize for the last eighteen plus years of a little happiness out of the more than forty years that Ruth and I have been married, well, you're not going to get it."

Herbert had worked himself into a state of frenzy and now that he was on a roll he was going to have his say. "You get on and off those damn trains of yours and ride from here to Chicago, Detroit, down to Richmond, and anywhere else the rails will take you, and then you return to a home filled with love and respect. Now you can say what you want, but by damned, Martha is a hell of a lot more wife than Ruth has ever dreamed of. I don't mean to complain and put Ruth down, she works hard in the store, keeps a fine house for Daniel and me, and she is a good upstanding woman in the community. No one can ever accuse her of not being a good mother. But when it comes to wifely duties, she missed the boat!"

Herbert tapped his pipe against the side of his leg and finally holding it in the air pronounced to no one in particular, "this damned thing, by God, Daniel brought it back with him the last time he went into Chicago and it sure as hell isn't worth the tobacco it takes to fill it." With that, he got up and threw the pipe in the trashcan. He turned to Thaddeus who had sat patiently listening while he tried to vindicate himself for his years of deceit and adultery. "How about we walk over to the diner and get a cup of coffee and one of their hot muffins? I know that you don't want Daphnia to return to Huron City, so why not just have her visit for a while, she won't have to stay? That might be the answer for everyone concerned. If I do nothing else in this life worth doing, I have to keep at least this one promise."

Thaddeus said not a word. He stood and placed his arm around the smaller man's shoulders. As they walked across the street, he thought about all he had heard his friend say.

As they reached the other side of the street, Thaddeus stopped and turned to the smaller man. "If she comes back for a visit, Herbert, and if she doesn't like it then she will return when she is ready with no amount of begging or guilt being laid on her, understood!"

"That's all I can ask of you or her, okay, Thaddeus, I'll give you that."

"And, what about Melissa? How long should Daphnia have to plan to stay around? I mean, how much longer do you think Melissa will live?"

"How the hell should I know that? As far as I am concerned, I hope she lives another thirty or forty years, by God. You of all people, Thaddeus, I can't believe you would even ask such a thing. Why not just go over there and put one of those pillows across her face and find out?"

Herbert was outraged and wanted no more of this conversation. He stopped abruptly and turned back toward the Gazette before they reached the diner. His anger soon turned to fear and he began running back across the street and yelling at the top of his lungs, "Oh, my God, Oh My God, Oh, no, no, no."

Thaddeus turned to see his friend at full stride entering the newspaper office where billows of black smoke were finding their way out through the window and door. He immediately began to run toward the burning building. Herbert ran and pulled the fire bell while Thaddeus entered the office and started pulling out as much equipment and files he could get his hands on until he finally saw the trash can ablaze and remembered the pipe. Herbert reached the doorway just in time to see his friend throw a rug over the flames, "that goddamned pipe" he muttered under his breath.

People began lining up passing pails of water and the fire was soon distinguished. Thaddeus helped his old friend assess the damage. The building was pretty much intact and most of the equipment was salvageable. There was some damage but mostly due to smoke and water, the structure seemed to be in good shape. Herbert arranged to have a team of horses, some wagons and a couple of strong young men move the salvageable equipment over to the basement of the house on Pine Street. Daniel was on his way to the Gazette when he heard the ruckus and rushed toward the building. He hurried in to help clear the smoke and clean up the debris. He spent the remainder of the day sorting through the papers and files looking for what could be saved.

Thaddeus returned to the hotel and cleaned up before once again heading over to his friend's house. He wanted to say good-bye and to leave without any hurt or anger between them. Entering the yellow house, he heard no voices from inside. He tapped on the door, "anyone home? Herbert? Ruth?"

"Come on in Thaddeus, I was just sitting here trying to gather my thoughts. You seem to be all packed and ready to head home. How about if I walk with you? Would you mind?"

"Of course I wouldn't mind, Herbert, that is why I came over. I was hoping I would have a chance to apologize for any hurt or anger that I may have caused you over all of this. My train will be leaving in an hour, so if you aren't ready to go right now, that is okay. I will catch up with you on my next visit, or when Daphnia comes, if she comes, of course.

"I'm ready, Thaddeus, now is a good time. Ruth, I am going to the station with Thaddeus."

Ruth came into the room only to see the backs of the two men closing the front door behind them.

As they walked along, the tension soon faded between them. Their moods were somber and they both knew that the fewer words spoken the better. Once they arrived at the station, Herbert shook his friend's hand. "I'm sorry Thaddeus, please believe that. Whatever decision you make is yours and I won't second-guess it. Just let me ask that you allow Daphnia to make up her own mind. She thinks that Melissa is her mother, rightfully or wrongfully, and you owe it to her to let her find out the truth from Melissa."

"I agree that setting the record straight is long overdue, we should have done this year's ago. Right now I just want us to do what is the best for Daphnia. I know that if she comes here, whether for a visit or to stay longer, that you will protect her and help keep her safe. There is no one in this world that I trust as much as I do you, Herbert. What has my stomach in knots is how she might handle things once she finds out the truth. I am afraid, Herbert, I am afraid that she will hate me. It pains me to say so, but whatever happens, you are right, she needs to know. Let's consider it a visit, for now? I'll be in touch." He slapped Herbert's back, picked up his valise and boarded the train... ... ...

Chapter Four

Now, standing on his front porch with the smell of Lilacs and Honeysuckle, he was once again faced with the reality of all that had happened and his fear of what lay ahead. With the thoughts and memories of his visit to Huron City in the forefront of his mind he couldn't help but to look away as Daphnia came up onto the porch from the rose garden where she had left Martha with a shawl to keep away the chill.

She could see his jaw clinched and his temples working. She knew that he was struggling with his feelings about her leaving. "Are you all right, Papa? I am worried about you; you look so tense standing there."

"I am tense, Daphnia. I want you to think about your life now and all that you have here and all that you will be doing without in Huron City. Why, it isn't even a city really, not like Lansing or Chicago, or even Detroit. Huron City is more like four rows of stores and shops all facing the town square with the backs of the buildings facing alleys littered with drunks and garbage with the "colored quarters" off behind the squalor. There is a school, but it is small; and, the lumberyard and the cabins for the men to live in are not suitable for family life. Why Melissa has stayed there for so long is beyond me. She should have returned to Boston years ago. It is a shabby little place where everyone is suspicious of everyone else and everyone's business is gossiped about and nothing is sacred. Why even the church and cemetery are locked up behind an iron fence that is only open during the day and is locked every evening at dusk. There is truly no reason for you to leave everything and go there, but I know you will do what you want, and what you want is to go to Melissa's side and help her to atone for all of these years of neglect."

"I think you may be somewhat biased in your assessment of Huron City, Papa. While I have not been in Huron City for sometime I do remember happy times. I remember flowers and blue skies. I know it will be different from these rolling hills and beautiful countryside, but I remember it as a quaint town with a great deal of charm. Besides, happiness is not about where we live but how we live and who we are.

I can't stay here knowing that Mother is ill and has called for me, regardless of her reason. I cannot turn away from her now even though that is what she has done to me."

"You are right, Daphnia. Melissa is very ill and she has asked for you. I know that you must leave, but I don't like it." For Thaddeus, this was a difficult time. He was not someone who went looking for trouble, but when it found him, he dealt with it promptly albeit not comfortably. He was a quiet man and didn't care too much for spending words he didn't need to spend. Watching her stand before him, he knew that letting her go was not going to be easy. He didn't want her to leave, but he knew he had to let her, and even convince her if necessary. Now was the time for him to be as open as possible, but not too honest. This did not sit well with him.

So many thoughts were going through his head. Thaddeus wondered if Daphnia would ever forgive him when she found out the truth. He prayed silently that Melissa would be gentle with Daphnia when the time came for her to reveal their secret. He was torn between breaking his promise to Melissa and telling Daphnia everything himself, but he couldn't bring himself to do it.

He looked around the porch nervously for something to pick up and start whittling; reaching in his boot top for his knife, he simultaneously picked up a piece of rough cut wood that was standing in a pail near the swing for just such a time as this. With one long slow push of the blade, he breathed in deeply.

"Daphnia, just because Melissa has asked for you to come and spend some time with her, doesn't mean you have to. But, in all fairness to both you and her I understand your feeling of responsibility and obligation. And, of course there is more. Herbert has offered you a position at the Gazette as well as the apartment above the office. He assures me that the apartment is very nice. As for the paper, well, you have to decide that on your own. He would like a two year commitment from you should you decide to take him up on his offer, and after all, two years is a long time. If you are planning to marry William next spring, that might be something you will want to talk with him about."

"He wants me to work at the paper? Why does everything have to happen at the same time? But, you are right. I have a job, and I am planning to marry William in the spring."

"You have to make the decision for yourself, Daphnia. As for the two-year commitment, I don't believe Herbert really believes either you or I would agree to anything like that right now. He is a reasonable man. But, you don't have to go. You must make this decision out of what you believe to be the right thing, not out of pride, or guilt, or dreams."

"Papa, you and I both know that to work in a newspaper office is a dream come true for me. You have obviously known that for a long time since you must have spoken with Uncle Bert about it. Regardless of that, Mother has never asked for me in all these years, she needs me now, and I need to go. Even if I go for only a short time I simply cannot stay here and not go to her. I'm not worried about pride, guilt or even right or wrong for that matter. I just know that if she has asked for me, I must go."

Thaddeus turned his face toward the sky. "Daphnia, dear, I need you to trust me and to believe that I love you as much as if you were my very own. You have always been everything to both Martha and me and I would walk from here to Detroit over cut glass if it would keep you from feeling pain or sorrow. If you decide that you must go to Huron City and spend Melissa's last days with her, of course I will understand. The Gazette is a fine paper and Herbert will be more than fair with you. You don't have to accept his offer to work with him at the paper or to live in the apartment. Melissa has offered to have you stay with her and Eloise. Herbert has made a very generous offer, and you might want to consider it. He's a good man. We go back a long way. We have been friends for almost as long as I can remember, there have been many things pass between us, we are connected through promises made and secrets kept." He laid the piece of wood down and put the knife back into his boot, then standing he turned back toward her, "I need you to trust me, I think going to Huron City and learning the newspaper business under the tutelage of a man such as Herbert Bernstein is not a bad thing. Going back because of Melissa, well that is something else altogether. I have a note for you from Melissa." Handing her a small white envelope, he turned and walked off the porch and out toward the barn.

Sitting on the swing, she watched him walk away and wondered if she could really leave this farm and the two people she had grown up loving as her Mother and Father. She picked up the white envelope that had been closed with a gold seal and the raised letters *"MAF"*. It was neatly addressed with the blue ink; it looked the color of blueberries. Her heart was pounding. She held the envelope close to her face and took in a deep breath, she imagined what it must say and how happy she was just thinking that her mother wanted her, really wanted her to come back after all of these years. Her hands were trembling. As she opened the note she could smell the sweet scent of lavender. The tears streamed down her cheeks, she was smiling with delight and anticipation of the loving words that she were written just to her. After a look toward the heavens and saying a short prayer, she read the letter.

> *Daphnia,*
> *Any rights I once had to ask anything of you have long ago vanished. You must surely know by now that I am not well. Before my life fades away completely, I feel the need to see your face and feel your spirit around me. Please understand that it is only through you that I can once again feel the closeness of your father and the bond between us. I beg your forgiveness and understanding of my actions over these past nineteen years.*
> *I am hopeful that you will find it in your heart to visit me.*
>
> *Warm Regards, Melissa*

She felt as though someone had reached inside her and removed her heart with one quick and mighty pull. The tears that were once flowing freely form delight and happiness were dried up, and there was a frown where her radiant smile had been. She suddenly felt cold and began to shiver. She had expected something more from her mother after all this time. As happy as she had been before reading the note she was now equally angry and sad. She had expected so much more. She expected the letter to talk about love and time lost now needing to be made up somehow. She expected the letter to be signed, *"Mother"* certainly not Melissa. She had expected words of love and a longing to see her now grown up daughter, but they weren't there. She felt a stillness about her that was unsettling. Her heart slowed, she felt no pain and no emotion; she simply felt numb. She sat on the porch swing watching the last of the setting sun and the disappearing pink and purple streaks across the sky. She felt as if she was dreaming, nothing seemed in focus. Everything that she had known and come to love was changing and she felt that her emotions had been mixed together with Aunt Martha's wire whip that she used to mix her cake batter. Her ability to concentrate was momentarily lost. She closed her eyes and tried to get a grip on what she had just read. She tried to imagine Melissa Flanders old and sick. She could no longer remember what she looked like, but she could remember the sweet smell of the lavender toilette water and the cold lifeless voice telling her that her father was dead. Those two things were the memories she had of her mother; every other memory was gone. She would return those to the deep crevices of her mind to be opened again later along with the note written in the bluest of blue ink. She would soon tuck away her memories and this note in the little cherry wood box and carefully place it between her cotton petticoats in the black trunk. It would be only a matter of days before she would take the long train ride away from these rolling hills and the smell of Aunt Martha's apple dumplings to the gray wet place known as Huron City. She knew she would go. In spite of what Papa Tad said, pride and dreams would win and she would leave Sunshine Acres. She turned her eyes toward the sky and vowed that if nothing else, it would be her pride that would pull her through this. She would be strong not for Melissa but for herself. And, after all, she would have the newspaper. She would graciously accept the offer of a job and living above the Gazette; she would commit to the two years, William would be through with the Army by then, they could wait to get married.

She sat back holding the letter in her hands. She closed her eyes and thought of arriving back in a place where she had spent the first four years of her life. Those first four years were as different from the next twenty as different could get.

In Huron City, she had played quietly without other children, with no one to talk to or to laugh with. There was Aunt Ella who would sometimes read stories to her, or sing songs with her, but those times were rare and usually only when her mother was away or outside of the house. It was these thoughts that caused Daphnia a sense of fright and dread of returning to Huron City. The memories of flowers and blue skies that she had just spoken with her Papa Tad about evaporated and just now it seemed that all she could remember was the coldness and the wetness of the streets and walkways, the dark back porch and the earth itself that was always cold. Even the walls would weep with moisture in the summertime and icicles would form along the outside of the windows in the winter. It was at Sunshine Acres where she learned to laugh out loud and run and skip and play. It was here with Papa Tad and Aunt Martha that she felt warm and dry and secure. It was here where she could sing and dance and everyone laughed out loud whenever they wanted to.

Putting the note from Melissa aside, she looked around at her current surroundings. If her aunt or uncle asked to see it or asked what it contained she would respond casually and without emotion. She would not discuss it other than to say that it was a brief and simple request that she return to Huron City. Her mind was made up, she would go all right, but she would let her mother know why she returned. She would be sure to let her know that it was for the opportunity of working in a newspaper office that brought her back. After all, Melissa had sent her away for someone else to care for, why should she not return because she cared for something else.

These thoughts and many others continued to run through her mind until she could stand it no longer. Trying to sort through the sudden rise and fall of her emotions, wanting her mother to want her for who she was and knowing that it could never happen broke her heart. She put her head in her hands and cried until her sides ached and her eyes felt sore and burning. She finally stood and walked numb up the stairs to her room closing the door and falling into bed where she slept fully clothed until morning.

Chapter Five

The sun was making its way through the lace curtains and its rays spilled over Daphnia lying across her bed. Before going downstairs she retrieved the letter from her mother and placed it in the little box. Her aunt and uncle were waiting for her as she entered the kitchen.

Thaddeus had told Martha of his and Daphnia's conversation the previous evening not knowing that she had overheard most of it. He confirmed for her what she had already surmised, that Daphnia would be going to Huron City and probably very soon.

Martha's heart was breaking but she knew that she must not let Daphnia know of how deeply hurt she was. "You must be starved, dear. Here, have some breakfast before it gets cold."

Daphnia was anything but hungry, but she knew that eating would give her Aunt Martha great satisfaction, so she ate. "You make the best biscuits Aunt Martha, I will miss these in Huron City. I'll bet Ruth Bernstein doesn't even know how to make biscuits. She probably only makes bread in hard, round loaves."

"You will have to teach her some of the finer ways of eating, Daphnia. Just think, they can teach you to be a newspaper woman, and you can teach them about biscuits and apple dumplings."

Thaddeus could hear the two women talking and laughing. He was glad that they were able to overcome their sadness if only for a short time. " So, Daphnia," he began, "have you thought about when you will be leaving for Huron City?"

"I have thought of little else, Papa. I just can't seem to get my thoughts going in the same direction. I am going with mixed emotions, and frankly I am not real sure about anything except that I need to go. Who knows how long Mother will last, and I owe it to her and to me to be there for her."

"For what it is worth, Daphnia, I think you are doing the right thing. I know it will be difficult for your Aunt Martha and me, but you wouldn't be satisfied staying here knowing that she has asked for you regardless of her reasons. And, who knows, I get down that way from time to time, maybe I will get down to see you before you know it."

"That would be wonderful, Papa." She spoke with such confidence that both Martha and Thaddeus found themselves wrapped around her as well as one another laughing and crying all wrapped up together.

"Oh, Daphnia," Aunt Martha said with a laugh, "you are the most changeable young lady I have ever known. William is right, you are a Daffy Girl."

Thaddeus took Martha in his arms and the two of them danced across the kitchen floor with him singing at the top of his lungs, "Oh Daffy Girl, Oh Daffy Girl' to the tune of O' Susanna." Daphnia joined in with the dance and the singing until they had run out of rhymes and were exhausted.

"I must go upstairs and begin to pack. There is much to do and I have to think about all of this calmly. I was wondering, though, what is Mother's illness? And, what about Eloise Barnes, is there no other family?"

"Well, Daphnia I'm not sure I really know, to tell you the truth. About Melissa's illness, it seems that she took ill before Matthew was killed, and it has just gotten worse over the years. I never asked for the exact cause or what it is for that matter, but whatever it is, I believe it is real. As for other family, I can't rightly tell you much about that either."

"You mean there is only Aunt Ella and me?"

"I guess there could be others, but I have never pried into Melissa's family history, just what I have heard or what she has volunteered. Other than Eloise, I never met any of them. Eloise lived with Melissa's Mother before she died, and then came on back to Huron City with Melissa after the funeral. Frankly, I am not even sure that she is a true cousin, but I believe she was a ward of Melissa's Mother. Melissa had two sisters and one brother, the brother and one sister are both dead, and the other one lost touch with Melissa some years ago. As to whether or not any of them had children of their own, I just don't know." Thaddeus leaned back in his chair and closed his eyes. He removed his pipe from his vest pocket and filled it with tobacco.

Daphnia watched the smoke rings and breathed in the sweet smell. She wished he would just sit and smoke and stop talking for a while. She wanted to be able to roll the words over in her mind and sift through some of the emotions she was feeling. She knew that there would be many things said this day that would bring her closer to Huron City and further away from the security of this comfortable home, and she wanted to stretch out this moment for as long as possible. She was beginning to feel the pains of a deep loss that she was certain would grow through time. She watched her uncle smoke his pipe, she traced his profile with her eyes as if she was burning his image into her mind where she could call upon it to surface again at some future moment.

"As for brothers or sisters of your own, dear, you are an only child, and so was Matthew." He spoke slowly and deliberately. He thought he could hear his voice trembling and hoped that neither Daphnia nor Martha noticed. His only concern was that Daphnia not ask questions that would force him to reveal more than he absolutely had to. He was doing what he believed he had to do in order to keep his promise to an old friend, and a bittersweet memory secret to himself.

"I guess there will be only Aunt Ella, Mother and me then for Sunday dinners." Daphnia said trying to sound cavalier.

Thaddeus did not hear the comment, he allowed himself to think of Melissa and the letter she must have written to Daphnia begging her to come to Huron City. How dare she ignore Daphnia all these years and now reach out to her from her bed of death and reclaim her when she wasn't even hers to claim? For what? Just to hurt her and rip her heart out by letting her know that she was the illegitimate child of a lonely widow and a man who was bound by his own ego and selfishness? Goddamn her soul right to hell, and Herbert Bernstein's right along with it for forcing him to be a part of this conspiracy all of these years. And, Goddamn young love and clear moonlit nights and farewell to the forbidden love that started it all. Herbert had played his final ace and Thaddeus knew in his heart that he would lose this hand. Now he watched the face of his beloved Daphnia and he knew there was no way that that he could talk her out of leaving.

"Was Uncle Joshua your only brother, Papa? Are you saying that I am the end of the line of Flanders?"

"I guess I am Daphnia. There was my brother Joshua and of course Sarah, Joshua's wife and Matthew's mother, your Grandmother, there are no others. You look like Sarah, Daphnia. You remind me so much of her at times."

As he said this last phrase he closed his eyes and inhaled deeply on his pipe. He stopped talking and felt himself slide into sweet memories of passionate love.

"Papa, did you go to sleep?"

"I'm sorry, Daphnia, I was just thinking for a moment. Joshua was a lot like Matthew only not as good looking. He was a little on the wild and spirited side. He would often take long trips down south or back east. He didn't mind just up and leaving Sarah whenever he got the urge. Oh, he always came home again, and I can't really say that he was gone all that long. Martha and me, we would look in on her and make sure she had everything that she needed. He meant well, he was just not one to stay put for very long. Martha, do you remember ......"

"I remember perfectly well how he would take off and leave her for weeks at a time. Why the winter she was expecting Matthew I don't think he was home more than two weeks. He always had someplace else that he needed to be. And, for what, that's what I would like to know? Why if it wasn't for you, Thaddeus, Lord only knows what she would have done. I think you were over at her place fixing, and taking care of things as much as you were taking care of things here. It was you and me who was with her when Matthew was born. I remember it just as clear. I can still see you there holding her hand telling her that it was all going to be okay and begging her not to die. But she just couldn't hold on. She tried to be brave, but I remember her lying there begging you to hold her. She said she was so cold. She died right there in your arms with Matthew sleeping next to her. No, I'll never forget it. Then Joshua came bustin' in the door and grabbed Matthew up. Why he walked around that room like he had done all the doing that there was to be done; he pranced around like a peacock. Like he had done something special. There she was lying there dead and he didn't even act like he cared. He raised Matthew to be just like him, and he did a good job of it, I have to give him that. It didn't matter none how much you tried to get him to let you raise Matthew, Joshua did what he wanted, and Matthew turned out to be just as careless and carefree as Joshua ever dared to be."

"Now, now, Mart. You are getting too wound up. I know you never really cared much for Joshua, but he was my brother and the truth be known he had it a lot rougher than we might imagine. He and Sarah had a rocky start, and I don't think he was ready to settle down when they married. But, Sarah was kind and gentle. She loved with all of her heart, and she suffered for that love. They're all gone now, all long ago passed away, and we must be kind to the dead."

"It seems so final, death. How is anyone ever supposed to know whether or not they have lived their life as they should have, or if grabbing the brass ring and living for the moment is the better way. Just look at Grandmother Sarah and my father, they sound like two very different people yet they both ended up dead before their time. Then look at my grandfather, well, what about him? Who knows if he was happy or sad or if he lived every moment for its glory or because of how tough life was to him? And then there is mother, how long did you say she has been ill?"

"I truly don't know exactly what her sickness is or exactly how long she has been sick. It seems that she became ill shortly after Matthew was killed and she has continued to weaken over the years. Eloise said that it is as if the disease has spread throughout her body. She is still as beautiful as ever, and she has some good days, but most of her time is spent in her bed. She is very weak. The doctor sees her often, Herbert takes care of her financial affairs so he checks on her regularly, and Eloise is the real caretaker. I don't know if she will die tomorrow or ten years from now. There just is no way of knowing."

"Oh, dear Lord, Thaddeus, did you say she could live for ten years? Daphnia will never come home if she lasts that long?"

"Now, Martha. I think you are being a little unfair to Melissa. After all, where is your compassion? I visited with Melissa and Eloise for quite a spell when I was in Huron City. I also talked with the doctor. I certainly don't wish Melissa any bad luck, and I hope and pray that she gets better and lives a good long life."

"I'm sorry, Thaddeus you know I didn't mean that to sound as it did."

"The place is really not bad, Daphnia. I spent a great deal of time talking with Herbert and looking over the newspaper office. It is really quite nice and you should be comfortable there. The town, of course, is not where I would want to live, but you might find it exciting. I don't know how they can call that little village a city; it is barely more than half a mile from one end to the other. There is a hotel, at least a couple of taverns, a feed store, the usual little shops, a bank that is hardly secure enough to keep out the squirrels and mice in the winter, and of course the Gazette with the Mercantile right next door; Ruth runs that along with the post office. The Gazette itself is a fine little paper and the office is actually very neat and bright. Especially now that it is being repainted after the fire we had."

"Fire! You didn't say anything about a fire, Thaddeus." Martha had been only half listening, but she heard this.

"It wasn't much, Mart, just a little trash fire that erupted when Herbert threw what he thought to be an unlit pipe into a barrel of paper and debris from the office. Everything is fine now and it wasn't much to start with."

"What about the apartment, Papa, how was that?"

"To tell you the truth, Daphnia, It looked nice from what I saw of it. That was the reason for me going to the newspaper office, but with all of the commotion, I just didn't have a lot of time to actually go through it thoroughly. Herbert tells me it is very nice, and I am sure that it is. Now, if you don't mind, I am a little tired." He stood and left the room without saying another word.

Reaching across the table and taking the hand of her Aunt Martha Daphnia suggested that she begin to get her things together. "Do you want to help me Aunt Martha, or should I get started without you?"

"You go ahead and get started dear, I will straighten things up down here then I will be up."

Chapter Six

As she cleared away the dishes, Martha watched Thaddeus walk toward the barn. It had been more than a few years since he had come home from a trip this upset and full of mystery, but in those days he was younger and he was more in control of things. Seeing him now taking his long strides across the pasture she was worried. He had changed since he returned to Sunshine Acres this time; he was worn out. She could not remember a trip that had left him more exhausted.

She stood at the window looking out at him as he spoke with Carl, their long time overseer, she thought of his recent return. Her excitement to see him had melted away when she saw that it was Carl who was driving the big automobile and not Thaddeus. When the automobile stopped, Carl had to open the door and help Thaddeus from the vehicle. It was Carl who brought in the valise and packages. This was unlike Thaddeus to allow Carl to drive when he himself loved to be behind the wheel of the shiny black automobile. And, Thaddeus never had allowed anyone but himself to bring in his bags, and certainly not his packages and gifts. As he approached the steps, she took over for Carl and walked arm in arm with Thaddeus through the front door and into the parlor... ... ...

... ... She remembered how he responded when she asked how he felt and the excuses he gave her of just being tired. "Are you feeling well, Dear, is everything okay? You look a little unsettled, so you may as well go ahead and tell me, Sir is it your fortune or mine that you have lost in the gray wet city near the lake?"

"I'm afraid it is our hearts I lost, my dear. I am afraid that I have lost our hearts to the gray and wet city. I am so tired lately and I just can't seem to shake this feeling. Won't you sit here with me a while, Mart. I need to rest some, tell me about all that has happened while I have been away."

This was not like Thaddeus, not at all she thought as she watched him now approach the barn and go inside. It always seemed to her that everything happened at one time and never at the time she would have preferred. She would worry about Thaddeus later, right now she had to go upstairs and help Daphnia.

She would tell Daphnia that she could not leave and that her uncle was getting old and tired. She would go right up and tell her to stop packing immediately!

Climbing the stairs she rehearsed what she would say to Daphnia, 'Daphnia, put those things down this minute, you cannot go. You must stay. Melissa is a selfish woman, she is not even your mother. You must stay here with us.' There, she had it.

"I see you made it up here, Aunt Martha. Thanks. Here, what do you think? Should I take this blue coat or the red one? Can you help me with this trunk? It looked so big before I started putting all of this stuff into it. Isn't it exciting? I mean, just a little bit? You and Papa will have this house all to yourselves again, and I can come back for the holidays, oh what fun we will have catching up on all the gossip. So, what do you think? You seem, rather quiet, are you going to be okay?"

"Oh, I am just not as excited to have you leave as you seem to be to go, but I understand. Why not take both coats, one never knows which one you will need, and the blue one is heavier."

Supper was served and eaten with the usual fanfare of rituals, Thaddeus teasing, Martha fussing and Daphnia trying to make sense of it all. It wasn't until much later as she soaked in the big tub with the aroma of lavender floating in the air that she took the time to piece it all together.

Chapter Seven

The next couple of days were uneventful at Sunshine Acres. It seemed everyone was busy preparing for Daphnia's trip to Huron City. Carl was busy as well, there were things that needed doing before his missus took to the labor bed, and with Mr. Flanders going off again, he knew that he had to have things in good condition should he need to spend some time on his own place for a couple of days. Carl had been with the Flanders since he was a boy. He had grown up on Sunshine Acres. He lived humbly and learned to listen to the things around him, how the wind moved through the tree tops, the colors of the sunsets and the way the crickets and pond creatures sounded when storms were in the offing. Lately he felt uneasiness along his spine and it was more than his wife getting ready to deliver their first child. He had been studying the skies and he didn't like the way the sky was looking these days, the dark clouds were coming up much too suddenly and it seemed that this was a hotter start to the summer than what he had remembered. He had heard about some terrible wind and rain west of Lansing, and he was sure that they were headed for some rough weather. He was busy! He had talked to Thaddeus about the changes in the weather just this very day. But, as usual, Thaddeus didn't seem too concerned.

It wasn't that he didn't care about Carl's aches and pains, he believed they could be a fair prediction of the weather, it was just that he had spent a lot of time in town lately with the railroad and the new rail that they were trying to get laid to the North; there were also some rails that already needed repairs between Lansing and Grand Rapids. While he was content with the activity and his need to stay busy, he wasn't oblivious to what was going on. He had listened to Carl and he too was aware of the changes in the weather and the storms that had been popping up lately.

He had gone into town to make passage for Daphnia and to send a wire to Herbert of her arrival time. Now on the way home, he thought of the many trips he had taken along this road, but today he felt more tired than usual. He smiled as he thought of Martha and how a cold glass of lemonade would hit the spot.

Pulling up to the barn and closing the automobile inside, he looked back over his shoulder only to see the clouds rolling with what looked like black and purple rage and more dangerous than he remembered, it seemed so hot. He quickly walked up to the house. As he entered the house the sky opened up and the rain came down in torrents. There was lightning, wind and rain that whipped across the pastures like walls of water; the roaring was like that of a train entering a tunnel.

"Mart, Daphnia, help get these windows shuttered, hurry there is a storm coming, let's get this secured and down to the cellar. Hurry up Martha, C'mon Daphnia."

Martha and Daphnia were up in her room where Martha was pinning up the hem of the dress that Daphnia would be wearing on her trip. Dropping the fabric and taking the pins out of her mouth, Martha nearly froze with fear.

"C'mon, honey, get your shoes on and let's get down to the cellar with Thaddeus."

"Come on Daphnia, get your shoes, let's go," Aunt Martha cried as she heard a crack and saw a large branch from one of the big Pine trees fall to the ground. She quickly pulled the shutters closed, and grabbed Daphnia's hand and began to pull her out of the room with Daphnia dancing trying to get her shoes on while running and hopping down the stairs and into the kitchen where Thaddeus had closed the shutters and was coming out the door toward them. He quickly grabbed Martha and pushed her toward the cellar door then grabbed Daphnia by the waist and lifted her off the ground with one shoe still in her hand and the other sliding off her foot and falling behind the door.

"Get into the cellar, get into the cellar, now, go, go, go" he shouted as the three of them entered the cellar and he pulled the cellar door closed behind them.

They were in the cellar for a long time before they no longer heard the wind. Thaddeus went back up the cellar steps and opened the door. The house appeared to be intact and he motioned for Martha and Daphnia to come up from the cellar. They went from room to room and found that there did not appear to be any damage, and they carefully opened the shutters and looked out.

The grounds were not as preserved as the house appeared to have been. There were limbs and debris everywhere. Thaddeus immediately went to the out buildings and barns to check on the livestock. Martha and Daphnia went to the wells and looked around the great porches and the chicken yard. Other than a few boards blown off the roof of the barn and some shutters broken and split, there didn't appear to be any real damage. The livestock had been spared and it seemed that this storm was over as soon as it started. Thaddeus saddled his horse and rode over to see Carl to make sure that he and his wife were safe as well.

Carl had been on his way home when he too had seen the black clouds, he was able to get his wife into their cellar in time, and they were safe. Like the homestead of the Flanders', Carl's home had been spared and other than a little debris and a few tree limbs here and there his place was undamaged.

The rest of the day was spent cleaning up the debris and checking on the livestock. Thaddeus was glad to have something that required so much physical activity to keep his mind off Daphnia's leaving. He felt energized and was glad to know that when he needed to be the extra hand, he could still pull down his share of the work. But he was tired. He could see that as he rode up to the house, Martha and Daphnia were both busy getting things back together.

"Well, it looks like we got through that one without too much damage. Carl and his wife are fine, we didn't do too badly, I guess. Did you and Daphnia check around the house and the orchards?"

"Daphnia is out checking the cherry and apple orchards now, she took the gelding and I think both of the dogs are with her as well. I have checked on the windows and looked over all the shutters on the first floor, it looks like the only one that is loose is the one in the back next to the bathing room; it seems that side of the house is always the one that gets hit the worst. Maybe we should plant some of those fir trees along the fence row over on that side next spring, what do you think of that Thaddeus?"

"We'll see, Mart. I think I will go inside and take a look down in the cellar. You want to come?"

"No, you go ahead, I think I need to go check on my roses. She watched him go inside before she went down the steps and across the yard to her favorite spot on the entire farm, her rose garden. She had nurtured and pampered the lovely flowers since she and Thaddeus first came to live on this place. There were roses of all colors, but her favorite, the yellow roses were planted near the graves of her mother and father. She was anxious to see her precious flowers and spend some time in prayer with her dear parents; she needed to talk.

As she picked at the flowers and pulled up the unwanted weeds, she thought of Daphnia and her leaving for Huron City. She was certain that this decision was surely fraught with heartache. She thought of what Thaddeus had said about her taking the train with him to Huron City for a visit, but she knew that she would never leave her home again let alone get on a train. The last time that she took a trip with Thaddeus, she was a nervous wreck and she longed to return to the safety and comfort of her home and her flowers. Even going the few miles down the road to church on Sunday was more upsetting for her than she let on. Her days of leaving Sunshine Acres at all were over and she knew it. She was grateful that Thaddeus and Daphnia were able to come and go so freely, but when she thought of just going into Lansing she would become physically ill. No, she would not take the train to Huron City, even to see her precious Daphnia. They would understand.

Lost in her thoughts, and 'playing with her flowers' as Thaddeus would say, she soon lost track of time and was caught off guard when she suddenly saw Daphnia standing above her.

"Why, Daphnia, you ought to say something before walking up on someone like that. You nearly scared the beejesus out of me," she said. She quickly began to gather her skirts about her and stand up only to trip on her petticoat and land right in the middle of the rose bush where she had just finished pulling the weeds.

It took all of Daphnia's strength to help her stand again but before she could regain her balance, she was again rocked backward and this time with Daphnia falling right on top of her. With Martha squirming beneath and Daphnia laughing and squirming above, it is a wonder they ever got up. If it hadn't been for Carl hearing the commotion and coming to their rescue, they may have been there until dark.

When Carl arrived on the scene, he wasn't sure just what to make of it. Martha was squirming and fussing and Daphnia was laughing and struggling to get up but every time she would put her hand down to gain leverage, she would place it on a thorn and then pull back only to have to start all over again. Carl quickly grabbed Daphnia by the waist and pulled her up and off Martha then both he and Daphnia each took a hand of Martha's and pulled her up right on her feet.

"What a mess the two of you are. Why, I thought that a bear or something had come down and gotten a hold of the both of you. You better get on up to the house and get cleaned up. Miss Daphnia, it looks like you have a few good scratches on your hands and arms there, you better get those taken care of pretty quickly." He then looked over at Martha and just burst out laughing. "Why Missus Flanders, I am not sure but I do believe you have left the back side of your dress down there with them roses, and it appears that your petticoat is not in too good a shape either, here, mamn, let me get a blanket from the wagon there and you can wrap that around you 'til you get on up to the house." He left to get the blanket. When he returned, Daphnia had retrieved the torn articles from the rose bushes and was trying to clean up the broken limbs and leaves. He gave the blanket to Martha and while putting his hand to the brim of his hat said, "Good day, ladies." Then he turned and walked back to the wagon, got up on the seat and with a quick sounding "giddyup" to the team of horses, he rode away. Martha and Daphnia could hear him laughing until he got out of sight.

As they walked back to the house, they too were laughing with the blanket wrapped around Martha's backside and Daphnia carrying the pieces of torn cloth.

Their laughter could not keep Martha from thinking of Thaddeus and the trip he and Daphnia were about to take. They went about cleaning up themselves and getting things ready for their evening meal. It had been a long couple of days and Martha was hoping to turn in early this evening. The train would be leaving early tomorrow morning and Daphnia would be on it.

Part II

Our intentions, they deceive us
dreams and nightmares
our suffering thus
unrequited, and often...
... just!

Chapter Eight

Morning came much too early at the Flanders' house on Thursday. Martha was standing at the headstone of the grave of her mother almost before the sun rose. It was times such as these when she felt she needed the support of her memory and to know that she was not alone. She had awakened early, and she quietly slipped from beneath the soft comforter and tiptoed out of the house to her rose garden and the small family graveyard. It wasn't just the graves of her mother that she visited, she had long ago felt the need and received comfort from the rest of the family, an aunt and two uncles, several cousins, nieces and nephews and one small tiny headstone with the name Thaddeus Allen Flanders, Jr., December 3rd, 1868 - March 1st, 1869; he had been born early and was so very tiny; his little system could not fight off the sickness and fever that stayed with him for his short life. Thaddeus had made the coffin in which he was buried and they laid him there next to Martha's mother. But the one gravesite, which Martha avoided, was that of Sarah Flanders, the wife of Joshua. When Sarah was alive she and Martha visited often, but there was an estrangement that Martha never quite understood. She had suggested that Thaddeus bury Sara and Joshua closer to their place on the other side of the farm, but he had insisted on including them in the family cemetery, so she gave in. She tended their graves as she did the others, but it was Thaddeus who generally spent time with the two headstones of Matthew's parents, his penance he would call it when questioned. The headstones had been put in place for Thaddeus and Martha just to the right of their only child. She often thought of what it must be like down there, so dark, so cold and so very still. If she thought of it long enough she could almost feel herself being pulled down into the earth itself. But, she wasn't scared; she would let herself imagine being in the arms of her mother and feeling a quiet peacefulness about her. Although she never said so, she longed for the companionship and comforting words of her mother and to once again hold her baby boy even if it meant leaving this life. She thought of it more often than she cared to admit, and there were times when she actually longed for the hereafter.

As she stood thinking of her little son, her mother and her father she wondered what advice they would give her about Daphnia and what words would they say to her about how to let her go. She stood quietly and prayed for guidance. She needed to be strong but she wasn't sure exactly how. Opening her eyes she told herself that she must shake off these feelings; she must get on with the reality of life. Shaking her head as if to remove all thoughts, she took a deep breath and then gently pressed her hand against each tombstone and turned and walked back toward the house stopping only to wipe her eyes and blow her nose.

Thaddeus had awakened to find her gone from their bed and went into the kitchen then out to the porch and finally looked over toward the small knoll where she was standing among the roses. The mere sight of her made him smile. He thought Martha to be beautiful and he felt himself lucky to have her to love and hold onto at times like these. He had found himself to be not so strong lately and the strain of it had taken its toll; he felt the tightness in his chest more often than usual and it seemed that he frequently had a hard time holding on to the piece of wood he was whittling. Just the simple act of breathing wasn't as easy as it used to be. By God, he was starting to feel old; he was almost seventy. He was glad he had delayed his trip until Daphnia was on her way to Huron City. It would be difficult for him to get caught up, but he knew that Martha would need him close for a while. Watching Martha make her way from the garden he walked out to meet her.

"Now, now, Mart," brushing the strands of fine white hair away from her face with his hand, "it will all work itself out, you will see. You know it has been a long time since I have had you all to myself, I might get to liking that special way you use to spoil me all over again." He teased her as he touched her cheek and kissed her soft pink lips. Then with a pat on her backside, he suggested that some biscuits and ham might be just the thing he needed to get started on his day.

"Honestly, Thaddeus, you have but two things on your mind and at your age. You will get your ham and biscuits sure as preaching, yes sir, just as sure as preaching, but don't you go looking for anything else this early in the morning, I have plenty to do to get Daphnia up and ready so that she is on that train on time. Now, be on with you, get from under my feet, now, get on out of here." She squirmed from his arms while loving every minute of him holding her; just before she was totally out of his arms she gave him a tight hug about his waist and winked as she wriggled free.

"No need to worry about getting me ready, Aunt Martha, I am already packed up, and have most of my things by the bedroom door," she said as she kissed her Papa Tad on the cheek and gave her Aunt Martha a side ways glance then looking back at Thaddeus she winked, "I guess I should have made more noise coming down the stairs, huh?"

Martha blushed from head to toe then laughed and hugged Daphnia. "Daphnia, I do declare, you are as bad as Thaddeus," she said as she held her.

How breakfast got prepared, served, and eaten with the chaos of that morning was unknown to Martha. Once Daphnia had finished eating, she and Thaddeus got up and went up the stairs to begin bringing down the trunk and Daphnia's valise and other items that she would be taking with her. Martha left the dishes and went up to help out.

"Here, let me help you dear," Martha was saying to Thaddeus, as he appeared to be struggling with the trunk. "I thought that Carl was coming in this morning to get things loaded up. You don't think Arlene went into labor do you? Oh, my, this would not be a good day for that," Martha said almost in a whisper.

Thaddeus had finally gotten the trunk out of the door and was headed down the stairs with it when he heard Carl at the door. "Come on in, Carl; we're up here."

Carl entered the house and took one look up the stairs. He quickly took the steps two at a time, squatted down and lifted the trunk up and onto his back then stood and went briskly down the stairs and out the front door where the carriage was waiting. He loaded the trunk onto the back of the carriage and strapped it tightly then went back into the house to see if there was anything else. While no spring chicken, Carl was in his prime at thirty-seven and the soon to be proud father of what the doctor said could be twins.

As he entered the house this time Carl saw Daphnia coming down the stairs with her valise, a shawl and one other small bag. She stood at the foot of the stairs. He had to catch his breath when he saw her. He had never seen her looking this way before. He took in a deep breath and thought to himself, now, this is a woman to be considered.

"Good morning, Miss Daphnia," he said as he took off his hat and bowed gracefully from the waist. "You're certainly something to behold, Miss, are you sure you should be traveling alone?"

"Well thank you Sir," Daphnia said as she curtsied back to Carl, "so, do you think I should have an armed guard, then? Well, maybe you can help me talk Aunt Martha or Papa Tad here in to coming along with me," she said teasingly while handing him her bags and shawl, "you know that Papa Tad has decided to let me travel alone while he stays here and takes advantage of this quiet and peaceful house with Aunt Martha all to himself, don't you?"

"Now, Daphnia, you know that I am not ready to go away again so soon, and besides you will be fine. You will have Herbert there to meet you at the station, and Melissa and Eloise are there, if you really want me to come with you, I can, but I don't think I need to, now do you really think you aren't old enough to go alone? After all, you are going to be twenty what your next birthday?"

"I guess, I don't mind, really. But, it will be strange arriving in Huron City not knowing anyone. It has been so long since I saw Mr. Bernstein and I truly don't remember much about Daniel. You will be up to visit soon, won't you?"

"Not immediately, but I will be up before you know it. You just take good care of yourself, and don't let anyone or anything get you down. If you really need us, just send word and I'll be there on the next train. Or maybe I can get Martha to drive down with me in that black automobile she dislikes so much. But, remember, Herbert Bernstein is my dearest and oldest friend, he is more like family than not, so you keep that in mind when you address him. You always called him Uncle Bert when he came to visit here, so unless you feel that you are too old to call him that now, he might appreciate you calling him that when you see him. Although, I can't honestly say whether or not Ruth feels the same way."

"Well, what about you Aunt Martha? Will you be coming to visit me with Papa Tad?"

"As much as I will miss you, I am not going anywhere anytime soon, now I don't want either one of you to get the notion in your heads that I will do otherwise! I am not going anywhere, and especially not in that black smoke spitting, start and stop noisemaker you call an automobile."

"Now Martha, I think you are being a little unfair to that fine piece of machinery that we don't use near as much as we should. But, Martha's right, Daphnia I will be there soon, but not right away. Things are getting busy around here right now, the crops are starting to come in and I need to be here for Carl with Arlene in her condition. But, I'll be there soon, now don't you worry. Besides, what would people think you having to have a chaperone?"

"You're right, of course. I promise to write often, and I will take full advantage of the telegraph office if I think I need to. You'll both do the same, won't you? If you need me, you will let me know. What do you think, Carl? Are you ready to look after these two all by yourself?"

"It sounds to me like I don't have much choice, Miss Daphnia. After all of these years of working along side Mr. Flanders here I don't think they will take up too much of my time."

Daphnia hugged and kissed her uncle and aunt, and allowed Carl to help her into the carriage. Looking back she watched as the house grew smaller in the distance and she could no longer make out the faces of the two people standing on the porch waving good-bye. This was going to be a challenge, this trip, the not knowing what to expect of her mother or Herbert Bernstein or of Huron City.

Once at the station, Carl unloaded her trunk and other large bag; he handed her the valise and her wrap. He hailed a porter and gave him an envelope with specific instructions for the ticket master.

"You take care of yourself, Miss, do you need me to stay until you get boarded?

"No, no, Carl, I will be fine. Good luck with those babies on the way. Don't you let Aunt Martha spoil them too much now, will you?" She gave Carl's arm a slight squeeze, took the envelope from the porter and went up to the ticket window to secure her passage.

The train ride from Lansing west to Grand Rapids and then back east again to Detroit was close to being boring. Even with her creative imagination, she found herself napping on and off. It always seemed to her that there should be a route somewhere that would allow the trains to go straight through and without having to connect with another small station somewhere so that she wouldn't have to go west to go east, but there never was. It seemed insane for her to have to go away from her destination only to double back some four or five hours later. It wasn't' that she minded riding, it just seemed out of the way. When she wasn't sleeping she found herself thinking of William and how much she loved him and missed him. She watched the other passengers go about their business of talking to one another, or reading the newspapers. It had always amused her the way strangers treated each other in a more kind and accepting manner than they often did their own families. Nonetheless, when the train made its stop in Detroit before going on up to Huron City she was grateful. She got off the train briefly to stretch her legs and get some air. It had been some time since she had been to Detroit, and much had changed. The station seemed busier than she remembered; there were more people, and the trains seemed louder and closer together than before.

It was not just the trains and loading platforms that were crowded, the entire station proper was crowded both outside and inside. On the porch and near the rails people were milling about. Trunks, boxes, and crates seemed to be stacked everywhere. She could hear the bellowing of cattle and could smell the pungent odor of the stockyards nearby. The hurried smiles, fast talk, and easy persuasion of the hustle and bustle were exhilarating to her. She played a game of imagining what the people were like based on how they were dressed or the way in which they acted toward one another.

As she looked about the porches she saw a tiny dark woman sitting on one of the benches near the entrance to the station; there were two children standing close by, a boy who was the larger and a small girl. There was a ticket agent talking loudly to the black woman as if he was trying to reason with her, but she didn't seem to be concerned. She just stared past him. Without any conversation, she merely opened her bag and gave him their riding passes. The smaller child looked frightened, but the young boy looked as if he was braced and ready to defend the woman if he had to. The agent took the piece of paper and once again began yelling at the woman. She gathered the small child to her and then nodded as if to accept whatever he had told her. Daphnia tried not to stare at the commotion but she couldn't pull her attention away from the woman and her children. It seemed that the ticket agent wasn't willing to allow the black family of three to ride with the passes they had presented. The woman didn't argue, but made it clear that she intended to get on the train. Finally, after much animation on the part of the ticket agent and little or no conversation he hustled the little woman and her two children off to one of the freight cars near the end of the train. He reluctantly helped them aboard the freight car and was very clear and loud as he reminded them that they were not to mingle with the other passengers nor would they be afforded the luxury of moving about the train. The little woman nodded her understanding as she moved the children inside of what appeared to be a boxcar more suited for transporting cattle than people. Daphnia felt sorry for the woman and children. The trip to Huron City wouldn't be a long one, but long enough for one to become uncomfortable sitting on a bale of hay with the wind blowing in through the boxcar's wooden sides. She would be sure to mention this to her Papa Tad when she wrote next.

Once resettled in her seat, she could not forget the black family, especially the children. She had not seen more than a dozen darkies at any given time, and never had she seen any darkie children up close; Aunt Martha called them "Coloreds" but Daphnia was always confounded by that term. Papa Tad just called them Negroes. There had not been a lot of discussion about the matter, and now to see three of them right here in the train station and riding on the same train as she, this was something. She didn't understand why people treated others so badly just because of their skin color. She felt the pangs of a lack of worldliness and sophistication; for the first time in her adult life she suddenly felt inept and ill prepared for a life on her own. She said a quick prayer that her naiveté would not be too obvious to those in Huron City. A city with nightlife and a daytime of fast pace with the lumberyard, the mill and industry coming in. Huron City was not a hole in the wall little village that was stuck next to the lakefront. It was small, maybe, but it was busy. There were a lot of comings and goings and people with a mission, and a past that they might want to keep hidden. She knew these things to be true regardless of how dull and shameless her uncle had tried to make it out to be.

As the train pulled away from the station, she could not help but to remember her trip so many years ago. She thought of riding away from Huron City at that time, not to it. She could still hear her mother's voice telling her how fine things would be, if only she could go back there, she thought. She wondered why her mother would send her away. With tears filling her eyes she shook her head and tried to think about happier times. Her mind raced to her last days in Lansing and to what she might find in Huron City. She allowed the steady motion of the train to lull her off to sleep.

Chapter Nine

Back at Sunshine Acres, Carl had returned to his own home, Thaddeus and Martha had made a busy day of it and decided to call it an early evening.

"I do believe I am coming down with something, Mart. Maybe it is the finality of these last couple of weeks and Daphnia's departure for Huron City today that's got me so tired, but I am turning in."

"I'm right behind you Thaddeus, just let me check the doors and windows one more time. I'll be up shortly."

As Martha came into the room he could not help but smile.

"What's that grin for, Thaddeus? What wheels have you got turning in that head of yours?"

"I was just watching you come up the stairs, Martha. Did I ever tell you about the first time I saw you?"

"If this is another one of your tales to get my mind off worrying you can just forget it. I am worried and I will stay worried for as long as I want to."

Ignoring her, he continued. "Well, you were standing near the Dogwood tree in the front yard of your father's old house down in Lansing. Those dogwood trees were the most beautiful trees to be found anywhere. Well, you were standing beneath the one over by the rock garden; there was a little brook nearby and yellow daffodils were growing among the rocks and next to the bank. I thought you were beautiful. I was with Herbert Bernstein and I fell in love with you at that very moment."

"Go on with you now. You never told me this before and besides what does that have to do with you calling me Martha instead of Mart?"

"Well, I'll just tell you what, it has everything to do with it, that's what. Herbert and I were talking with your father and trying to bargain for some work when I looked over and saw you standing there. Well, your father invited us to come up on the porch and when he went inside, I pointed you out to Herbert."

"Take a look at her, Herbert," I told him, "Isn't she something? She looks like she belongs there next to that beautiful tree all surrounded in happiness. I'll bet her name is that of a flower, like Violet, or Rose, or maybe angelic like Mary. Those names just fit her."

Herbert told me that I had lost my mind, and had obviously been smitten with Cupid's arrow." He was chuckling under his breath as he spun this story for Martha.

"And, just what did you do when you found out my name wasn't that of a flower at all, but I was just a plain old Martha Louise?"

"Just wait a minute, now, just you wait a minute, don't you want to know what Herbert had to say?" He walked away from the window and picked up his pipe from the table trying to buy some time so that he could continue with his story and get her into a happy mood. He wanted her to relax and forget about Daphnia going away, if only for a short while.

"Okay, then what did Herbert have to say?"

"Herbert looked me straight in the eye..."

"Now, Thaddeus, you know full well that Herbert Bernstein couldn't look you in the eye if he was standing on the porch and you on the ground, you're making this whole thing up," she said pushing against him and wiping her eyes while trying hard to keep from laughing.

"Okay, so maybe he got to the top step before me, okay? If you don't want to hear this just say so."

"Of course I want to hear the rest of your story or should I say tale?"

"All right, but stop interrupting, I'm trying to tell you something you might want to hear."

"Now, let's see where was I, oh, I know, it was then that I saw your sister Adele walk by and all thoughts of you and that Dogwood tree just flew right out of my head. By the way, you didn't happen to bring up any cookies and milk with you by chance? I am suddenly starved." He moved around her and started toward the door.

Martha was left standing there stunned and wondering what had just happened, she didn't even know anyone named Adele and she didn't have a sister.

"Thaddeus! Thaddeus Flanders, you come right back here this very minute. You are truly a cad, Thaddeus, I swear you are absolutely bad to the bone." She was scolding and following after him as fast as her fat stubby legs could carry her.

Thaddeus whirled around only to have Martha run right into him. Laughing and putting his arms around her to keep her from falling, he held her close and once again declared his love for her. But, Martha was having none of it, she demanded that he finish his story if for no other reason than to make him sit with her a while.

"Herbert was astonished," he started over again as he walked over and sat down on the window seat. He took out his pipe and proceeded to light it.

Martha sat down next to him eager to hear him spin his tale that she was sure was being made up as he went along. "Why was Herbert astonished, Thaddeus?"

"He was surprised that I would even notice you at all, since I was eager to enter into a business deal with your father, and secondly, I think he was shocked that I knew anything about flowers let alone their names. So anyway, Herbert took one look over at you standing there beneath that cherry tree ..."

"Cherry tree? I thought you said it was the dogwood tree! You're making this up! I knew it. You are bad, Thaddeus Flanders, mean, bad, and insensitive."

"I'm sorry, Mart," he said laughing now while holding his sides and the tears running down his face. "The reason I said 'cherry' tree was because that is what Herbert said he thought your name was, Cherry!" He had to stand as he said this for the pain of the laughter required that he be able to stand and walk around some. After catching his breath, he bent over and kissed her cheek. "I sure am glad your name was Martha, now what about those cookies and milk?"

"No, I did not bring up cookies or milk. There are plenty of cold biscuits and some ham on the sideboard down in the kitchen. You go on down there and make yourself up something from that, making a fool of me and me so scared and worried about Daphnia, why you should just be ashamed of yourself, Thaddeus Flanders." Martha left the room, walked across the hall and then down the stairs.

He could hear her sobbing and blowing her nose and he felt bad for teasing her. He got up and went after her. As he walked down the stairs and into the kitchen he saw no signs of her but saw the cellar door was ajar. He slowly pushed the door open and he could see her sitting on one of the steps holding something and crying quietly.

"What you got there, Mart?"

"Look Thaddeus, its one of Daphnia's shoes, it must have been one she lost during the storm. Do you think she will be okay in Huron City? Do you think Melissa will break her heart again? Do you think Melissa will tell her about Grace?"

"I don't know, Mart, I honestly don't know. Melissa is a selfish woman, but she is also proud so maybe we can pray that whatever she tells Daphnia and when she tells her about Grace that she will do so with some sense of compassion and understanding for what Daphnia will be going through. She will have to convince Daphnia that Matthew was taken in by Grace instead of it being the other way around. She'll need to save face and we can hope that she will be gentle."

As he moved down the stairs and closer to Martha he looked around the earthen cellar. He didn't come down here often, and was always surprised to see how uncluttered it was. As he stepped around Martha he could almost stand up straight since the cellar was just six feet from floor to ceiling. It smelled of dirt and moisture, there was no light except for that coming in from the kitchen above, there were no windows and Martha had not bothered to light the kerosene lantern. He squinted to make out what he thought was a bundle of rags, blankets and . . . what was that?

"What you got down there behind those stairs, Mart? What is all of that? Has somebody been sleeping down here in the cellar, Mart? What the ...."

"Now, now, Thaddeus, that is nothing but a bunch of blankets and things that I have to sort through, I have just been piling them back there beneath the stairs, it seemed like a good enough place, I need to get down here someday and clean it all up, don't you worry. I come down here now and then and just sort of fiddle around, sorting through first one thing and then another, I'll get it picked up. What about those cookies you were wanting, I'll get 'em for you. Come on now, let's go back upstairs. Here take my hand, I feel a little wobbly." He took her hand to help her up and the two of them went back up to the kitchen.

"How about those cookies, Thaddeus, sit down, sit right here and let's just take a minute. How do you think Daphnia is doing? I will write her tomorrow, you don't think it will be too soon do you? Why aren't you eating your cookies?"

"I don't think I'm hungry anymore Mart, I'm sorry, C'mon let's go, upstairs. We'll get a good night's sleep and things will make more sense come morning."

"Oh, that's okay, you go ahead I'll put this stuff away and be right up." She breathed a sigh of relief as she watched him leave the kitchen. She was grateful that he had not pursued the blankets and boxes that she had placed beneath the cellar stairs.

Chapter Ten

Daphnia awakened to the sound of rain hitting the window. She loved the rain; it seemed to agree with her need for peace. She stretched and then again settled down in her seat to watch the rain washing over the countryside rolling past her. She allowed her thoughts to return to the train ride that she had taken on that cold gray morning almost twenty years ago. She remembered feeling safe and warm but very little else. She drifted off to sleep again while trying to remember the events of her life leading up to that ride and the years since, but nothing was clear to her.

In one of the freight cars toward the back of the train was the frail little Negro woman and her two children. The children were lying against some loose hay that their mother had managed to brush into a pile. They had fallen asleep after eating a cold biscuit with apple butter that Clarice Hayes had brought along. She had carefully wrapped the biscuits in the flowered printed flour sack and then again in a burlap sack that she had cut down and sewn with a flap that she could fasten with buttons. The children had drifted off to sleep covered with a quilt made of rags and pieces of a wool horse blanket that Clarice had stuffed into a tapestry bag. Looking over at her small children she prayed that all would be as she had been promised.

The little family had been traveling for over two weeks. They had come up from a small mining town in West Virginia through Pittsburgh by riding on the back of a corn wagon where they finally boarded their first train. Since then, they had been shuffled from one boxcar to the next, at one point they were forced to ride in a car that had sheep on one side and themselves and two other families on the other. Clarice's father lived in Huron City and their train fare had been paid by a man she had never met, but who knew Mr. Hayes. He had promised to pay the full passage for Clarice, Michael and Ruby and to help get them situated. She knew he was not doing these things out of the generosity of his heart, but she needed to be with her father, and more than that she needed to get out of Morgantown with its cold winters and hot summers. But, mostly, she needed to get away from the men who worked in the mines. She especially needed to get as far away as possible from Horace Bloom before he decided to put little Ruby to work in the back of his saloon the same way he had done with her once her own father had left and her mother had died. She couldn't let that happen, she had to save her children if not herself. It had taken her a while to find her father and beg him to take them in, but once he came down to Morgantown and saw Ruby and Michael he had agreed to help her. He had assured her that things would be better for her in Huron City with no one knowing of her past or that of her children's fathers. She would no longer have to trade her body for food for her children, or allow herself to be sold for the night by Horace. For once, she could live respectfully and raise her children with no one knowing what she had been or how she and her children had survived. Her father told her that Mr. Daniel had promised to give her a housekeeping job for a fine family, and young Michael could work at the General Store and Gazette sweeping up, and taking care of the trash. Clarice could repay him for the cost of the passage a little each week. She closed her eyes and thought about the generosity and kindness of this man, she allowed herself to smile and to dream of walking down the street and feeling respect; he must be the most wonderful man alive. She said his name over and over in her head, Mr. Daniel Bernstein, Mr. Bernstein, or Mr. Daniel as her father referred to him in his letters. She smiled as she drifted off to sleep with dreams of happiness and laughter for her and her children.

The rain stopped and as the sun was rising Daphnia awakened to its warmth. The train was nearing the station at Huron City. She could feel her heart begin to pound. She quickly got up from her seat and walked to the back of the train. She once again pinned her hair up beneath her hat and tilting the brim with its feather at just the right angle, she took a deep breath and pushed her chin forward.

She stood at the door of the train car and looked out at the hustle and bustle of all the people, automobiles and horses, but she did not see anyone that she knew. She approached a porter to make arrangements for her trunk to be delivered. She looked about only to see the black family being loaded onto a buckboard, there was a small but very finely dressed man with them giving instructions to the woman and a large black man who was up on the wagon seat with the reigns in his hands. The man giving instructions was obviously someone of power and full of self worth since he was barking out orders and acting in a very authoritative manner, he was small in stature but big in voice. Daphnia thought the whole thing quite odd since the small man was loud while the large man was quiet. It was some scene, with the little man acting excited and shouting his orders as if everyone in the station needed to hear him; the little black family and the large black man acted on his every command with their heads held down so as not to look at the overly excited person as he waved his arms about accentuating his every command. They went about their business of loading the wagon and climbing onto the seat without saying a word. Daphnia wondered if the loud little man was at all concerned with their obvious lack of interest in his own exaggerated movements. She chuckled as she turned back toward the porter who had been handling her things; she thanked him as she placed two bits in the palm of his hand along with the address for the delivery of her trunk.

She could feel the excitement in the air of the station and was caught up in the activity and conversations about her. It was as though she could not capture everything with just a glance, people were moving about; she could hear the voices shouting, crying and laughing, smell the steam coming from the train engines, and feel her body tensing as she stood there watching, listening and feeling all that was going on about her. She was lost in the station's wonder when she heard someone calling her name. As she turned toward the voice, she was surprised to see it was the same little man who had been giving the orders to the black family in the wagon.

"Daphnia, Daphnia Flanders," Daniel called as he waved his hands wildly from within the crowd of people nearby.

She turned to the porter, shrugged her shoulders and waved back at Daniel. As he approached her, she extended her hand and thanked him for coming to meet her. She explained the arrangements she had made with the porter only to have Daniel look at her with disgust.

"What? You have money to throw away? I have heard plenty about you Flanders' and it is obvious to me that the apple didn't fall from the tree with you. Everyone knows that Matthew was a gambler and an irresponsible womanizer; guess you are of the same cloth. Come on and get in the automobile, unless you would rather pay the porter to hire you a coach." He opened the door for her and held her hand as she stepped inside the shiny black Ford, then he yelled over to the porter to deliver the trunk and any other belongings of Miss Flanders post haste.

Daphnia could see that people were staring and she felt the blood rushing through her neck and face. "Why did you do that? I am perfectly capable of taking care of myself. Please don't intervene on my behalf again unless you are invited to do so. As for my father, whatever he was has nothing to do with you so please don't bring him up again. Maybe I should take a coach," she opened the door and began to step out.

"Please don't. I am sorry. It has been a very long day, and maybe we should start over. Besides my father would never forgive me if I didn't bring you home. I'm Daniel. Daniel Bernstein. I guess under different circumstances we would be considered more like cousins than anything else. My father and your Uncle Thaddeus have been like brothers for years, I believe they think of themselves as such, and it would be a shame if you and I didn't get along. Please forgive my outburst, and my rudeness."

She had an immediate feeling of dislike and distrust for Daniel. She felt that there was something mean spirited about him, but didn't know why. Trying to regain her composure she decided to make an attempt at being less forthright and accepting his apology.

"I am sorry, also. I had no right to flare up like that. I know this is probably a little awkward for you. After all we don't know one another. I am Daphnia, and I am very happy to be here. You are right, we are probably as close to being family as possible without actually being such. By the way, who were those colored people you were talking with at the station?"

"You mean that nigger family? Well, the woman is the daughter of a friend of mine and the children are hers. Her name is Clarice Hayes and I believe the boy is named Michael and the little girl goes by Rosie or Ruby, something like that. I have known her father for some time.

His name is George Hayes and he lived with his woman in the quarters outside of town. Now and then they would do some odd jobs for us. Then the woman up and died. Just like that, no warning, he got up one morning and she was lying there dead. Anyway, he took it really hard. He told me about his girl, Clarice living down in Morgantown and said that she would like to come live with him if she had the promise of a job. Since Lillian had passed away, I figured that his girl could take on those jobs so I agreed to bring her and her kids on up. She has those two kids and no husband so living here will be easier for her and for her father. I don't expect that you will meet many "coloreds" as you call them, and certainly you wouldn't become friends with any of them since the quarters would not be a place that you would ever have reason to visit."

"The Quarters?"

"Yeah, that's the part of town where all the niggers live, they don't' live near the regular folks, and you won't see them too much unless they come in to buy something or do some work for white folks, I expect that is what Clarice will be doing, working for a white family or two. And, of course that boy of hers might be in sweeping up and doing odd jobs now and then. Now, how was your trip?"

"It was truly uneventful." She talked about the various incidents or lack thereof of the train ride, but through the meaningless conversation she could not help but wonder about Daniel. He did not fit the image she had of him, and as hard as she tried she could not ever remember him visiting at Sunshine Acres. She remembered his parents had been to visit them several times, but where was Daniel? She had only visited Huron City a couple of times over the past twenty years herself, and even then she remembered very little about Daniel. She remembered there being a young boy around, but for whatever reason she could not remember much about him at all. There was something hard about him, and she could sense an element of cruelty and anger. She was curious about the real association Daniel had with the father of the pretty little dark woman.

The automobile finally arrived in front of the Gazette. "Here we are. What do you think?" he asked holding out his arm for her to take.

She didn't know what to think. It was much smaller than she had imagined and it was nestled between the General Store and a small alleyway with the bank on the other side. She was excited when she looked up and saw bright red Geraniums and a mixture of white and purple Petunias growing from a window box below an upstairs window. The gray skies and drizzling rain could not dampen her mood once she saw the beautiful flowers. "Is that the window to my apartment, Daniel?"

"It sure is, Daphnia, my father loves flowers and he has the greenest thumb of anybody in town. He plants them all over the house inside and outside." Daniel was chuckling as he told her the story of when Herbert had planted flowers all spring and summer a few years ago only to be too sentimental to leave them to die with the coming of fall so he dug them up and replanted them inside the back porch of the newspaper office using wooden crates. "It was like a jungle all winter, people from all over town would come to him to pick flowers. "With the fertilizer, the wood burning to keep the room warm, kerosene lamps lit for light, and the soil everywhere, the place started to smell like a barnyard. In a rage one day, mother came in and threw them all out into the snow and made me help her clean the porch with lye soap and water. Father didn't speak to either one of us for weeks after that." Daniel was having fun telling her the story.

"What did your father do when your mother threw out all of his flowers? Was he able to salvage any of them?"

"He was furious. I have never seen him so mad at Mother. He moved out of the house for months and stayed upstairs that is how the apartment came to be. Before that it was just an attic and storage space. That was also the last time that Mother came into the newspaper office for anything."

"You mean she hasn't been back into the Gazette since then?"

"That's right. Father removed the door between the General Store and the newspaper office and filled in the space with wall board, painted it and then moved shelving in front of it." He was telling the story to Daphnia almost without emotion. "She did come back just today to be sure that you had everything that you needed upstairs, but Father wouldn't let her go up. So, don't take it personally if she doesn't come over it doesn't have anything to do with you."

"Now, maybe you can explain something to me. Why are you staying in that apartment when you should, or could stay with your Mother? Isn't that the real reason you came here in the first place?"

"Yes and no. I guess knowing that Mother needs me was the push I needed to move out of Aunt Martha's and Papa Tad's house and be on my own. But, your father made a very generous offer. He said he would allow me to work at the Gazette and provide me with my own living quarters where I could be somewhat independent but still be available to help Mother. According to Papa Tad, Mother is almost bedridden and she and Eloise have things in place there, having me move in might upset her routine and do her more harm than good. So, here I am."

"And, here we are. Are you ready to go in?"

"Yes, I am ready, at least I'm as ready as I'll ever be."

Daniel took her valise and other small garment bag and led the way up the walk and into the newspaper office where Herbert and Ruth Bernstein were waiting for them.

One look at Daphnia and Herbert caught his breath, "Welcome, my dear, we are so happy that you are here with us."

Daphnia leaned into him and lightly kissed his cheek. She could feel herself instantly bond with this kind and gentle man.

"Thank you, Uncle Bert, I'm happy to be here." Then turning to Ruth, Daphnia extended both of her hands and leaned toward the birdlike woman with the very plump backside only to have Ruth take Daphnia's hands and then pull away not allowing the peck to the cheek that Daphnia was about to endow upon her.

"Welcome, Daphnia," Ruth said with her high-pitched voice. "We hope that you will be comfortable here. I know that it isn't as large as the home you enjoy with Thaddeus and Martha, but there is a pump upstairs, and you have a water closet complete with a porcelain tub and washbasin. The kitchen is fully equipped with a wood stove and plenty of light. I feel that it will be comfortable enough for a short period of time anyway. Bring her things, Daniel," she directed as if Daphnia wasn't there at all. "Come with me," she said to Daphnia without looking at her but turning toward the staircase that led to the apartment upstairs. "I'm sure you will want to get settled in and have a little rest before you begin your work down here. After all, this is not a free ride or a ticket to leisure land, I understand that there is a definite need at the paper or you wouldn't be here at all. I tried to talk Herbert into just putting on that young man, Tom, full time, but he took off for parts unknown and Herbert insisted that you be given this opportunity; I just hope for his sake that you don't prove me right. So, I imagine you will want to get unpacked and downstairs just as soon as possible. You will want to see Melissa, I suppose, but that can wait until you get settled in here first, isn't that right Herbert?"

"Well now, Ruth, let's give her a chance to at least unpack. I will see that things that need to be done get done for now. How was your trip, Daphnia? There is plenty of time to get familiar with the things that need to be done at the Gazette. I know you will want to unpack and settle in; you just take your time."

"Thanks, I really need to just catch my breath and become familiar with my new surroundings. And, of course I would like to wash up and change my clothes before I go over to see Mother"

"From all that I hear from Herbert, there will be a full day of work right here, Daphnia, before you begin your socializing, at which time I am certain that someone will be happy to instruct you how to get to Melissa's. I know this isn't a farm where there are only a couple of buildings, but surely you can find your way around this small City." Ruth opened the door to the small apartment and led Daphnia inside.

The larger room had two windows facing the front of the street looking out over the roof of the newspaper office; it was beautiful. The furniture looked as though it had been transported from a country cottage. The covering on the chairs and the davenport was of soft purple velvet with pink and white roses; the accents in the room were of soft beige's, pink and crimson flowers. The walls were papered not painted and there were hints of elegance throughout the small but comfortably decorated rooms. Within the larger room there was a conversation area as well as a cozy dining nook carved out between the two front windows, the kitchen was located in one corner of the room with cupboards and counter tops made of light oak and trimmed with fresh white paint. The pump was painted white and was positioned in such a way to allow Daphnia to look out the window while washing the dishes or preparing her meals.

"You have thought of everything, Mrs. Bernstein," Daphnia said as she ran her fingers along the large crystal bowl of fresh fruits and vegetables sitting on the counter separating the kitchen space from the dining area.

"Herbert took care of the details, Daphnia, you can thank him." Ruth replied with enough indignation to crack the paint on the ceiling.

Daphnia continued to explore the room walking around it and touching everything. She felt at home here with these things and wished that Ruth would leave so that she could get to know her new home privately. As her eyes soaked in her surroundings she could see that the room had been divided into three very separate living areas, elegantly furnished yet simple and very livable. There were plants and fresh flowers everywhere. Even on the top of the small icebox there was a vase filled with fresh roses. Daphnia could not resist going over and leaning into the beautiful blossoms to soak in their fragrance. Her moment of reverie was interrupted with the shrill voice of Ruth Bernstein explaining the functionality of the well-appointed kitchen and the icebox as if Daphnia had been raised in the back woods of some deserted village.

"That is for keeping milk and such cold enough not to spoil, Daphnia. Herbert or Daniel will bring up ice for you when you need it. As for milk, butter and eggs, well the milkman will deliver these twice a week. He will place these through the milk door located on the back porch of the office. In spite of what my foolish husband believes, the porch is also used for storage of boots, shovels for the snow and other tools and equipment needed to maintain the building and the grounds immediately surrounding it." As she explained the various necessary logistics, Daphnia could only hope that Ruth did not expect her to take care of the shoveling of snow and maintaining the grounds around the building.

It wasn't the way that Ruth explained the various conveniences to Daphnia that was confusing, but rather it was the sense that Ruth was seeing the apartment for the first time, just like Daphnia. Daphnia was curious about this woman and wondered just what kind of a life she must share with her husband and son. It certainly could not be one that was filled with love and laughter like that of her Papa Tad and Aunt Martha.

As they completed the tour of the front room, Ruth opened the door on the east side of the large room. Through the cherry wood door, Daphnia could see what looked like the bedroom of a queen. The large four-poster bed had a canopy made of lace and satin the color or pale pink roses with a dust ruffle and spread to match. The bed looked as if it were a cloud of rose pedals, so soft, plump and luxurious. There were at least a half dozen pillows of all different sizes and shapes leaning against the headboard. There was a small fireplace on one side of the room with a marble hearth and a mantle made of the same dark cherry wood as the bed and other furniture in the room. Off to the side of the fireplace there was a writing desk and chair with a bookcase above it filled with books. On the other side of the fireplace there was a large soft chair with a matching ottoman and a table with a lamp for reading. One corner of the room had painted vanity screens standing to protect a large tub for bathing, a brass pump and basin, a dressing area and toilette. Her bathing room at Sunshine Acres was nice by most standards, but even there they didn't have indoor plumbing like this. She could see the pipes leading from the tub out through the floor and where she would assume was down and out the back of the building. There were mirrors on the walls and a dressing table with hand mirrors, brushes, and combs. She felt sure that this was the most glorious bedroom anywhere. And, Ruth Bernstein must have thought so as well for when she entered the room she gasped and held her hand to her mouth.

Ruth was not gasping at the beauty of the room, however, it was the pictures on the wall above the bed that caught her eye. There, as if displayed for a showing, were what looked like dozens of paintings and old photographs of people, some looked familiar and some did not; it was as if Herbert had used the wall as a gallery of sorts filling it with every picture and photograph he could find. In the center was a large painting of a young man who was obviously her father-in-law. Ruth had met him only once in St. Louis when she and Herbert were first married. The woman, whom Ruth had never met, must have been Herbert's mother. There were two small children in the picture as well, a little boy standing and a slightly younger little girl. Ruth was certain that the little boy was Herbert, but as for the little girl, she did not recognize her; she didn't remember Herbert ever speaking of a younger sibling. But, when she turned and looked at Daphnia, she felt faint. "Air, I must have some air!" Ruth barely spoke above a whisper as she turned and bolted from the room. She was almost out the door when she heard Herbert and Daniel coming up the stairs with Daphnia's things. "She is all set, just leave her things, I believe she is tired, I must finish up a few things at the store. Stop by before you leave."

Daphnia was shocked, what could have gotten into Ruth all of a sudden; it couldn't have been something she said, she hadn't said anything. She could hear Herbert and Daniel coming up the stairs and she wanted to tell Herbert how appreciative she was. She had expected a humble parlor with some cooking conveniences, but certainly nothing like this.

"Thank you Uncle Bert, I appreciate all that you have done, it is beautiful. You really went too far, honestly, you really should not have done all of this for me. It is beautiful."

"It was my pleasure, Daphnia. Besides, most of these things actually belong to you. I just took them from storage and had them cleaned up a bit. I'm glad you like it. You should be comfortable here. It is a warm and sturdy building."

"Speaking of being warm and snug, I know that it is barely summer, but when it does get cold, where is the wood and coal stored? And, how do I get it up here? I see there is a pump for the water, but do I heat it on the stove or in the fireplace?"

Ruth was still standing at the head of the stairs leaning against the doorframe. She was wiping the perspiration from her brow with the hem of her skirt without regard for her petticoat, which was made of what looked like pure silk with ribbons and lace everywhere flouncing up and down as she pulled and tugged on the shiny fabric.

"The place doesn't come with a man servant Daphnia. You won't have that handy man waiting on your every whim here like you have back in Lansing. You will soon learn that you have to get by the same way most everyone else does, Daphnia, you will have to go downstairs to the back room and carry up whatever wood and coal you need in one of the buckets over there by the hearth. How you heat the water is up to you of course, you can choose to use whichever method suits your fancy. I suppose you will learn soon enough what it is like to do for yourself. Maybe you will reconsider staying over there with Melissa and Eloise, after all. If not, I guess you will be happier then that this place is a little on the small side, won't need as much wood and coal to carry up them stairs. I suggest you keep a goodly stockpile of both of them up here - that'll take elbow grease. When the wood runs low in the back room, there is more out in the shed out back - you will want to be careful going out there though, lots of rats they come in from the cold in the winter time. You'll be sure not to bring any in with you now won't you? But, I don't suppose rats will be a problem for you, though will it? I mean, rats don't scare a farm girl like you now do they?" Ruth was enjoying this opportunity to be a little cruel. "Do you think you can handle that, dear? I mean carrying in your own wood and coal?" she asked only to turn toward the door at the bottom of the stairs to see the porter from the train station bringing in the trunk. "Well, I can see that you are planning to be with us for a while, looks like you brought enough stuff to at least stay the winter. Guess you will have plenty of time to get know some of those rats by name. Herbert, Daniel, put that stuff down in here and let her put it away on her own; she can handle it. Of course I will be as helpful as I can be, but I am a very busy woman what with my own responsibilities over at the store and keeping things under control in the big house and all. You call if I can help out in any way. You won't be totally alone, I will see if I can find time to visit now and again. Now, Herbert, you leave those things and get on back to work, you too Daniel. After all we all have responsibilities and the sooner we get back to them the better we will all be. As for me, I have left things under the eye of Mrs. Blaine long enough, I have to get back over to the store." She walked out the door and down the stairs without saying another word.

Ruth was in a tizzy. She could hardly help but relive the memories of her time spent in St. Louis with Matthew Flanders. Those days and nights were as clear to her now as they ever were. She wanted to go back upstairs and just sit and watch Daphnia. She couldn't shake the images from her mind. Daphnia definitely had Matthew's charm, if not his face. It was her face that had gotten Ruth so riled. The truth be known, Daphnia was the image of the picture of the little girl in the painting, but that was impossible! She was just so much like Matthew that Ruth couldn't get her image out of her mind. There was something about the way she held her head, and the sideways glances she gave to Ruth when she was explaining the icebox; it was eerie. Even with the lack of pure physical resemblance, Daphnia was Matthew's daughter and Ruth could feel his presence when she looked at her. She wanted to take the young woman in her arms and tell her the wonderful things about her father that she was certain no one else could, his sense of humor, his zest for living and his gentleness, she wanted to tell her how much in love with him she had been. She would not let this happen, however, because as much as she would like to love Daphnia because of what she had felt for Matthew, she had as much disdain for Melissa. No, Ruth would never let Daphnia know how much she would like to befriend her. She would keep her distance. Besides she still had not figured out what Herbert was up to, and why he had been so insistent that Daphnia come here and stay above the newspaper office. But, she was here and they would all make the best of it and she would figure this out in due time. She tried to go over the pictures that were hung on the wall in her mind. Herbert had said that much of what was in the apartment had belonged to Daphnia's mother and grandmother, so surely the pictures must be of Melissa's family as well as Matthew's mother and father. Besides, the picture was very old and she was more than fifteen feet away from it, it was more than likely that of Melissa. Daphnia did favor Melissa, too. Yes, that was it; it was a picture of Melissa and her family. Surely she had been mistaken about Herbert's father being in the picture, and of course that could not have been Herbert if the little girl was Melissa. She would figure this out in time.

Herbert had listened to Ruth and was annoyed at the manner in which she spoke to Daphnia, but he was so taken aback that he couldn't find it in him to stop her. Now, however, he knew that he had to find a way to reassure Daphnia. "Don't you even think about starting to work today, you can start Monday, Daphnia," he told her. "You need to get settled and spend some time with Melissa, that is what is important right now. Here, let me show you what Ruth most likely failed to do." Gently touching each, he showed her the well stocked ice box, cupboards and all of the fine linens and china he had put into place for her to use and to have. "This is your place, Daphnia. Everything here belongs to you. Most of what you see here belonged to your grandmother and some of it is from Melissa. But, generally all of the things that you see around here once belonged to people and a time that is connected to you. I am sure Ruth showed you some of my family heirlooms; things that once belonged to my Mother and your grandmother; some of these things came from Melissa's cellar and they had been stored away for years. Let me show you around. Over here on the mantle is a clock that was brought to this country by your great-great-grandmother. This is her in this photograph, I had it touched up a few years back, but it is still faded I'm afraid. I know that it isn't very clear anymore, but it is her just the same." He took down the photograph in which the face was almost unrecognizable and he handed it to Daphnia. "The china is from your Mother as is the silverware, crystal and all of the utensils in the kitchen. Your bedroom has been furnished with furniture from three different homes along with the curtains, lamps, quilt and the privacy screens. You will see little touches of your past everywhere." Herbert began to stare off into the distance as he fingered the face in the painting. Daphnia could barely hear him and it was difficult to understand what he was saying. Barely speaking above a whisper he gently dropped his hand by his side, "She always loved fresh flowers and bright surroundings. You remind me so much of her. I can hardly stop myself from staring at you. You take your time to get settled and then come on downstairs and I will show you around our little town and take you by to visit with Melissa."

"Thank you, Uncle Bert. You have gone to far too much trouble for me."

He took her hand and pressed it to his chest. He could barely keep the tears from flowing out of his eyes as he breathed in the scent of her. He said a silent prayer and thanked God for bringing her back to him, and he vowed to never let her go.

Daphnia was sure that this wonderful man was somehow connected to her, and wondered how someone like him could be married to such a nasty unhappy woman as Ruth Bernstein. As for Daniel, he didn't seem to be like either one of them. Thankfully he had followed his mother down the stairs. She felt a special closeness to Herbert and thought that Daniel's presence seemed to cause the older man a sense of anxiety and stress. Pulling back she looked into the face of the man and tried to shake off the feelings of coming home.

"Thank you, Uncle Bert, thank you for everything."

As he closed the door behind him, Daphnia stood alone in the nearly exquisite apartment with her trunk and bags stacked in a heap in the middle of the bedroom floor. She put water into the teapot and placed the pot on the wood stove, lit the wood beneath the burner and started unpacking her things. She took her time putting away each piece of clothing she had brought, and stopping along the way to sip her tea and become acquainted with the things in her apartment.

It was after sunset when she was startled by the sound of someone knocking at the door. Ruth Bernstein was standing at the door with a dinner tray covered with a linen cloth. Before she could speak or invite her in, Ruth brushed past her and over to the dining table.

"I have brought you some dinner, Daphnia. We had hoped that you would join us for dinner this evening but Herbert says that you are tired and I tried to tell him that if you were too tired to pay your respects and show up for dinner, then you would probably prefer to eat alone. It is not like you are a child. Surely you are able to fix yourself up something to eat if you're hungry. But, he insisted that you were not trying to be disrespectful, that it is understandable that you would be tired after your trip. He worries about everything and everyone, why one day he brought home a sickly tabby kitten that had obviously been beaten up by something or someone. He nursed that cat back to health, and then do you know what happened? Well, the ungrateful thing just up and ran away. That's the way things happen, it seems. If he would just stop and think before he goes to all the trouble to take care of people and things that don't give a hoot about him anyway he wouldn't get hurt all the time like he does. Just take what he has done here for you, and you probably won't stay past fall. Then, what will happen to all of his efforts? I'll tell you what! He will sulk and work himself to death, that's what. He always puts more stock in making everybody else happy. If he would just give me and Daniel a little of his generosity, but he never has and never will. So, anyhow, just in case he is right this time, I didn't think you should be faced with preparing your own meal on your first night in Huron City. I put together some dinner for you, it isn't much, and probably not what you are used to, but a little pot roast, potatoes and gravy never did anyone no harm. I can stay for a while if you would like." Then uncovering the tray of food, Ruth walked over to the chair facing Daphnia and sat down. "Surely after being here alone all afternoon you will want some company. I will be happy to stay for a while if you would like. We can talk awhile and I will tell you about ... well, I knew your father, and I do know Melissa, although not as well, I must admit. I don't know much about the newspaper business, but let me tell you, I know a lot about what goes on in this town. I can tell you where to buy the best cuts of meat, and who to sit next to in church on Sunday. There are all sorts of goings on here what with them men yelling timber at the top of their lungs and the tree harvesting at its peak. All of them lumberjacks in town have really raised up a ruckus. You might be interested in where to go on Saturday night; I can tell you who is married to whom and who not to bother to associate with. But, if you would like for me to stay or to go I will be happy to do either one. You should plan to attend the town social next Friday evening, though. There will be everybody in town there, lots of young men to meet, plenty of goings on, I promise, and you do need to get out and meet some of the young men, and women too, of course. You can't expect my Daniel to always be your escort to these things in the future, although I have told him I thought it would be only proper if he would be so generous as to show you around on Friday, this being your first one and all. So, shall I stay and visit with you a while? How is Martha, anyway? I know that she must miss the daylights out of you. Now, you just go ahead and eat your dinner, and we'll have ourselves a good visit." Ruth sat back in the chair and put her feet up on the ottoman nearby.

"I don't mean to sound ungrateful, Ruth, but honestly I just need a little rest. Thank you so much for all that you have done. Everything is wonderful. And, I would like to catch up on all that is happening in Town, but some other time. Thank you again for the pot roast, I am sure it is delicious. So, if you will excuse me," she was still standing at the door holding it open.

Ruth didn't know what to say. She got up from the chair, smoothed her skirt and nodded to Daphnia, "good night Daphnia." She heard the door close behind her and the latch click into place. Yes, she thought to herself, this is Matthew's daughter all right. As she walked home, she could once again feel his arms about her and she could almost feel his lips on hers.

143

Chapter Eleven

Morning came early, and Daphnia was ready for it. She dressed and was out the door barely after sunrise. She had a small gift for Eloise Barnes and a box of handmade handkerchiefs for Melissa. Walking up to the doorway, she took a deep breath and prepared herself for the visit that she had been waiting for. In her mind were the words of Melissa, *"Please understand that it is only through you that I can once again feel the closeness of your father and the bond between us."* She knocked on the door.

"Come in, Daphnia. We've been waiting for you."

"Aunt Ella, why I would know you anywhere. You look exactly as I remember you. How is Mother?"

"She's waiting to see you, dear. Go down the hall and the last door on your left. I'll be right in with some tea."

Walking down the hall Daphnia felt that the house had shrunk. It seemed so much smaller and closed up. As she entered the bedroom of her mother, she could see her leaning against a large satin pillow. She looked frail, but certainly not like she was on her deathbed.

"Come in Daphnia, I am awake and I have been waiting for you. You look wonderful, so much like your father. Come sit, how was your trip? Have the Bernstein's made things comfortable for you? You are welcome to stay here if you would like."

"I guess that everyone just assumed that it would be better if I stayed over the newspaper office since my comings and goings might be disturbing to you, Mother. I promise to come visit often, though. You look beautiful. I have tried so many times to close my eyes and see you, but I never saw you as beautiful as you truly are. How are you feeling?"

"I am feeling better today, Daphnia. Everyday is a new day and I try not to plan or predict. Hi Eloise, come on in. Have a seat. I am tiring already."

"Well, here is some hot tea for the two of you. I brought some sugar cookies if you feel up to having one, Melissa. Daphnia, go ahead and have your tea, she will probably fall asleep before she finishes hers."

"Now, now, Eloise, I will try to stay awake for a while longer. Maybe we can just sit quietly and I can regain some strength."

Daphnia poured herself some tea only to look over and see that Melissa had closed her eyes. She motioned to Eloise that she would leave and come back again, and then she gently kissed her Mother and tiptoed out of the room. Eloise removed the pillow that was propping up Melissa's head, closed the window shades and left the room behind Daphnia.

"That's the way she is, dear. She wants to visit, but she gets so tired so quickly that she simply goes to sleep. Please try to understand. When will you come again?"

"I understand Aunt Ella, I will come tomorrow. Maybe I should come a little later in the day. Please let her know that I will see her tomorrow. Thanks for the tea."

❦

For the next two days Daphnia spent her time trying to reacquaint herself with the town. She made it a point to stop and visit Melissa each day, but on each occasion Melissa was either sleeping or not able to stay awake for any meaningful visit to take place. Trying desperately to fit in and find her place, she took long walks down by the river and through the small town first up one street and then down another. She was trying to remember the town and the houses but they seemed strange and yet like home to her all at the same time. She was both confused and at ease with her surroundings and walking along these narrow tree lined streets seemed as safe to her as walking in Aunt Martha's garden at Sunshine Acres.

She spent her first evenings sitting by the fireplace in her bedroom and reading long into the night. She was trying to come to terms with why she was here and it wasn't easy for her. All she could think was that her mother had called her here not because she loved her and wanted her nearby, but because she wanted to feel the closeness of her father before she died. She had hoped that it was to beg her forgiveness for giving her away, but she knew that wasn't the case.

Trying to find some answers, she searched the faces in all of the pictures that were on tables, bookcases, and those placed upon the wall in her bedroom but could not find any of her mother and father together, or any of them separately. As a matter of fact when she looked at the pictures upon the wall she felt an uneasiness, it seemed so strange to her that there were so many pictures of what appeared to be the same people, but none of her mother and father, or at least none that she recognized. It seemed like in every photograph and painting, there were the same people over and over just at different phases of their lives. No one had bothered to tell her who the people were, and other than the one photograph of her Aunt Martha and Uncle Thaddeus none of the others looked like anyone she had seen before. As she explored the pictures on her third night in Huron City, she had become more and more uneasy when looking at the one with the family of four. When she looked into the faces of the faded photograph she felt goose bumps along her spine. When she looked into the eyes of the little girl in the picture she felt it was like looking into a mirror of long ago. She removed the picture from the wall, covered it with a piece of linen and placed it in the closet. In its place she hung swags of dried flowers tied together with a silk ribbon.

Although she had been to see Melissa each day since her arrival, she felt like today would be different. As the sun was creeping into the little apartment, she started a small fire in the belly of the wood stove, she needed just one cup of the dark coffee she had come to enjoy before getting started on her way over to the modest house on Maple Avenue. She had been in Huron City for exactly three nights now, and it was time to "face the devil" as her Aunt Martha would have said. She quickly dressed, said a silent prayer then out the door, down the stairs and before she could stop she was out onto the street and on her way. The morning was cool and damp; there were few people out so early. There was a slight mist in the air and she wondered if she should have worn a bonnet instead of just pulling her hair up into a twist on the back of her head. No matter, she was going to see her mother today and she was going to feel good about it. As she walked she softly hummed a tune that reminded her of a lullaby, but she wasn't sure why.

Walking up the path to the house in which she had spent her first four years of life, she thought she saw the curtain move in one of the front windows. Nothing looked the same to her, and it all seemed so much smaller and older, it needed a fresh coat of paint. She could feel eyes watching her and she knew that she must be strong today. She proudly walked up to the door and knocked soundly. Eloise Barnes came to the door. Without any warning whatsoever, Daphnia put her arms out to the older woman and hugged her; there were tears in her eyes as she held onto the woman.

"I'm sorry for being so forward. I have been thinking a lot these last few days, and I can't help it if she is sleeping or needing to sleep, or doesn't even want to wake up, but today we need to talk. I need her to be awake. Will you make some tea?"

"Of course I will dear. And, you are right. She needs to stay awake, you have been over her everyday and she has practically slept through your entire visit. Today she will sit up and take notice. Leave it to me. Go ahead in and open the curtains and even the window if you want. I'll be in with tea and I made muffins this morning."

"Thank you."

"There's no need for the two of you to stay out there and talk, come on in Daphnia."

Daphnia and Eloise both jumped, they weren't prepared for Melissa to hear them let alone call out to them. She was actually standing not ten feet from them.

"Come in, come in here Daphnia, I would like to see you, please come in, don't be surprised, I told you I had some good days and some not so good. Today is a good day."

As Daphnia followed her back into her room she could see just how frail she actually was. She walked ahead of her and turned back the bed covers and fluffed the mountain of pillows. Melissa got back into the bed and for a brief moment, she closed her eyes. Daphnia watched her as she settled in against the pillows. She was beautiful. Her hair was pulled away from her face and held in place by two large turtle shell combs, her hands were folded neatly across her abdomen and there was a golden chain with a locket wrapped about her fingers.

Before sitting or speaking, Daphnia opened the curtains and raised the window shade. Melissa opened her eyes and smiled.

"Good Morning, Mother. I'm so happy to see you. I was worried about coming over so early, but I can see that you were ready for me after all."

"I was hoping that you would come early today. Go ahead and open the shade all the way so that I can look at you. Eloise please light the lamp so that I can see what a fine young woman our Daphnia has grown up to be."

Eloise lit the lamps and pulled open the remaining curtains. "I'll bring in some of those fresh muffins I made, you two go ahead and visit."

"That sounds wonderful, Aunt Ella."

"Daphnia sit over here so we can talk and I can look at you. There is much that I would like to talk with you about. I am sorry that I haven't been up to actually visiting before, but I am feeling better this morning so maybe we can have a good visit today to make up for it. So, you got my letter. I wasn't sure that Thaddeus would actually give it to you; he can be so stubborn and self-righteous." Then holding her hand up to keep Daphnia from speaking she continued, "I know you want and will continued to want more from me Daphnia than I can give you. I can't ask you to understand, but I can ask that you forgive me for what some would call my selfishness. You need to know that sending you to live with Thaddeus and Martha was the best thing that I could have done for you. Were you happy with them?"

"Of course I was happy, Mother. Papa Tad and Aunt Martha are wonderful. I have had a marvelous life with them. That doesn't mean that I didn't miss you and wonder how or why you could send me away. But, I am back now. We can start over. I am all grown up. I will be twenty-four on my next birthday. That is long enough to carry around pain and unhappiness, don't you think. I am here now. For whatever reason you asked for me, you did ask for me. Let's make the best of it, shall we?"

"I know there must be a lot of questions you would like to ask, and we will get to those, I promise. Right now, I just need to look at you. You have grown up to be quite a beautiful young woman. Now, tell me about you. I hear that you are in love with a young man from the hills of Lansing. Is he tall and dark like your father? Your father! What a man! You look like him, Daphnia. You have his confidence and excuse me for saying so, but it appears that you may have his arrogance as well. You have a sense of self-assuredness that most young women rarely, if ever, develop."

"I really haven't heard much about my father, Mother. What was he like? What were the two of you like?"

"We were like peaceful sunsets and stormy seas, Daphnia. When we were together it was like honey butter on a hot biscuit, everything just melted into everything else and became one with each other. Every morsel was pure heaven. But, when we were apart, or when he was getting ready to leave for one of his trips as he often did, it was like a violent storm upon the ocean. Nothing was calm and everything would well up from the very bottom of my very soul and it was a tumultuous time. Once he was gone from me, I would sink into a cavernous pit of darkness. He was my light, Daphnia. He was my only love."

"Your only love, Mother? He has been dead a long time, was there never anyone else?"

"I can truthfully say that I have never loved anyone other than Matthew. He was something special. I knew that I loved him the minute I saw him. He was visiting a friend in Boston where I lived at the time. He was handsome, dark and tall, full of life, laughter, adventure and childlike wonder. Nothing frightened him nor intimidated him. He was like the heroes you read about in books with just a hint of danger yet filled with a lovable kind of warmth and an endearing smile that was mostly mischief. Matthew was the life of every gathering and the light of my life."

"I wish I could remember more about him. I have only a couple of vague recollections of him, but I guess I was just too young. Papa Tad has also told me that I resemble him a great deal, but not always in how I look but in how I act. How can that be? What is it that makes me so much like him and not like you?"

"Oh, honey, I think it was his strength of character and attitude, not that it was always the best mind you, but there was just something there. He had an air about him that brought about envy from others, but his charisma and charm would win even the hardest of hearts over eventually. I always forgave him regardless of what he had done or was about to do; he knew that I would no matter what happened. And that's the way it was with most people who knew him. It seemed that everyone would get upset with him from time to time, but eventually they would forgive and forget and all would be right again."

"Why did he go away so much?"

"I guess I was just never enough for him and my love couldn't hold him. I hated the gossip and stories about him, I tried not to listen and even when the truth was staring me in the face, I would tell myself that it was just Matthew's way, and I would see him again and it would all be alright."

"What gossip? Why would he leave you so much if he loved you? And what about me? Didn't he love me?"

Melissa closed her eyes and Daphnia could see the tears escaping from her long lashes and running down her cheeks. She wanted to reach out to her, to hold her, but she sat still hoping that they would continue talking. She had waited for so long to see her again. To sit with her now and to hear her talk about herself and her father, this was like an answered prayer. Melissa dabbed at her eyes and cheeks and then continued.

"Daphnia, there is a lot to talk about and we will have many mornings like this. The one thing that is certain is that whatever has happened, I never stopped thinking about you or caring about you. I have been sick for a long time, and I am not getting any better. Right now, though, I am a little tired. Will you come back again real soon, please? I want to get to know you. Eloise will show you out, just call to her when you enter the hallway," she closed her eyes and patted Daphnia's hand before she turned her face away.

"You rest now, Mother. Don't worry; I will visit you everyday if you want. I am glad you asked for me, I am here now and we can be together. I will be back tomorrow."

Melissa struggled to open her eyes again and look at Daphnia once more, but this time with the sunlight shining on her face. As she saw the fine features, the golden hair with auburn and brown highlights, the green eyes and the full soft mouth, she held her breath. She closed her eyes and held her hand to her mouth hoping that Daphnia wouldn't notice or hear her as she muttered to herself, "she doesn't look at all like Matthew, oh my God, what have I done?"

Chapter Twelve

The walk out of the house and down the lane was a blur to Daphnia. She could not help but to sob as she hurried away from the house. Feeling the cool damp air against her face she tried to put the morning into perspective. Her mother was sick, it was only natural for people to want to make things right before they pass on. She was glad she came to Huron City and she was glad she saw her mother today. She wanted and needed to know more about her mother and father from her mother, not through the whispers and gossip from the churchwomen and smartalecs like Daniel Bernstein. Wiping her eyes, she vowed to forgive her mother and to love her. She was determined to put any bad feelings or worries behind her. She would begin building a new life... a life with her mother and her work that lay ahead at the newspaper office. She stopped at the end of the walkway and picked a few of Eloise's roses and wrapped the stems in her handkerchief.

She walked along organizing her day in her head and listening to the awakening sounds of the birds and town's people. As she neared the corner of Maple and Pine, a little Negro boy ran directly into her. "Well, where are you going in such a hurry?"

"Please, Please mamn, it my mama and she hurt pretty bad. She done got the bone in her leg broke 'n she bad, I needs to get the doctor."

"I'll help you get the doctor, where is your Mother, where do you live? Come with me." Daphnia took the little boy's hand and headed back toward the Town Square where the Doctor had his office as well as living quarters in the back of the building.

"I live down in the quarter with my family, my mama and my sister. We just come from Morgantown to live with my granddaddy," he pulled her along the street toward the square.

"What is your name?"

"Name is Michael Hayes."

The little boy seemed familiar to Daphnia but she could not remember why. She hurried over to the Doctor's office with Michael almost running to keep up with her. Daphnia called to the doctor as she knocked on the door.

"Yes, yes, just a minute, I'm coming," replied the voice from the other side of the door. "Well, now what do we have here?" Doctor James asked as he opened the door while fastening his suspenders and looking at the strange pair standing before him.

"Good morning, sir, I am Daphnia Flanders, and this young man is Michael Hayes. It seems his mother has been injured somehow and needs some immediate attention down in the quarters."

"She hurt real bad, please hurry." Michael begged as he tugged at the man's hand.

Grabbing his coat and hat as well as his black bag, the Doctor took the little boy's hand and pulled the door closed behind him; he took off with Michael down the street and toward the quarters. Daphnia was left standing on the porch of the Doctor's office watching the two strangers walk and sometimes run until they had turned the corner and were out of sight. She once again gathered her thoughts and went back to the newspaper office where she sat at her desk and worked into the late afternoon.

Chapter Thirteen

Daniel was not at all satisfied with the half-assed answers he had been given to his questions about why Daphnia had come to Huron City. Every time he broached the subject with his father he was given some flippant reply and was even told not to worry about things that were none of his business. When he tried to discuss her with his mother he was left with more questions than answers. There had to be something more than her just coming to sit with a dying woman. He knew that prior to her coming to Huron City his father had made a special trip to St. Louis – a place where he had sworn he would never go again. He also knew that several trips had been made back to Boston over the last year and too many deliveries of furniture and household items had been made to the small apartment after hours. He walked into his father's office.

"Good morning, Father. Just a few quick questions and then I will be on my way. I have decided to follow-up on a story that I heard about down at O'Connor's just the other evening."

"Oh, and just how can I help you with a story that came from that cesspool of drunks and whores?" Herbert asked as he put down his pencil and looked at his son. "What kind of story could get started in that place that would be worth any space in the Gazette?"

"I think you will be surprised to learn that the roots of the story lie in a back alley of St. Louis some nineteen or twenty years ago. I believe you know something of the times back then, you growing up and living in St. Louis and all. And, isn't that where grandfather's estate remains? I know that it has been a while since you spent any real time there, but weren't you there just a few months or so ago?"

"Get on with your questions, Daniel, I am rather busy and don't care too much about your grandfather's estate or St. Louis. Yes, I went back there in March, but it was business, nothing more. So let's get on with it, what is it that you want to know?"

"I want to know how Matthew Flanders died, why he was left bleeding to death in a back alley and by whom. What was it like,

Father, back then I mean? Was it really as wide open as they all say it was?"

"Matthew Flanders was the father of Daphnia, Daniel. If you are determined to dig up any dirt to shame her with I suggest you forget it. He was shot, he died, that is all anyone needs to know. Melissa was left to deal with a situation that is still painful for her to this day. There is no need to dredge up any bad feelings or hurt. Now, if you are planning to take this any further, you do so at your own peril. I'm busy; please shut the door behind you I don't care to be disturbed anymore today. And, Daniel, don't ever ask me about Matthew Flanders or St. Louis again."

Daniel stood at the doorway just long enough for Herbert to see the smug look on his face. He grinned and closed the door behind him and walked out of the building. His mother would be happy to answer his questions, he was certain.

Hearing the bells clink together as the door opened, Ruth looked up to see Daniel coming into the general store. This was something that he did not do often and she was pleasantly surprised, "well good morning, Daniel, to what do I owe this pleasure?"

"Just stopping for a few minutes, Mother and to ask a couple of questions. I am going to St. Louis tomorrow and want to follow-up on a story about Matthew Flanders that I heard down at the pub the other evening. What do you know about him? Do you know how he died? I understand that he was shot and left to die in an alley back in St. Louis, but do you know by whom or why? Did you even know him?"

"I am really busy, Daniel, why are you asking all of these questions?

"I am asking these questions Mother because I heard a story that has piqued my curiosity. Did you know him or not?"

"I knew him. He would come into the store now and then. But, he wasn't around a lot."

"What was he like? Who killed him?"

"He was like no other man I had ever met. He was charming, I guess. But the truth is, Matthew Flanders was a womanizer. He never met a woman he didn't want to spend time with, and he spent time with most every woman he met. He loved Melissa and as for Daphnia, well she was everything to him. I don't know how he died or at whose hand. If I had to guess I would guess that he got himself shot over a woman. Now if you are planning on going into St. Louis to open a can of worms that has been closed for a long time, then you better think twice. I am just as curious about Daphnia coming here as you are, but digging up dirt on Matthew ain't going to satisfy that curiosity any. You better stick to what's going on around here and leave the dead and buried alone. Don't close the door too hard when you leave, it has been sticking lately." She turned away from him and began to stack some dry goods that had been lying on a chair nearby.

Walking out of the store he knew he had to go to St. Louis. With both of his parents trying to put him off the scent of a real human-interest story like this all because of who the central figure was didn't sit well with him. His next stop was the train depot and information on the next train to St. Louis via whatever route it needed to take. The next train would take him through Detroit, into Lansing, down to Chicago and end in St. Louis. It was scheduled for departure the next morning at 7:10; Daniel booked passage.

Chapter Fourteen

When the train pulled into the station at Lansing, Daniel was eager to spend some time in the city learning as much as he could about the Flanders clan and especially about Matthew. He immediately went to the ticket master and told him he would be staying in Lansing for a few days and would catch a later train on to Chicago. He asked for directions to the nearest boarding house and whether or not there was a city courthouse with historical records. Once he got the information he requested he was on his way. He felt like he was seventeen and couldn't keep himself from whistling as he walked.

The clerk at the courthouse was eager to help. She showed him the room where all birth and property records were kept and left him to his own devices as to how much he looked at, copied, or took with him. But, there was little to find. It seemed that Thaddeus Flanders had lived a remarkably quiet life; Daniel could find no ghosts. He found that Matthew had been born to Joshua and Sarah Flanders August 1, 1855; Sarah died giving him birth and Joshua died some seventeen years later. There was no record of Matthew's death. There was also no record of Daphnia. Going out to see the clerk, Daniel put on his most charming façade.

"It looks to me like there is not much to find in there about the man I am interested in. Maybe you can help me out some? What do you know about the Flanders family, specifically, do you know anything about Matthew Flanders?"

"Oh, no sir, I really don't. And even if I did, why I just couldn't participate in gossip like that. Best if it is that kind of information you are after that you go down to Miss Ann's, I am sure some of the ladies down there can help you. You can't miss it, just behind Frankie's Tavern on Main Street. Good luck."

Daniel thanked the homely woman whom he decided must surely be a spinster of some fifty or more years. He would go to the tavern first, and then visit Miss Ann's.

Upon entering the tavern he knew immediately that these men were unlike those back in Huron City. He ordered a whiskey and looked about the room. There were a couple of men sitting over in the corner playing cards and one or two standing at the bar, but none that looked too friendly. He finished his drink and left the tavern for Miss Ann's, he was certain the ladies would be a bit friendly and easier to get to know.

Miss Ann and her girls were having a slow day of it and at least two of them greeted him as he stood at the door to take in the sights. "Good afternoon, sir, how can we help you?" the busty woman asked as she sauntered up to him.

"Just a little relaxation, maybe some conversation, a drink or two," he replied while gently stroking the shoulder of the redhead holding onto his arm. "I was wondering, though, no intent to offend this sweet young thing here, but my preference is someone with a little more years on her so to speak, and maybe a little more cushion such as yourself, would that be possible?"

Miss Ann blushed as she looked into his eyes. She wondered just what he had in mind, but she was certainly happy to oblige him. Not too many of the men were interested in someone of her age or girth for that matter, and she welcomed the compliment. "What are you drinking, sugar? You go ahead first door on the right at the top of them stairs, I'll bring up a tray."

"Whiskey," he replied as he patted the backside of the redhead, winked and went up the stairs.

Miss Ann had been around for some time, Daniel reasoned that she must be well past forty and hoped that he had not made a mistake. What he wanted was information and knowing that she most likely thought he was interested in something else gave him pause. Maybe he could just get a few drinks into her and cuddle her up some and that would be enough.

Coming into the room with a tray holding a bottle of her finest malt whiskey and two glasses, Miss Ann smiled. "Now, young man, I been around the block a few times and I know full well that what you want from me ain't got nothin' to do with experience between them sheets or a softer cushion to push yourself against. So, how about we just sit here and talk a little. What is it you are after?"

"You sure get right to the point, I'll give you that. Here let me pour us a drink and you can tell me all that you know about Matthew

Flanders. I figure he might have been around when you were younger, no offense, and I am with the Gazette Newspaper down in Huron City, we're doing a piece on unsolved murders and the like. It seems he has a daughter who stands to inherit a fortune and we just want to make sure it is rightfully hers."

"What did you say your name was?"

"Daniel, my name is Daniel Bernstein. Here take a look at my credentials. My father and I own and operate the Gazette, have for years, and it seems that Flanders spent time between here and there, among other places, and I can't find too much about him down at the courthouse. Anything you can tell me would be appreciated, and I will keep your name out of it. I promise total confidentiality. Did you know Matthew Flanders?"

"Yeah, I knew him. You're right. I was barely eighteen when I first met him. He used to come around this way some. And, of course, when he moved in at his uncle's place out at Sunshine Acres with his baby daughter some years later, I got to know him real good. Like all the girls around, I thought I loved him, but to him I was just a warm body for a few short hours every now and then. He would come into this place and it was like a free for all with each of us vying for his affection, we couldn't help ourselves. But he let everyone know that he had no love to give after the dying of the baby's mother. We knew he just used us, but somehow that was okay."

"What do you know about the baby's mother? Was she from around here?"

"No, she was from back east, Boston I think. To hear him speak of her, which he did constantly, she had to be a saint."

"What happened to her? And, what happened to him?"

"I think she died shortly after giving birth to young Daphnia – that's her name, Matthew's daughter I mean. She came back here when she was just a little thing and was raised by the same uncle and aunt that tried to raise him. She just left here not long ago; I think for Huron City is what I heard. Just what are you up to? If Daphnia Flanders is in Huron City and if you are who you say you are, and if she is to inherit a large sum of money, just who is she getting it from? The last I knew Mr. and Mrs. Flanders are both still very much alive. What's your angle?"

"I have no angle, Miss Ann. Daphnia Flanders is in Huron City, you are right. She thinks she is there because of her mother, but the woman she thinks is her mother isn't her mother after all and she is dying. What do you know about her real mother?"

"I know she died in Boston shortly after Daphnia was born. Now, how about we stop all of this talking and get down to what you are paying for?"

"Let's have another drink first. Do you know how Matthew died, or why?"

"It was tragic. There were a lot of different stories flying around at the time. Some say it was his uncle who pulled the trigger, but nobody who knew Thaddeus Flanders believed that tale. Thaddeus loved that boy, couldn't have loved him more had he been his very own. Other folks talked a lot, but there was never any murderer named that I know of. It could have been anybody the way Matthew flaunted his womanizing. He didn't hold too much for places such as this, his favorite past time was teasing and pleasing women married to men who had long forgot why they married them. Now, how about you? What's your pleasure? I'm not too old to still give a man a good turn around that featherbed over there, I ain't reached my prime yet, so to speak even though I might look like I got a few miles on me, ain't so many as you might think. So, come on Daniel, how do you like it?"

Daniel knew that he was not going to get anymore out of her without giving something in return. He unbuttoned his shirt and pants, stripped down to his socks then turned down the covers on her side of the bed and with a sweeping motion of his arm he invited her in. Miss Ann was right, she knew how to please a man and Daniel was pleased plenty before he nodded off to sleep.

Miss Ann slipped from the bed, retrieved her things and left the room with Daniel sleeping soundly. When he awoke he saw that it was dark and he was alone, he would leave for Boston tomorrow after all; he should probably go there before heading to St. Louis. He needed to know more about Grace Humphreys.

Chapter Fifteen

As the train pulled out of the station in Lansing, Daniel felt like a child waiting for his birthday. He had a feeling about this trip and it was good. Miss Ann hadn't given him the information he had hoped for, but she did put some ideas into his head; the first being that he would go to Boston and find out about the widow.

When he arrived in Boston it was colder than he had expected. There was a mist in the air and he thought of how his father might react if he knew where he was at this very moment. He stopped a constable who was shaking the doorknobs of the shops lining the town's square and asked for directions to the courthouse. Upon arrival at the stone building he took a seat on the steps and waited for someone to open the doors.

He spent most of the morning going through birth records before he found that of Daphnia Jean Flanders born February 11, 1880 to Matthew Flanders and Grace Humphreys. Going to the death records he found that of Grace Humphreys dated March 18, 1880. He couldn't believe what he saw written on the certificate of death, the names of Grace Humphreys' mother and father were those of his very own grandparents. His father and Daphnia were listed as her only living relatives. He dropped the court record book with its handwritten entries. He needed a drink.

Walking down the street toward the nearest tavern, Daniel was practically in shock. People stopped and stared at him as he passed them, but he didn't notice. He wondered why he hadn't put all of this together before. Now he knew that he had to get to St. Louis, he had to see the death entry for Matthew, he turned from the tavern without going in and went to the train depot and booked passage on the next train heading west.

Awakening as the train pulled into the St. Louis station Daniel was still seeing the handwritten image in his mind with the names of his grandparents and his own father. What a tremendous secret his father had kept all of these years. He wondered how much his mother knew, if she knew anything at all.

Leaving the train station he could barely keep himself from running to the courthouse so he could begin his search for the death certificate of Matthew Flanders. After some digging through boxes and shelves in the dusty closet, the court clerk graciously gave him the record book of births and deaths for the year 1884 explaining that she did not have time to help him further, but he was welcome to look through the book on his own. Daniel took the book to a quiet corner of the room and began his search. Finally, there it was 'Flanders, M. 1884, Feb.04, died of gunshot'. This was not what he wanted to see.

"Excuse me, Miss, but is there anything that explains what type of gunshot killed Mr. Flanders or whether or not it was murder or self inflicted?" he asked the less than interested clerk.

"Can't say, sir, you might want to check with the coroner's office. What you see is all we got here," she responded without looking up.

"Where is the coroner's office?"

"You can see the constable on the other side of the building, don't know what they will have there, but I believe they can direct you."

Daniel walked out of the office without thanking the clerk, and went to the office of the constable. After asking a number of questions he was directed to the room at the end of the hall where the records of suspicious homicides were kept. He was met with another clerk who shared the same disinterested and unhelpful attitude. He was directed to a closet with shelves of leather bound record books. Each book had a to and from date on the spine and he soon located the one containing records for the year 1884. There was no record of Matthew Flanders. He went to the previous year, still no record. He then pulled the book for the years 1885-1887, no entries with the name of Matthew Flanders. Frustrated, he went back to the clerk, "excuse me, I am with the Gazette Newspaper out of Huron City, Michigan. I am investigating a murder that took place here in St. Louise in February 1884. I can't seem to find anything here with the victim's name, is there some place else I should be looking?"

"If you can't find anything, then there ain't anything, mister. If you are trying to find out something that happened twenty years ago, then good luck. Them records back there are all that I have."

"I understand that you might not have any other records, but do you know who else I should be talking to?"

"Can't say that I do, if the poor bastard was murdered as you say, then there would be a record of it, since there ain't no record here guess you are barking up the wrong tree. Sorry I can't help you. But, if I do say so, it seems to me that if it is a story you are looking for you would go to the St. Louis Tribune, they might have something in their archives that we don't."

"Thanks!" he said as he ran from the office. Why hadn't he thought of that? Then he doubled back, "where is the Tribune?"

"Thought you might come back with that question, over on Maple, about three blocks from here, go down the street to your right and turn left onto Oak, keep heading south and you will turn east on Maple; it'll be about half way down the block.

He walked into the St. Louis Tribune and straightened his jacket before going up to the information desk. "Excuse me, I'm with the Gazette in Huron City, Michigan and I am here trying to follow up on a story. Where can I find information about a possible homicide that took place here back in 1884?"

"The archives are located down in the cellar, you can put in a request and we can look it up for you or you can go back there on your own. Being in the newspaper business you probably know what you are looking for, so let me show you the way."

Daniel followed the man to the archives. Everything was labeled and appeared to be in order. He thanked the clerk and took down the first stack of papers marked with the year 1884. He meticulously went through each paper starting with January 1st of that year. It was noon before he finished the month of January and was ready to start on February, he could feel his pulse racing and he thought he might need to take a break, but he was too excited. February 1st, 2nd, 3rd and there it was finally, February 4th – he took a deep breath and started reading slowly, but there was no mention of any homicide involving Matthew Flanders. His heart sank. There was no paper for February 5th through February 18th, 1880. What could have happened to those papers? He went back to see the clerk at the information desk.

"Excuse me, but there is a gap of missing papers from the fifth of February through the eighteenth, can you tell me where I might find those papers?" he asked as politely and calmly as possible.

"Yeah, I can tell you. It seems that during that time there was some sort of problem and the entire City was pretty much shut down. Some kind of storm, I think. You might go ahead and look at the papers after the eighteenth, they probably covered the important stuff."

"Thanks." Daniel went back to the archives and looked at the remainder of the papers for February through to April, but still nothing about Matthew Flanders. Disgusted, he left the newspaper office and went back to the office of the constable. Maybe there would be someone there who would remember what happened; after all it wasn't all that long ago.

"Good afternoon, is there someone on duty who was here maybe twenty years ago who might remember something about a homicide back in 1884?" he asked the clerk at the desk.

An older gray haired man looked up, "yeah, I was here back then, whaddaya want to know?"

"My name is Daniel Bernstein, and I am co-owner, co-editor of the Gazette back in Huron City, Michigan. I am following up on a story about a man, Matthew Flanders who was shot and killed here back in 1884. I want to know why he was shot and who did it? Do you know anything about that?"

"You Goddamned right, I know about it, and the only thing I can say is he got what he deserved. He was cattin' around every woman in town and some of the ones from somewhere else for that matter. He got what he deserved, and that's good enough for me."

"Of course, I understand that, but who did it?"

"Who cares? He was found face down in the mud with the sleet and snow covering him over. He had been shot in the heart point blank, and by the time anybody got to him, he was already gone. They celebrated over at the Red Dog, and I was there to buy the drinks I can tell you that."

"Did you shoot him?"

"Me? I wished to hell I did, but no, I think it was somebody who was braver than me, and good for him, I say. You better go on back to Huron City or wherever you came from, young man, ain't nobody around here who was there that night gonna have anymore information that what I done give ya. Matthew Flanders was shot for doing what he hadn't ought to have been doing with somebody he hadn't ought to have been doing it with, and he got what he needed to get, and so did she."

"What do you mean, so did she? Was there a woman involved? Was she killed also?"

"Of course there was a woman involved, she was the wife of the town Sheriff, and she hanged herself when news got out that Flanders was dead."

"Did the sheriff kill Flanders?"

"Cain't say one way or the other, but one thing for sure, nobody else can say either."

"I can't find any records anywhere. Did the records get destroyed?"

"Cain't say, lots of things go missing over the years. I gotta go, you take care."

Daniel left the office and walked around the corner to the hotel where he took a room and decided to wait until morning to decide what to do next.

He didn't have to wait until morning. When he registered at the hotel the clerk looked at him and questioned, "I knew a Bernstein once. Her name was Ruth or Rose or something like that. You any kin to her?"

"Well, my mother's name is Ruth, but I don't know how you would know her."

"My grandmother ran a boarding house here years ago, she's dead now and the boarding house is gone, but when I was young I remember a woman named Bernstein staying there one summer, thought you might be related, is all. You here on business?"

"Yeah, you can say that. I own a newspaper back in Huron City, Michigan and I am here following a story, or at least I think it could be a story. You ever hear of anybody named Flanders? Matthew Flanders? He was shot and killed here about twenty years ago and nobody seems to know anything about who shot him or why."

"That Ruth Bernstein woman, your mother I think you said, she used to go out with a man named Flanders. I remember him calling on her at the boarding house. I don't remember him getting shot, though. Course I was young when your mama was staying at my grandmothers and then I went away for a while down south, so I don't know nothing about anybody getting shot. Why don't you ask your mama, she must know something?"

"I think you must be mistaken, my mother would never have been seeing another man when she was here. Why, she and my father have been married over forty years. You must be mistaken. Do you know how I might find out about this Flanders fellow? It happened about twenty-three or four years ago."

"I could be mistaken about your mama, like I said, I was young. If somebody got shot around here that long ago I don't expect too many people to have forgotten. Maybe you ought to go over to the Red Dog Saloon, there should be somebody there who knows something. I'm sorry again about saying anything about your mama, I didn't mean to offend you."

"No offense taken, mistakes are easy enough to be made. I'll go on over to the Red Dog, thanks."

Taking a deep breath, he entered the Red Dog Saloon and ordered a shot of whiskey. He looked around the room and finally saw an older man with gray hair and a beard that looked like it might have bugs living in it sitting in the corner of the barroom. "Excuse me sir, mind if I sit a minute?" he asked as politely as he could. The older man just looked at him and grunted.

"I am here trying to find out some information about a murder that took place about twenty-three or four years ago, man named Matthew Flanders. Word has it that he was shot out back here and left to die without anybody ever knowing who shot him or why. Any chance you might know something about it?"

"I know it wasn't me that shot him."

"Do you have any idea who did?"

"Yep, maybe the sheriff whose wife he was bedding. Could have been some stranger who had a beef with him, and then again, it might have been the husband of some woman he was messing with from back east. Could've been most anybody, I suppose."

"Were there that many people who wanted to kill him?"

"Yep, he didn't have too many friends exceptin' the ladies."

"Well, wasn't there ever an investigation? Wasn't anybody ever charged with his murder?"

"Yep. The sheriff investigated."

"Well, what did he find?"

"He found him dead and closed the case, wasn't no need to question anybody, wouldn't nobody snitch on the one who did it even if they knew who it was. Guess you won't find too many answers for your story. You better just chalk this one up to a mystery that can't be solved and let it go at that, unless of course you can find one of them lumberjacks still around somewhere who might know more."

"Was Flanders working with the lumberjacks when this happened?"

"Yep."

"Do you know any of their names or where I might find one of them?"

"Nope. Now if you will excuse me, I prefer to drink alone so if you don't mind ...."

Daniel thanked the man and left the saloon. He would take the next train home. It seemed that he had as many questions about Matthew Flanders now as he did when he left Huron City. The only problem was he now had questions about his father, Grace Humphreys and his mother. This was a lot to take in.

Daniel returned to Huron City ready to face his father and mother about what he had learned. When he entered the office of the Gazette he was met by Daphnia who told him that Herbert had taken some time off to settle some business with her Uncle Thaddeus in Lansing and that his mother had decided at the last minute to join him, they weren't expected to return for at least another week.

The news of his mother and father being away just when he was full of questions and even a few answers did not sit well with Daniel. He stormed out of the newspaper office and went to O'Connor's. He needed some action and a few drinks. Daphnia was left to do whatever needed to be done.

Chapter Sixteen

The time spent alone in the office was of no real consequence to Daphnia. She had developed a routine of awaking before sunrise, and going downstairs to her work. She took time during the middle of each day to visit Melissa. They would sit on the porch or in Melissa's room and drink tea while talking about things that didn't really seem to matter much to either one of them. Daphnia told her of William and her short-lived teaching experiences. Melissa spoke of her own dreams as a young woman and of how she had traveled to Europe and met the Royals of England. It was strange to Daphnia how different they were from one another. Melissa was concerned with the proper things in life and being considered as being proper herself. She had not concerned herself with making her own living or standing for principle and fairness. While Daphnia on the other hand was concerned with the right and wrong of things and the happiness that only living life to its fullest and working for the pure pleasure of working could bring. The women would frequently speak of these things only to have the conversation end by eventual polite disagreement. It would be times like these when Daphnia would say good-bye to Melissa and visit with Eloise.

"Do you have a few minutes, Aunt Ella? I can stay for a while if you would like. Mother has gone to sleep and it is so beautiful outside today."

"Sure, honey, I can sit for a spell… I just made some tea, won't you have a cup?"

"I really shouldn't, but yes, I would like some tea. I don't know where the time goes when I come to see Mother. I have been remiss, I am sorry that I haven't had a chance to spend much time with you."

"Good. Good then. Come on, let's sit here, I'll go get the tea. I baked some sugar cookies just this morning, I'll bring a plate out."

Daphnia like sitting outside on the front porch. The air was fresh and smelled wonderful to her, she breathed deeply and allowed herself to lean back in the rocker and close her eyes.

As she sat waiting for Eloise to return she felt peaceful. She had finally come to terms with her untypical mother-daughter relationship with Melissa. She had resigned herself to being comforted in whatever love her mother showed her and in whatever manner she chose. She was committed to doing the right thing for Melissa no matter what. Hearing Eloise come from behind her she stood and offered her help.

"So, Daphnia, tell me about the work you are doing at the Gazette. What is the news of the day? I just don't see how any news can be worth printing around here. Why all that's goin' on is the shenanigans down there by the river and them coloreds living over in the quarters always a'comin' and a'goin' what else is there?"

"Well, I dare say that there is much more than that. What about the starch plant that is expanding up river? And, there is news of the railroad. The feed and grain has almost doubled in size over the past two years, or so Mr. Bernstein tells me; and then there is the mill that is supplied by the vast forests in these parts. This little town is bustling, Aunt Ella. It might not be much now, but it is going to be. You sound like Daniel Bernstein. All he is concerned about is that lumberyard and the "river winches" as he calls them. I don't know much about the coloreds, but I met one young man when I first came here. I finally figured out that it was he and his family who were actually on the same train with me when I came in from Detroit. He seemed polite to me. As for my work, well I don't get much involved with the actual newspaper stories or printing. My job is trying to keep the bills paid and enough ink in stock. Uncle Bert, I mean Mr. Bernstein, is a very gentle and kind man. He has been very helpful to me. Do you know that he actually keeps flowers and greens growing all year long? He has made the porch on the back of the building into a year 'round garden of sorts. He heats it and has holes cut in the roof and covered with plates of glass to bring in the sunshine during the winter. It is really amazing, it doesn't smell too nice, but it is interesting."

"So, that's where he gets all of those flowers that he brings over here when everything is covered with snow. So, tell me, what's this I hear about that young man of yours? Melissa tells me that he is in the Army or is it the Calvary?"

"Yes, he is in the Army, but he is assigned a position out west, so I guess technically that could be considered the Calvary. We plan to marry next spring. He is a good man, Aunt Ella. He is kind, and compassionate and I love him very much. He has been my best friend since I was a little girl, and he is my only love. I miss him terribly."

Having said this, Daphnia turned away as the tears welled up and ran down her face. The two women sat quietly for a while each consumed by their own thoughts.

"Tell me about my mother and my father, please Aunt Ella, there is so much about them that I don't know and I would really like to understand them and their relationships with one another. And, I guess I want to know where I fit in, if I ever did."

Eloise straightened herself in her chair and then rose and walked about the porch. She fumbled with the hem of her apron, poured herself more tea, and then eventually sat back down. Taking Daphnia's hands into her own, Eloise began.

"Well, honey, I know it has been difficult for you. It has nothing to do with you, though. None of what happened was your fault and don't you ever believe anything any different. Circumstances sometimes take the form of a bucket of minnows and what comes out of that don't nobody know why. Now, as for Melissa, she was from an upright and church going family. Her mother was from England and her father worked his way over on one of them big ships out of Italy. They were hardworking and God fearing folks. They made good money and lived as proper as any family in the whole of Boston. Melissa never wanted for anything. She had done more traveling and seen more of what most folks only dream about before she was ever sixteen years old. She was the heart and soul of her Father. He died too young, worked himself to death most likely. He gave everything to Melissa and her Mother. When Melissa met Matthew she thought he would do the same for her that her father had always done, but they were from two different pieces of cloth so to speak. Not that he didn't love her, he just didn't love her enough. That is what has almost killed Melissa. She was used to being the center of the universe, and in Matthew's universe, he was the center and he had lots of stars that he chased and longed for."

"I am not sure I understand. I have heard the rumors that Father had many other women, but he loved my mother, didn't he?

"Loving your mother had nothing to do with it. Your father, my dear, was quite the rounder. I don't know how much to say to you, but I know you won't accept anything less than certain honesty, so here goes.

There is no way that I can sugar coat it for you, I wish that I could, but it is the truth and a matter of record, that he was a womanizer, selfish and filled with more charm and passion for living than anyone I had ever known. He had a way of walking into a room and bringing life to everything inside. It didn't matter how much he had hurt Melissa, or how he had left her alone, when she took one look at him all of her anger was washed away. His passion and zest for life was contagious, he was fun and filled with just enough good to cause you to forgive the mischief he could get himself into. He was handsome and strong, Daphnia, and he knew how to use it to his advantage; especially with the ladies."

"Maybe I am just too old fashioned, myself, Aunt Ella. But, if Father loved me and if he loved my mother, then what happened? How could he leave us?"

"I don't think in his mind he did, honey. As for loving you, he loved you more than life itself. I think it is fair to say that he didn't love anyone as much as he loved you, except of course himself. I must admit that his love and devotion to you bothered Melissa some. When you came along, her place was relegated to a lower level. When he was here, your place was either in his arms or riding on his shoulders once you were big enough to sit alone. He would spend hours just rocking you and telling you secrets and holding you close. He was not ashamed of his love for you and he made certain that everyone knew that you were the apple of his eye."

As she spoke, she looked off into the distance just beyond Daphnia's gaze. Eloise told Daphnia these things carefully and with deliberation. She did not want to be the one to tell her that it was his love for her that caused Melissa to become so bitter and unforgiving and to blame an innocent child for something that she had nothing to do with. And, she especially didn't want to be the one to tell her about Grace Humphreys.

"If he loved me so much, then why did he leave?"

"Work, I guess, honey. He had to work. He sent plenty of money back here for Melissa, he sent gifts for you and came home as often as he could. He worked with the railroad, in the lumber mills, took his turn at the gambling tables on them riverboats that wind up and down the Mississippi. Huron City was not a "City" back then, why it was barely a stop along the way. So, he left to work. Melissa wouldn't budge from here. She loved the slow pace and its quaintness. Being from Boston one would have thought this place would be too small and uninviting, but when she saw this house and this place she said she would never live anywhere else, and she hasn't. But, Matthew, he needed flash and excitement. He would become sullen and bored after only a few days here; she wouldn't go with him so he would go out on his own. This would often lead to stories and gossip, they would argue and she would go off to her room locking him out for days until he would either leave completely or wait her out and seek forgiveness until he would become bored again. He made good money and he spent good money. He worked hard and he lived passionately, and for a lot of years he got away with it. He was a man that craved excitement and change, and as for the women, honey, they craved him right back. He loved life and all it had to offer, and that included ladies that didn't belong to him. He was a fun loving man. I guess if I had to sum it all up I would just have to say that he was a rounder, honey, that's all I can say."

"How exactly did he die, Aunt Ella?"

"You know how he died. What? Do you think there is another story? Of all the gossip and rumors that have gotten around about Matthew Flanders, the only one that is the absolute truth is the one you have heard over and over again. He was shot, Daphnia. Shot in the heart in one of the back alleyways in St. Louis. No one knows by whom or for what, but he was shot just the same. I guess it was late, I have heard many different versions of what happened but I figure if there was a doctor around no one could find him, or else he didn't want or care to be found. Matthew died laying in the mud with the rain coming down and no one around to help him but the local blacksmith who also was considered to be the next closest thing to a doctor the place had."

Fearing that she had said just enough and anymore would lead to a greater disclosure than she wanted, Eloise stood and held her arms open to Daphnia. "Well, it doesn't look like that kitchen floor is gonna get washed with me sitting out here. You better get on back to your work and me back to mine. I'll see you tomorrow and we'll talk again."

"Thanks for the tea, Aunt Ella, and thanks for conversation."

Walking back to the Gazette, she tried to remember the different stories that she had heard about her father, as she attempted to compartmentalize the varying slants depending on who was talking, she found herself feeling alone and abandoned all over again. Pulling her shawl about her she felt suddenly chilled. It seemed that no matter how bright the sunshine, the air was always cool and damp, and she thought that with summer so cool that maybe Eloise was right autumn would be early this year.

Turning off Pine Street she walked along the waterfront as she had done so often since her arrival. There was peace in the listening to the water lap against the rocks and dirt of the shoreline. She felt a sense of harmony with this place and herself as she sat quietly on the rocks and looked out over the still waters. She found comfort in the manner in which she had adjusted to her new life and to Huron City. While she definitely missed her Aunt Martha and Papa Tad, she had come to enjoy her many conversations with her Uncle Bert and the freedom of living alone. She felt at peace in spite of her mother's lack of compassion and warmth toward her. She whispered to herself and all that was silent around her that this would change, her mother did love her, she would be able to show it eventually.

Leaving the shoreline and returning to the Gazette she found things just as they had been when she closed up earlier. She went about the business of the day and then pulled the shades, locked the doors and went up to her apartment. She thought of Daniel and wondered what he was up to since he had not spent much time in the office, and the next edition of the Gazette would be due for publication in just two days.

Daniel was thinking of things other than the next edition of the Gazette. His mind was on the warm and yielding body of Clarice Hayes. He longed to feel her next to him and to enjoy the rhythm of their bodies joined in an easy motion like the rocking of the boat on the gentle river. He could almost feel the rise and fall of her beneath him and taste the sweetness of her breath against his mouth. He walked over to the small house in the quarters, opened the door and asked that young Michael take his little sister over to visit their grandfather for a while. He brought along some stale rolls that his mother had left for him to eat along with a jar of honey for them to take along to the old man.

Daphnia looked out of her window and saw the moon bright and full in the evening sky. It was a beautiful evening and one that made her think of love and William. She heated a kettle of water and prepared for a long hot bath.

A thousand miles away, William too was thinking of Daphnia. He loved her and knew that she loved him, but he also knew that they would never be together. They were different; she was accustomed to finer things and a life of carefree days and moon filled nights. He was used to hard work and always having to hold his head down and work too hard for anything and everything that he or his family got that was pleasurable. His father had been known as the town drunk, and his mother did little more than keep house and make babies, three of which had never lived past their first birthday. It was a hard life, and Daphnia would never fit in. At least not until he made something of himself; not until he became a doctor with a big white house with porches and kitchen help. As he closed his eyes and laid back on his cot he thought of Daphnia and her sweetness, the smell and the feel of her, the way she whispered along his neck and caressed his shoulders and back. Yes, he loved Daphnia and knew she loved him, but would it ever truly be possible? Could they really ever come together and be happy? He missed her, and he knew right down to the soles of his feet that he always would.

A sense of restlessness did not give of itself only to the young this evening; Martha and Thaddeus were feeling their own discomfort. The full moon and the passing of spring into summer with the onset of Autumn was like a cloud engulfing those of "The House of Flanders" with melancholy and a need to withdraw to within themselves for comfort and solace. Herbert and Ruth had been visiting for almost a full week, and the house had started to feel a little small. Thankfully, they had gotten onto the train headed back to Detroit and he and Martha were once again alone.

Thaddeus took his pipe out to the front porch and stood tapping it against the palm of his hand. As he lit the sweet smelling tobacco, he watched the smoke rise up and disappear into the evening. It was getting cooler at night and soon the crops would be ready for harvesting. With Herbert coming to Lansing, there would be no need for him to make his planned trip to Huron City next week, he had written a letter to Daphnia explaining why he needed to stay home, she would understood. As he stood staring out into the evening's twilight he could see Martha walking back from the roses; she had been visiting the family cemetery more often lately and the roses were not the reason for her frequent trips out to the small stone bench. Martha was suffering from the loss of Daphnia, but she also seemed to be more withdrawn, and Thaddeus had overheard her talking as if to be carrying on conversations with persons long since gone.

Coming from the garden she looked up to see him watching her. "Now just what are you standing their watching me for? I must look a sight. I've been thinking about them twins due any day now to Carl and his wife. And, I been thinking that maybe I will take a ride with you to see Daphnia. Do you think that would be alright?"

"Well, of course I think that would be alright. I was thinking of canceling my trip since Herbert and Ruth have come here, but we can still go next week. Would that work for you?"

"Oh, no, not next week. Maybe later, but not next week, oh no, that just would not do. Let's go on inside. I'm getting tired. I think I will go up to bed. Are you coming? Maybe we should go ahead and just forget about going for now anyway."

"Okay, Mart, whatever you say. You go ahead to bed, I'll be there shortly. I just need to sort through a few things first." He re-lit his pipe and sat down on the steps; he needed to think. He had received a message from Miss Ann that a young Daniel Bernstein had been in asking questions. She said that it had been a while since Thaddeus had been in to see her, so maybe now would be a good time for a visit. He would have to work this out somehow. He was curious about what Daniel was asking about, and even more so that he had come to Lansing and not stopped in for a visit, especially with his mother and father in town as well. He would have to get into Lansing tomorrow and see Miss Ann.

Chapter Seventeen

It was good to get home. Herbert went straight to his office and Ruth went home alone. She unpacked and took a look around the house before settling down with her knitting. Her mind wandered to her visit to Sunshine Acres where the four old friends had spent a lot of time visiting about nothing of real importance. At least nothing that Ruth wanted to talk about. She had not had any of her questions answered, and was still trying to figure out the conversations and outcome of Thaddeus' last visit to Huron City. Things just didn't add up for her. When she had tried to engage Martha in conversations about Daphnia or Melissa, she was met with a change of subject. Sitting with her yarn and needles, she allowed her mind to once again go back to Thaddeus' last visit to Huron City.

She was so lost in her thoughts that she did not hear Herbert walk up the stairs and enter his room until she heard his door close. Too late! She put her knitting away and went into the kitchen where she sat down at the kitchen table and finished off the remainder of the chocolate sheet cake that Daniel had not eaten. She would have to find another time to talk with Herbert. She wondered what was going on with him, and where on earth was Daniel these days. Surely he knew they were coming home today. She would talk with him tomorrow.

<hr/>

Daniel had been in a stupor since returning to Huron City from St. Louis. His mind was working overtime and his need for answers was eating away at him. He had spent much of his time down at one of the local pubs trying to let the whiskey help him make some sense out of it all. It was there that he overheard a group of the older lumberjacks talking. They were spinning their tales about romance and travel through the northeast and Midwest. When he heard one of them mention working just outside of St. Louis he sauntered over to listen. But he learned only that lumberjacks are like every other loud mouth man who has nothing to do but swig whiskey and talk big. Disgusted he left O'Connor's and went to the little frame house nestled between the big pine trees down in the quarters.

"Hey there Clarice, get them brats outta the house, I'm coming in, and you better be ready."

Clarice hurriedly put jackets on Michael and Ruby and sent them out the back door to their grandfather's telling them to stay there for a while. She then straightened things up as much as she could before he came through the front door and started tearing at her clothes and pushing her down onto the bed. He was drunk, and when he was drunk he was mean, she knew to be ready for what was surely going to be a painful encounter. The only good thing about him being drunk was that he would allow his rage to take over and he would pass out before he could inflict too much pain on her.

Michael and Ruby got to their grandfather's house, but he wasn't home so they came back just in time to see Daniel slap their mama and then take her in a manner they had never witnessed before. He saw them standing there watching and this only served to ignite his anger; he was more brutal than even he thought he could be. Oddly, he found pleasure in hearing her screams and watching her children watch him. Michael came at him but only to be pushed away. Clarice begged Michael to take Ruby outside and wait for it to get quiet.

As the children huddled against the back door, they heard the man have his way with their mother against her will. Once he was satisfied and physically drained, he was eager to rest; he pushed Clarice from the bed.

Michael listened for silence and then he and Ruby crept back inside. Clarice tried to cover herself from her children's gaze while gathering her clothes from the bed covers now tangled around the man's legs. Once she was able to get dressed, she crawled over to the hearth. She called the children over and the three huddled together in front of the fire. She whispered and sang to them softly so that they wouldn't awaken the hateful man lying drunk in the only bed that they had. Her lip was swollen and bruised where he had bitten it earlier in the evening, and there were purple and blue lines around her left eye and on her cheek from his fist.

She had thought that once here in Huron City things would be different than they were in Morgantown. In fact, they were worse. At least back in Morgantown her children didn't have to listen or watch her sell her body to meanness, at least she was left with a little pride. This man had all but drained the very spirit out of her and her children as well. How long before he would be after little Ruby she thought. Then what would she to?

Michael was angry and he made no secret of wanting to kill the man while he slept, he whispered this to his mother as he held out the tattered blanket for her; Clarice was scared. She knew that she could not kill another man no matter what he did to her. The last time was the last time for her, and no matter what happened she would not do it again. She pulled the children close to her and straightening the blanket so it could be wrapped around Michael and his sister she cradled them against her. The little loud man snored, turned over and grunted but did not awaken. Clarice hoped he would sleep until morning then he would be too anxious to get out of her house without anyone seeing him, this was the only way she could be assured that he would do her no more harm this visit.

Michael prayed silently that the man would drown on his own saliva and save him the chore of killing him and bringing sorrow to his mother. He had planned his method of taking the life from this mean man, he could close his eyes and see himself pushing the butcher knife between Daniel Bernstein's shoulder blades and feeling the life drain from his pasty white skin. At his young years of ten, he knew what it was like to take a life, he had helped his Mother kill his own father, and he could certainly kill this son of a bitch and enjoy it. He carefully slipped from beneath the blanket and walked over to the wooden table only to see the sleeping figure stir and finally stretching his arms and rubbing his eyes he sat up. Once he was able to focus he scratched his head, belched loudly and then rubbing his belly, the man in all of his nakedness rose from the bed and walked over to the pot and pissed without concern or respect for Michael's mother and sister who had been watching him stirring about and hoping that he would not fully awaken.

Daniel looked around at the small woman and her little girl and grinned. He didn't seem to mind that Clarice had been forced out of her bed and left to comfort her children on the hearth. She had sufficiently satisfied his need and now he was awake and most anxious to leave and return to his other life, one of respect and dignity. Pulling his clothes on, he turned and saw young Michael staring at him from the other side of the room. He suddenly felt the hair on the back of his neck stand on end, and for just a moment he was scared.

"What are you doing, Michael?" Daniel asked the young boy who was now standing in the middle of the room with the knife in his hand. "What are you doing with that knife boy?" Michael demanded while buttoning his trousers and tucking his shirt inside his belt.

"I was just goin to cut me a piece of that there bread, you want some?" Michael asked pointing the knife over toward the loaves of bread that Clarice had baked earlier in the day and set out on the cupboard.

"No, I don't want any, I must be leaving now." Then kicking Clarice in the back he growled at her, "Get on up here girl, I'm leaving, don't you want to say goodbye to your man?" he roared. Clarice did not move although she felt the toe of his boot hit her between her ribs and almost take her breath away. She tightened her body in preparation for the next blow that she was sure was coming.

Daniel, not getting the expected reaction from the frightened black woman, spit into the fire and letting go with his foot again he swore at the woman as he pushed the toe of his boot into the plaster cast on her broken leg, "stay there then you nigger whore, I'll be back for more when you are in a more willing mood to please me." He turned and walked across the floor to rub Michael's head, but stopped short as he caught the eye of the young boy. Every bone in his body froze and a wave of fear came over him. Quickly he opened the door, he could feel the wind pick up and he heard the sound of blowing leaves and the lower branches scraping against the roof. He left the door standing open as he went out. He felt the dampness in the air, and the smell of the wood burning in Clarice's open fireplace made him smile, "it's the middle of summer, autumn is just around the corner, Tom Saunders will be back," he said out loud to no one.

Michael hurried to close and bar the door behind Daniel. As he turned back toward the inside of the house he could see that Clarice was sobbing as she tried to stand. He dropped the knife and ran over to help his mother. Once he had gotten his Mother and little sister into the bed he tucked the covers in around them and then patting his Mother's shoulder he kneeled down next to her and gently rubbing her back he whispered, "I'm going to kill that bastard, Mama. You just don't worry none, but I'm gonna drive that there butcher knife right through that son-of-a-bitch's heart." He then stood and walked to the other side of the bed and once seeing that his little sister was covered, he prepared a pallet on the floor for himself in front of the fire. Listening to the crackling of the wood, he once again checked to see that his Mother and sister were okay. He turned toward the fire and watched the red and gold flames lick the logs. He lay awake far into the night thinking and plotting so that when the time came he would be prepared to end the life of one Daniel Bernstein.

❦

Walking from the little shack and onto the streets of Huron City, the cold air felt good to Daniel as he let it rush over him, he whistled as he walked thinking of his friend returning soon. Maybe then he would have someone to talk with who would understand him. Maybe then, he could unload some of his frustrations. Maybe then he could sleep without awakening every hour or so. He felt unsettled these days. It wasn't just Clarice or young Michael that disturbed him it was everything. He was working too hard at the Newspaper Office, and what he had learned about the connection between his Mother and Father and Matthew Flanders preyed on his mind. There was so much still that he didn't know and that he couldn't quite figure out. He wasn't too eager to get to know anymore about Daphnia that he already had, but he was curious just the same. He had some powerful ammunition now and he had to decide when and how to use it. If Tom would just hurry and return he could talk to him about everything. He found himself smiling at the thought of Tom meeting Daphnia. He wondered how they would hit it off. Now, that was something to think about. He could just see them now, Tom with his tall good looks and more charisma than any three men Daniel had ever known and Daphnia with her arrogance and beauty that was only outdone by her brains. Now that would be a relationship worth watching. The thought of these two meeting and the many places that he could take those thoughts caused him reason to laugh out loud and he soon found that the trip home was almost too short.

Opening the door to the large yellow house, he could see the light shining from the kitchen. He remembered that his mother and father were returning today, but he wasn't ready to involve himself in a conversation just yet. He needed a plan and tomorrow would be soon enough. He walked quietly up the stairs glanced over at his father's bedroom door to see if the light was on. He stopped in his tracks, his Father had not spent a Tuesday evening at home for years, and now it seemed like he was home every evening, Tuesday or otherwise. How long had this been going on he wondered? Then he quickly did some calculations and determined that since the arrival of the Precious Daphnia his Father had changed some, not the least of which was that he no longer found it necessary to spend Tuesday's out of the office or Tuesday evenings away from home. Something was different, but what. Maybe a little conversation with his Mother would not be such a bad idea; he would join her in the kitchen and share in one of her late night feasts; he was always amazed at how much his Mother could eat after dinner when during dinner she seemed to do little more than push the food around from one side of her plate to the next. Eating with her made him nervous and he made it a point to do so as infrequently as he could get away with it. He turned and went back down the stairs only to meet Ruth coming up.

"Mother, I was just coming down to visit with you. How was your trip? I wish I had known that you were going away. I had to hear it from Daphnia. Did you have a good time? Come back down to the kitchen with me, tell me all about Lansing."

"Another time, Daniel, I'm tired and would like to go to bed. We'll talk tomorrow, good night." She then finished her climb up the stairs went into her room where she changed into her nightdress and crawled into her bed. Ruth did not sleep, however, she lay awake listening to the sounds of the house resisting the wind as it rattled the shutters and blew the low hanging limbs of the big pine tree against the window. She thought she could feel a chill in the air and could sense the coming of fall, it seemed to her that summer had just begun and she was already thinking of the falling leaves; it would be a cold winter.

Daniel proceeded down to the kitchen anyway and searched the cupboards until he found a loaf of bread and some cheese. As he took out one of his mothers' knives he had a flashback to the look on the boy Michael's face, chills ran up and down his spine. He laid the knife down on the table and leaving the cheese and bread out as well, he practically ran from the kitchen to the hallway where he took the stairs up to his room two at a time.

He was scared and he knew it, and he knew why. He could see and feel the black eyes laughing at him, he felt they had pierced his very soul and he couldn't shake the feeling of having looked into the depths of hell through the young Negro's smile and those two laughing black eyes.

Covering his head with his covers he couldn't escape the fear. Sleep had been his enemy for sometime now, and tonight was not going to be any different. He tried staying awake but battling the fears of consciousness was almost impossible, but sleeping was worse. The dreams haunted him, and he awakened more than once soaking wet from sweat. He finally got out of bed and lit the wick in the lamp on his bureau as well as the one on the table next to his bed. He gathered as many pillows as he could find in his room and sat against them leaning into the headboard. He did not want to sleep, but his tired and aching body wouldn't let him stay awake. This night was filled with demons lurking in every corner of his mind and all he could see through the darkness were Michael's eyes. Asleep he was tormented with fear of being chased through the woods and onto the rocky beach where the young black boy stood waiting for him and holding the butcher knife in his hand. Each event was more frightening than the last and each time he awoke gasping for air as he felt himself falling from the cliffs and into the lake. He thought he heard his mother knocking at his door once or twice, but he was too frightened to leave the security of his bed to answer her; rather, he just ignored her calls and prayed she would go away. It was not until he finally saw the streaks of morning that he was able to fully breathe. He finally felt relief with the dark of night being washed away by the dawn; he removed the pillows, put out the lights and slept.

PART III

...... and, what kind of shoes do Angels wear
as they tiptoe in so silently
and take those I love away from me?

Chapter Eighteen

It was already the second week of September and autumn seemed to have arrived early. The leaves were beginning to turn and the lake had become a slate gray. The men in the lumberyard had made themselves known to all who had shown an interest; Daphnia was not among them. Their rough and raucous ways would soon end, however. Most of the trees had been harvested and the men would be pulling out before the first snowfall; there were very few things left for them to bother with in Huron City.

Daniel had made several attempts to discuss what he had learned about Matthew Flanders and Grace Humphreys, but on each such occasion he was rebuffed. It was obvious to him that his father had no interest whatsoever in discussing this with him, and he was still trying to figure out some things in his own mind first. He had made fewer in-roads with his mother than his father. She was in a state of frenzy these days, especially since her return from Lansing. He had one more lead before he was truly ready to insist on a conversation with his father, but then no matter where that lead took him, he would get his answers. He was determined to unseat Daphnia from the pedestal his father had placed her upon and to reclaim what was rightfully his.

Ruth remained focused on trying to coerce Daphnia into attending some of the town's socials but to no avail, nor had she managed to find what she would consider a "suitable" escort for the young woman. This continued to prey on her mind. She thought it strange that Daphnia was content with her life as mundane and boring as it appeared to be to Ruth. She was equally puzzled that she and Daniel had not become kindred spirits of sorts, but Daniel had shown little other than total disregard toward Daphnia since her arrival. When he was forced into speaking of her at all he would turn up his lip and refer to her only as the "the Princess of Independence." Somehow this suited Ruth, for she had the same impression.

Daphnia and Melissa had formed a unique bond. Eloise often watched the two women silently, and usually from behind a door or over the top of a book that she would pretend to be reading. She thought the relationship was curious, but she vowed to let it run its course. She had provided Daphnia with as many answers to her questions as she dared, and had tried to remain scarce or at best busy during Daphnia's visits to the small house.

As for Herbert, he had become almost obsessed with Daphnia. In his mind she was perfect and could do no wrong. He prayed that she would never find out of his secrets and wrongdoing. He would sometimes close his eyes and dream of what might have been had he not taken things into his own hands; if only he had waited and thought about the possibilities; if he could only take things back.

During his visits with Melissa he would find himself telling her of Daphnia and her skill with managing the office. He would speak with genuine love of her smile and her laugh. He tried to fit these things into conversations, but found comfort just saying her name. In spite of his enthusiasm, he tried to be ever conscious of Melissa's feelings, and was sensitive above all else to how she thought of Daphnia. It seemed so unfair to him. How could the two women whom he loved so much bring such conflict and harmony to him at the same time?

He had learned to balance his visits with Melissa. He would sit for hours and hold her hand while she slept; or he would read to her from Browning or Dickinson or tell her of the waterfront and how the weather was changing. He loved Melissa; he had loved her since the day he first saw her at the train station. It was amazing to him how she and Daphnia had lived here in this very town for almost four years prior to that day, and he barely knew she existed. Pondering this oddity had become almost an obsession with him for years, now it no longer mattered. How could he thank Melissa for bringing Daphnia home? She would never understand. And, how could he ever speak of any of this to Daphnia. She was sophisticated and naïve at the same time. One minute she seemed to be in total control, and the next she would be confounded and astonished about some brutality that had taken place at the local pub or a not-so-rare promiscuity of the "ladies" down in the quarters. And, yet, she seemed to be adjusting well to her new surroundings, and to Melissa.

Herbert was right, Daphnia had settled into a routine of her own in Huron City. She had found a sense of belonging and felt that for the first time in her life she was actually needed. Her days were filled with awaking early, eating and dressing and being downstairs in the newspaper office when Herbert and Daniel arrived. She habitually worked through lunch so that she could leave in the mid-afternoon to go for her visit with Melissa. She had come to enjoy walking the streets of Huron City and listening to the shopkeepers and businessmen talking. The sounds of the people with their bustling and fussing about brought a smile to her face and she looked forward to witnessing the day-to-day happenings of the townsfolk. She made mental notes of the changes she noticed and the different people she would meet so she could share these with Melissa.

The conversations between the two women had expanded to things beyond their mutually agreed up topics. They found that they could discuss opposing interests as well as agree to disagree. Daphnia had begun to share her personal joys and plans about William, and Melissa would on occasion give her a piece of motherly advice or a more mature opinion. They would talk about the events of the town, the people and the world beyond. Regardless of the topic of the day, however, Matthew was always lurking about the edges of their conversations and forever lingering on their minds. His name and his memory would frequently enter into their conversations almost without thought or deliberation. On even the most shallow of conversations, he would creep into the crevices of their meanderings without warning. Before either of them would realize it, Melissa would smile and begin a tale about one of his escapades or a frown would come upon her and she would stop talking altogether. But, despite Matthew and his devilish ways of intruding upon them, they had grown. They had learned things about one another as two strangers might. Their respect and a genuine caring for one another had evolved to beyond what one might expect of a mother and daughter, they had become friends.

Daphnia felt good about who she was and she had learned to accept, although not necessarily understand, Melissa. She was glad she came to Huron City, but she missed Sunshine Acres, her Papa Tad and Aunt Martha. She missed William and their time spent together. She missed the smell of the grass and the sweet crispness of the apples bursting with flavor. Daphnia was homesick!

Although Thaddeus had sent word back with Herbert that he would be visiting soon, he never made it. Life at Sunshine Acres was more demanding than he had expected and she received a letter from him advising her that with the coming of Carl's and Arlene's twins it didn't look like things would slow down anytime soon. He suggested that she consider making a trip home. When she mentioned this to Herbert he readily agreed that she could use a vacation. As for Daniel, he was downright gleeful. He couldn't wait for Daphnia to be from underfoot so he could have his father to himself.

"You go ahead, Daphnia, don't even think twice about things here. Father and I can take care of things, and I am sure you will enjoy your time with your family," Daniel spoke up without being asked.

"Thanks, Daniel, I believe I will start making plans to leave in a week or so," she was perplexed at his eagerness for her to leave after complaining about how much work he had to do.

She discussed her plans with Melissa during their afternoon visit, and then quickly penned a note to her Papa Tad that she would plan to leave Huron City in two weeks for Sunshine Acres.

Ruth was at the counter of the general store when Daphnia entered. In addition to running the store, Ruth was also the postmistress and operated the telegraph station. If there had been a gossip-processing window, Ruth would have been in charge of that as well. She was centrally positioned within the town and made it her business to keep up with the "goings on" as she called it. She was definitely the next best thing to the Gazette. There were times, in fact, when Herbert would run a piece of news by her before he published it just to test its gossip versus fact quotient.

"Well, well, you are certainly in an excited state, Daphnia, what has happened, a piece of type get stuck somewhere?" Ruth chirped.

"Oh no Ruth, I am sending a letter home to let Aunt Martha and Papa Tad know that I will be coming for a visit. I won't be leaving until the end of the month, but I am a little excited, I guess. It's a beautiful day isn't it? Just think, I will have been here for over three months on Monday. Where has the time gone? Isn't it a beautiful day?"

"Yes, it is dear, it is a beautiful day." Ruth replied while thinking that with Daphnia out from under foot for a little while she could have some time to query Herbert and maybe even pay a visit to Eloise Barnes. And of course, there was Daniel. He had been acting rather strange lately and on several evenings he had stopped her and wanted to talk;

but his timing was always so wrong. He would want to talk when she was dealing with some piece of information or question in her own mind that could unlock some of the mystery surrounding Daphnia and Herbert. Now, she would make it a point to find some time for him. "Yes, yes, dear, it is a wonderful day." she said while walking over to help the young lady and to be sure that the letter was posted properly. "I'll see that this goes with the next mail freight. I know that Martha and Thaddeus will be anxious to hear from you. What about Herbert? You know, Daniel is very busy right now. Are you sure that you leaving for a while won't put extra work on him? I just hate it when he has to work too hard. He is so sensitive."

"I am sure that everything will be fine. I will only be gone for a short time and Daniel won't have to work too much. He never actually comes into the office when I am there anyway, and Uncle Bert is the one who will be keeping up with things. I don't think you have to worry about Daniel being overworked, Ruth, not when I am gone or when I am here, for that matter. Besides, I heard that his friend, what is his name – Sawyer, Saunders, Smathers? Anyway, I heard that his friend would be returning soon to help out. Thanks for getting this on the train with the other mail. I'll be seeing you before I go, after all, it won't be for a couple of weeks."

"Don't worry, Dear, I am sure that things will be fine without you, after all they were fine before you came so why should your leaving for a couple of days make any difference now? It will be for only a couple of days, won't it? I don't want to overburden Herbert or Daniel."

"Have a good day Ruth!"

Chapter Nineteen

The second Sunday of October was cool and clear as Daphnia snuggled further beneath the comforter on the large feather bed. She was excited about returning to Lansing, Sunshine Acres, and seeing her Papa Tad and Aunt Martha. She could almost smell the cinnamon and spices Martha used in her apple dumplings; she could close her eyes and hear the laughter of the great house. She must see Melissa early today. She had bought her a china cup and saucer with lavender lilacs and a gold rim from which to drink her tea. She would give these to her today along with a book of poems tied with a white ribbon. Maybe Melissa would be up to sitting on the back porch this morning, because Daphnia didn't feel like she could be inside today, she was just too excited.

Herbert had also awakened early. He was feeling melancholy, and wishing that Daphnia was not going away. He was missing her already and knew that the days would drag without her. He dressed and headed over to the Gazette, he wanted to see her before she left.

Daniel had spent the evening at O'Connor's talking it up with a group of lumberjacks. They had told him of an old man who used to work with them and travel from camp to camp out in St. Louis and over to Nebraska. Seems that this man followed the same route every spring into fall; that was his territory and he had outposts of what one might call friends along the way with whom he stayed. Daniel wanted to meet this man, and he believed that he held the key to the mystery of how Matthew was killed without anyone caring enough to find out who did it. He knew that there was something tying Thaddeus, Daphnia, Grace, Melissa and probably his own mother and father to his demise, and he was obsessed with the notion of finding out just how they were all involved and to what extent.

"What did you say the name of that old lumberjack was?" he asked the group of men.

"Don't rightly know his real name, but I think he went by the name of Red," one of the lumberjacks spoke up.

"Naw, now Rufus, his real name was Konrad, and they just shortened it to Rad, not Red," corrected the woodcutter sitting next to Rufus.

"Do you have any idea where this Rad might be today, or even if he's still around?"

"What's your interest, mister? He's gotta be pretty old by now if he's stil livin' which I don't expect he is. Last I heard of him he was staying with some Indian squaw up in Omaha. But if you're planning to go looking for him, you better take along someone a bit bigger than you, cause he might be old, but he was the size of a bear when I seen him last, and I don't expect he shortened up any. Unless he's dead, of course," the woodcutter put down two bits and left the bar.

Daniel knew he would go to Omaha and find this Konrad; he had to. Daphnia promised not to be gone long; as soon as she gets back he will leave. He was excited; he had to solve this mystery.

⁂

There was excitement at Sunshine Acres as well. A pounding on the door and the frantic cries of Carl awakened Martha and Thaddeus. Daphnia was not the only one to be going home this day.

"Excuse me, Mr. Flanders, Missus Flanders. Don't mean to be bothering you, but it seems like Arlene has gone into labor and it will take me a while to go in and get the doctor, I think she is having a real bad time. Do you think, Missus Flanders, that you could go on over to the house and help her out some while I go and get Doctor Brewer. I just don't know what happened, she seemed pretty good last afternoon when he was there."

Martha began to tremble and the beads of sweat popped out on her forehead. She was afraid that this might happen, and she was hoping and praying that it wouldn't. She knew she had to be strong and she had to go. "Yes, of course, Carl, I'll get my things together and go right on over there, Thaddeus will take me over in the carriage. Do you think Arlene will be okay until I get there?

"I hope so, Missus Flanders, I surely hope she will be. But, you will hurry right on over there now won't you?"

"You take the automobile, Carl. We will take your buckboard over to your place. You will make better time that way. And, don't worry, Carl, we will be there shortly," Thaddeus said as he tried to push the man along and out the door. Turning to Martha, he could see the distress she was feeling. The round little woman had suddenly become a shivering, bundle of flesh. "Come now, Martha. We can do this. I will be right there with you. Don't you worry, you go ahead now and get your things together."

"No, I don't think I can go, Thaddeus! You go ahead, you know what to do. I need to stay here and get things ready for Daphnia. Please go without me, Thaddeus, please don't make me go. I don't think I can do it. Honestly, Thaddeus, I just can't go," Martha sobbed as she held onto his arm and pleaded with him to leave her there in the comfort of her kitchen and the safety of her secret place beneath the cellar stairs.

"You have to, Martha. You don't have a choice, just like I don't have a choice. Now go get your things, we'll be leaving directly." Thaddeus spoke with firm determination; he knew that he had to.

Coming down the stairs with her bag packed, Martha was as nervous as a cat. She was flustered and scared and didn't like having to leave the safety and comfort of her home. She was not too good at helping others who were in pain, and especially with child bearing. She didn't like the sight of blood and she had a real adversity to watching others suffer. Where was the doctor? Why did men just assume that because she was a woman that she would know what to do? She didn't have a clue as to what to do. If the truth be known, she had never delivered someone else's baby or even seen anything be born. What was it with Thaddeus thinking that she would be okay with this? Didn't he realize that whenever it was calving season, or when the new piglets that Daphnia was so fond of were born that she was never anywhere around? Where did he think she was and just what did he think she was doing? What was the matter with him? Didn't he know these things about her after all of these years? Didn't he understand that this was an impossible task for her to do? Didn't he know that she had never seen anything but her own baby boy be born, and that the memories of that still haunted her? She was puzzled as to why Thaddeus, if no one else, had not noticed this by now. What was she going to do? Her hands were sweaty and she felt like her legs were made of stone. "Thaddeus, can you take this bag please. I want to cut some of those roses to take with us. I think they will cheer Arlene up. There is just nothing like a bouquet of fresh cut flowers to make a woman smile. Now you go ahead and take this bag and I will be right along."

"She can do without roses, Martha. You can do this. Let's go." Thaddeus took her arm and held her close to him. "You can do this Martha, Arlene needs us. She needs us now. She doesn't have time to wait for flowers to be picked or for you to talk to your mother's headstone." He ushered her to the seat of the wagon and climbed in beside her. Within a matter of minutes they were on their way. Thaddeus felt a sense of urgency, and he didn't like it.

Martha was trembling. She was glad that Thaddeus had insisted on Carl taking that loud, belching automobile; she hated riding in it. It seemed ridiculous to her that a piece of steel could be as comforting as the two dependable horses with their broad backsides swaying in a steady rhythm, she was accustomed to the sounds of their hooves landing on the hard dirt road; oh, why did things have to change? Her thoughts were of anything but Arlene and the possibility of her trying to birth twins. "Oh, God Thaddeus, I don't know nothing about birthing twins – I sure hope the doc gets back here before long."

"Now, don't you worry, Martha. I know you are scared. I know. I understand. I'll be right there with you. Now you don't want me having to worry about you and Arlene? You come on now, what if this was Daphnia? Wouldn't you be right there, first in line, helping out, reassuring her that everything would be okay? Now, you just think of Arlene as Daphnia, and you will be just fine." Thaddeus was pushing the horses as fast and hard as he dared. "Lord, I do wish we had brought in some of that dirt from behind the barn and filled in the ruts in this road." He whipped the horses and whistled for them to move along.

Thaddeus was worried and not just about Arlene or Martha. He could feel his chest tightening and there were times that he could barely catch his breath. He pulled the horses off to the side of the road. Getting out of the buckboard, he slowly leaned over and breathed in as much air as his lungs could hold. "I think I'll try walking these horses for a while, Martha. There are so many ruts in this road that I'm afraid if I don't try to lead them through them we might lose a wheel on this buckboard. Damn, if I could just catch my breath," he muttered. Standing straight again, he began to walk slowly leading the horses around the hazards of holes and mud accumulations that looked more like small craters and lava deposits.

"How long do you think it will take us going this slowly, Thaddeus? Don't you think it would be better if you unhitched the horses and rode one of them on in to Carl's and Arlene's?"

"You might have something there, Martha. Maybe I should consider doing that. But, what would I do with you? Do you think you can get up behind me? I sure can't leave you here," he spoke haltingly between gasps. "Maybe I better ride awhile, the road seems to be a little smoother now." He climbed back onto the seat of the buckboard. The sweat beads had popped out on his forehead and his back was soaked. He couldn't hide his heavy breathing any longer; he had to let it out.

"Thaddeus? Are you all right? You don't look too good."

"I'm fine, Mart. I just need to catch my breath. Walking along trying to avoid the pitfalls of this road with its dried mud and rocks takes a lot out of a man. I'm fine. Let's try to get there with as little extra exertion as possible, what do you say? Let's not worry or bring anymore onto each other than we have to right now."

Pulling up in front of the house, Thaddeus had once again regained his composure and his breathing had finally returned to normal. "Let's go in now, Martha. Whatever we see, or whatever state Arlene is in, we won't make a fuss. We will be calm. Are you okay, now? Can you hold it together for Arlene and the babies?"

"I'll be fine, Thaddeus. I can do this. Don't you worry. I won't make a fuss. I'll be fine." Martha was scared. She felt her knees collapse as she stepped down from the buckboard. She could feel her blood racing through her veins. She thought she might faint dead away. "I'll be fine, Thaddeus, just like you said, if this was Daphnia, I would be right there without any worry or fear, and I will be like that for Arlene. Now, let's go in."

Arlene heard the wagon and the horses. She was relieved that someone was here, but she was scared as well. It seemed like hours since Carl had left her all alone in the house and the pains had become a steady and dull ache; there were no longer sharp contractions along her sides and beneath her belly, she felt sleepy and terribly cold. She had as many white cloths as she could find all washed and folded on the table next to the bed. She had prepared the bedclothes and protected the mattress and linens with heavy quilts and a woolen blanket under the muslin sheet. With each minute that passed she found herself biting her lip to keep from screaming out, she was frightened and she wasn't sure she could remain brave. She had been losing large quantities of blood since she came back inside last evening from the porch, and she knew that this could not continue. She found herself floating in and out of consciousness as she prayed, "Dear God, please let my babies be okay."

Again, she collapsed into a foggy sleep. This lightheadedness of moving in and out of reality was becoming all she knew. It seemed she was in a dream state and could barely feel any sensations in her feet and legs or lower body. She awakened when she heard Thaddeus and Martha come inside, but she was too weak to call out or to even look up, and before she was able to realize there was help on its way she was once again unconscious.

As Martha and Thaddeus entered the modest cabin Arlene looked so small and weak. Her face usually full of life and laughter was now drawn and looked like it had been painted with a gray paste.

"Good morning, Arlene, how ya doing, hun?" Martha asked while checking for the woman's pulse and laying the back of her hand against her cheek to check for a fever.

Arlene could not answer, she tried to smile, but couldn't quite manage it. She was so cold, her teeth were beginning to chatter and Martha put another of the heavy blankets over her. "There, there now, Arlene, you just relax and don't you worry. Thaddeus and me are here to help you. Carl is on his way with Dr. Brewer. You just rest."

"You better get those linens ready, Thaddeus, I might need your help here." Martha said in full voice to Thaddeus who was already getting the necessary things together and preparing for a difficult delivery. Birthing babies wasn't strange to Thaddeus; he had done it many times over his lifetime not to mention the dozens of calves and colts that he had helped into the world. Martha, on the other hand, was surprised at herself at the way she took control. It was like she was standing by watching this woman she didn't recognize take charge. In the past she had always just been a hand wringer and worrier when it came to anything that was related to blood or pain.

Thaddeus couldn't have been more surprised at Martha's strength. She had never been the one to take care of anything or anyone who was hurt. Even when Daphnia was small if there was a cut, bruise or scrape,

Martha was usually the one who needed the taking care of more than Daphnia. Martha had never been one to deal well with these things. He shook his head, who was this woman?

Martha took charge. She gently went about checking Arlene out and getting her into position so that she could help get those babies out of their warm comfortable home and into this one, it wasn't going to be easy. Arlene was weak, and Martha was worried about how she would hold up through a sure to be difficult labor. She turned to Thaddeus, "I might need you here, hon, this ain't going to be easy."

Thaddeus came up beside Martha and whispered to Arlene, "now don't you worry, I have done a lot of this sort of thing, ain't nothing to it; you just relax and between Martha and me we'll help those babies along." He had handled some breach calves but not any breach babies, and he had never delivered twins. These babies were more than likely both of those things. Taking a deep breath and trying not to start wheezing and coughing, he said a silent prayer.

"Relax, Arlene, don't push. Just try to relax and the doctor will be here soon." Thaddeus was speaking as softly as he could, he didn't want to alarm her, but he knew that this was a bad thing. He tried to calm her.

As he began to check her out he saw that one of the babies was on its way, he gently urged it along with all the tenderness he could manage. Bringing the baby up he handed it to Martha who cleaned it, wrapped it and had it crying at the top of its lungs before he knew what had happened. The next baby was on its way and the two worked like a team with many years of experience between them.

Once the babies were snuggled next to their mama, Martha went about pulling out soiled linens and covers from beneath Arlene. Dabbing her forehead with a cloth, Thaddeus reassured her that all would be okay and the doctor and Carl would be here soon. Arlene held her babies close and slept peacefully.

Martha went into the kitchen and made a pot of coffee. She and Thaddeus sat and watched Arlene with her two little babies, "there is nothing as precious, is there Thaddeus?" Martha asked.

"No, Martha, there is nothing like a new baby and a healthy mama holding it close."

By the time Carl and Doc Brewer arrived Thaddeus and Martha had cleaned up the cabin, Martha was making up some gingerbread cookies, and Thaddeus was standing on the front porch with pipe in hand and a sense of contentment about him. Carl took one look at his trusted friend and then bolted into the house where he took Arlene and the babies into his arms and cried into her shoulder. He held his babies, laughed, cried and hugged everyone in the small house. Doctor Brewer complimented Thaddeus and Martha on their fine work after he checked Arlene and the babies out. He had a few things left to do, but mostly they had done a good job.

Martha told Carl that she would send over supper and Thaddeus would see to it that things were taken care of over on the farm, so he should just stay here and be with his new babies and Arlene.

Once word of the twin's birth reached the neighbors, casseroles, soups and desserts began streaming into the house. It seemed that once the first wagon of visitors arrived, the whole town began to follow. The streams of friends and neighbors appeared almost endless.

Carl wasn't too sure what to make of everything. Arlene wasn't in any condition to get out of bed, and the twins seemed to take turns needing feeding and diapering. By the time night fell, he was exhausted and ready for some peace and quiet. "We sure won't go hungry around here, Arlene, not for days and days anyway," he said to his wife as he brought her a tray of food. Then putting his arm around her shoulder he gave her a slight squeeze and sat down in the rocking chair. He smiled as he watched her with the babies.

Thaddeus had taken the time to speak with the doctor about his own problems after the excitement of the twin's births, and Doctor Brewer had not held back. He told Thaddeus how sick he was and that getting his house in order would be a wise thing to do. He was happy that Daphnia would be coming for a visit, and he made it clear that Carl needed to get back to work just as soon as possible. Watching the doctor leave with a cloud of dust blowing up behind him, Thaddeus thought about what the doctor had said. He filled his pipe with tobacco and determined that it was time he talk with Daphnia and get some help in the house. He wasn't afraid of dying, but his greater fear was what was going to happen to Martha once he was gone. He knew that she would never be able to live alone nor would she likely keep her senses about her. He smiled as he thought of her bustling around the kitchen making breads and cookies and such while everyone else was openly grieving out in the parlor. She would never accept his death and that lack of her ability to face reality would be her undoing. The smile left his face and he knew his death would hasten hers. It seemed so unfair to him, she was so innocent and so honest.

Once back home on his own front porch, he took out his knife and began whittling, the tears fell silently and his breathing was heavy as he sat there quietly sobbing and grieving the soon to be end of two wonderful lives. He had always tried to be philosophical about death and the act of dying, but just now as he sat on the steps of his porch thinking of what he knew would soon be the end of his own life and that of Martha's soon after, he found that he could not be philosophical. He had tried to believe in her God, and he tried to be faithful and a good person, but the seeds of sins did not stop with his brother Joshua. And, if the truth were known Matthew had come by his way of living honestly. Until this very moment, the hereafter was something that he had never thought about. Thinking about it now made him just a little frightened. He wished that he could talk with her about this, but he knew that he couldn't. He got up and walked into the house and all but ran up the stairs to the sound of her singing. Taking her in his arms and holding her tight he kissed the top of her head and whispered into her hair, "know that I have loved you since the minute I saw you, Mart, and I will love you long after I am dead and buried out there under all those rose bushes. I love, you Martha Flanders, I love you."

As the tears streamed down his face and onto hers, they stood in the room soon to be lived in again by Daphnia and cried holding onto one another. He knew why he was crying, but Martha was not sure, except that it just felt good to stand there leaning into him and releasing all of the emotion that had been bottled up for the past twenty four hours. Then pulling away from him, she wiped away his tears with the corner of her apron. "Now, now, Thaddeus," she said, "everything is going to be just fine come tomorrow, Daphnia will be here. Look don't you think her room looks just like springtime?" she asked holding out her arm as if to show off the bed and bureau. "Now, let's the two of us lock up and turn in for the night. Tomorrow will be a big day, I think maybe I will ride into the station with you, how'd you like that?"

She seemed to speak in a sing song manner and Thaddeus knew she was speaking from her excitement, there was no way that she would get in that automobile and ride into the train station with him. "Okay, Mart, let's get things locked up and settle in for the night. I will want to leave pretty early tomorrow, so you will need to get your beauty sleep. Let's pack a little lunch to take in with us and we can stop along the way and picnic in that grove just outside of town. Any of that chicken left from supper?" he put his arm around her shoulders and guided her out of the room and across the hall.

Once in bed, he decided that he would stop and see Miss Ann before he picked up Daphnia at the station. He had not had time to find out what Daniel had been asking her about and now would be a good time. He wondered if Herbert knew that Daniel had visited Lansing.

Chapter Twenty

Daphnia spent the night on the train leaning against the window and watching the fields and trees fade into a blur of colors across the night sky. She allowed herself to think back to happier times of summer afternoons and crisp fall evenings walking with William and sharing each other's dreams and fantasies. She wondered if he ever thought of these things, and where he might be. As she let her thoughts wander she fell asleep only to be awakened by the noise of the train station in Detroit. She remembered the last time she rode the train through Detroit with the little black family. She wondered how they were. She promised herself that when she returned to Huron City she would make some inquiries and find out how the young Michael and his family were getting along. Thinking of the young man, she soon dropped back off to sleep as the train rocked and moved along the tracks.

Her sleep was not a quiet one, however. The dreams turned into nightmares and the nightmares caused her to awaken, again. She was startled and frightened. She dreamed of Sunshine Acres, but it was a shambles, a pile of debris, and the only thing identifiable for her was the small cemetery and her Aunt Martha's rose garden. She tried to block out the nightmares and think happy thoughts, but she could not seem to shake the feeling of something terrible about to happen, she had a strange urgency to return home.

***

Thaddeus had awakened early and dressed before Martha was out of bed. Giving her a quick kiss he told her that he was on his way into Lansing where he had several stops to make before Daphnia's train was scheduled to arrive. Then out the door and down the road he told himself the first place he would stop would be that of Miss Ann's.

Upon arriving at the stately looking white washed house he knocked on the front door. A young Negro woman opened the door, "Yessir, can I help you?"

"I came to see Miss Ann. I believe she is expecting me. Please tell her that Thaddeus Flanders is here and I would appreciate it if she would step out here on the porch where we could talk."

Ann Bennington came out onto the porch, "Well, Thaddeus, so now I know what it takes to get you to come around, I suppose you are here because of that note I sent you about that Daniel Bernstein. Who is he anyway?"

"He's the son of my oldest and closest friend, Herbert Bernstein from Huron City. What was he doing here? And, Ann, what kinds of questions was he asking?"

"I don't know why he was here. He came in kind of quiet like, said he preferred someone with a little more padding and who was older than my other girls, then he invited me to spend some time with him. He wanted to know at Matthew and how he died. He asked a lot of questions like who killed him, why wasn't anybody ever tried for his murder. But, the oddest question of all was about Grace Humphreys."

"What did you tell him?"

"I told him I didn't know who killed Matthew or why, and as for Grace Humphreys I thought it was pretty common knowledge around here that she was the mother of Matthew's baby girl that you and Missus Flanders raised. He left here and I think he went on over to Boston, at least that is the impression I got from what he said."

"Thanks, Ann, I appreciate you getting in touch with me."

"Thaddeus, wait a minute, my time ought to be worth something, I know you probably don't have in you what you once did, but if you want to come upstairs ….."

"Thanks, Ann, but my days of coming upstairs are long ago over." Then placing two folded bills into her hand, he winked and walked down the steps.

Leaving the porch he wondered about Daniel. Just what would provoke him to make a trip all the way out here and start asking questions? He decided that he would send a message to Herb with the conductor and let him know what Ann had told him. He was sure that Herb would want to contact his attorney in St. Louis and ensure that any information would remain under tight security. "Damn it! Damn Daniel for getting all up into business that he had no right to get involved with," he said aloud as he pondered just what to say and how to say it to Herb.

His next stop was to that of his attorney, John Morgan where he made some updates to his will, and then it was to the office of his accountant where he had to sign some papers. Once he arrived at the train depot, he penned the note to Herb and had it ready to give to the train's conductor. He could see the train pulling into the station and breathed in a deep sigh of relief.

Stepping off the train, Daphnia was glad to be home. Lansing was so clean, the air was crisp and the sky was a robin's egg blue. It didn't seem possible that she had been gone for only a few months. She was eager to be home and to awaken in her own bed with Aunt Martha downstairs making gingerbread cookies, and Papa Tad whittling and puffing on his pipe out on the porch. She looked out and saw him standing there; she was home.

Martha was home fussing and fixing for Daphnia. She was happy and singing as she walked along the path to the garden. It was a brisk morning, and the dew was heavy. The thoughts of these past months had been put behind her for now and she was enjoying the thought of having the house filled with the laughter and excitement that only Daphnia could bring.

On the ride home, Thaddeus and Daphnia got each other as caught up as possible on the various happenings. He told her of the babies born to Carl and Arlene and how Martha had been such a take-charge person through it all. He told her too of what the doctor had told him about his own health, and the preparations that he had made with his attorney and accountant. The only stone left unturned as far as he was concerned was the woman he had hired to come into the house and help Martha. He was certain that would not sit well with her and hoped that Daphnia could help him convince her that it was for the best.

Daphnia told him of her visits with Melissa and how the two of them had become close. She spoke enthusiastically about her work at the Gazette and how beautifully her apartment had been decorated. She spoke of Herbert and Ruth and how comfortable she was in Huron

City. She made sure that he understood that she would be staying on at the Gazette and would not be returning to Lansing to live. This was difficult for him to accept, but he assured her that he understood. He asked that she not speak of this to Martha just yet.

Martha watched as the black automobile came up the roadway toward the house. She waved and wiped her hands on her apron before running out to greet Daphnia. "Welcome home, honey, it has been so long, just let me look at you. Why, I don't believe you have changed one bit. Come on in, you must be starved, do you want biscuits and eggs or would you rather have something more filling?"

"Well, hello to you too, Martha," Thaddeus said with a wink toward Daphnia. "I believe some eggs and bacon would suit me just fine. Do you have any coffee to go with those biscuits or should I draw some water from the pump out back?"

"Oh, my word, Thaddeus, I don't know where my mind is. I have just been in a tizzy waiting for you to bring Daphnia home. I hope everything is done up okay, it seems to take me a lot longer these days to do the simplest of things." She said this without realizing what she had said and regretted saying it immediately.

"That is exactly what I want to talk with you about, Martha. I've been thinking," he began. "I think it is time that we have someone come up here and help you with the house. It is so big and there is so much that needs to be done, I just think it is time that you have help around here, what do you think? How do you feel about it, Daphnia?"

"I agree with you Papa, Aunt Martha needs to kick back and be a lady of leisure now that I am out from under foot. Besides, she will be wanting to go play with those new babies and won't want to be working herself to death around here."

"Now just a minute you two. Is there something that I am not doing that you want done, Thaddeus? Or you, Daphnia?" she asked. "I know that you didn't have your breakfast on the table all served up proper for you the minute you walked into the kitchen, but I wasn't real sure what you would be wanting."

"Oh, Aunt Martha, I am glad you were out front to meet me. I am so happy to be home and whatever you serve is good enough for me," she said as she gave her aunt a hug.

"Well, what about you, Thaddeus? Don't you think bringing someone in to help out is a little extreme? Is there something else, because if I have been neglecting you or some part of my duties around here I just wish you would come right out and say so, yes sir, I just wish you wouldn't beat around the bush none about this? Now suppose you just tell me, Sir, what it is that you want done that I am not doing? Is your bed not as warm and inviting as it used to be, is that it? Do you feel a little mistreated or abused in any way? Looking at you just now, you sure don't seem to be wanting for meat and potatoes. So, tell me Thaddeus, just what is it that you think I need help with? This is my home, your home and Daphnia's home. Haven't I always managed it without any help? Is there something that I have missed?"

"That's not what I am saying, Martha. You have done a wonderful job making and keeping a home for us. But, you just said yourself that it takes you longer to get things done than it used to. I just thought you could use some help, is all."

She was hurt and he could see that the way she was behaving he had somehow managed to do just exactly what he had not wanted to do.

"Thaddeus, I have done everything that I know to do around here, isn't that enough?"

"You have been doing everything and more, Martha. That is just the point you do too much. You have worked so hard all of your life and it seems that you are up before dawn every morning, and it is well into the evening before you settle down any. There is too much, Martha, neither one of us is getting any younger and we can afford to get a little more help around here. I have already spoken with Carl and we agreed that it is time for me to hire someone else for the farm, and if the truth be known, we probably need at least two men. I just thought that you might appreciate a little help around here as well. This is a big house, we don't even use half the rooms, and what with fall right here and winter just a short while away, it might be nice to have someone help with getting things covered and bundled up before the snow and ice sets in. What do you think? Let's kick back a little and take advantage of relaxing out there on that porch swing. Or sitting by the fire and enjoying the quietness of the evening without having to clean up this big old house." He walked up and took her into his arms.

"We'll see, Thaddeus, whatever you think you need to do, you just go ahead and do it. I'm not ready nor none too eager to share my kitchen with another woman, but if you are thinking that to bring in someone to help with the windows, floors and rugs and such then I guess that wouldn't be such a bad idea," she acquiesced, "But" she continued "who ever you get to come in here you make sure that they know this is my kitchen and I'm not ready to turn it over to anyone else, not just yet, anyway, I promise that your breakfast won't be late again." Then wiggling free of his hold on her she got up and walked out the back door.

Taking a handkerchief from her pocket she blew her nose and wiped her eyes, he was right, she wasn't getting any younger and she didn't have the energy she once did. She stood there sobbing, but not really crying. She was just so full of excitement and she wanted to have everything just right for Daphnia. This was going to be a good day. As she leaned against the porch railing she looked out across the yard, she could see Carl. He was already up and out working. She wondered how much sleep he had gotten last night, if any at all. Then thinking of Arlene and the babies she smiled. She would take some fresh bread over to them today; she could get Daphnia to go with her. She was happy to know that there would be babies running around on this place again. It seemed that she had been so busy with getting things ready for Daphnia that she hadn't thought much about Carl and his family. Now seeing him out there with the morning mist around him and the sun peeking up over the horizon, she thought of what a good man he was and how much he and Arlene meant to one another. Thaddeus came up and sat next to her. Taking her hand in his he told her he loved her and that everything was going to be okay.

As he hugged her close to him, Thaddeus saw Carl walking toward them; he had a smile on his face. As he whispered to Martha, Thaddeus straightened the both of them up and then speaking out to Carl he stood "good morning there Carl, what's got you up and out so early?"

"There's a new baby calf Mr. Flanders, yes sir, there's a new baby calf born just after midnight to 'ole Bessie. I thought that I should check on her last night and sure enough she was ready and between the two of us we popped that calf out and they are both just fine this morning. Unusual as hell ain't it? Seems babies of all kind are popping out everywhere" he said as he slapped the older man on the shoulder. "that coffee sure smells good, Ma'am, would you mind if I shared a cup with you?"

"Of course not, Carl, come on in and tell us about the calf. How about some bacon and eggs, I just took out a pan of biscuits and we have fresh apple butter, won't you come on in?" Martha said with glee. She was so grateful for Carl, it seemed that he always came at the right time. And regardless of his own need, it seemed that he was always there to make her feel better or to rescue Daphnia from some danger or something. He was the most unselfish man she had ever met.

"Where's Miss Daphnia?" Carl asked looking around the kitchen.

"I'm right here, Carl. How is Arlene? I heard about the twins, I can hardly wait to see them. Maybe I can take a ride over later? Do you think Arlene is up to some company?"

"I think she would like that, Miss."

Thaddeus pushed his chair to one side and took out his pipe as he filled it with fresh tobacco he spoke quietly, "I've told Martha about what you and I have been thinking, Carl, it seems that this place gets bigger and more to care for everyday. Not just out there with the animals, crops and the out buildings, but in here as well. When Martha and I first moved into this house we had planned on a big family with a dozen or more children, and eventually grandchildren, well that hasn't happened and it isn't likely that it will. The long and the short of it, Carl, is that it is just more than we can take care of anymore. Now, you, you are younger than me, you have worked this land right along with me and you treat it as if it were your very own, I trust you, and I know that you feel at home right here. I know that you will make the decisions that need to be made if I am not around, gone for some reason, or just need you to pick up the slack or make a decision that I would make if I were around to do so. I would like for you to accept a bigger responsibility, Carl. How would you feel about signing on as a part owner of this place? It's a gift from Martha and me to you, Carl. I'm not asking you to buy into anything. I want to give it to you. I want you to be part owner of what you have helped to build. I've set up a meeting between the legal minds and myself for tomorrow, I have seen John Morgan and I have already put some things down on paper – I've freed up some of the burden of this place so to speak. Daphnia and I have talked about this and we are in agreement on how we think things should be. Besides, this would be a good opportunity for you what with your two new babies. Your place is so small, and you can stay there of course, but if you want to build a bigger place here you just name your spot." Then turning to Daphnia he asked, "Daphnia, do you have anything you want to add to this conversation? Do you have any concerns?"

"No, Papa, I feel comfortable with what we discussed earlier, and I am in full agreement with whatever you and Carl decide."

"Well, Carl, what do think?"

Carl sat there looking at the older man and wondered just what was going on in his head. He had always admired Mr. Flanders, but had never really thought of him in any other way than as the boss. Now, it seemed that something had changed. He knew that he was trusted, and he knew that he was thought of favorably, but as a part owner in this farm? That just didn't add up. "Say, Mr. Flanders, I don't think so well sittin', how about if me and you take a little walk and maybe talk about this man to man, so to speak. Miss Daphnia, would you care to join us? No offense, Missus Flanders, I just need to walk while I talk, I seem to think better when I'm moving around a bit?"

"No offense taken, Carl. I understand about men talking business. You all go ahead and get out from under foot, I have plenty to do right here and what is decided will be just fine with me." Martha was glad to have them leave her alone. She was feeling tense and needed to put some things in place in her own mind.

Daphnia had talked about this with her Uncle and had agreed with his gift to Carl. She had no need to walk with them, "Carl, you and Papa go ahead, if you don't mind I think I would like to ride over and see Arlene and the babies."

"She'd like that, Miss."

The two men left the house and Daphnia went out to saddle her horse. Martha was left alone with her thoughts and her baking.

As they walked out toward the barn, Thaddeus told Carl what was really on his mind, "I guess the best way to say this Carl is to just come out with it. I know the timing is bad, but I haven't a choice. Doc told me to get my affairs in order, he doesn't give me a lot of time and I need to know that you will be here to keep an eye on Martha for me. I know that with Arlene just having two babies she won't have a lot of time to help out, but anything the two of you can do will surely be appreciated. I know this won't be easy for you running this place as your own, but, Carl, this isn't going to be easy for Martha."

"I've signed forty-nine percent of this place over to you. I want you to fix up your place, or move on up here if you want. We have plenty of room. We can even build you a new place anywhere on the property that you choose. Of course, Daphnia will get the remaining fifty-one percent, but I don't expect her to ever come back here to live. I know that she and that young Johnston will end up marrying, but who knows where they will settle. You will be the one running the place and I don't think that will bother Daphnia none at all."

"Now, just a minute, Mr. Flanders, you seem to be taking a lot of things for granted. Daphnia just might want to come back here and raise her family. She might have different ideas about who runs this place, so to speak. I think that William Johnston might have a thing or two to say about who will be in charge once they marry. Have you run this past Daphnia?"

"Yes, Carl, I have. She has assured me that she doesn't have any objections, as a matter of fact, before I finished telling her of my plans, she suggested the very thing herself. Daphnia is a smart young woman and she knows what's going on."

Carl grew quiet, maybe he needed to listen and hear this thing out. Thaddeus continued. "Tomorrow you will need to hire at least one new man, if you find two go ahead and hire them. You also need to bring one of the men over from the dairy to help you here. And, Carl, that orchard is getting to be more and more work every year, maybe we should take down some of the apple and cherry trees; but, you make that decision later on your own. I expect that you and I will be spending a few weeks just going over the books and you learning what it really takes to run this place. Does that sit alright with you?"

"Well, so far, I guess I can give it a try. But, I'm still not sure that I'm ready to spend more time behind a desk full of papers and less time out here with the animals and the crops."

"Good, there's one other thing. I'll want a woman to come in here and stay with Martha and help her out around the house. I've already planted the seed, but she is going to put up a fuss. I want her to have some time to get used to having someone else around. The woman you hire should be someone that won't want to make a lot of changes. She needs to be calm, quiet, sort of keeping to herself so to speak. Martha won't accept any busybody or some woman who wants to be up into her business. I was hoping that you and Arlene would want to move in here and let Arlene sort of begin to take care of things easy like. I know that Martha wouldn't object to that." He was talking fast and low for fear that Martha would decide to come after them to see the calf herself. "I spoke with John Morgan this morning and met with the accountants. I have already written a letter to Herbert Bernstein and will send it in with you tomorrow. You will need to take it to Bill Raines in Lansing; he's the engineer for the 2:15 that leaves here on Saturday. He will deliver it personally to Herbert. Herbert is a reasonable man, but sometimes he gets caught up in his own dealings and I want to be sure that he will understand if and when I have to call Daphnia back on short notice."

With that said, Thaddeus put his hand on the shoulder of his new partner. "You've been a good friend, Carl; I appreciate you and what you have done for my family and me over these years. In case, I haven't said that often enough, please know that I am saying it now."

Carl didn't know what to say. He was faced with a sense of loyalty and dedication to his old friend, but wasn't one to act hastily. He wanted to talk this over with Arlene, and he still had some questions in his mind about how Daphnia might feel. After all, she was blood. The other thing that worried him was how Mrs. Flanders would handle things. He had seen her when she was all a dither, and he didn't relish the thought of having to handle her should something happen to Thaddeus. Finally, after several minutes of silence Carl finally had enough courage to speak, "how long does the doctor give you, Mr. Flanders?"

"Not long, he told me when Daphnia left in June that it could be as few as a couple of weeks and as long as six months, but that I should prepare for it to happen, and happen suddenly. I have been to the bank and the lawyers and all of the financial papers are in order, I have left you your house, the land extending out twenty acres in all directions around it and have given you forty-nine percent of the rest of the properties, designated you as the manager of Sunshine Acres as you have been doing with the exception of the business decisions; those will be made by yourself, John Morgan and Herbert Bernstein. The remaining fifty-one percent will be in Daphnia's name and it will all be placed in a trust for her with the exception of what it will take to run this place and make the appropriate repairs and expansions." Thaddeus stopped and leaned against a tree stump. "Damn, has that barn moved? It sure is a lot further out here than I remembered" trying to catch his breath he sat down on the ground and leaned against the stump. Taking out his handkerchief and wiping away the perspiration that had formed on his brow, he looked up at Carl, "now don't you start worrying about me already, I'll be fine, just a little winded all this walking and talking at the same time just got me a little tired is all. Now, I mean to do right by you Carl, what do you think of what I have said so far?"

"Now, Mr. Flanders, you know that I will do whatever you want me to do. Of course I think you have done right by me, I just don't know if I can accept all of this without first talking with Arlene." Carl spoke softly. It bothered him to talk about such things as money, wages and being given something that he had not properly earned. He stood there next to the man he had come to know and respect for what he stood for as much as for who he was and as he dug his toe into the ground and felt more like a teenager than a grown man in his thirties, he stammered a little, "you see, I'm just not so sure that I have earned all that you want to give me. I don't know if you understand that or not."

Thaddeus understood all right, he understood that he just needed to be patient. "Of course I understand, Carl, you don't have to worry. We do need to go ahead and get those men hired tomorrow and that letter delivered, though. Now, let's go see that calf, we still have a lot to do." He picked up a fallen branch and used it for a cane as he walked the rest of the way to the barn.

Entering the barn with its smell of hay and oats and the animals, it was what this place and Thaddeus was all about. He breathed deeply taking in the smells of his surroundings. Walking over to the stall where the new calf was nuzzling 'ole Bessie, he looked up at the rafters and thought of the craftsmanship that went into building this barn. Then kneeling down to pat the head of the red and white calf with its coarse curls and wide-open pink mouth, he said to Carl, "you know, I think we will need an addition to this ole barn next spring. What do you think, should we build off to the side or out back there?" he pointed to beyond the stalls where Carl was standing.

"Well, I don't like the idea of going off to the side there, sir, that stand of pines is just too close for comfort for me and I think if we go out back here we will have more space to spread out and maybe put in that little corral that we've talked about for so long. Course, if you want to go off to the side ...." Carl let his voice trail-off, he knew that Thaddeus had only asked the question to see how he would respond. "Damn it, Mr. Flanders, I love this place, it is my home, I can't imagine ever living anywhere else, I guess I'll just have to lay it on the line with Arlene the way you have done with me. I guess you got your answer all right. We'll stay out at our place as long as we can, and then when we need to move in up here, we will. In the meantime, I will bring someone in from town to help out Missus Flanders." Then closing the gate on the stall Carl and Thaddeus turned and walked back to the house without speaking more.

Martha had been watching the two men make their way out to the barn. She was curious as to why they stopped, and when she saw that Thaddeus was using a stick to balance himself, she started shaking and could not stop. She went down into the cellar and sat very, very still in the corner beneath the stairs. She took one of the old quilts from a table nearby and wrapped it around her shoulders. As she sat there with her teeth shattering she stared off into the space in front of her. She had sat here many times before. Times when Thaddeus had left and Daphnia was away in school and the weather looked bad. Or the time when she heard the cattle moaning as a wild fire raced across the pasture and burned down the first barn they had built. There were cows and calves inside, Thaddeus and every hired man on the place had fought the fire with all they had, while they had won in the end and managed to put the fire out before it reached the house, it had taken the lives of twenty head of cattle, one farm hand and a black mare with her new foal. She had spent many nights here huddled in this very corner with Daphnia and Thaddeus upstairs sleeping not knowing that she had awakened from a nightmare and could not let them see her fear. Martha trembled but she did not cry, she was too scared to cry. She refused to close her eyes because she knew if she did she would see the image of Thaddeus limping out to the barn leaning against a broken branch, something was wrong, yes, she was sure that there was something dreadfully wrong. She heard his footsteps up in the kitchen, he was calling out for her, but she just sat very, very still. He would go out the front near the roses, he always did, and then she would be able to stand again and go back up to her warm kitchen. She would be okay in just a little while, she just needed to sit here for a minute and be sure that it was his voice she heard and his footsteps walking across the floor, she could imagine him, his tall muscular frame, his tan skin, his eyes, and the laugh line around his mouth. Thaddeus, so full of life, yes she would be okay. As she heard the front door close behind him, she stood, folded the quilt and placed it back on the table. Then straightening her dress and apron, she pushed the loose strands of white hair back under the combs and walked back upstairs as if she had just been out back picking a tomato from the garden, or sweeping off the back steps.

Thaddeus returned to the house back in through the front door as he had left. "Well, it is all settled, Mart. Carl and Arlene will move in here with those new babies in a few weeks, just in time for winter. Won't it be wonderful to have them around? We have so much room in this big old house that we need to fill it up. I'll open the back of the house upstairs and make a room just for them. Arlene and Carl can sleep in the room across the hall, and won't it be wonderful Martha?"

"It does sound good, Thaddeus. But, they don't have to wait. They can move on in now. That way, I'll have Arlene here to help out with things and you won't have to bring in some woman from town. I like Arlene a lot, she is like me, she minds her business and that is important. You tell Carl not to worry about two women in the kitchen, I will be happy to share my baking pans with Arlene."

"That sounds good to me, Martha, I'll be sure to tell him how you feel. Arlene might not be ready to move just yet though, we'll work it out. Is that Daphnia coming up the back? Maybe I'll go talk with her and let her know what we've decided." Then giving Martha a pat on the backside, he left the kitchen and walked out to meet Daphnia.

Martha watched him walk out to where Daphnia was standing and then she went back inside. Humming a tune and taking the combs out of her hair only to replace them and then out again and back in again until she finally took them all out and laid them on the kitchen table. She opened the cellar door and ran down the stairs and over to the table of blankets and quilts. Taking out a favorite quilt she once again returned to the corner beneath the staircase. She gently removed a block of wood and lifted from behind it a small metal box. Opening the box she began to sing a lullaby as she fingered each of the small things laying inside, first a little shirt with blue embroidery and then pressing it to her face she held it there and breathed in softly. The tears streamed down her cheeks as she continued this same ritual with each and every item that had been so gently packed, unpacked and packed again into the safety of the silver box.

Chapter Twenty-One

Daphnia was happy to hear that Carl had agreed to the proposition of her uncle. She felt good about Arlene coming to live in the big house and knew that she would get along well with her aunt. She felt that the decisions that needed to be made were made and now it was a matter of waiting. She hugged her uncle and told him she loved him, she knew that she would miss this man and she told him so.

Martha did not hear the back door open and was awakened by the laughter and voices of Daphnia and Thaddeus coming into the kitchen. She woke up startled and somewhat disoriented. Trying to remove the blankets and stand up, she bumped the table upsetting the rest of the quilts stacked on top of it and then with her feet numb from being tucked up beneath her for so long, she fell onto the heap of blankets and quilts. Reaching for something to save her, she knocked over a box of canning jars she had placed on the table and the noise carried up to the kitchen.

"Mart, Mart, you down there? Are you all right?" Thaddeus called down the basement stairway. Then in a full run with Daphnia following behind him, he went down the stairs and stopping only to light one of the lanterns hanging on the wall, he rushed over to where she was lying in a heap of blankets and canning jars with her apron over her face. "Oh, Martha, are you all right, Oh, Martha." Thaddeus cried and laughed all at the same time. "What on earth are you doing down here? Why didn't you have a lantern with you if you were coming down here after canning jars? Oh, Martha," he said as he helped her up laughing and hugging her while trying to wipe away the hair from her face.

"Oh, Aunt Martha, it is so good to be home. You are just the same as always. I could smell your ginger bread cookies before I ever got inside the house." She said as she hugged and kissed Martha, and laughed with her Uncle. Nothing had changed here at Sunshine Acres, nothing at all, or so it seemed, and somehow she could feel the sense of good-bye in the air. It was the unsaid words, the exaggerated laughter that seemed a little forced and nervous and it lasted a little too long, it was in the emphasis of the word love, and the hugs that were too tight. There was fear that emanated from her aunt and a dread that was like a black cloud over the head of her uncle. No, nothing was the same; everything had changed.

Martha soon regained her balance, but not her dignity. She was more than embarrassed; she was also a little ashamed of letting them believe she was actually getting canning jars when that was never her intent. She turned and walked up the stairs. Grabbing the combs off the kitchen table she pushed them into her hair.

Thaddeus went up after her. He knew they had startled her. He wanted to tell her that he had known about her secret corner for a very long time now, but he didn't. He had found it many years ago after their little baby boy had died. He remembered it as if it were just yesterday. He had awakened in the middle of the night to find her gone from the bed. He looked into every room and even went out to the cemetery, but he couldn't find her. Then as he came back inside he saw that the cellar door was ajar and he tiptoed down the steps only to see her sitting in the corner covered with the blankets and quilts holding a blue and white bundle and softly humming while rocking the empty blanket. He could see that she had been crying and this would not be a good time for him to call out to her. She needed some time to be alone with her loss and grieve for the baby that she wasn't allowed to keep. He checked the corner from time to time after that, but never violated her space or the things that she kept there. Even during times when the weather would turn bad and they were forced to take to the cellar for shelter, he made it a point to avoid the corner, he never mentioned it nor did he ever look at it. It was hers, and he respected that. But, today was a little different, he had heard the clamor of Martha falling and things falling around her and he had to go to her, he could not take the chance that she might be hurt. Now, as he walked up the steps behind her, he was sorry that he didn't call out to her or make more noise coming in to give her a chance to save her dignity. He was just so excited; he didn't expect her to be anywhere but in the kitchen.

As he reached the top step he patted her on the shoulder, "sure hope those canning jars aren't too badly damaged, it would sure be a shame to miss out on that applesauce that you had planned to put up in them." He just kept walking straight down the hall and out the front door where he stood and looked out over the rolling hills called Sunshine Acres.

Down in the cellar, Daphnia refolded the blankets and quilts and placed them back on the table. She picked up the last quilt and noticed that it had been laid out onto the floor as if someone had been sleeping on it. She stooped down to look at where the quilt had been and she found one of her shoes propped against the wall, a box with some letters that had been written by her Papa Tad years ago before he and Aunt Martha were married, a small crocheted blanket of blue and white yarn, and a tiny stuffed toy. There was also a small box of dried rose petals and a baby bootie. She looked at all of these things that were stacked or folded neatly in a metal crate, she determined that this was more than a place for her Aunt Martha to store canning jars and blankets, it was her special place and there had indeed been a pallet of sorts made with the quilts on which her Aunt Martha had been sleeping. Replacing the quilt to the stack with the others, and returning the odd collection of things to their sacred place, she went back upstairs. She was concerned about her Aunt Martha, was this really the same person whom she had known all of these years. Now, it seemed there was something more to her Aunt's flusters than she had previously thought. She decided that she would discuss this with her Papa Tad later.

Thaddeus came back into the house and taking her into his arms he held her close and whispered, "I love you," in to her ear. "We must talk with Daphnia while she is here, Martha, it is time that we let her know the truth. I should never have let her go off to Huron City like I did without telling her myself. Now, I know I may have waited too long, but what is done is done, and I have to fix things."

"Now, now, Thaddeus, you just go on so, you are making way too much of this. There is enough going on here to worry about. Daphnia is just fine with whatever it is that she knows and don't know. Now come on over here and help me with this jar of peaches, I can't seem to get the lid off"

"Please listen to me, Mart, I need your help with this. You know that I love Daphnia as if she was our very own, but she isn't and it is time that she knows the truth. Who knows, she may want to know something about Grace Humphreys and who she was and from where she came, God only knows there is enough mystery there." He was pleading with his wife; she continued to ignore him and went about her way humming and talking to herself about how much cinnamon, and where was the nutmeg, and such.

"Martha, listen to me. Daniel Bernstein has been to Lansing. He stopped and spoke with a woman in town who knows me and she told me that he was there asking questions. I don't believe Melissa has said one word to Daphnia about who she really is, and if we don't do it I think Daniel will. And, believe me, he won't be so concerned with how she might feel about things."

"I don't want to talk about this right now, Thaddeus. You do what you think you should, after all it isn't like you have ever asked me what you should or shouldn't do before, now you are asking me what I think about two different things all on the same day. As far as I am concerned she is here for a while and I intend to enjoy it."

Daphnia had stopped on the top step; she wanted to know more about what it was that Melissa didn't say and that Daniel might. Yes, she would have her answers before she returned to Huron City, she would talk with Papa Tad, he wanted to tell her, and she wanted to know. Coming into the kitchen she saw that her Aunt Martha was busy trying to straighten things up and ignore Thaddeus as she fussed with her baking pans and rolling pin.

"Okay, Mart, but you need to be ready when she starts asking questions," he said as he spun around to see Daphnia standing within three feet of him. "Good Lord, Daphnia, where did you come from you startled me."

"I have just been busy down stairs trying to straighten up that pile of blankets and those canning jars. Whatcha cookin' Aunt Martha?" Daphnia asked as she went over and embraced her aunt. She had missed the goodness of this place and the warmth and love that seemed to abide here with them. "Those ginger bread men sure look good," she said as she took one off the sideboard where it had been left to cool earlier in the morning. "Sit with me, Papa Tad, let's enjoy these and pretend that they are still warm."

"Well, I will sit, but there is not a chance that I will spoil my dinner, besides I want you to walk with me out to the barn, there is a new calf just born last night, and there are some things that we need to discuss," he said this while sending Martha a sideways glance. Martha kept working like she didn't even hear him.

"You will have to go upstairs and get some of those things unpacked before you go tramping off to look at anything, Daphnia. There will be plenty of time to get serious and talk about things that have rested quietly for a long time without bringing them up now and causing hurt and pain now Thaddeus. And, I don't want another word about it until tomorrow." Then wiping her hands and untying her apron, Martha threw the apron down on the table and walked from the kitchen and out the front door. Thaddeus and Daphnia knew where she was headed, but they also knew that they needed to do as she wanted, at least for now.

Finishing the ginger bread man and her milk, Daphnia put away the dish and glass and then giving her uncle a little wink took her uncles arm; the two of them went out the back door and to the barn. "What has you so troubled, Papa?" she asked.

"Let's sit over here, Daffy Girl on this bail of hay, there are a few things we need to talk about."

"Daffy Girl" she was suddenly frozen. How long had it been since anyone had called her that she wondered. That was the name that William gave her. God she missed him. She closed her eyes and thought of their last picnic together. She could still remember the way he touched her, the way he smelled and the smoothness of his back. She could almost hear his laughter. A tear fell from her eye as she remembered too the last time she saw him, and kissing him goodbye; she would write to him this evening and go over to see his Mother and brothers and sisters tomorrow.

"Daphnia, Daphnia, are you listening to me, there is a lot that we need to talk about and it requires you to listen at least."

"Oh, I'm sorry, Papa, I guess I just got lost in my own memories for a moment, please forgive me, now what were you saying."

"I was trying to tell you about what I have asked from Carl. A lot has happened Daphnia. For one thing the farm is too much for me to manage alone anymore and I am too old. I can no longer stay on top of things the way I once did. Carl will stay on, I'm giving him forty-nine percent of the place with the exception of our home and the immediate area surrounding it. But, he doesn't have some of the business experience and decision-making abilities that he will need to keep the farm in good order and to make sure that things are taken care of like they need to be. I am having the lawyers and accountants take on more of that end of, and I am depending on you, Daphnia to keep an eye on things as well. After all, the other fifty-one percent is yours. I am sending Carl into Lansing tomorrow to hire at least one new man and also a woman to come up here and help out your Aunt Martha until Arlene feels like she can move in with the babies. Martha needs to have someone around to help her keep things in order here in the house. She is not strong, Daphnia, and when I go ..."

"What is it exactly, papa?

"I am old, Daphnia. Some of my parts don't work the way they used to. Doc Brewer has been upfront with me and he has told me to get things in order. I don't expect to die right here and now, but I'm not going to live forever, and some days it seems like making it to sunset is all I can hope for. But, this is not about me. It's about your Aunt Martha and this place. It's about you and my legacy, or what little legacy I might have. This place is what I have poured my blood and sweat into for more years than you have been here on this earth, and I don't plan to leave it to the jackals to tear apart with their probates and court expenses. I want things in order now, today! I want to make sure that Martha is taken care of, that you are taken care of and that I leave a footprint on this earth that means something. Now, I don't want to talk about me right now, it is enough that you know the doctor has told me to get my affairs in order and that's what I am going to do."

"What do you want me to do?" She walked away from him and looked out over the land as the tears filled her eyes and spilled out over her cheeks. "What will we do without you? If Carl is not ready to take on the responsibilities of managing Sunshine Acres, and with me down in Huron City ... maybe I should come home. I'll come home, Papa. I'll go into Lansing and wire Uncle Bert. I'll tell him that I need to stay a little longer. I won't leave again."

"Daphnia, now don't you go making plans to stay here and wait for me to die. We are going to go on with our lives. We are not going to stop doing what we normally do. Martha knows we need more help around here. She has even agreed to have someone come in and help her around the house, and she likes the idea of Arlene and the babies moving in. So, let's not jump to conclusions. I don't think I could stand it if you were here just waiting for me to pass on. You have a life. If you decide to stay here because that is what you want then good, but if you are staying here just to wait for me to die, then don't. I don't want you to argue with me about this."

"Okay, papa."

"Now there is something else that is more important than the legal issues and whether or not Martha will accept help around here that we need to discuss."

"I am worried about her, Papa, she doesn't seem herself to me. And, there is a silver box in the cellar with mementos, and one of my shoes, it is eerie; I think she has been sleeping down there."

"I know, dear, it has been there for over forty years. It is not the finding of her pallets and precious memories that upset her, it is the fact that we found her there, the combs out of her hair on the kitchen table, the half finished ginger bread men, the apple cobbler still not in the oven, the little things that she does or doesn't do trouble me. I worry about her too, and I don't think she will last too long after I am gone, Daphnia, do you understand why you must remain strong?"

"I have always known that she doesn't handle pain or blood well. Does she know what Doc Brewer has told you?"

"No, she doesn't. After Carl took you to the train station last summer, while I was upstairs feeling like my chest had one of them red hogs sitting on top of me, she was downstairs making cookies and tea. She just can't handle reality and she thinks that if she ignores it that maybe it will go away. It won't, Daphnia. You must be strong. Doc Brewer told me back then that I was looking at not more than one or two months; both of them are gone already. How long are you staying?" He asked trying to change the subject.

"I will be leaving on the train out of Lansing a week from Thursday, that's not real long, but I plan to come back for Christmas."

As Thaddeus took out his knife and picked up a piece of wood to start whittling, he looked back toward the house and saw Martha standing on the back porch.

Chapter Twenty-Two

Martha had overheard the doctor asking Thaddeus how he felt when Arlene's babies were born, and she had heard them talking right after Daphnia left for Huron City. She had been trying to prepare herself for the inevitable, but it wasn't easy. She knew that he didn't think she knew what was going on but she did. She worried about how she would survive without him. She knew that was the reason that he wanted to hire more people to help out. She was glad that Daphnia had come home now, God forbid that he leave her at all, but she prayed that if he was to go that he do it when Daphnia was close by. She wanted to stop all of her thinking and stop the spinning of her mind, but she could not. Everything that she touched and all that she said included a farewell, she knew once he was gone she would lose her mind and that scared her almost as much as being alone.

She watched them walking toward her. She wondered what they were talking about? Her, probably! Maybe he was telling her about Grace and Melissa; or maybe he was telling her about his frequent gasps for air, and the pain in his chest. Watching the two of them coming toward her, she knew that they had been talking, and she hoped that he had gotten it all out because she didn't think she could handle much more of it. She had already scratched away much of the skin on both of her forearms from worry and nerves and she just couldn't continue this way. She was going to walk out to meet them and tell him so, too. She had had quite enough. Walking off the porch and putting her hands on her round hips she looked at them both, and with a matter of fact tone that she had rarely used, she stood tapping her toe, "Thaddeus, Daphnia, have the two of you solved all of the problems of the House of Flanders? Because if you haven't you just stay right out here until you do, because let me tell you both something right now, I have had enough. Do you understand me? I won't hear another word about sickness, dying, who is the mother of who and not another word about Melissa, Grace Humphreys, or Matthew either for that matter. This house has had just quite enough and that's all I have to say about it. So, Thaddeus, if there is something that hasn't been said, you just better get it said, and I mean now." She turned and went back inside the house and slammed the door behind her. Thaddeus and Daphnia looked at each other and shook their heads.

Before they could regain their composure, the door opened almost as quickly. Returning to the porch and wiping her hands on her apron and in the same matter-of-fact manner she looked at Daphnia, "Daphnia, you are going to need another blanket or quilt tonight, so you might as well go on up to the attic and get it out now. As for you, Mr. Flanders, I have a lot to do and don't want you worrying me to death about things that are done and can't be undone, we have our family together for just a little while, let's enjoy it. Daphnia, come on in here now and help me get things finished up so that I can get supper started." She turned and went back inside. As she heard the door slam behind her she stopped to look back at them staring after her. "Well, Daphnia Jean, get it on up now and let's get to work, there is enough to be done that will take us right up to sunset if we let it, come on, I need your help," she opened the door and stood there waiting for Daphnia to come inside which is exactly what Daphnia did without saying another word.

As they went into the kitchen, Daphnia had not remembered ever seeing things in such a mess, there were ginger bread men on the sideboard, a half put together cobbler with a mixture of peaches and apples, (she wondered how that would taste), and then there were dishes from morning still on the table along side one of Martha's combs. This was definitely not like her Aunt Martha.

"What's the matter, Aunt Martha? What has happened to get you into such a state?"

"Oh, Daphnia, there is so much that has happened. Arlene and them babies and Thaddeus being so sick, I just know he is going to kill over dead any day now, Doc Brewer told him a couple of months at best and it has been all of that, then with that Daniel Bernstein about to tell you all about your father and Grace Humphreys, and you up there in Huron City all alone knowing that your whole life you believed Melissa was your mother who didn't love you, now to find out that she was never your mother after all and your real mother was a widow woman that Matthew took up with while Melissa's own mother was laying there dying. Then to top it all off, Grace Humphreys, died leaving Matthew alone with no one to help raise you, and nobody knowing the first thing about her or where she came from. I am so sorry for not letting Thaddeus tell you when he wanted to, but I just couldn't stand to see you hurt, can you forgive me. Why would that young Daniel get hisself involved with all of this? What's it to him, anyway? I am so sorry that I didn't tell you when you was little. Daphnia, please say that you forgive me. I can see now that I was wrong, you are going to hear from a total stranger that your life was all a lie. I should have listened to Thaddeus, but I was just afraid, and for no reason at all." She put her arms around Daphnia and held her close. But Daphnia did not hug her back.

Daphnia was emotionless. It was like hearing the man in the uniform say that her father was dead. She was numb. She could not feel any pain. She could not feel anything. She heard her Aunt say that Melissa was not her real mother, and that it was a woman named Grace Humphreys. That is what Melissa kept hidden from her. She had heard the name, and she had heard rumors, but what was this she was being told? Is that why every time she would ask about being a baby, or her father, Melissa would skirt the issue or change the subject? So, that was what Melissa wasn't telling her. That was why Melissa looked at her so mysteriously, that was why she didn't look as much like Melissa as she did Matthew. But, the real truth was she probably looked more like Grace Humphreys than either of them. How could she have been so dense, how could she have not known this sooner? How could they have kept this from her for so long? And, of all people to ferret this out, Daniel Bernstein! How dare he! What was her lineage to him? Was he that jealous of her? She sat down to keep from falling, she felt faint, and she needed a drink of water but she couldn't speak.

Martha, seeing Daphnia's reaction, realized that it wasn't until this very minute that Daphnia knew the truth, and she had been the one to blurt it all out in one fell swoop without giving one minute of thought to the proper timing.

Daphnia felt ill, she knew she was going to be sick, she got up and bolted out the back door where she ran into the back yard and leaning against one of the pine trees she allowed herself to give way to her body's need to release itself of her stomach's contents. Then she walked out across the pasture and into the barn where she unhooked the dipper form the peg next to the water bucket, she dipped it into the cool clear liquid. As she held it to her mouth to drink she allowed some of the water to run down her chin and she wiped it across her neck, the coolness of it was refreshing to her.

"Need a rag to dry off with, Miss?" Carl said as he handed her a rag. "Its good to see you back home, your Uncle and Aunt sure enough missed you while you was away. Did you see the new calf?" He asked as he pointed over to the stall.

"Oh, Carl, thanks, but I saw the calf earlier. Did I tell you congratulations? I have only been home for a little over six hours and it seems that there has been enough said to last weeks." She said as she touched his shoulder. "I'll help you throw down the hay if you want."

Walking over to the stall where the calf and Ole' Bessie were sleeping peacefully, Daphnia felt so grown up, it seemed that for whatever reason, she was no longer the young girl who left here with her head filled with romantic dreams. She was a woman who had, in just a few short hours found out that the man who had raised her was dying, the woman who had loved her and treated her as if she were her own was losing control of her senses, and the woman she had always thought to be her real mother was not at all, and that Daniel Bernstein a man with whom she had little regard was about to use information about her that he had no right to. Surely, she was dreaming because she was too calm. With all of this how could she be so calm she wondered?

As Daphnia and Carl were getting ready to pitch the hay into the feeding troughs, she looked up to see Thaddeus standing next to the stall door. "Oh, Papa why didn't you tell me? How could you allow me to go to Huron City believing that I could convince Melissa to love me, she never really wanted me and I was such a fool, and you let me make such a fool of myself, how could you let me, who was Grace Humphreys, and why didn't you tell me sooner? Why have you left this to that miserable and mean Daniel Bernstein to be the one to shatter my beliefs?" she sobbed.

"Let's go back to the house, Daphnia, it is getting cold out here and Carl has work to do before the sun sets," he said as he started walking with her across the pasture.

As they approached the steps leading up onto the back porch, Thaddeus stopped, and turning to face Daphnia he placed his hands on her shoulders, "Daphnia," he began, "we should have told you long ago, but it just seemed that there was never the right time. In the beginning we waited for you to get old enough to understand, and then it just became too easy to put it off. All the while that we were waiting for that right moment to arrive, we were digging ourselves into a deeper hole and it was soon obvious that there was never going to be a right time, so we may as well just wait. Please try to understand, we didn't want to hurt you, we didn't want you to suffer, we always just loved you, it is just that simple. As for Daniel, well, I have sent a letter to Herbert and I can only hope that he will see to it that Daniel gets his comeuppance!"

"Oh, Papa, I am so confused right now. All my life you have taught me to be honest and fair-minded, now at my age to find out that my whole life has been a lie is a little much. I grew up believing that my mother didn't want nor love me and only to find out that I was right, but not because my mother didn't want nor love me, but because the woman I thought was my mother was not my mother at all. For years I would cry myself to sleep at night wanting her to come and get me and to hold me and sing to me. I wanted to be loved by her. I used to look at myself and wonder what I had done to make her give me away. The pain of all those years never had to be. I never had to grow up feeling like there was something wrong with me because my very own Mother had given me away. While you were trying to keep from hurting me and waiting for me to grow up so you could tell me the truth, I was tearing myself apart. Don't you see, don't you see the pain and suffering you have caused me by not telling me? Oh, Papa, I know you and Aunt Martha love me and that you did what you thought was for my own good, but my God, what a lie I have been forced to live and at such a price. And, just who the hell is Grace Humphreys?" She pulled back from him and walked away toward the orchard. She had to be alone. She had to think about this and all that had been said.

She sat in the swing that her uncle had made for her when she was a little girl. She was startled as she saw Carl sitting some ten feet away leaning against one of the other trees. "How long have you been sitting there, Carl," she asked.

"Oh, a few minutes ma'am. I been watching you and thinking that you're in some sort of pain. Anything I can help you with Miss?"

"Well, if you can sort out my life for me and help me to understand how the two people with whom I grew up loving and trusting have lied to me for all these years, then yes, maybe you can help. But, if you can't do that, then I think there is nothing else that I need."

Carl picked up a piece of dried grass and while twirling it between his fingers, he said, "if you don't mind me saying so, Miss, you have to look beyond your own needs and your own pain. You need to look out for the one thing that you can't see right now but that is standing there right in front of your face. Later on when you settle down some, you'll see it for sure. I've known you since you came to live here and you've been raised with love and by two people who are kind and who care about you. Now if you want to believe that they somehow betrayed you and have purposely caused you pain, then you are just a selfish and foolish child. You aren't grown up at all. If you can't see them for what they are and for what they have done for you then you ought to get your things together and go back to Huron City, 'cause if you can't understand all that they have given up for you then your head is as cold and empty as your heart."

"It's not a matter of love, Carl." Daphnia said as she stood up and started pacing back and forth. "It is a matter of truth and honesty. And, how about trust? What about trust? I trusted them to not lie to me. I didn't think I had to be specific about what not to lie about. Do you know how much pain I have endured? If I had known that my real mother was dead, and that was the reason that someone else was raising me I might have been okay. But, that wasn't what I was told. I was told that my Mother was very much alive and I was the one who had to deal with that. I was the one who felt that there was something wrong with me, I was too slow, too difficult, too whatever, Carl, I have lived all these years not trusting others because I thought they would leave me or that I would be undeserving of them for some reason. A reason that never existed, because there was not anything wrong with me, my Mother did love me, and I was never allowed to know that or to know her. Who is Grace Humphreys? I don't even know anything about her, what she was like, how she died. That is what has been taken from me, Carl. It isn't a matter of love; it is a matter of trust. I trusted them! Don't you see that? And the bigger issue is that Daniel Bernstein, a man who hates me and is nothing more than a slithering snake has found out the truth and will wait until the most opportune moment to use it against me. My God! A man who despises life itself now holds the key to mine. Isn't that ironic."

Rising and walking toward her, Carl put his hand on her shoulder, "get up Daphnia. Life has given you a cruel blow, you are not who you thought you were. The woman you thought was your mama ain't and a woman you never knew was. Well, well, it seems that the misery of being the child of a mother who didn't love or want you is now more important to you than finding that your real mama did want you very much, she did love you. Seems to me that you've had some sorrow taken away and true love to fill its place. Don't be selfish, Daphnia, forgive Mister and Missus Flanders, they only loved you. It wasn't the lie of who your mother was that they were protecting you from, it was the infidelity and shame of being born to your father's mistress. Now while you sit out here and cry betrayal under the stars and the moon, you should stop and think a minute about what it was they wanted you to be grown up enough to understand and ask yourself if you are a woman yet who can face the truth. Now, I don't know this Daniel Bernstein, but if he is the kind of person who would go snooping where he don't belong just to cause pain to others then I don't suppose he is worth too much of your time.

But, I did know Matthew. He was a good man. He had a wild streak, but he wasn't mean. I was just a boy back then, but I remember him. He was fun and I used to look forward to seeing him ride up the path on that black horse of his. He would throw his head back and laugh like there was no tomorrow. Then he would ride up behind me and swoop me up and we would take off as fast as the horse could go. I don't know about the bad things people are telling you about him, but I know one thing, he wasn't all bad. If it means anything to you, Daphnia, I liked your father." He then turned and walked back across the yard to where he had his horse and wagon tied. He headed for his own home with his wife and two little babies.

Daphnia was left somewhat perplexed. She had never heard Carl speak that way. She was both surprised and embarrassed. He was right; she was being selfish. How would she have felt had she known all these years that her mother was not married to her father and that Melissa was left to raise her while Matthew went off to chop down trees and gamble on the river boats. Who was she so angry with anyway? Maybe it wasn't the fact that she was raised believing that her mother didn't love her, but finding out that her Father was not a hero, but truly a womanizer and a man who was self indulgent and shameless. The thought of Daniel Bernstein brought fury to her face, however, and she vowed to let him know it. Walking back to the house she could see that there was light coming from the kitchen and she knew that her Papa Tad and Aunt Martha were inside. She picked up her pace and pulling her skirt up so that she could run without tripping on the hem of her petticoat, she hurried up to the house and inside the warm kitchen.

As she entered the room she walked over and poured herself a cup of hot coffee. "I'm sorry, I have been behaving like a child. All of these years I prayed and cried begging God to let my mother come and get me and to love me. You are my mother for all intents and purposes, Aunt Martha, and you Papa Tad, well you are the closest thing to a father that I have had. Thank you both. Please excuse me, I will go up and get the extra blanket and quilt, Aunt Martha. Good night. I'll see you both in the morning."

Starting after her, Martha called out, "Daphnia, wait, please."

"Let her go, Mart, let her go." Thaddeus said to Martha taking her hand in his as she started up the stairs after Daphnia. "She needs to be alone and to think this out, she has to deal with it her own way. Besides there are a few things that we need to finish talking about." Then leading her back to the kitchen table and pulling out her chair for her to sit, he filled his coffee cup and sat down himself.

"Carl will be going into Lansing tomorrow. He is going to talk with a few men about coming out and helping on the farm here. He is also going to enlist the help of Spinster Martin about finding a good woman to come out and live here with us and give you a hand around this house." Then putting his hand up as he saw that she was about to protest. "Now, I won't hear one word against this, Martha." He spoke as sternly as he could and made it a point to look away so as not to see the tears welling up in her eyes. "Martha, we have talked about this and there is nothing more to say. This place is too big and too much for you to handle alone. Carl will be hiring a woman to come out and that is that."

"I guess this is where I salute and say yes sir, right Thaddeus. Now if you will excuse me, I need to clean up this kitchen before I go out there and say goodnight to my folks, so take your coffee on out to the swing if you don't mind."

Thaddeus stood and walked out to the front porch leaving his coffee cup on the table.

When he came back into the house he saw Martha wiping dishes and humming. She was content, he thought. He then went up the stairs and tapped on Daphnia's door. "You awake, Daphnia?" he called to her.

"I'm awake, Papa."

"Daphnia, I just want you to know I love you. Good night." he said. And as he moved away from the door he heard the doorknob turn and saw her step out into the hallway.

"I love you too Papa, I truly do. This will all work out, and don't worry about Daniel, he is just looking for gossip with which to hurt me, but now that I know the truth that won't be possible. Good night," she said as she put her arms around his neck and kissed his cheek.

"Good night, Daphnia," he replied. Then letting go of her he placed a gold key in the palm of her hand. When you are ready, Daphnia, this key will fit a trunk in the attic of Herbert Bernstein's study. There are things you will find in there that I cannot tell you about. There are answers to some of your questions and things that belonged to your grandmother, your father and Grace Humphreys. You will find letters that you might not understand, but I beg of you to take your time with them and be patient. Listen to your heart and remember that I love you." Moving away from her he touched her face and her hair then turned and went across the hall and into his room where he prepared for bed, he was tired and mentally drained

She watched him walk away and thought that his shoulders looked a little slumped, he was getting old and she hoped that Doc Brewer would be coming out for a visit soon. She went back into her room and as she crawled back under the comforter she said a silent prayer.

Finishing the dishes and putting away the last of the cooking pots, Martha took one last look around the room then grabbing her shawl from the hall tree, she hurried out the front door and down the path to the rose garden. As she sat on the alter, she held her face in her hands and prayed to God, her mother and her father begging for their guidance. After gently touching the headstones on the graves, she went back up the path to the house and inside and up to her room. Thaddeus was in bed, and sleeping soundly. She left the room again and went over to Daphnia's room. Calling to the young woman and tapping on the door, she listened for a response from the other side. Hearing none, she gently turned the doorknob and went inside.

"Daphnia, Daphnia Dear," she said to her niece as she sat down on the bed next to her and gently shook her shoulder. "Wake up dear, we must talk."

Opening her eyes and pulling herself up in the bed, Daphnia looked at her Aunt Martha. "Oh, Aunt Martha, I have been such a foolish and selfish nilly. Please forgive me."

"Oh, my dear, there is nothing to forgive. You have acted just like anyone would be expected to act. Let's go down and have some bread pudding. Whaddaya say?" Martha said as she pulled the covers back and began to tug on Daphnia's arm to get her out of the bed. "Here, put on your robe, Thaddeus is asleep so step quietly." The two women left the room and crept down the stairs and into the kitchen where Daphnia lit the lantern and set it on the table and Martha served up two bowls of bread pudding. It was still warm, since she had just taken it out of the oven before going out to visit with her parents.

Chapter Twenty-Three

"Tell me about Grace Humphreys, Aunt Martha," Daphnia said as she played with the pudding in her bowl.

"I don't rightly know a whole lot, Daphnia, mostly gossip and a few rumors, I suppose, but I'll tell you what I can," Martha replied as she brought over a cup of coffee and sat down at the table with Daphnia.

"Let me start when we first heard of her from Matthew. Maybe that will help you to understand. Matthew was always the wanderer. He was your Uncle Thaddeus' God Son and was the only son of Thaddeus' only brother, Joshua Flanders. Joshua had not always faired as well as Thaddeus and it seemed that trouble followed him wherever he went. He passed on while trying to fell some trees and clear a piece of land. Matthew was only a young boy then and him with no Mother left to help raise him . . ."

"What happened to his Mother?" Daphnia interrupted.

"She died, dear. She died right after Matthew was born. She died in Thaddeus' arms with me standing by holding Matthew. Joshua tried to do right by the boy, but he just couldn't seem to tame him none. Me and Thaddeus tried our best to get Joshua to let us raise Matthew, but he wouldn't do it. It wasn't that Matthew was a bad sort, he was just so full of tom foolery and a need for the forbidden. He was always out looking for a good time and paid no mind to settling down. Once Joshua died, Matthew had no other choice but to come here to live with us. Thaddeus tried to keep him in school, but once he came of age, it was the saloon in Lansing and all of the excitement of the City life that he was after. One day, out of the clear blue, he just saddled up his horse and headed west. He stopped just long enough to let us know that he would be in touch, but Michigan was no place for him. And, he rode off with nothing more than a hand shake and a tip of his hat." She stopped talking long enough to spoon out some of the bread pudding for herself and take a few bites. Then after another sip of her coffee she continued.

"The next time we heard from Matthew, he was in St. Louis. That is where he met up with George Barnes. George was the brother of Eloise

Barnes. It seems that the Barnes' had left Boston and gone on to Huron City and then George left there and went down to St. Louis. It was through this connection that Matthew eventually met Melissa. Melissa had grown up just outside of Boston and somehow she and Eloise had traveled out to St. Louis to see George, or so I seem to remember. Well, anyway, how they met and the comings and goings of such I can't say for sure, just mostly rumors, but what is certain is that Matthew fell head over heels in love with Melissa. He wrote to us telling us that he had married her in a small ceremony in Huron City. We were happy for him, but it was the first we had heard from him in almost five years. But, that is just the way he was, in your life one minute and out the gate the next. He told us he loved Melissa and we had no reason to do anything but to wish him well."

"If he was so in love with Melissa, how did he end up with Grace Humphreys?"

"I really don't know the details about all of that, Daphnia. I do know that Matthew was happy for a while and then Melissa's mother got sick and she had to go to Boston to take care of her. That is where he met Grace. What went on back there only Matthew and Grace would know for sure, but whatever it was we have you and I will always be grateful for that. As for Melissa well she was heart broken. Once she could leave Boston and the gossip she left. Matthew didn't seem to mind, he stayed on with Grace for a while but eventually he got bored and went to Huron City and Melissa. That is the way he was, he had no regard for time nor the worry of others. He moved in and out of the lives of people who loved him, never thinking that he should love them back." Martha stopped talking again. She rose from the table and began to clear away the dishes as though that was the end of the conversation.

"Wait, Aunt Martha, you can't just leave it there, you must go on." Daphnia demanded as she got up and went over to where her Aunt was standing. "Please, Aunt Martha, you must go on."

"Okay, if that is what you want. But, sitting isn't easy for me and sometimes I just need to move about a bit. Now settle down. Let's see, where was I. Once he went back to Huron City, he wrote to tell us that he wanted to visit us and to bring Melissa with him. He said that it was all over between him and Grace and that he surely loved Melissa.

He said that she had forgiven him and all was right with the world. So, Thaddeus sent him a letter and told him to come on home that there was a wedding gift waiting for him. That brought him back and we could see that he was surely taken with Melissa, but I don't think he loved her, not really. He did things and said things that might have sounded like love to somebody else, but not to me. She loved him all right, though. She would look at him and it was clear that she didn't see anything or anyone else. It was also clear that she didn't see him for who and what he really was. He was a reckless fun loving womanizing man that you couldn't help but to love and adore. Even the men couldn't stay mad at him for long. He had something about him that caused you to love him in spite of hisself." As she said this last statement she looked away like she was remembering someone who had been very special and a smile came across her face. Then she chuckled right out loud. "Honestly, Daphnia, he was the most lovable and wicked man that ever walked, I do declare he was, but your Papa Tad and I, we loved him like he was our own. We would get so mad at him and then he would come in with his hat off to one side and that cockeyed smile of his and it would melt our hearts. We'd just take him in our arms and hug him and whatever we had was his. That's just the long and the short of it. He was a reckless man with a good soul. He never meant no one any harm, and he was always right there to apologize when he realized that he had hurt you, but somehow he never learned from it. I guess that is what made the women so crazy after him, and Melissa she just pretended that all the gossip and the rumors weren't so, even after what she had witnessed first hand back into Boston. I knew when they left here that it was just a matter of time, and once he heard that you were on the way, well, that was the beginning of the end for them.

"Tell me about Grace Humphreys, Aunt Martha, Please tell me about my Mother. You don't know how long I have wondered why Melissa didn't love me and why I felt so inadequate, like I was missing something. Now I understand why she is the way she is. I know the reason she wanted me to come back, it was because she hoped that I would remind her of my father, but I didn't. That broke my heart and I have always felt ashamed of the fact that my very own Mother didn't want me. Now to find out that she wasn't my mother at all, and my real Mother died, it is like part of my self has returned, I am not inadequate, there is a sense of pride that I really was loved and I wasn't rejected. What was she like, Aunt Martha? Did you ever meet her?"

"No, dear, I never met Grace Humphreys. From what I have heard, Matthew was so in love with her, people say he was just like a little sick puppy. She was a good ten or more years older than he, but I heard that she was still a real beauty. She lived alone since her husband had passed on some years before, just how many I don't know. He was a slave runner or something on the dark side like that in his earlier days. He had lived outside the law from time to time and her family had disowned her. Feeling the shame for what he had done as he grew older he needed to find a way to protect her from the gossip and his sins. So, he stashed her up in Boston in a little white stone cottage that she had inherited from her mother just on the outskirts of town for safe keeping so to speak. Then he went on and died, word has it that he was old enough to be her father hisself! They never had no babies of their own before he died. I heard that he didn't leave her anything in the way of money; and she didn't have nothing except that house. They said it was covered with roses in the summertime and the yard around it was like a sea of flowers. I used to hear these things and could just see a picture of a little white stone house with a whitewashed picket fence and one rose bush right after another. I could almost smell the sweet fragrances and the Honeysuckle and Jasmine growing up the side of the house as an invitation to all the Humming Birds." Again Aunt Martha looked up toward the ceiling and sat back and took in a deep breath like she was in the middle of the garden. Sitting back in her chair and folding her hands across her plump chest she smiled and closed her eyes.

Daphnia was listening to every word and was waiting for the next, "Aunt Martha, Aunt Martha, don't stop now," she gently shook her Aunt's shoulder. "Continue, please continue."

"I'm sorry, dear, it is just that it reminds me of my own Mother's garden and how she loved the smell of the roses and the fluttering movements of the Humming Birds. You would have loved her, Daphnia. She was wonderful. She was strong and sure of herself. There was nothing that frightened her or that she couldn't face. She was taller than me, but not my much. I used to stand in front of her and look up then taking my hand I would measure from the top of my head to hers. I always wanted to be just like her, but I fell short in more ways than my height. So many things frighten me, Daphnia. I am so unsure and I am scared about being alone. I know that Thaddeus is not well and if something happens to him, I just don't know what I will do. I know that I won't want to go on without him, Daphnia, I can't." She took out her handkerchief from her pocket and wiped her eyes and blew her nose. Then rising, she said, "don't you think we have talked enough tonight, dear? Aren't you tired?"

"Oh, please, Aunt Martha, just keep talking for a little while, please."

"Okay, but I really don't know much about facts, I can only tell you the gossip and rumors that I heard myself and you will have to decide what you want to believe, then." She continued. "Grace made a living by taking in sewing. She had a family either down south or out west somewhere, no one was ever sure just which it was. But, the long and the short of it was that she made time with Matthew. Matthew watched Melissa pack up and go on her way back to Huron City just as soon as her mother passed on. I have heard many stories in my time, but my guess would be that Melissa couldn't endure the shame of it all and went to Huron City to live with Eloise Barnes in order to get away from the gossip. Thaddeus tried to talk with Matthew and even went to Boston to talk to him. Matthew did go back to Huron City with Melissa for a while, but eventually he left her and returned to Boston. I think this was when he learned that Grace was with child. He had offered Melissa a divorce before she left Boston, but her pride wouldn't let her go through with it so he decided that he would just do the next best thing. As long as Grace Humphreys would let him live there with her, then that is what he would do. In his mind he had tried to do the right thing by Melissa and she refused, so he had no choice. Living with Grace, Matthew was in his glory. We must've got letters from him almost every time the train ran between there and here. Eventually, he made the trip back to Melissa, but that didn't last for long. The minute he found out that you were on your way he left Melissa without a second thought. When he got back to Boston, he wouldn't leave her side and word has it that he waited on her hand and foot. She, being so much older than he was and having such a difficult time and all, he stayed right there. Lordy, I remember when we got the word that you were born. He sent word across the wire and it sounded like he was just bustin' right out with pride. We'll have to go lookin' for them letters and things tomorrow. I think they are up in the attic somewhere. Course bringing you into this world took just about all Grace had right out of her. She never got up from the bed again. They had a woman come in and care for you until Grace passed on. Then, of course, it was harder for Matthew to stay there without her, and it was harder to get good help for you. He came here for a while and we fell in love with you from the minute we laid eyes on those beautiful golden curls and your contagious smile. But, he wasn't happy here either. He got restless and had written a letter to Melissa asking her forgiveness once again. And, she forgave him like always." Martha stood once again and arched her back and yawned. "Don't you want to go on to bed, dear, we can finish this tomorrow? I just needed to let you know that I love you and I am so sorry for causing you pain. I think those letters are in a box up in the attic. I am sure we can find them. I believe they are up there in that trunk with the other things that belonged to Matthew; you know the one in the back of the attic, I think it has his name on it. We'll go up there tomorrow and look for it. Can we go to bed now?"

"I know you are tired Aunt Martha, and, I know that you love me. I'm tired too, and you are right, we will have all kinds of time to talk tomorrow and the next day and the day after that. Come on, let's go up to bed."

As the two women started up the stairs Daphnia was startled when she heard the clock strike one. "My goodness, we have been down here a while, we'll never get up before Papa Tad tomorrow morning," she said as they laughed and went up to their rooms.

Chapter Twenty-Four

Daphnia awakened with the sun streaking across the room. It must be eight o'clock she thought as she jumped from her bed and grabbed her robe. Stepping out her door into the hallway she saw that her Aunt and Uncle were also still sleeping. There were no aromas coming up from the kitchen; no coffee or wafts of bacon cooking. She looked down the hallway and saw that the only light was that from the sun shining in through the windows. She crept down the stairs and into the kitchen. Lighting the wood stove she proceeded to fill the coffee pot with water and scoop the fresh ground coffee beans into the basket. Then setting the pot onto the stove she went into the bathing room and freshened up. As she walked back into the kitchen she saw Martha sitting at the table in her nightgown. "What's the matter Aunt Martha, are you alright?" she asked putting her arm around her aunt's shoulder.

"I feel a little out of sorts, Daphnia, guess it is 'cause I never slept this late before, Thaddeus' stirrings usually awaken me before the rooster crows," she said dryly.

"Where is Papa Tad, Aunt Martha?" she asked.

"He's still sleeping, dear, I don't think he is feeling too well, he seemed cold to me and I put another quilt on the bed, but that didn't even warm him up, I think he will probably need to sleep a little while longer. How would you like some mashed potatoes with that coffee? I know what I'll do, I will go out and bring in some fresh tomatoes from the garden, they are about ripe now, and we can have fresh tomatoes with our roast beef. Or, how would you like it if I braided your hair before you go off to school today? Wouldn't you like one of those sweet yellow bananas?" She asked. Then she got up and walked outside onto the back porch in her bare feet.

Daphnia ran up the stairs and opened the door to her aunt and uncle's bedroom. There he was, her dear Papa Tad, lying there with every quilt and blanket that Martha could pile on him heaped up one on top of the other. She began to pull the things off and as she got to the last quilt she could see that her Papa Tad would not be getting up this morning or any other. She fell to her knees beside his bed and holding onto his hand she cried. She kissed his hand and prayed for his soul, Aunt Martha's and her own. And then remembering her aunt, she immediately became aware of what she must do. She knew she had to keep her from coming up stairs and seeing him. She straightened the blankets and quilts then gently tucking the covers around him, she kissed his forehead and walked out of the room and into her own. She quickly dressed and took down some slippers and a robe for her aunt.

"Here you are, Aunt Martha. I brought you down some slippers and a robe. Papa Tad is sleeping just fine for now. He said that he thought he would stay in bed for a little while longer, but that he isn't feeling too well so maybe I ought to go in for Doc Brewer. How would you like to go with me?" she asked while helping the little woman into her robe and putting her slippers on her feet.

"Oh, dear, you go on ahead for Doc. I'll be just fine here, I need to get breakfast going and besides I don't want to leave Thaddeus here all alone when he doesn't feel well. I will go back up and check on him, maybe take him up some breakfast after a while," she said sounding almost normal

"No, Aunt Martha, Papa Tad said that he didn't want to be disturbed. I must go out and hitch up the horse to the carriage and get into town." She knew this too had to be done and it would take a while for the horse and carriage to cover the 25 miles to town. Then she would have to find the doctor and then get back. That would leave her Aunt here all alone with nothing but time on her hands and she felt that Martha knew Thaddeus was dead. "Aunt Martha, you must promise me that you won't go upstairs and bother Papa Tad, he is sleeping peacefully and he wouldn't like it too much if he was awakened before he was ready. Now, you promise that you will just let him be until I get back." Then squeezing her aunt's hand, she hurried out of the house.

Rushing out to the barn she got the horse from his stall and hitched him to the carriage. Then with a slap to his broad hindquarters she trotted him out of the pasture and on up to the house. Martha was standing at the front door waving goodbye. Daphnia got down off the seat and went to her aunt and holding her very close she said, "Aunt Martha, I need for you to promise me that you will let Papa Tad sleep and you won't go up to your room. You don't want to disturb now, do you?" she asked.

"I won't disturb Thaddeus, dear, we have been together for so long why one of us is half of the other, we're not a couple, Daphnia, we are one. Now you go on and get the doctor and bring him back here with you. I love you Daphnia, and your Papa Tad he always loved you too. Now, go on Daffy Girl, go on into town there," she pulled away from her niece and wiped a tear from Daphnia's eye.

Daphnia climbed back into the carriage and waved goodbye then slapped the horse and steered the carriage out and onto the main road toward Lansing. She pushed the horse as hard as she dared, she knew things were not right with Aunt Martha and she was more scared for her than for anything else. She knew the urgency was to get back there with her; the doctor would do no good for Papa Tad now.

Once the carriage was out of sight, Martha went back inside and started to straighten up the kitchen. She wasn't hungry and not in the mood for coffee, she poured the whole pot out. Then going into the bathing room she began to ready herself for her day. Once dressed and with the turtle shell combs in her hair she took a pan of warm soapy water, a towel and a washcloth up the stairs and into the bedroom she shared with Thaddeus. Setting the pan of water on the night table, she looked around the room. She remembered when he first brought her here. She was a young girl of only sixteen and so innocent. She had always loved this room she walked around it and touched the curtains, she felt of his shirt and held it close to her face so that she could take in the smell of him. She went over to the bed and sat next to him. Then she bent down and gently kissed his eyelids, his face and his mouth. She caressed his ears and let her hands move slowly down the side of his face as she traced his jaw, his neck and his collarbone. She loved this man, this man who had brought her such happiness. She laid her face against his chest and let her fingers do a whisper dance across his abdomen and his thighs. She prayed to him to come back to her, she kissed the palms of his hands and cried on his shoulder for the last time. Then she got up and stripping the covers away and removing his nightshirt she bathed him. This man who had been everything to her she loved him, she caressed him and she bathed him. She lathered his face and she shaved him, she dressed him again in a clean nightshirt and combed his hair. She rolled up several of his handkerchiefs and placed them beneath his chin so his mouth wouldn't gape open and she placed his hands in a prayer-like position over his abdomen. Then taking away the pan of water and cleaning the room so that it would be most presentable she went back downstairs leaving the door open.

As she entered the kitchen everything seemed to be in a haze to her. She set the pan down and went out to her alter and the roses and prayed. She touched the headstones of her Mother, Father and little son, and then she went back inside. She cleaned up the pan, and towels in the bathing room. Before she replaced his shaving mug to its place on the shelf, she took it in her hand and remembered how she had always watched him shave she remembered how he loved to tease her; she could almost hear the sound of his laughter... ... ...

"... ... ... Now, Mart just what is it that you like so much about me shaving?" he would say. "Is it the fact that I soap myself all up so you can pretend that I am somebody else, or is it because you just like it when my face is soft and smooth against your skin? Cause if it is the latter, you won't ever have to remind me to shave, I will do it morning noon and night. Would you like that Mart?"

"Oh, Thaddeus, you are just so bad. I just like the closeness of you, and it is always amazing to me that you never cut yourself with that there razor."

"Well, I couldn't cut myself with this, Hon, I wouldn't want to get blood all over that cute little belly of yours, now would I?"

She could hear his laughter and see his eyes twinkle.

"Tell you what" he would say wiping away the remaining lather and directing her out to the other room and up the stairs, "let's just keep the bacon sizzling down here and we can take a minute or two to sizzle ourselves."

She tilted her face upward and could feel his soft touch again, just like before as he patted her backside and gently caressed her cheek... ... .

240

Martha reached over and took down the leather razor strap. Holding it close to her face she felt close to him somehow. She hung it back on the wall and picked up the ivory handled razor, she watched the sunlight as it flashed across the blade. She left the bathing room and crossed the kitchen she opened the cellar door and went downstairs to her blankets and quilts next to the canning jars. She sat down and took out the box of her secret memories; she picked up each one and looked at it. Then she put everything back as it was. She held the blade of the razor to just beneath her left ear, and opening her eyes and looking to the heavens with one final prayer and gasp of air she pulled the knife across the soft white skin beneath her chin and to the other side of her throat. She heard singing, and felt the soft warmth of her little baby boy in her arms, Thaddeus was smiling and her mother and father were standing next to him. Martha closed her eyes.

PART IV

.. Sometimes even Angels weep
for promises made which we can't keep
and footsteps follow us which we cannot hear
until their silence gives way to fear . . .

Chapter Twenty-Five

How Daphnia survived the next several days that rapidly ran into weeks, she didn't know. When she got into Lansing she found Doctor Brewer and told him what had happened. Before heading back to Sunshine Acres, they went over to John Morgan's and left a message for Carl to come home right away. The Doctor pushed the horse as hard as he dared. Once back home, Daphnia started running up the walkway only to be held back by the doctor. "Daphnia wait a minute. I think it would be better if I went in first, don't you?" He asked of her as he caught her arm.

"No, I don't think it would be better if you went in first, thank you just the same," she quipped. Then pulling her arm away she ran inside the house and into the kitchen, then up the stairs to her Aunt and Uncle's room. Martha was not there, but Daphnia saw that she had been. Thaddeus looked as if he was sleeping with this fresh nightshirt and the blankets tucked around him. His hands were folded as if in prayer. She turned to see that the doctor had come in behind her.

"What will we do without him, Doc?" she sobbed allowing him to hold her in his arms. Then pulling back, "we must find Aunt Martha. You check the roses and I'll check out back."

As they reached the bottom of the stairs he went out the back door but she turned and saw the cellar door ajar, and she knew that was where Aunt Martha was. Sitting there on her pallet of quilts and blankets with all her precious treasures around her. She smiled as she opened the door and quietly went down the stairs.

"Aunt Martha, you down here?" she called out as she was about half way down. "Aunt Martha?" she called again feeling her throat tighten. As she walked over to the lantern she took it down, lit it and walked over to where she knew she would find her Aunt. She just didn't know that it would be like it was. Seeing her Aunt lying there covered in blood with the razor next to her was more than she had been prepared to handle. Daphnia screamed and collapsed.

Doc Brewer heard the scream and took off in a full run back to the house. By the time he reached the back door he could smell smoke.

He ran down the stairs and saw Daphnia lying next to her Aunt. He lifted her over his shoulder and carried her up the stairs and went back down for Martha.

Martha was much more difficult to handle and as he was struggling to get her into his arms Carl came rushing down. They wrapped her with a blanket and the two of them managed to get her body up the stairs.

Doctor Brewer filled a bucket with water and started down the stairs when Carl came in from outside with one in each hand. The two of them together put out the fire and went back to check on the women.

Daphnia had regained consciousness and she saw her aunt lying on the floor wrapped in the blanket. Using a towel from the cupboard, she began to wipe away the blood; her tears fell onto the gentle woman's face and neck. "Aunt Martha" she sobbed as she lifted her aunt's head and shoulders and cradled them in her arms. Daphnia sat on the kitchen floor rocking her aunt while she cried with all the emotion and hurt that was inside of her.

The two men came back upstairs. Carl brought up the box of Martha's treasures as well as the ivory handled razor. He and the doctor went about cleaning themselves up and filling their lungs with fresh air. They walked out to the porch and sat on the steps.

"This is what Mr. Flanders was so worried about, Doctor. What do you think I should do now?" Carl asked.

"Well, Carl, Thaddeus had things pretty well in order. His death was no surprise and I agree with you, he always knew that Martha wouldn't stay long once he passed on. Daphnia is going to be truly alone for the first time in her life, now. I imagine she will survive, but she sure has been dealt a cruel blow at such an early age. Thaddeus filled me in on his plans of splitting this place up with you having a big chunk of it. Even with Daphnia the major stakeholder, I imagine this place will be left for you to take care of, she more'n likely will return to Huron City. Though, God only knows why unless it is because she thinks that it is best to be there where her mother is. Some mother!" he said under his breath

"No sir, she knows the truth." Carl told the doctor of the events of the night before. "I think she's lost a lot, and all at one time." He shook his head and stood up. "I think we have given her enough time in there, it sounds like she has calmed down some. Maybe we ought to go back in."

As they went back into the house, Daphnia had managed to regain control. She had wiped away most of the blood from Martha's face and had placed a bandage of sorts around her throat to cover the gaping wound and keep any blood that remained from seeping out. "She was so good," she said to Carl as he helped her up and Doctor Brewer took over attending to Martha.

Carl got her inside the bathing room and sat her on the stool there. Then filling the basin with water he took a cloth and bar of soap and cleaned her up. He took the jacket and blouse off of her and wrapped her in a robe that was hanging on the back of the door. Then lifting her up into his arms he carried her upstairs and placed her in her bed where Doc Brewer gave her a sedative. She slept the rest of the day.

Carl and Doc Brewer took care of Martha, then cleaned up the mess that had been made in the kitchen and bathing room. Carl left the Doc there while he went over and told Arlene what had happened. He asked her to start packing up some things and to be ready to come to the big house and stay for a while. He then went back into town and made the arrangements for a proper wake and burial. The coroner had the coffins all ready that Thaddeus had picked out earlier in the month and he left right away to take care of what he needed to do. Then Carl stopped by the telegraph office and sent a wire to Herbert Bernstein in Huron City. Then going over to John Morgan's office he handled the necessary business there. His last stop was to the house of Earl and Helen O'Riley. The O'Riley's had been long time friends of Thaddeus and Martha. "Of, course they would come out straight away." Earl O'Riley had said. Carl told them he would be stopping at his place to pick up Arlene and the babies but would be back at Sunshine Acres as soon as he could. When the O'Riley's arrived the coroner and doctor were there taking care of their business at hand. Leaving Mrs. O'Riley to go to work doing the things that she needed to do. Martha was cleaned and dressed in her Sunday Best, Thaddeus was laid out in his finest suit with his pipe in his hand. The two were laid out in the front room with their coffins end to end.

Carl walked up to where Thaddeus was lying looking so peaceful and placed his whittling knife in the top of his boot and a fresh branch of cherry wood near his side. "Just in case you get up there and find yourself with some spare time, Sir," he said through his tears and with a lump in his throat. Then walking over to Martha he placed a bouquet of wild flowers mixed with what roses he could find. There were hardly any roses left in the garden. Next to her side he laid in her rolling pin and a small jar of apple butter. Carl's heart was broken. He had loved these two people as if they were his own blood and he just couldn't imagine what his life would be like without them to care for. Arlene came up behind and squeezed his hand, she promised to be there for him no matter what, just as Martha had always been there for Thaddeus.

Chapter Twenty-Six

Once Arlene and the babies came, Mrs. O'Riley helped her to put their things in the downstairs bedroom and then the two women began preparing for the many people who would be coming through to pay their respects to Thaddeus and Martha. They found Martha's kitchen well equipped and spotless. They remembered Martha as they went about preparing for the onslaught of people to come. It was easy for them to imagine Martha standing there next to them, hands and elbows covered with flour and little specks of sugar on her cheek. They laughed as they thought of the little wisps of hair blowing about her face and her fussing and laughing all at the same time. These two women loved Martha, everyone did.

Wiping her eyes, Daphnia felt as though she could not wake up, she was dreaming of running through fields of wild flowers, but she was crying, it was like she was trying to come home, but the big house was nowhere around. Then when she found the house her Aunt and Uncle were dead. Sitting up in her bed Daphnia was suddenly awake. "Thank God," she said out loud and jumped up and ran down the stairs to the kitchen. "Aunt Martha, oh Aunt Martha," she sang out. "I was having the most horrible dream, I ...." Her voice trailed off as she saw that it was not her aunt who was laughing in the kitchen, it was Arlene and Mrs. O'Riley.

"Good Afternoon, Daphnia," Mrs. O'Riley said as she walked over and held onto the young woman. "Come on dear, let's go back up to your room and get you some slippers and a robe. You don't want to get sick at a time like this." She then steered Daphnia back up the stairs and into her room where she helped her with her things. She brushed her hair for her and tied it back with a blue ribbon. "Daphnia, I want you to know that your Aunt and Uncle were the best friends that Mr. O'Riley and I have ever had. They were like family to us, and you, my dear, are family as well. We watched you grow up, and we are here for you."

Daphnia thanked Mrs. O'Riley and went down the stairs where she kneeled beside each coffin, first one and then the other. She cried, prayed and talked with the two now lifeless bodies as if they were very much alive. Finally wiping away her tears she rose to the sound of Doc Brewer coming inside the house. He again took her in the kitchen and had her drink some tea that he assured her would help her sleep. But, she didn't want to sleep. She wanted to stay with her aunt and uncle. She wanted to sit by their sides and talk with them. The tea won out, however, and Daphnia was once again put to bed.

The memorial service was the following day with bright sunshine and crisp blue skies. It seemed like everyone within 100 miles came to say farewell. Herbert Bernstein arrived just as the coffins were being lowered into their graves. He had driven from Huron City to Detroit and then took a train out of Detroit to Lansing. He had not slept much, but was wide-awake when he spoke with John Morgan, Doc Brewer and Carl. Doc was right; Thaddeus had taken care of everything.

Carl managed to get Herbert alone for just a brief while, "Mr. Bernstein, I think we need to talk about that son of yours coming into town and trying to stir up some trouble for Daphnia. Do you know anything about it?"

"Yes, Carl. I received a letter from Thaddeus, and I plan to deal with Daniel just as soon as he returns. He left the day after Daphnia for some place up in Omaha, Nebraska. I don't know what he is up to, but I assure you that I plan to find out and deal with it. You don't have to worry, I will protect Daphnia."

"Thanks, that's all I need to know," Carl said as he turned and walked away.

The next several days were filled with the coming and going of people that Daphnia had not seen in years, many of whom she had never seen at all. With Arlene settling in and taking care of the household responsibilities, Carl taking care of the running of the farm itself, John Morgan and Herbert managing all of the financial matters, Daphnia had little to do except be alone with her grieving. She went through the house as if she had never lived there but was exploring it for the first time. She went through the dresser drawers, desk, bureau, pantry and all of the private places. She read the letters and notes from Thaddeus to Martha and her to him. She looked through all their private and personal treasures and held them close to her face breathing in their lingering fragrances. She packed away the things that she wanted to keep and take back to Huron City with her, and the other things she placed in neat stacks and took them down to the fireplace in the parlor and burned them.

William had sent a telegram stating his sorrow, and apologizing for not being able to come home and comfort her. His words were like so many of the words that she had heard and read before, she knew this was one more mountain that she would have to climb alone; it had always been that way and she didn't expect it to change. William loved her, she knew that, but when things were difficult he was nowhere to be found, it seemed that there was always something else that took precedence. She would manage.

After almost three weeks of grieving and saying hello and good-bye, it seemed that the legal matters were well on their way to being settled. Arlene and Carl had properly settled into the big house and this suited Daphnia. Even with all of the care that Thaddeus had taken it still took a while to settle things with the estate. Herbert left after only one week, with both Daphnia and Daniel out of town, he was anxious to return to the Gazette. Daphnia told him that she would be returning to Huron City as soon as she could.

She went into Lansing with him to see him off on the train. It had gotten very cold and there had already been a couple of ice and snow episodes. Bundled together in the carriage she held onto his hand. "Don't worry, Uncle Bert, I will be back soon enough. There are just so many things left for me to do here. I want to leave as many things taken care of as possible. I know that Carl and Arlene will do fine. I am happy that they will be living in the house. So, don't worry, I'll be back soon enough. The only person you need to worry about is Daniel. When I get back I plan to have a talk with him. Do you have any idea what he is up to?"

"No I don't but don't worry, I will deal with Daniel. The only thing you need to concern yourself with right now is making sure that returning to Huron City is what you want to do. You have a beautiful home here in Lansing and I am sure that if you decide that you want to stay right here, everyone, including me, will understand."

"No, I want to return to Huron City. For some reason the apartment over the Gazette seems like home to me, and I enjoy what I am doing. There is one thing you could do, if you don't mind, Papa gave me a key that he said fits a trunk stored in your attic above your study. Is there any way you can have the trunk moved to the apartment for me?"

"Of course, I will have it moved as soon as I return. Now don't worry about anything, you just stay here for as long as you think you need to." Then giving her a good-bye hug he left her and went into the train depot.

As she rode onto the property again she could feel the air against her face, it was cold and she could see snowflakes starting to flutter to the ground. She knew it wouldn't be long before the snow would be covering everything with its whiteness.

The tears streamed down her face as she thought of leaving the big white house. She let the horse go at his own pace with no regard to the wind or the snowflakes that were starting to fall. A smile came over her face as she heard her Uncle's voice calling to her … … …

"…… … roll the snow around and around like this, Daphnia, pat it down good, that's it roll the snow balls on the ground so they will get big and fat."

"What about his hat, Papa, can he wear yours?"

"Sure, he can wear mine, here let me lift you up so you can put it on his head. How about if I let him smoke my pipe, too."

Then standing back they admired her first snowman. She was happy and clapping her hands, and he was beaming ear to ear. He taught her to lie down in the snow and make snow angels until it was hard to tell the difference between the snowman and Thaddeus.

She could hear her Aunt Martha calling to them, "Come on in now, Thaddeus, before the both of you catch your death out there rolling around in that snow. Bring in some of what you haven't been tramping around in and we'll make some snow cream, how would you like that Daphnia? Come on in now, Thaddeus, I have done decided to take your little playmate inside."

Life would never be the same, and she missed them terribly. She arrived back at the house and took the horse to the barn where Carl took care of putting things away for the night. Before going into the house, she went out to the little cemetery. For the first time she understood her Aunt Martha's visits, she sat on the stone alter and talked to Thaddeus and Martha. When she went inside the house she could hear the babies crying, Arlene was in the kitchen with one of them in her arms and the other one lying in a basket filled with blankets and pillows. Arlene had made a shepherd's pie and a fresh pot of coffee. Dinner was not like she had been used to, but it was wonderful to see Arlene and Carl together with their babies. She felt good about leaving the house with them taking care of things.

After supper Daphnia helped to clean the kitchen and then she told Arlene how she felt, "I'm glad you will be staying here in the house, Arlene. Please know that this is your home and you should do whatever you want to do to make it comfortable for you. I would like to ask that you keep my room as it is if you don't mind. I may come back from time to time, and would like to be able to stay here."

"Of course, you will want to stay here, Daphnia. No matter what changes I might make they will be small ones just to accommodate the babies. I won't disturb your room or that of Mr. and Mrs. Flanders. This will always be your home, and you will always be welcomed back with open arms for as many times and as long as you want."

"Thanks Arlene. I will be leaving in a few days, there are just some odds and ends that I need to get taken care of. I want you to know how much I appreciate all that you have done."

"Don't mention it, Daphnia."

Daphnia went to her room feeling relief. She was tired but not ready for the nightmares. She tried to think of pleasant things, but all she could do was cry. Finally she slept. She dreamed of the newspaper office, and her small apartment. She dreamed of William and Herbert, and she dreamed of drinking tea with Eloise Barnes. For the first time since their deaths, she did not dream of her Uncle and Aunt until just before dawn. She had awakened, but soon fell back to sleep when she thought they were with her once again and they were walking on either side of her and holding her hands. The three of them were walking out into the pastures and over to the meadow just on the other side of the small stand of blue spruce trees. It was then that she saw the creek and as they waded into it her uncle stood in the middle of the cool water and held her close. Then letting go of her hands he took the hand of Martha, "we must go to the other side alone, dear, you must let us go." She heard him as if they were standing right in the room next to her. Then, Thaddeus and Martha walked through the creek. As they stepped onto the other bank they floated up and away from her.

Finally she felt a sense of peace about her. She rushed to the window and looked out to see the sun rising and the last glimmer of the morning star.

Daphnia was down in the kitchen making coffee and putting a pan of biscuits in the oven when Arlene came into the room.

"Daphnia, I hope the babies didn't keep you awake last night, I think they may be a little colicky. You look rested, I guess you are ready to get your things packed up here and back up to Huron City."

"Yes, I am. I know there is still much to be done here, but I feel good about leaving things with you and Carl. I looked out the window this morning and the sky looked so clear, but look now, it has started to snow again."

After breakfast she went about the business of packing the things that had meant so much to her Aunt and Uncle. She did not want to go through this process again. She tried to stay focused. She put aside the boxes of letters, her Aunt's diary and other little mementos that she knew she would want to take time and care with. She placed these things in the big black trunk and would have them brought back to Huron City with her.

It took several days before she had done what she felt was a thorough job of sorting through, packing up, and giving away the things with which she had grown up. She saved the basement for the last. With tears streaming down her face she knew that it was time. She went down the stairs and to the special place where her aunt had kept her mementos. She gathered up her Aunt's special treasures and took them back upstairs with her and packed them in the big trunk.

She had two trunks in which she had packed all of the things she would take back. One was filled with some pieces of fine china, and linens and the other was filled with small mementos, a box of letters that she had found in her Aunt's closet and a few pieces of the wooden toys and dolls that she had played with as a child. There was a photograph of her Aunt and Uncle on the day they were married, one of her Father sitting on a horse and holding her when she was an infant. There were little silver bells and teaspoons that her Aunt had collected and which had been brought back to her by Thaddeus from his trips. These were things that would be important to only her now. She had carefully packed the silver box of treasures next to several jars of her aunt's canned fruits and apple butter.

Thursday came before she knew it, and Carl had loaded the things she wanted to take to Huron City with her in the automobile. The two of them set off for Lansing without much conversation. Everything had been said that needed to be said, and now they would keep in touch as any two partners might.

She knew that once she returned to Huron City her first task would be to find out what Daniel was up to. Then she would go to see Melissa and let her know how she felt and that she understood. She thought of the trunk in Herbert's attic and wondered if he had gotten it moved yet. There were so many questions that had been left unanswered for her. Maybe she would take a trip to Boston in the spring. But for now, she needed to be busy with her hands and her mind. She welcomed the steady rocking of the train.

Chapter Twenty-Seven

Sunshine Acres was not the only place where people felt forced into an action that they weren't excited about doing. Daniel was on his way home from Omaha where he had spent the last couple of weeks. He learned almost too late that his questions were getting under the skin of some of the locals. He was practically tarred and feathered by friends of the woodcutter, Konrad. He had asked around the bars and taverns about him and was about to give up when on his way back to the hotel one evening he felt the hair on the back of his neck stand on end and he heard footsteps coming up fast behind him.

"Hey, buster, stop right where you are."

Daniel felt his knees weaken and he slowly turned toward the gruff voice, "yes sir, what can I do for you?"

"You been askin' around about me and I want to know why?"

"You're Konrad?" Daniel asked as he looked into the face of the tallest man he had ever seen.

"Yeah, I'm Konrad, what do you want with me?"

"I just want to ask a few questions. You see a friend of mine is the daughter of a man who was killed back in St. Louis some twenty years ago and no one seems to know anything about who did it or why. I was told back in Huron City that whoever did it got paid to because it seems that Flanders had plenty of money on him when they found him. I was told that you might know something about it. Do you? I mean do you know anything about who killed Matthew Flanders and why?"

Konrad picked Daniel up by his necktie with one hand, "now you listen to me you little son-of-a-bitch, that was a long time ago and I think we should just let the dead stay dead, unless of course you want to join Flanders."

"No, no, I just want to know who killed him. I can't find anything out from the coroner's office, the newspaper archives or the county records. I'm not accusing you if that is what you think, I just thought that if you knew something that maybe you could tell me so I could find out who did kill him."

"If I did know who did it I would thank them, not snitch on them to someone like you. You want some advice, son?"

"Yeah, yeah sure, anything you want to tell me, go ahead, I'll listen."

"Get the hell out of Omaha and don't come back. And, whoever you are, you better forget you ever heard of me, saw me or spoke to me. What happened back then was a long time ago. I was only one of the men that Flanders played for a fool. Everybody needed a little extra money back in them days, and whoever did kill him did the world a favor, and there ain't no amount of money to get me to say another word about it. You might find that there are a lot of people who claim they did it or know who did it, but there is only one man who knows what happened that night, and in case you don't get it boy, he ain't talking. Now you get out of this town, and you forget about me and what I said here tonight." With that he threw Daniel away from him and turned and walked away.

Daniel was left trying to gather his wits about himself and wondering just what had happened. Had he found the killer of Matthew Flanders? But, if Konrad was the killer, then why? Did someone pay him to do the killing? He had to get home to Huron City. He had to talk to his father about all of this. One thing was for sure, he wasn't going to waste any more time. He would catch the next train home.

When Daniel arrived back in Huron City, his parents were home and in their beds. He had traveled for two days on the train and he, too, was tired. Sleeping at home was the same for him, however, as it was when he was in Omaha. His fears had kept him awake during the darkness and the comfort that it was supposed to bring never arrived.

Getting out of bed and dressing, he left the house and walked around the corner and down the side street to O'Connor's Pub. He had been working way to hard for his way of thinking, and he was tired, tired and dry. He was still trying to get things straight about Matthew Flanders' killer and Grace Humphreys being Daphnia's mother, and it was all getting jumbled up. He decided that if he could just stop by the pub for a drink maybe he would get the courage to go to the quarters and see if he could stir up some interest among some of the young Negro women who had arrived on the latest wagon up from Atlanta. He needed a diversion, and a fresh young woman would do it for him every time.

Stepping up to the bar he ordered a whiskey. Then it seemed as if out of nowhere that he was stopped dead in his tracks at the sight of young Michael who was sweeping up the place for ole' Ian; Michael's eyes caught his, and Daniel froze with the glass not quite to his lips.

"What you doing here?" Michael asked putting his hand against the chest of Daniel and holding him there by staring up into his face. Michael knew that Daniel was afraid of him. He could feel his heart beating and see the sweat popping out on his forehead and temples. "You didn't hurt her again, now did ya? Cause if you did I thank its about time that I start giving you some of your own medicine. So tell me, sir, did you hurt her?"

"Now, now, son, you know that your Mother is the sweetest thing that I have ever known, why would I want to hurt her? Besides you know that I haven't been over to your place in weeks. And, listen boy, you better be careful, making threats and such against me, and especially for no reason. Who you been talking to, boy?" Daniel asked trying to keep his voice from shaking. "Just what are you thinking touching me and making threats? Just because you are close to becoming a man yourself gives you no right to even talk to me, let alone touch or threaten me. Do you know what one word from me to the constable would do to you and your family? Well, you would be sent to jail somewhere, and they don't take kindly to niggers where you would end up, and your mother and that little sister of yours would be right back there in the midst of those coal miners in Morgantown. Now, you just better think before you touch me or threaten me again, do you understand me, nigger?"

"I understand. I understand plenty, and if I see you sniffing around my house you won't have to worry none about the constable, cause you wont have a breath in your body to drag your sorry ass to see him. Now, let's get things straight between us." Michael spoke through gritted teeth with his hand holding firmly against Daniel's chest. "Now, I ain't been talking to nobody, I just know that I ain't letting you hurt her again, cause if you do I'm here to tell you that I, sir, will carve your heart out and shove it up your tight skinny white ass." As he made this last remark, he pushed his hand hard against the chest of Daniel and then pulled it away just as fast. Seeing Daniel's face turn even whiter than usual, he spat on the floor and walked past him toward the back of the pub.

Coming face to face with the angry black boy had scared him to where he was afraid his heart would jump out of his chest. He had never seen such hatred and arrogance in the eyes of another human being like he had seen in Michael's.

Daniel was frightened. He couldn't go home, because he couldn't sleep, and he couldn't see Clarice because he was afraid of Michael. Now, O'Connor's was off limits, too. He headed down Pine Street and over to "Joe's Brewsky" for some light entertainment and a shot of whiskey. Surely he would be able to find some peace there. He shuddered as he entered the small establishment with its dirt floor and dimly lit lights. It was more of a cavern than a building.

Stepping inside of the smoke filled room where there was barely enough light to see one's own hand in front of their face, he squinted trying to focus. He could barely see the men sitting around the card tables and standing at the bar. The place was loud with raucous language and bawdy laughter and the smell of stale whiskey and ale that had been spilled and left to sour on the dirt floor brought little comfort to Daniel; but, he knew the men who frequented this place understood his superiority and would regard him with respect. He strode up to the bar as if he owned the place. He ordered whiskey straight up and then taking the small glass in his hand, he closed his eyes and took in a deep breath and swallowed the warm liquid. But, he didn't keep his eyes closed for long. The minute he felt the whiskey slide down his throat, he had visions of the reflection of the young Michael in the mirror. It was as if he could feel the young black boy standing behind him and breathing against his neck. He felt the glass slip from his hand and was startled at the sound of it shattering onto the bar. He wore, not drank the pungent liquid and putting two bits on the bar, he left the tavern without a word and walked down by the river.

Finally, he was alone with his thoughts of Clarice. As much as he had tried, no other woman really satisfied him the way she did. He would sometimes close his eyes and pretend that she was white and that he could bring her home to a meal with his folks, or take her out on the town. In spite of the fact that she was a Negro, he actually thought that he could love her if everything was right. He had had many women, and certainly his share of them over the last month or so, but none could compare with her. He found himself hating the other women and himself as well for being with them. He would drink too much and become angry and abusive toward them. He walked along the St. Clair River bank and allowed himself to imagine what it could be like if she just weren't a nigger.

He had managed to shake the sight of Michael out of his head, and was able to focus again on what it was that he needed. He could wait no more. He knew that Michael was working so he would be free to be alone with the small black woman. He would risk it. As he walked back toward the quarters he could feel his need for her and the anxiety of his wanting brought firmness to his loins and he hurried his pace into a trot then a full run.

He rounded the corner of the shanty and as he stepped up onto the porch he could see that she had company. Her father was sitting there at the table with the little girl Ruby on his lap. Clarice was busy dishing up some chowder of some sort. He could never go in with the old man there. That wouldn't do at all. He stepped down quietly from the porch and pulling his collar up around his ears he walked back to the big yellow house on Pine Street. Another night without sleep, he thought as he went inside and up to his room.

Morning did not arrive soon enough for Daniel. Coming down the stairs he walked through the parlor where his parents were sitting and into the kitchen without speaking to either of them.

"Daniel, Daniel come back here, son." Ruth called to him. "You won't believe who stopped by yesterday. That young man Tom Saunders is back in town, and you will never believe it, he brought himself a wife."

Daniel stopped in his tracks, "Tom? Tom is back?" he asked in disbelief. Then coming over to where she was sitting he took hold of her shoulders "Tell me, where is he? When did he get here? How do you know this?" But before Ruth could answer, Daniel looked over to his father, "Father, is Tom really back in town? Is he coming back to work? I could sure use him around there. When does he start?"

"Sit down, Daniel. You sound like a schoolboy. What's got you so excited, you look like the devil himself has been after you, son? Are you okay? Ruth, come over here and take a look at this son of ours, why those circles under your eyes Daniel are as dark and puffy as I have ever seen. You lost some weight? What's got into you, son? Didn't you eat anything while we were gone, and while you were away on your fact-finding escapade?"

"I'm okay, Father, just haven't been sleeping very well lately, and there has been a lot of work. As for my fact-finding escapades as you call it, you are right I did find out some things that might interest you, and you to Mother. But, there is just one more detail that I need to challenge first before I discuss what I have learned with either of you. Now, tell me about Tom. When did he come back?"

"He came in the Gazette late yesterday afternoon, Daniel. He looked just fine. Said that he decided to return, Alabama didn't suit him at all. He asked if we still had a job for him and I told him he could start tomorrow. He is starting Monday, that will be soon enough. He said he got married down there and his wife is expecting a baby. Can you just believe it, Tom Saunders married and soon to be a father? That just don't seem possible to me, he was always so wild, and such a man for the ladies." Herbert sat back down in his own chair and again took up his paper and started to read.

Ruth looked over the top of her glasses at her son and his father, "Yes sir Tom Saunders is back and I'll bet there will be plenty of hearts broken when they find out about his new family. He sure didn't change much, still tall and handsome as ever. Those dark eyes and soft dark hair, and that sideways smile of his that shows just enough of his pearly white teeth to make you forgive and forget any of his foolishness, yes sir, he is just as tall, dark, and handsome as he was the day he left, maybe even more so. Now, don't you think you should have a bite to eat Daniel, you look terrible, are you sick or something?"

"No, Mother, I am not sick, and I don't want anything to eat. I just need a cup of coffee. I'm going to go out for a while, I'll see you both later."

"Daniel, aren't you coming into work today," Herbert asked?

"I'll be in. But, Father if things are so busy, why didn't you let Tom start today or tomorrow? I need him to pick up some of the work especially with Daphnia still gone. She said she would only be gone for a week or so; so much for honesty on the part of a Flanders. How long does it take to bury her aunt and uncle, for God's sake, how long does she plan to grieve anyway?"

"Just how long has it been since you have been to the Gazette, Daniel? Daphnia got home here last evening. As for picking up her work as well as your own, I was gone for only a short while and both times you found it necessary to hang a sign on the door and leave town yourself. Just what are you up to, Daniel?"

"I told you, there is one last detail that I need to resolve before I talk with you about this. But, what I can tell you is it is a story that goes back over twenty years, and it will shake some declarations of honesty to hell and back along with those that took part in it. Murdered people stay buried, but sometimes their stories find a way of breaking free of the coffin and when they do, the secrets break free as well. Just like a rolling wall of thunder, Father, silence is never really silence for too long." Putting his coffee cup down on the table next to his father, Daniel walked out of the yellow house and toward the waterfront and the shanties of the lumberjacks and woodcutters.

Chapter Twenty-Eight

Daphnia awakened early and went downstairs to the newspaper office to see what needed to be done. There were stacks of papers and wastebaskets overflowing everywhere. She went about cleaning things up and trying to make some sense of what needed to be done first. By the time Herbert came into the office she had already done several hours of work, and she was glad to see him and equally happy about the interruption. The two talked about Thaddeus, Martha and her welcome return. Herbert had brought bread and cheese from home and the two shared their noon meal amidst talk about business, what Daniel might be up to and what plans she had made, if any. There were no problems solved and no promises made, but she was glad to be home.

***

Daniel saw two of the lumberjacks sitting on a log eating; he stood quietly and watched them for a while until one of them finally spotted him.

"Hey you there! What are you doing here? What do you want?"

"Nothing, I'm just standing here. I was taking a walk by the river and this is where I ended up. You men are here a little late in the year, aren't you? Shouldn't you be getting back down south by now?"

"What's it to you, whether we stay or go? Who are you, some sheriff or something?"

"Now, that's funny. No, I'm not a sheriff. I work for the Gazette. It is a newspaper here in town and I was just wandering around here looking to see what was going on. I heard there was some activities going on here at night that I might like to join in on, as a personal nature that is, no newspaper reporting or anything like that."

"Well, you heard wrong. And, I always say once a newspaper reporter always a newspaper reporter. If you see it, hear of it, think it, eventually it will show up on one of them printed rags and everybody will be thinking it is gospel just because it is in print and someone read it. You get on outta here, now, this ain't no place for you even if something was going on, which it ain't."

"Yeah, boy you better get on outta here before Rufus sees you, he'll make short work of you for sure. You take your pencil and paper and get a move on back to where you came from."

Daniel knew from the tone in the men's voices that he had intruded and had said too much. He felt like maybe he better leave these men alone for now, he would question them about Konrad later when he sees them at O'Connor's or Joe's. He left the way he came and decided that maybe he should take a chance and see if Clarice was available.

Going through the back alley he stepped up onto the porch and knocked at the door, Michael opened it.

"What you want?" he asked with a grin on his face.

"I was, I was just wondering if maybe you would like to come to work at the Gazette, sweeping up and taking out the trash, stuff like that," Daniel stammered.

"Where you been, man, I done been doing that stuff since Miss Daphnia came to town, don't you know nothing?"

"What? Why didn't I know about this? How many jobs do you have anyway? When do you work at the Gazette?"

"How many jobs I have is my business. I work for Miss Daphnia, and you can ax her your questions. Now, what do you want?"

"Is your mother home?" Daniel asked humbly.

"No, she ain't home. She went in to see the doctor about Ruby's sore throat and them blisters on the back of her mouth, doctor thinks we might be contagious. You wanna come in?" he asked with a nodding motion toward the inside of the cabin.

"No, tell Clarice I came by, hope your sister is okay. Guess I'll be seeing you around."

"Oh, you'll be seeing me, Mr. Bernstein, you'll be seeing me most everywhere you go," Michael said with a smile this time and he chuckled as he closed the door.

As Daniel turned to walk away he heard a voice come from inside the cabin causing him to spin around.

"Who was that, Michael?" Clarice asked.

"Oh it weren't nobody mama, just a man asking for a handout. I told him we barely had enough for ourselves let alone give it away to some fool beggar." Michael knew that Daniel was standing outside so he shouted as loudly as he could. "Come on, Ruby, let's go outside and play. I'll play kick the can with you if you would like."

Daniel walked away knowing the young boy had gotten the better of him again. He would speak with his father about Daphnia hiring someone to help clean up around the office without letting him know about it. How dare she, he thought. As he walked back toward town, he decided that maybe the key to blowing the story of Matthew Flanders' murder wide open was in the little gray house with Melissa Flanders and Eloise Barnes.

It was Friday afternoon and he didn't expect anyone to be there at this time. He walked up the path and knocked on the front door. He was greeted by Eloise.

"Mr. Bernstein, this is a surprise. What can we do for you?"

"Well, actually, Miss Barnes, I was hoping that you could maybe answer some questions for me. Do you mind if I come in?" he asked as politely as he could.

"Well of course you can come in. Can I get you some tea or something to drink, Daphnia and I are having a cup of ginger tea and some lemon cookies, would you care to join us?" she asked.

"Daphnia is here? Maybe I better come back another time; I wouldn't want to impose on her time with Mrs. Flanders. I'll stop again," he said as he replaced his hat to his head and turned and walked away from the house.

"Now, isn't that just the strangest thing? Daniel Bernstein coming here just as big as you please saying that he wanted to ask some questions. What do you think of that Daphnia?" she asked as she returned to her seat on the davenport.

"He has been asking questions where he should leave things be, Aunt Ella. He has been up to Lansing, out to St. Louis and the Lord only knows where else. I think he has found out that Melissa is not my mother and he wants to use that information to hurt me in some way."

Daphnia had told Eloise about what she heard from her Aunt Martha about her father and Grace Humphreys. The two women had discussed every detail at length. They promised that they would not tell Melissa of this just yet, she had not had a very good day and Daphnia agreed that no good would come from upsetting her further. They were just getting ready for Daphnia to leave when Daniel appeared.

Leaving the two women sitting there looking all smug and knowing everything irritated Daniel. He walked back toward O'Connor's; he needed a drink for sure. The Gazette could wait until Monday for him to make his re-entry into how things were managed and going to be managed in the future.

Daphnia went in and said good-be to Melissa and then gave Eloise a hug. She walked down the pathway feeling a relief that she had not known in a very long time. Finally, she knew who she was and she felt good about her decisions. She loved Melissa, she couldn't help herself, but she loved her for who she was not for the woman she had believed her to be. Walking up the stairway to her apartment, she vowed to begin going through the trunks and boxes of letters tomorrow. Now, she would sleep. She had found peace.

Daniel drank at O'Connor's until they suggested he leave so they could close up and he could still walk home. The cold wind on his face served to help sober him up on his walk back to the big yellow house on Pine Street. By the time he arrived there he knew that sleep would not come easy for him regardless of how much he had been drinking. And he was right. Sleep was almost impossible for him, and as for finding peace or any semblance thereof, the big yellow house had seen its last and the coming of morning would not bring anything but harsh daylight.

Daniel awoke with a start. He had spent most of the night sleeping in the chair in his room and he was stiff and aching from being slumped over. He shook his head and wiped away the sleep from his eyes. "My God," he said out loud to no one, "Tom is back, hallelujah, he has returned. I have to get dressed. Now I don't care what Daphnia does, who she hires, or who her mother is! Finally, Tom is back!" as he stood, his legs felt wobbly and it felt as if someone had beaten him over the head with a board. He sat back down, groaned and closed his eyes. There was plenty of time, he would try to just sit and rest for a few minutes. He leaned back in the chair and once again slipped into a restless sleep.

It was almost noon when he awoke for the second time. Although not feeling totally well, he went about washing up and putting on a fresh shirt and pressed trousers. Tipping the glass and drinking down the remaining whiskey from the night before, he smiled. He was whistling as he grabbed his jacket and skipped down the stairs. He could smell the fresh brewed coffee as he came through the parlor. Going into the kitchen, he touched his mother's neck, "good morning, Mother, that coffee sure smells wonderful. You got any rolls and jam to go with it?" he asked pouring a cup of the hot coffee.

"Well, well, you sure are in a better mood than you were last night, but for your information, it is no longer morning. And, even with a clean shirt and freshly washed face you still look like you've been run over by a tribe of Indians. I wish you would take better care of yourself, Daniel, you know you are all that your Father and I have and there is a lot riding on your being able to handle things once we are gone. Whether you want it or not, you have some major responsibilities. We aren't going to be around forever, your Father is getting up there in age and I am right behind him. It won't be long before you are left alone and having to fend for yourself, and we don't have the wherewithal to leave you like Thaddeus and Martha left Daphnia. Lord knows that girl don't have to work another day in her life."

"She doesn't have to work, Mother, but look at her real good. Just what's she got? Yeah, she has money and property, but she doesn't have family or friends. The entire time she has been here in Huron City she hasn't made one friend. Now with Thaddeus and Martha dying she doesn't have family anymore either. All she does is sit behind that desk during the day and visit Melissa in the evenings. Does that look like someone who has it all? And, Mother, you know of course that Grace Humphreys was nothing but a whore, shacking up with Matthew Flanders the biggest whoremonger around? Why, the way I heard it, he had his way with every woman he met, even had one taking care of him so to speak before Daphnia was even born out in St. Louis and the whole time keeping time with Melissa. Yep, Matthew Flanders didn't leave nothing behind but a bunch of broken hearts and the child of a woman he wasn't even married to. You wouldn't know anything about any of this, now would you Mother?" he asked as if he hadn't seen the blood drain from her face the minute he mentioned Matthew's name.

Ruth was shaking. She sat down at the kitchen table and pretended to drink her coffee, "Daniel, I don't know where you hear all of this stuff. I don't know nothing about Grace Humphreys or Matthew Flanders. I think you better drop this right now. As for Daphnia, you're right. She'll be an old maid, just like Eloise Barnes, working just to have something to do. Ain't no life, no life at all. Now if you are interested in figuring out a mystery, leave Matthew alone and find out what it is that is so important to cause your father to insist Daphnia stay here. I swear, there's something going on that I just can't quite put my finger on, with that young woman, but I will, you can bet your last dollar that I will. Now, sit on down here and eat something. My God, Daniel, you look terrible. I think you better see the Doctor. Are you sleeping at night? You better start taking care of yourself, your Father and me won't be around forever to take care of you so you better start looking after yourself. You are the only heir we have, ain't no bastard children hanging around our alleyways. Are you listening to me, Daniel?"

He was drinking his coffee and hoping that the pounding in his head would stop soon. At the same time he was trying to listen but he couldn't be sure if she was telling the truth or not, she was so flustered. He held his hand up to her hoping that she would stop for a minute and just shut up, but she continued. As he was trying to shut out any unnecessary conversation or noise of any sort, his Father came into the room slamming the door behind him.

"Good God, woman you aren't on that again, are you? Pour me some of that coffee Daniel. Ruth do you have anything to eat or are we just supposed to exist on coffee, rolls and jam? They look like what was left over from breakfast. And, I wish you would stop this nonsense about getting old and dying. I'm not ready for the grave, Ruth, maybe you are, but there is a little of life left in this old body whether you think so or not. Glad to see you up and about son, I was worried about you last night. You want to walk back to the Gazette with me, there is a lot to talk about and we need to make some plans for Tom's return on Monday." Then sending a look toward Ruth he took his coffee cup and walked out of the kitchen with Daniel close behind him.

"Here, let's sit here a minute and finish up this coffee and then we can go. What have you been up to Daniel? What is going on with you? Where have you been? I know that you were in Lansing visiting with Miss Ann, and I believe you went out to St. Louis and back east to Boston. Is there some place that I have missed? What is it that you are looking for? You have been back just three days and you haven't been home two. Where have you been spending your time in the evenings? You sure don't look well, and I know it isn't because of how hard you are working. I saw how you left things while I was away, even before Daphnia left, why you took off the very day after your mother and I went to Lansing. When you are here you barely spend six hours a day at the office and from the stories you have brought in lately you aren't spending too much time out on the streets or down at the mills. What's going on?" Herbert asked the young man. It was clear that time had taken residence between the two and he realized he didn't know his own son very well.

"That's a lot of questions, some of which I don't believe you have a right to ask. Which do you want me to answer first? What have I been up to? Well, let's see, I have been working on a story that started a long time ago. I believe you are aware of it. Does the death of Matthew Flanders ring a bell for you? I want to know the who and the why of it, and I want to know why nobody was ever charged with his murder. Do you want to talk about it now, Father? Or would you rather that I just tell you I have been working, just not the kind of work that keeps me sitting behind a desk all day long seven days a week? I'm looking for answers, does that satisfy you? As for being in the office and keeping things going, well you have Daphnia. Your precious and perfect Daphnia! Do you know that she has hired that nigger boy, Michael Hayes to work at the Gazette without me even knowing about it?"

"That young colored boy, Michael Hayes, has been doing a heck of a lot of work around there. You had no idea he had been hired because you are never there. I am sure there are plenty of things that go on around the office that you are unaware of, because you don't seem to care," Herbert was glad to change the subject. "I am worried about you, you look terrible, and I think you are spending too many nights at the taverns."

"I am fine, I am not sick, I just have not been sleeping well for quite some time now. As for my evenings, well they are mine, aren't they? If you are bothered about me coming in late, I can always take a room at the boarding house. Now that Daphnia has moved in over the office, I can't really stay there, now can I?"

"There's no need to start that up again, Daniel. You didn't want that apartment. I tried for years to get you to move in up there and start taking on some independence, but you didn't want to. Now that Daphnia has moved in that is all that I hear from you and your mother, that I gave away what was rightfully yours. Well let me tell you something Mr. High and Mighty, she has as much right to live there as you do, and she at least appreciates it. That's more than I can say for you. Now, come on, let's get down to the office and see what's happening, maybe Tom will come in today instead of waiting for Monday. At any rate, you and I need to get some things settled down there about who is going to do what. The Gazette is my paper, it is me, it is what I have worked my entire life for, and I don't intend to let it get run into the ground. Now, you talked about them lumberjacks down by the river. They'll be moving out soon now with winter upon us. Just what is it that you think needs to be addressed in our paper? Is there something illegal going on down there? Are you mixed up in anything, Daniel?"

"Good God, Father. Just what has been going through that head of yours? You sound like I am keeping time with the Devil or something. No. I am not mixed up in anything illegal. If you don't like my work, just let me know and I will move on. The Gazette is not my life, it is not what I am working for, it doesn't represent me. It is no more than a means to an end and some money in my pocket. You need to know that those doors will close permanently the day they lay you in the ground, if it is up to me. I need to move on, I want to see other things, meet new people, smell new smells and taste the salt of the ocean. I'll be here for as long as you want me to be, but when that changes you just say the word. I can be out of here tomorrow. I know there are a few dollars put away for me from Grandfather, and I will be happy to oblige him and use them any day you say."

"Well, maybe it is good that we had this talk. When you feel froggy, Daniel, you jump boy! You can do whatever you think is right for you. You're of age. Your Grandfather's money is sitting there you can take it whenever you want. You can leave today, you don't need to wait until tomorrow or the next day either for that matter. As for what's been going on in my head, I hear things. I know about your drinking, you're patronizing the quarters. You better watch out, son. You aren't as well regarded as you might believe."

"Don't worry, Father. I'm not ready to move on just yet. I'll stick around for a while anyway. Besides I, like Mother, am interested in seeing how this thing with your precious Daphnia works out. I agree with Mother, there is some special connection between the two of you and I plan to be the one to break the story. And, for my money, it all has to do Matthew Flanders. Did he owe you some money or something? Maybe it involves his whore, Grace Humphreys, is that it? Was she your woman and he stole her away?"

Herbert could barely contain himself. He came at Daniel with his fist clinched and his eyes red with, "now you listen to me, if I ever here you mention the name of Grace Humphreys again you won't get a choice of when you leave, and you won't get a chance to say good-bye. Whatever it is you are looking for you stay away from anything having to do with her or her memory."

Daniel jumped back and away from his father. He had never seen him angry like this before and he had a sinking feeling in the pit of his stomach that he had finally happened upon the key that would solve the mystery.

Ruth came into the room and saw the two men standing mere inches apart and she was somewhat perplexed. "What's going on out here?"

"Nothing, Ruth, just talking about the things that are happening around town, that's all," Herbert said as he moved away from Daniel. "Now, Daniel, tell me about those lumberjacks, what is going on? Is this something that you want to work on or should I give it Tom on Monday?"

"As for the lumberjacks, Father, I can handle them without any help. But maybe I should discuss some of the other things with Tom. Hopefully he won't wait until Monday to stop by. It will be good to lift a few ales with him."

"No need to expect that Saunders boy to be running around from tavern to tavern with you this time, Daniel. He is done married and expecting a baby, I imagine he is settled down and acting like a man with a family ought to act, yes sir, he is done gone and gotten himself married, Daniel, you will have to find yourself another best pal to carouse around with. Now, here ya go, I buttered you up some of those rolls to take with you down to the Gazette. You two are going back to work today, aren't you? I closed up the store to come here and check on things, but I can't leave it closed forever." Ruth left the two men and went back into the kitchen.

Daniel took the sack of rolls and putting on his coat and hat, he held the door for his father. "What do you think of the activity down at the lumber yards, Father? Do you think they are working too far into the season? It seems to me that they will soon have a hard time determining which trees to cut and which to leave standing. They are sure a rough crowd, those lumberjacks. Why those shanties they live in aren't much better than down at the quarters, no telling what all is going on down there. I think we should make them clean up some of the trash they got piled up around. Why don't you go over and see the judge today? I know there is a story there, I can smell it."

Herbert was listening to Daniel but the words that lingered were those of his connection to Daphnia. He did not want him messing around trying to uncover things that were best left alone.

"Oh, now, boy, leave them be. They will be out of here soon enough and then the place will be so quite it will seem dead. All the woodcutters and lumberjacks bring excitement and it don't last all that long. I don't think there is much to the goings on, let's just drop it. Now, we best be thinking about whether or not the Gazette can afford both you and Tom, so I need to know where you stand. Daphnia will be taking on more responsibility and I will want to include her in the partnership very soon."

"Daphnia! Daphnia! What will we need her for once Tom gets back into the swing of things? She's been gone long enough that we have just about gotten back to where we were before she came. Besides, now with both Tom and me working full time you can go back to keeping up with the paperwork that Daphnia was doing while you were doing some of the typesetting and writing, maybe she can work with Mother."

"That's not likely to happen. Besides, like I said the Gazette is as much her right as it is yours."

The wind was brisk and Daniel felt cold from the inside out. Both men were having difficulty fighting the wind and keeping their minds from wandering in different directions. They were talking, but not necessarily listening. They were caught up in their own secret charade and hoping the other wouldn't find out before it was time.

Arriving at the Gazette, Herbert stepped ahead and unlocked the door. Daphnia was not in today, but it was obvious that she had been. Herbert went to his office where he closed the door and remained working in silence until late into the afternoon. Daniel, on the other hand, worked in his office with the door open and stayed past sunset but Tom didn't come by.

It was Saturday evening and instead of going into O'Connor's, Daniel decided to go straight home. As he walked the wind whipped the leaves against him. He could feel the two black eyes on the back of his neck, and his walk was more of a trot and a skip than the walk of a fearless man.

Feeling the wind whipping about his collar and hearing it howl through the treetops and around the corners of buildings only made him more frightened. The darkness had always been his friend, but no more. With the night came the hushed whispers of young Michael against the back of his neck, and the boy's eyes peered from around street lamps, corners of buildings and from the very sky above him. To say that he had come to dread the darkness of night would be an under-statement. He knew that he would spend this the same way as he had spent the last several; he would stay awake praying for morning and the routine it would bring.

Upon entering the yellow house, he went immediately up to his room. He needed a drink and he needed to begin his vigil of keeping away the demons that floated from every corner of his mind while he was awake and the nightmares that haunted him when he slept. Ruth had come up to check on him only once to leave a tray of food for him outside of his door. "God why couldn't she leave him alone?" he muttered as he ignored her knocks at the door and her calls to him.

Chapter Twenty-Nine

Daphnia had spent most of the day going through things she had packed away in one of the large trunks. She did not see the trunk from Herbert's attic and would ask him about it again on Monday. In the meantime she enjoyed the unpacking of the precious treasures and reliving some of her fondest memories. It was late when she decided to go downstairs and to the general store to pick up some things.

There was a steady mix of rain, sleet and snow falling against the door as she left the Gazette and went to the next door over to the General Store. She saw only one dim light, but the door was unlocked, as she pushed it open and called out.

"Well, good evening, Daphnia," Ruth's shrill voice cut through the silence like an ice pick being drawn against a piece of glass.

"My Goodness, Ruth you startled me. I thought someone had broken in, there are no lights on, what are you doing here so late?"

"I came down to get a handle on the inventory, dear. I don't always get to the paperwork end of things during the day, and with Herbert gone doing whatever he does and Lord only knows where he does it half the time, and Daniel out doing whatever it is that he does on Saturday evenings, this is a good time for me. But, I should ask you, too, what are you doing coming down here so late?"

"Honestly, I lost track of the time and when I decided to come down here, I was hoping someone would be here, but was prepared to leave a list of whatever I took and the money as well," she held out her hand showing the list of items she was planning to purchase along with her coin purse. I figured that I could settle up any differences with you later. I didn't realize how long I had been away and I guess I didn't leave much in the way of staples upstairs. I do hope you won't mind."

"No, no, of course not. You go ahead and take whatever you want. This is a good time for me to tell you in person just how sorry I am about Martha and Thaddeus. It has been especially hard on Herbert. He has been working far too hard with you away for so long. You know once you make a commitment, you have to honor it, dear; and you have made a serious commitment to Herbert I hope you realize that."

"Well, of course I do. I am sorry that I was gone longer than I had originally planned, but then I can't be held to the original agreed upon time frame considering the fact that I have just lost both my aunt and uncle, now can I?"

"Of course, dear, I understand. I am so sorry about Martha and Thaddeus, such a shame, such a shame. Now you are all alone for sure, except for Melissa, of course, but then she is expecting to go just any day now, just any day. Then what on earth will you do? You won't want to stay around here with no family, will you? Commitment or not! I know that Herbert wouldn't expect you to stay here and would understand if you went back home. Surely you will want to return to that farm where life for you will be easier and you can marry up with one of them hands. Well, of course, there you go dear, you can go home and marry up with one of them young farm boys and raise a whole litter of farmers; you're still reasonably young and healthy enough and with all that land there will be plenty of room for them to run and play. I know that Herbert said you had let that hand and his wife move into the big house, but surely they would understand if you wanted to go back home. And, besides, with all of your money you could build another house. My, my you sure didn't get too much, let me go ahead and settle up with you on that now, I mean I can put it on your tab. But, since I am trying to complete the inventory it would be easier if you just paid for everything while you're here. But, of course if you didn't bring enough money, well then …. are you feeling well, dear? Here you better take some of this cod liver oil up there with you, looks like you are in need of some rest. I do declare, Daphnia, you haven't said more than two words. Here let me take those things and I'll just put them on your bill, I don't want to have any mistakes with me trying to get the inventory done and all."

"That's okay, Ruth, just keep my purse down here and take what you want out of it. I'll go ahead and take these things back upstairs. Here is a list of what I have. I'll let you settle up with me at your convenience."

"No need to do that, Daphnia, we can settle things now."

Daphnia wrapped the items as Ruth added the charges. Once things were paid for Daphnia started out the door, but before she left she turned to Ruth, "I appreciate your advice and understand why you might think returning to Lansing is the right thing for me, Ruth, but I have my own plans. I plan to stay right here for as long as I feel that it is the right thing to do. And, as for getting married, I am engaged to marry William Johnston in the spring."

Once back inside of the cozy apartment she went about putting the purchases away. The wind whistled about the eaves of the building making a moaning sound like she had never heard. Even though the apartment was warm and comfortable, she didn't sleep well, and spent much time pacing the floor thinking about what Ruth had said about marrying one of the farm hands and raising a litter of farmers. What a cruel woman she was, thought Daphnia, how dare she make such assumptions?

Chapter Thirty

Monday morning was a welcome coming. Daphnia awakened early from a night of fitful sleep. She was ready to get started downstairs. The road and walkways were covered with snow and there were icicles hanging down from the porch roof. She unlocked the door and started a fire to heat the office before Daniel and Herbert arrived. She filled the coffee pot with water and the basket with fresh ground beans, then setting the pot on the black pot belly stove she went about raising the green window shades and taking the latest news off the wire. She was glad to be back at the Gazette and was determined not to let the snow and dreary sky dampen her spirits today. She was going to get on with her life. She needed to move forward and no matter what Ruth Bernstein thought, she was not going to pick up and leave Huron City. She wanted to be a newspaperwoman, and this is where she would fulfill that dream.

Going over to her desk, she resumed work on the mountains of paper that had been left for her. She had not been able to get to everything on Friday, and behind her desk and against the wall there were papers piled up in separate stacks with some leaning against the legs of the furniture. Pouring herself a cup of hot coffee, she sat down to begin work and was soon lost in the business before her. She didn't hear the door open and was startled to look up into a stranger's face; she caught her breath.

"Good Morning, what can I do for you?" she asked putting down her pencil and standing up. "Mr. Bernstein is not in yet, is there something that I can help you with?"

"Well, now, let's start with first things first. Who are you?"

"My name is Daphnia Flanders, I am a friend and employee of the Bernstein's. I live upstairs and work here. Who are you?" she responded coming from around her desk.

Before he could answer, the door opened and Herbert came in shaking snow off his coat and hat and nodding over to Daphnia. He walked over and took the hand of the man and shook it firmly, "Good morning, Tom, I see you have met Daphnia."

"Well, we have not been formally introduced, we were just getting around to finding out each other's names when you came in. So, this is Daphnia. Good to meet you," he said while bending slightly from the waist and taking her hand in his.

"Daphnia, this is Tom Saunders. Tom works for us. He is Daniel's best friend, and he has been away in Alabama, but he is back now and ready to go to work, I hope. Tom, Daphnia is the niece of my dearest and oldest friend and she is learning the newspaper business. You two will get along splendidly. Got anymore of that coffee, Daphnia, I brought some fresh rolls and jam. Daniel should be along any minute. Here, Tom, pull up a chair and let's get down to business, you have been gone awhile, and Daphnia has just returned from Lansing where she buried her … never mind, let's have a cup of that coffee," he said as he put the rolls and jam on the back table.

"You are only saying that because you want me to pour it for you and bring it in to your office. Where'd you get the rolls? Don't tell me that Mrs. Bernstein was up and about this early," she said as she poured coffee into a mug for Herbert and refilled her own cup.

Before Herbert could answer the question about the rolls, the door opened and in came Daniel without so much as a good morning, he walked over took the mug of coffee out of Herbert's hand and then walked into his office and closed the door.

"That's okay, dear, Daniel has always been more like his Mother and her side of the family in the mornings." He went to the cupboard above the table and got down another mug and poured his own coffee. "Maybe this way I'll get to drink this one. Come on over here, Tom, get yourself a cup of this coffee, Daniel will be back out in a minute, he hasn't been in a very good mood lately. I'll go in and get him." Herbert then walked over to the closed door and gently tapped "Daniel, come on out here, Daniel. You walked right by your best friend without so much a hello, come on out here Daniel."

Daniel knew he walked past Tom, but he wanted to make him think that he didn't care that he was back. After all, Tom had been gone a long time out having fun and getting married without so much as a letter, why should Daniel make a fuss over him now. Besides, with Daphnia and Tom both back, nobody would even notice him anyway. Getting to his feet, he walked across the office and opened the door and went back into the main office where he extended his hand toward Tom, "Well look who has returned." he said with glee and almost giddiness. He quickly walked over and shook Tom's hand first with one hand and then placing both of his own hands around the one of Tom's and shook it again. "God, don't you look just fine. Married life must agree with you." He added with a punch to the shoulder and a slap on Tom's back. "I sure hope you have returned to stay and are ready to come back to work. You have been missed around here. Father has been some help, but then Daphnia was here just long enough to learn the simplest of tasks and then she left too. So, you sure have been missed Tom Saunders and I'm glad to see you return. You just don't know how hard it has been with you gone, I have had to cover the news stories as well as handle most of the writing and typesetting. I've been working extra hours and there has been no time for ....." he suddenly realized that he was whining and about to say something that he didn't want to say, but in his mind he knew it was the personal pleasures found in the narrow bed with the tender Clarice that he had truly missed more than anything. Feeling his face flush, he released Tom's hands and went over to the stove and poured himself a second cup of the hot coffee. Then turning toward Daphnia he nodded, "welcome back Daphnia, it is good to see you. You look well, considering. Come into my office, Tom, let's get caught up on things."

"Wait a minute Daniel, I feel like I am in one of those Alabama windstorms. I would like to talk with your Father and discuss the terms of my employment, and I sure would like to know more about this new family member, Daphnia here." He said as he extended his hand in Daphnia's direction.

Daphnia felt her breath catch and her stomach tickle from the inside, her knees were suddenly weak and she thought she might faint as she looked up into his chocolate brown eyes and wide smile. "I will be happy to tell you whatever you want to know, but honestly there isn't much to tell. But, what shall I call you? Is it Tom, Thomas or Mr. Saunders?" she inquired.

One look at Daphnia and Tom knew that he had married Brenda Sue Gibson much too quickly. While he certainly loved Brenda, Daphnia took his breath away. He could feel the blood surging through him, and his immediate desire for this young woman with whom he knew would be forbidden to him was overwhelming. He could feel the guilt building before he even had a chance to extend his hand to her in a cordial greeting. As their hands met so did their eyes and there was no mistaking the sparks that flew between the two very different and star-crossed individuals. "Tom will do fine, Daphnia," he said while wishing he had said something more profound. Then turning to Herbert, "So you have finally hired someone in here who can make coffee and help keep the place in order, good for you." He winked at Daphnia and immediately wished he had not.

The interaction between Tom and Daphnia did not go unnoticed by Daniel. His earlier prediction that he would be a mere body in the room was confirmed, but what really upset him was seeing the sparks fly between his best friend and this "new family member" who had taken over his father's heart and soul. He vowed to watch the two of them and to speak to his Mother about Tom's new wife and the news his father had told him about papers being drawn up making Daphnia a partner in the Gazette. He shrugged as he walked back into his office without so much of a word from anyone.

Herbert and Tom retreated into Herbert's office and Daphnia went back to her desk and started to go through the stacks of papers. Regardless of the business at hand, each of them was merely going through the motions of the immediate task, while their thoughts were elsewhere.

Daniel was wishing that Daphnia had not returned and was silently damning her with each breath he took. He was determined to find out about her, her father and her real mother, Grace Humphreys.

Herbert was ready to get Tom out and about and on his way so he could spend some time trying to find out what Daniel was up to.

Tom was trying to come to terms with the feelings he had just experienced when looking into the eyes of Daphnia, and Daphnia was secretly rejoicing in the feelings of butterflies and smiles that she had not felt in a very long time.

At his desk Daniel sat pouting; he did not know what to make of what he had just seen. He had not seen Daphnia in such a take-charge mode before, and until now he had actually forgotten how competent she was and how seriously she took her job. He felt threatened and excluded. The thought of this made him feel ill, Daphnia Flanders, coming from a father who was a scoundrel and who took every woman he met, raised by a great uncle and aunt and now returning to Huron City to bury a woman she didn't even know and who had given her away. This Daphnia was someone he had not paid too much attention to before, but now things would change. He might have been remiss in his lack of regard for her earlier, but no more. He vowed to speak with his Mother this evening about what he learned in Boston, St. Louis and Omaha. He would also be sure to tell her of his father's plans for Daphnia. Damn he hated her. Just who the hell did she think she was anyhow? He knew that there was something more to this woman and her relationship to his father; he was determined to find out. He could see the pride swell up in Herbert today and he had seen this before, there was something familiar about her, he knew promises had been made, but what were they. He wondered about this confident young woman who was little more than a bastard child. Even the Flanders' bloodline could not erase the scandalous nature of her birth. Why did she have to come back here at all? And, what was it with Tom? Who the heck had he become, a married man expecting his first child giving the winks and nods to Daphnia as if he was telling her that he would see her later? God damn them both!

Herbert sat down at his desk and began to move around some of the papers. He was smiling, but he didn't exactly know why. He liked what he had seen from Daphnia. He wished that she had stopped by last evening, he wanted to come over and see her but Ruth was in such a state of ranting and raving that he felt it best to let it be. He would have some time to speak with her later. "Come on Tom, let's you and me sit down and talk business."

Once Tom closed the door behind them that was the last anyone saw of them for quite a while. The two men did not come out until almost noon and then they left the building. Daniel remained in his office all day even when Ruth brought lunch for everyone. She knocked on Daniel's door, but he refused to answer. She left his lunch on a tray along with the others.

Alone with her work, Daphnia found that she had missed working with the words, numbers, and business at hand. She was soon caught up in her own world and the time passed without effort. Herbert and Tom had returned and gone back into Herbert's office without saying a word and once again she was alone with her work. Before she realized it, Daniel was putting on his hat and coat and it was well past dusk. The snowflakes were coming down at a fast and furious pace. The wind was blowing and she could see icicles forming on the eaves of the building; she would need to finish up soon.

"Good evening, Daphnia," Daniel said as he opened the door and walked out into the cold damp air. He didn't wait for her response or acknowledgment. He was sullen from spending the day in his office alone working while his father and Tom were catching up on the affairs and news of the day. He could see that they were still at it by the light shining from beneath the older man's door. He shivered as he pulled his coat around him. He walked toward the quarters; he had to see Clarice.

Daphnia put away her things and was just turning out the lamp on her desk when Herbert opened his office door and he and Tom Saunders walked out. "Good evening, my boy, I am sure glad to have you back with us. I believe I have filled you in on the changes around here and what my expectations are of you, I'll see you tomorrow." Then walking over to Daphnia he said good evening and promised to speak with her tomorrow about some of the changes he would like to make. He buttoned his coat and placed his hat on his head and waved good night as he went out into the night for home.

"Well, guess that leaves you and me here to lock up. Just like the old days some things haven't changed," Tom said to her as he went about checking all the windows, the back door and pulling down the shades and turning out the lamps. "Good night Daphnia, it was a pleasure meeting you," he said as he took her hand and brought it up to his lips. He held her hand there just a second too long and suddenly felt his face redden, "Good evening," he said again.

Daphnia was almost speechless. She took in a deep breath and extending her chin she managed a smile, "Good evening, Tom. I am looking forward to working with you. I have heard so much about you from Daniel. Have a good night I can finish up here." She walked with him to the front door and helped him on with his coat. They needed no more words. As she watched him walk across the street she could see the flutter of snowflakes as they danced about the bottom of his coat that whipped about his boot tops.

Locking the door, she reached into her pocked and felt the smoothness of the small gold key. She had forgotten to mention it to Herbert again, she must remember to do so the very first thing tomorrow morning.

Part V

.... there are whims and fancies and pleasures a plenty,
but when met with deceit, its the heart that's left empty.

We convince ourselves we've no time to care,
while our emptiness echoes silent cries and dry tears.

Chapter Thirty-One

Daniel was disgusted with everything and everybody. He vowed he would show his father that he was "worth his own salt"; he didn't need anyone to tell him what to do or how to do it. If the Gazette were so damned important, then by God he would show everyone that he could make it into more than the simple one page rag that had more opinion and ads than news. He would prove that he could take it further and make the Gazette into a real paper, and certainly more than his old man had made it. He knew enough about when something was out of kilter to not bury his head in the sand; he knew enough to find out what it was. And, he knew that there was something wrong going on in that lumber camp. He also knew that no amount of digging for additional information about Matthew was going to solve anything just now. His father had made it clear that the subject of Matthew, Grace Humphreys and his precious Daphnia were off limits. He knew enough to know that the answers he needed lay with Konrad and his fellow lumberjacks who were around some nineteen or twenty years ago. He would go to the camp. Regardless of what his father said, he knew that those men had stayed far too long and there were too many questions around town about what they were doing. There were people coming in from across the lake to spend time in the camp – now did that make sense? Who would cross that lake in this weather, or travel for miles across the peninsula just to visit that camp? There was something happening and he was going to find out before his father assigned Tom the task. He knew that his father was curious, but just didn't trust him to tackle the story on his own. He could feel it.

He walked down by the shoreline and peered out across the precipice of land extending out into the lake. He could see fires burning off in the distance in the direction of the camp. He crept along the edge of the woods until he could hear the voices of the men. They were laughing and obviously there were more than just the usual lumberjacks, there were at least a half dozen or so horses tied up at the various posts and trees, and there were more than a couple buckboards and wagons hitched around to the side of one of the buildings. At least four or five of the cabins were lit up, but he couldn't see inside. Creeping closer he could hear the laughter and voices getting louder. He thought he could hear women laughing and there was music. He had to know more, he had to get closer.

On the edge of the clearing there was a larger cabin that the men used for their mess hall, and poker games. It was their private tavern of sorts and that was from where most of the noise was coming. He walked along the side of the building and tried to look into one of the windows, but the curtains were pulled shut. He noticed that around the backside of the building the door was ajar, if he could just sneak in through that door, he could find a place to hide and see what exactly was happening.

He slipped around to the back of the building, his heart was racing and he could barely breathe. Just as he stepped inside the door he felt a hand grab him by the back of his neck. Daniel wet himself.

"Well, look at what we got here. Just look at that, you done pissed yourself, Mr. Bernstein. Now, whaddaya wanna go an do a thing like that? You better come on in here and let's see if we can't fix you up."

Daniel was shaking. This was the biggest man he had ever seen, and he acted like he knew him. "Wait, wait, just a minute. Let me go. I just came to see what all the fun was about. Let me go, will ya?" Daniel squirmed, but the man kept holding onto him and dragging him along into the big room.

"Hey, everybody, take a look. We got company! And, what special company he is too. Ya'll know Mr. Bernstein, now don't ya?"

"Hey, Henry. Whatcha bringin' that sonofabitch in here for?"

"Now, quiet down, Rufus. We might just have a little fun this evening. Don't you know who this is? This here's the meanest little man in town. Why, do you know that he beats women and kicks little puppies?"

"Yeah, Henry, I know how mean he is. That piece of slime you got there is the man that whupped up on that sweet young Marylou the other week. You know the one, real cute, shy, red hair, all covered with freckles. She worked over at O'Connor's place, real good worker too! Ya'll remember her? She had to leave town she was messed up so bad. Well, this here is the fine gentleman who was responsible."

"Yeah, and she ain't the only one," came a voice from the back of the room. "What about that colored woman down in the quarters, she done tried to make a livin' for her kids and her old pappy. She's a decent woman, works hard. That boy of hers works plenty hard hisself. Whaddaya think the almighty Mr. Bernstein did to her, well he broke her leg that's what – busted up her ribs too. I saw that colored boy talkin' to him and I asked what it was all about. Bernstein here was plenty scared when he left O'Connor's, but I don't 'spect the boy scared him enough to keep him from hurting his mama again when he gets the notion."

"Now, whaddaya say to that, Henry? Whaddaya say we let him know just how much we appreciate what he done?" Rufus had begun to get the others wound up and in agreement with him.

"See, there Rufus, I knew you would think of a way to make Mr. Bernstein feel welcome," the man who had spoken up earlier guffawed. "Come on let's have some fun."

Daniel was shaking and he could feel himself leaning into the large man who was holding onto him. For some reason, he felt this man might actually keep him safe from the others. But, he was wrong.

The room was full of men and women; the men were jeering and laughing and jabbing at Daniel, but the women stood by watching silently. There were men that Daniel had never seen, and some whom he had. There were women that he had never seen either. Where did they all come from? He could feel their eyes staring at him, and smell the whiskey and stale beer on the breaths of the men as they all came closer and took their turns punching and pushing him. What must they be planning, he wondered? He knew that he couldn't show fear. He had to stand tall and hold his ground. Just then he felt himself being pulled away from the grasp of the big man. He was pushed to the floor, but when he tried to get up he was once again pushed down.

The cheers, whistles and laughter started growing louder. The men were jeering and mimicking him as he crouched and tried to jump out of the way of their fists and feet that were coming at him from all directions. The women were huddled together against the back wall and watching silently, they had no idea about what they were about to witness. One of the men walked over to Daniel and hit him open handed across the mouth. Another spat on his shoes, and then all hell broke loose.

Daniel felt himself being pulled and tugged from one set of hands to another; he was pushed and practically thrown across the room and back again. The men were slapping, hitting and kicking at him from all directions. Finally, he could feel himself falling down onto a cot, and suddenly a hand reached into the waistband of his trousers and ripped them from his body. He was laid out face down and spread eagled on the cot with his hands and feet tied to the respective legs of the bed. He knew what they had in mind, and he tried to brace himself for the onslaught that was about to come his way – but there was no way for him to prepare for what happened next.

Daniel fainted as one man after another assaulted him. When he awoke he was lying in his own vomit and blood. The stench was almost overwhelming, but nothing was as severe as the pain he felt. He felt as though his body had been ripped apart and that he would surely never stand again, let alone walk. There was no part of him that didn't hurt. Even his ears felt bruised and opening his eyes took all of the courage he could muster. Turning over was an almost impossible task. He was certain that his hips and pelvis had been dislocated along with at least his left shoulder; it felt that the fingers on one hand had been twisted and some of them were dangling in such a swollen state that he barely recognized them as his own. He tried to move his leg, but couldn't. Looking down toward the end of the bed he could see that one of his ankles was turned in an awkward position, but ironically that was the one thing that didn't hurt. With each breath he could feel the sharp pains emanating throughout his stomach and chest. His mouth was swollen, and he couldn't quite reach his lips with his tongue, just a little spit, he thought, just a little moisture, but his face was covered with dried blood and he couldn't feel the inside of his mouth let alone lick his lips. Just as he was beginning to actually realize what had happened, and began to shake the cobwebs from his mind, he heard footsteps coming toward him. He squinted against the light and tried to brace himself for the next attack, but instead of a pair of rough hands tearing at him he felt cold water being poured over him. It was both painful and welcome at the same time.

"There, that might make you smell a little better, now. It sure won't make you look any better, but some of that puke and blood will at least be washed away. Let's get him up boys, we better get him down there with them women afore somebody misses him and starts to look for him," the man with the shaggy beard and big hands said as he motioned to the others.

"Aw, come on now Henry, you know what he might do to them women? Let's just finish him off right here and be done with it. There ain't no way nobody will look for him out here, 'sides, we need to burn up some of that trash out there by the grove anyway."

It was Rufus; Daniel remembered his voice from earlier. God he hated that man, he was the first one Daniel saw coming toward him with his eyes filled with blood from the whiskey and his breath smelling like that of an open sewage ditch in the back of the quarters. He could still feel the rough hands of the man as he ripped Daniel's trousers from his body.

"Now, Rufus, you jest let that boy be. He's done hurt bad enough and I don't think he will tell anybody anything ever again. Why, just look at his face, them lips are so split it will take months for them to heal, and when they do, why it won't do no good, George took care of that. Mr. Bernstein here ain't never gonna tell anybody anything ever again, and as for writing them pretty words for that newspaper of his'n, well I don't expect his hands will work quite like they once did. Now come on, we cain't let him lay here and drown in his own filth. Let's get him down there and let them women take care of cleaning him up a bit afore we move outta here."

Three of the other men came over and together they got Daniel to his feet.

Daniel didn't know the details of what had happened, and he certainly didn't know how long it had gone on. All he knew was that he was being moved. Now he was being pushed and pulled toward a hole in the floor. He did not resist as the men grabbed hold of him. He actually welcomed the thought of being put anywhere other than where he was. As they got him on his feet he once again passed out and did not awaken from the nightmares of the disgusting men coming at him over and over until hours later. When he did awaken, he was in a dark hole; he could feel the earth against his skin and smell the wetness of the soil.

Opening his eyes he squinted to make out the images in front of him. There were several women sitting about three feet away; they were just sitting there staring at him. He tried to talk, but couldn't move his tongue. He felt as if there was a dishrag stuffed in his mouth. God his mouth hurt. He tried again to speak, but he couldn't move his jaw. Maybe if he held his hand to the side of his face he thought, but his hand was of no use to him. If he could just open his mouth, but he couldn't. His mouth had been sewn shut, and there was no longer a fully attached tongue. Oh my God, he began to pray. The tears streamed down his face and he tried to beg for their help, but they just sat and looked at him. His mind was screaming, and the tears were coming faster, he tried to stare at them, but he could only open one eye. "What's the matter with you women? Can't you see that I am hurt bad, I need help," he tried to yell, but nothing but muffled noises came from him. Again, he fainted.

"Bernice," one of the women whispered, "we have to do something. Look at him. He's in a bad way. If we don't get them stitches out soon, he won't ever be able to talk, or eat or nothing."

"He ain't never gonna talk agin no how, Doris. They cut off his tongue, don't you know what that means. That boy ain't never gonna say another word. But, yore probly right, we should take out them stitches and try to do him up so he can at least eat and breathe. My God, they made him look like a jack-o-lantern. Anybody got any scissors or needles or something?"

"Here, I got some thread but I don't got no scissors, you might hafta use a nail or stick or something to break away them stitches that's there now. Melanie, didn't you have a needle holding your skirt up the other day?"

"Yeah, but I don't think we ought to get involved. He took quite a thumping last night, and he's pretty messed up. I expect they will want him jest as they left him. No thanks. I ain't getting involved. I got my own troubles to worry about. Besides, I remember him. He's a mean sonofabitch – he's the one what nearly broke my arm about a month or so ago; he's little but he knows how to hurt a woman that's for sure. Naw, I ain't got no interest in putting myself on the line for that mean little bastard – what them men done did to him ain't no worse than what most women wudda liked to have done if given a chance. I ain't getting involved" The larger of the woman named Melanie said.

The others nodded in agreement.

Bernice came up on her knees and put her hands on her hips, "Now, look here. I ain't never asked nothing of none of you. I been a prisoner here just like the rest of you, but this man is sick. He ain't never done nothing to cause him to be treated this bad. Yeah, he beat up a few women and I give you that he deserved to get what he gave, but he never done anything to deserve this and I just cain't let him die here. Now we are gonna help him, and that's that. Melanie, you give me that there needle or I'm gonna have to take it and I don't wont to do that. Ellen, I'll take that there thread, if there is anyone here who has a pair of scissors then hand them over. And, I want petticoats, aprons anything that we can use to tie together splints for his leg and fingers. I ain't no doctor but I done bandaged up enough men in my day to at least get some of his bones back in a straight line. Phyllis, you find me some straight boards that I can use. Mary, go look around and find something that I can use on his fingers. Now come on, we have to work fast before he wakes up. This man is hurt, and he is hurt bad. And, we need water – I want every water bucket we got down here – we have to get him cleaned up."

Bernice began working on Daniel, and the others went about doing as she had instructed. Melanie handed over the needle and then went and sat in a corner – she had made up her mind, she wasn't helping.

Bernice leaned over Daniel again; she had to figure out just where to start. A pair of scissors appeared and there was more than one needle. She tried to be as gentle as possible so as not to awaken him, she did not want him to wake up with her leaning over him with scissors in her hands. The stitches did not come out easily. The men had double knotted each stitch. Once his lips and face were parted she opened his mouth and her hand flew to her face. Daniel's tongue was practically severed, and his mouth was filled with hunks of flesh and dried blood. How he had managed not to drown in his own blood was a mystery to her. She gently swabbed his mouth and reattached his tongue as best she could. She then went about trying to stitch his face and lips back as they were supposed to be. There was so much blood that she was not always sure she was sewing in the right place, but she continued. She had to get his face at least back together, she thought. She remembered a doctor back in St. Louis wiring a man's jaws together after a fight, and she considered trying this with Daniel, but decided to wrap his head and face with rags torn from the women's petticoats instead. At least this way his face would be held together and he wouldn't try to talk for a while. When she had finished with his face and head, she started to work on his arms and hands. God, what a mess; she was able to put his shoulder back into place and made a sling for his arm. It appeared that his arms had been spared – they were bruised and scratched up pretty badly, but the bones seemed to be intact. His hands were another matter. She held each hand as delicately as she could and did her best to straighten the bones and force the knuckles back into place. She made splints for his fingers and wrapped each hand as tightly as she could without cutting off the circulation. Then, she started with the ribs, wrapping his abdomen and forcing his hips and pelvis back into place. It looked to her that both legs had been broken as well one of his ankles. His feet were pretty bruised but otherwise didn't seem to be broken. When she finished with him he had so many pieces of boards, twigs and rags tied to him he didn't look like a man at all. One thing was for certain, he wasn't going to move around much, or talk either for that matter. She took what water was left and tried to wash him up as best she could, that's when he awoke.

He opened his eyes and could see the face of the woman leaning over him. He tried to scream but he couldn't. He couldn't move. He was bound so tightly that he thought he had been entombed like an Egyptian Mummy; he was frantic.

"Now, now, you just lay there and be quiet," Bernice told him. "You been hurt real bad, and I done all I could to put you back together, but its best you don't try to move around much just now, you just lay there and be quiet. Try to drink some of this here water." She held a cup of water up to his mouth and managed to get him to drink down about half of it before he passed out again. "He's lost a lot of blood, we got to get him to a doctor somehow. He's in a bad way."

The others just looked at her and sat silently. There was no way any of them were going to risk their lives for this man or any other for that matter.

294

"If we can get him to one of them wagons that's hitched out there we can get him to town, we have to give it a try," she said to the others.

"No," Melanie said, "we ain't getting involved. You want to risk your life to save him, then you go ahead, but we ain't movin. When them men come down here to get us tonight, we're gonna leave him right here, we can cover him up and they won't see him. They don't need to know that you done kept him from dying, but that's as far as we go."

The others nodded in agreement, folded their arms and turned away from Bernice and Daniel.

"Okay, we'll hide him. We won't say anything, we will just go on up there and make happy laughter and fun times for that bunch of cowards, and we'll tell ourselves that we are different," Bernice said hoping to make the others feel guilty, but she knew there was no use. She looked for a blanket or rag of some kind that she could cover him with; she didn't want him to die after all of her hard work to save him. But, her plan to keep him hidden would not work out as she imagined. Just as she got Daniel covered she heard voices and footsteps from above. The trap door swung open and there stood Rufus and Henry.

"Okay, you ladies, get yourselves ready. Don't worry about Mr. Bernstein, we're gonna let him live, we're leaving him down here. We're planning to pull outta here so get yourselves ready to move." Henry shouted down into what might be considered a root cellar by some, but more like just a hole in the ground by most.

"What are you gonna do with him?" Bernice yelled up toward the voice. It was too dark for her to make out just who she was talking to, "You can't just leave him down here to die."

"Now what's it to you? You getting sweet on him or something?" Rufus laughed.

"No, I just spent the last few hours trying to sew him up and straighten his bones, is all, and I don't plan to see my work be for nothing. Now, you men had your fun last night, you taught him a lesson, I don't expect he'll hurt nobody again – at least not like he used to. He needs a doctor, and I plan to see to it that he gets one. Now I want you to let me take him to town and drop him in front of the doc's place there and then won't no more be said about it." Bernice was shaking as she spoke, she couldn't believe that she was standing up to these men who had full dominion and ownership of her.

"Now, girly, you sound real sure of yourself down there in that hole with no way out but through this here door. I thank we're jest gonna hafta leave him down there and you with him, Missus Doctor herself." Rufus said.

The door was shut and Bernice could hear the sound of furniture being moved across the floor. She was certain that whatever they drug across the floor was now holding the door down. There would be no way out. The other women glared at her and whispered among themselves. Upstairs the men began preparing to pack up and pull out of the camp.

"We can't leave them down there, Rufus, you know that as well as I do! Them women are good women, they just saw too much and took pity on what they believed to be the underdog. We gotta let them out, and we'll take them with us at least to the next town where they will have forgotten all about what happened here and they will go on about their ways." Henry felt sorry for what had happened and he blamed himself for letting things get out of control. It was all of the whiskey and talk, and them men from over in London that had come down on the ferry that had egged everybody on. Now he was left to deal with it. "Come on, Rufus, let's get Bernstein up and drop him at the first corner of town that we come to. Then, we'll come back here and get the women and clear outta here, whaddaya say?"

"You're right, Henry, we should never had left things go this far, I'll get the wagon, and you get things straight with Bernice down there, she is a tough one, and I wouldn't mind taking here to more than one town, if you know what I mean."

"Thanks, Rufus, you go ahead and let the others know that there won't be no trouble from the women, and that we are just dropping off Bernstein. I'll square it with Bernice."

As Rufus left to get the buckboard Henry thought of all the years the two of them had spent together going from one tree stand to the next, chopping, rapid rolling and raising hell. But, he was getting too old for this life, he wanted to settle down, and he too had been keeping his eye on Bernice. She was a woman to reckon with and he sure enjoyed his time with her. "Bernice," Henry called as he moved the table and opened the trap door, "Bernice, we need to talk."

"Ain't no need to talk none Henry unless you plan to get this here man to a doctor," she called back.

"Well, that's just what I plan to do. See there, you think you are the only one with a conscience and you down here being so high and mighty. Rufus is getting the buckboard and we're gonna take him into town where he can be properly bandaged and taken care of. Do you want to come along, or can you trust me to do the right thing this time?"

"I never said nothing about not trusting you, Henry. I'm a might disappointed though by the way you acted last night and the way you let them other fellers act, wasn't like you, not like you at all. But, if you say you are gonna drop him at the doc's then okay, and yes, Henry, I would like to go along, just to be sure, so to speak, you can understand, cain't you?"

"I understand, Bernice." When Henry climbed down into the hole, the stench was almost overwhelming. How could these women have survived down here with this stench and in these conditions? A wave of guilt swept over him, and he shuddered as he realized what animals he and the others had become. His shame brought tears to his eyes as he reached out to Bernice. "Here, let me help you. Together we should be able to get him out of here. Come on, you women, come on out of there. Go on upstairs and get yourselves cleaned up. I am so sorry for making all of you live like this, God, I am so sorry."

They managed to get Daniel out of the hole. The other women followed. As they came into the large room, Henry heard Rufus open the door.

"Well, I'm here Henry, come on let's get this over and done with."

"Rufus, we were wrong, we owe these women more than just dropping them off at the next town, we gotta make things right. Have you ever been down there? Do you know what its like in that hole? We can't just let them go with nothing. "

"Well, what you plannin' to do? Give them our wages for all the hard work we done this here season? You might give them yours but you sure as hell ain't givin them any of mine and I'm betting the others will feel like I do. Now we said we was gonna take this here sonofabitch to town and drop him by the doc's and that's as far as I plan to go. What you do after that is your own affair, I don't want nothing to do with it. Now, lets get him in the wagon and be on our way. We gots lots of stuff left to do here before we pull out. We gotta get this place cleaned up and then go see Anderson and get our final wages – you might be wanting to hang around but I ain't. Georgia sounds pretty good to me right now and that's where I plan to be headin' before sunset."

The two men and Bernice loaded Daniel into the buckboard. Henry yelled back at the women, "Ya'll get yourselves cleaned up and if you have a mind to you might straighten this place up a bit. We'll be back as soon as we can and then we'll all head out down south. That is, if you have a mind to come along. I promise you I won't ever put none of you back in a hole in the ground like you wuz here, I promise. We'll be back soon." Henry tipped his hat toward the women as they stood staring after him.

Chapter Thirty-Two

It was Tuesday, not a particular unusual day of the week, but this one would be remembered for a very long time. Daphnia had awakened earlier than usual and decided that she would go see Melissa before she started her day at the Gazette. She had not been to see her the evening before and now felt a sense of urgency to see her. She had decided that it was time to let her know that she knew the truth. She was out of bed, dressed and out the door almost before the sun came up. As she placed a note on Herbert's desk that she may be a little late getting back, she left the building with a feeling of self-pity even though she didn't want to admit it. For the first time in her life she actually needed a spark, she needed a friend and she needed to cry, but that was not a luxury that she had allowed herself very often. She shook her head and tried to release her preoccupation with her own sorrow and grief and focus on her task. Locking the door behind her she was startled by what sounded like wagon wheels and men shouting. She rushed to look around toward the side of the building, but she didn't see anyone. She was sure that she had heard sounds from a wagon and horses. She shook her head and pulled her shawl around her shoulders.

She was not the only one out on the street so early. Michael had worked late the night before at O'Connors and was too tired to sleep when he got through at sunrise. He decided to take a walk down by the river. He was growing up despite what his mother told him and he felt like he had to do something about it. He couldn't stay here in this town and work emptying slop jars in the local pubs and picking up tips from the tables; he could head across the border to Canada and be somebody. He had been sitting by the shoreline of the river for several hours trying to plan how he would tell her he had to leave when he saw a wagon being driven by two men with what looked like a scarecrow and a woman in the back. The horses were going at full speed and the two people in the back were being bounced all over. Thinking they might even fall out, he decided to follow the wagon.

He watched the commotion from behind a tree and saw the wagon stop near the corner of the Gazette. That's where the two men got down from the seat and dragged the scarecrow looking figure from the back of the wagon and dropped him alongside of the road. Then they got back onto the seat and left just as quickly as they came. The woman stayed in the back holding on for dear life. Michael crept up to the figure and immediately put his hands to his mouth. "Oh my Lord in heaven, you is Daniel Bernstein, even beat up like you is, I recognize you, you sonofabitch, look what they done to you. What you go and get yourself mixed up in now? Did you beat up the wrong woman?" Then looking toward the heavens, Michael did a little jig and praised the Lord, "Thank you God! Good Lord, you done answered my prayers, hallelujah, somebody done give this man exactly what he deserve. Thank you sweet Jesus!" then looking down at the pitiful Daniel he whispered, "Damn I wished it had been me given you this whuppin." It was then that he saw the tears streaming down Daniel's face, and he felt sorry for him. Okay, let's get you some help. You stay here and I'll go get the doctor." Michael could still here the horses' hooves in the distance. He ran as fast as he could to Doctor James' office.

Pounding on the doctor's door, Michael yelled inside, "Doc James, you gots to come. Come quick. Bernstein done been beat up bad, you gots to come now." Finally getting the door open, he ran inside the building.

"Now wait a minute there boy, just hold on. What are you talking about? Where do I have to come to?" asked the doctor trying to get Michael to calm down.

"You gots to come quick. They done dropped that Daniel Bernstein off by the Gazette and he's hurt real bad. They got more rags and sticks tied to him, why he looks like somebody done made him into a scarecrow or something. Hurry up, he's real bad."

The doctor grabbed his bag and started out the door after the young boy. As they neared the corner of Elm and Pine he thought he saw a buckboard in the distance and he could hear the pounding of horses hooves and people yelling.

"Henry, you cain't leave him there like that. You promised to take him to the doctor's." Bernice tugged at Henry's arm. "You got to get him to the doctor, nobodys gonna find him here."

"She's right, Henry," yelled Rufus, "c'mon let's put him back in the wagon and drop him at the docs." The two men stopped and went back for Daniel. They threw him back in the wagon and headed toward the doctor's house when they saw young Michael and the doctor running down the street.

Henry smelled trouble. He pulled up on the reigns and stopped the wagon; jumping down from the seat he ran to the back and flung Daniel out and onto the ground. He jumped back on the seat and picked up the reigns in one smooth motion. He looked at Rufus and whipped the horses at the same time and with the same determination. "Don't even say a word, Rufus, we might have just sealed our fate right here and now. And, Bernice, you just shut up back there and keep down. The horses responded with a start to the crack of the whip.

"Stop, stop, come back here" Doctor James yelled to the two men going away in the wagon. But Henry whistled at the horses and slapped the reigns against their backs forcing them into a full run with the wagon bouncing along the roadway toward the lumber camp. The two men did not look back at the doctor nor did they allow the horses to slow their pace until they were safely inside the clearing of the lumberyard with the little wooden shacks set about with their cluttered entranceways and trash piled against the out buildings.

Exhausted from running behind the fleeing men, the doctor leaned against a tree until he could once again catch his breath. Finally, as he walked back toward young Michael, he looked at the boy with some disgust and annoyance, "Are you sure there was a man here in need of help, boy?" he demanded of the young Negro.

"Sure enough, doctor. It was that Daniel Bernstein; I'd know him anywhere. He was hurt plenty, too, all broken up and bleeding bad. I wonder what those men wanted with him?" Michael asked, scratching his head. "Do you think we should follow them?"

"No, I don't suppose it would do much good, I'll go over and speak with Herbert Bernstein myself and maybe he will know more about what is going on. More than likely, that young Daniel just got himself in with a rough bunch and he don't want his pappy to find out about it. I'll see him later today. Daniel will probably be back home by supper time with a few bruises, but no real harm done." Then thinking that he may have prejudged the boy, he smiled and rubbed the black boy's head before walking back toward his office. He was a little more than puzzled about this. That young Bernstein is always in some sort of trouble that his Father never seems to find out about. It would do him good if those lumberjacks showed him what for. Still, it seemed strange to him and as he walked away he thought that maybe he was just getting too old to maintain his perspective when dealing with young folks anymore. Maybe he should think of slowing down some. And then he saw him, "What the …?"

✦◦∾∾∾◦✦

As Daphnia turned the corner and crossed the street she glanced back to see young Michael running to the doctor's office, she hoped that there wasn't a real problem. She stood and watched as the two left the office talking and gesturing with one another. After watching them for a moment or two, she hurried toward the other side of the street and on to the little house where she had spent the first four years of her life.

Walking up the stone pathway, she thought of the many times as a child she had walked this very path. She could hear Melissa's voice … … …

> *"… … … Daphnia please stay on the stones. Don't walk in the flowers, Daphnia. Please come along, hurry dear, and please stay on the stones. There you go, you just can't stay away from the mud and the dirt now can you. Look at those shoes; you will be bringing in half the yard with you on the soles of those shoes. You sit right here on the steps and take off those shoes before you come inside, do you understand. I won't have you wearing those muddy things in this house."*

Shaking her head, she left the voice of Melissa behind and steadied herself before knocking gently on the door of the house she once called home.

Wiping away the tears and clearing her throat, she somehow managed a smile when the door was opened and she was face to face with Eloise Barnes. "Come on in child, my but it is early, I haven't had time to put the fire under the teapot. Come on in, Melissa ain't awake yet. Here take your coat off, sit down a minute while I get things going,"

Eloise said as she struck a match along the oven door to light the fire in the cook stove.

"What's happened with you, child? You look plumb thin, and tired . Just let me look at you a minute. Why, have you been crying, Daphnia? Daphnia, now what is it that's botherin' you? What's brought you over here hardly before the sun even gets up itself?"

"I guess there is a lot on my mind, Aunt Ella. How is Melissa? It has been so long, and there is so much to talk about. I have decided that I need to relieve her of her burden and tell her that I know everything and I understand why she did what she did. What time does she normally awaken?"

"Well, it's just too hard to say, dear. She hasn't been feeling well, and some days I don't know that she ever fully wakes up. She is bad, Daphnia, real bad. How she has lasted as long as she has is beyond me. She has suffered more than most, and I just don't know what it was she ever did to bring so much pain on herself. Why don't you tiptoe on in there and see if she is stirring some. Maybe she will hear you and if she is up to it, she might let herself wake up. It would be good for her to take some tea and nourishment. Here take in this tray with a cup of tea, I'll put a few biscuits on it too." Eloise handed Daphnia the tray and shooed her on down the hallway. "She'll probably wake up soon enough when she hears us out here, seems like most any noise at all wakes her these days. Although it don't last too long, but the slightest ruckus disturbs her some."

Daphnia shook her head, the images of the doctor and the young Michael still seemed strange to her, and she was certain that she had heard some commotion. Things just didn't seem right. She looked back over her shoulder and out the front door, not necessarily looking for anything or anybody, but just to try and clear her head and shake out the sight of the old and the young standing together with their arms and hands moving frantically and the one trying to convince the other of something.

"What on earth happened here?" Doctor James asked of no one in particular. Lying on the ground was the worst looking bundle of sticks and rags that he had ever seen, and they were tied and wrapped around what appeared to be a very badly beaten Daniel Bernstein. "Here, boy, come here and help me get Bernstein into my office. Michael? Michael come back here and help me get hold of this here man."

Michael had no intention of doing anything but following that wagon. He heard the doctor calling to him, but he kept running as fast as he could. He ran through the woods dodging the trees and brush until he came upon the camp. He watched as the men loaded the wagons with blankets, boxes and all types of saws, and equipment. He was out of breath, and he felt like his heart was going to explode. And then he saw the women. There were about six of them all dirty and ragged; they were being loaded into the back of one of the wagons. There was garbage and trash strewn about and Michael thought this was a strange way for the lumberjacks to leave the camp, they seemed to be in quite a hurry.

Doctor James pulled Daniel next to the building. "You just lay here and be quiet, now, don't you worry, I'll be back." Then he turned from Daniel and ran as fast as he could to the Bernstein house. By the time he reached the front porch he was out of breath, and his entire body was practically in spasm. "Herbert, Herbert, get out here, hurry," he shouted as he pounded on the front door.

"Well Doctor James, are you okay? Come on in and sit down for a minute. Would you like some tea? It sure is early enough for you to come calling. Is everything okay? I always said that you woke with the chickens, and I guess today you really did. Now come on in here and sit down, I'll go in and make you some tea." Ruth was saying without actually looking at the doctor, she seemed oblivious to his sense of anxiety or the urgency with which he had been calling to Herbert.

"Mrs. Bernstein, please, just get Herbert."

"Well, of course, Doc, but won't you sit "

"Mrs. Bernstein, get him now. NOW!" he shouted.

"What's all the fuss down here? Ruth what the blazes is going on? Doc, is everything all right? Is it Melissa? Come on, I'll get my coat." Herbert grabbed the doctor by the elbow and ushered him out the door as he grabbed his coat and hat.

"Now, wait a minute, Herbert, you can't just leave like that. Herbert, come back here, Doctor James, the both of you what's going on?" Ruth stood yelling as the two men hurried down the front steps and away from the big yellow house.

"Look, Herbert, it isn't Melissa. I'm afraid your boy has gotten himself into some trouble, somebody done beat him up pretty bad and it looks like they tried to fix him but they didn't do so good a job. We better hurry."

"Whaddaya mean, tried to fix him? What are you talking about?" Herbert stopped mid stride and took the doctor by the elbow. "Now, how about you tell me what has happened, no extra fancy words and no innuendos. What has happened to Daniel?"

"Well, I don't rightly know. The fact of the matter is that the young Michael found him laying along side the Gazette this morning and came and got me. When we got there we saw a wagon and some men trying to run off with him, but it seems they turned into my place and just threw him out of the wagon right there on the street. When I saw him, he looked pretty bad. He is all bandaged up and he has boards and splints tied to him. He's pretty bad, Herbert, I left him against the building, but I don't think I should leave him there for too long. We need to get moving."

The two men hurried down the street and Herbert asked no more questions.

Chapter Thirty-Three

Daphnia took the tray into Melissa's room and set it down upon the table next to the window. She opened the drapes and raised the shades. She spoke softly to Melissa, "Good morning, I brought you some tea." Looking into the face of the sick woman she could see that Eloise had not exaggerated Melissa's condition. Her eyes were sunken and there were deep dark circles beneath them. Her cheeks were shallow and drawn, and it sounded like each breath she drew in would be her last. How could she have gotten so much worse in just two days? Daphnia wondered. It didn't seem possible. She lifted the cup of tea from the tray and leaned over to Melissa. "Here, take a little sip of this warm tea, it will make you feel better."

"Sit," Melissa whispered as she pulled away from the teacup and motioned toward the chair. "So, Eloise tells me that you are staying here in Huron City. I am happy about that. I know you will miss Lansing and of course Thaddeus and Martha; they were such good people." Her speech was strained and it looked as though just talking at all was painful for her.

"Please don't try to talk. Let me do the talking today. There is something that I need to tell you, and I want you to know before I do that I have always loved you and I always will." Daphnia said as she took Melissa's hand in hers. "I have learned some things, and, well I . . . I know everything now. You did all that you knew to do and I know now what a struggle it must have been for you all of these years."

Daphnia got up from the chair and walked over to the window. "I will be twenty-four in just a couple of months, and I feel like I am eighty. So much has happened, it has all been so sad and frightening. I know about my father and Grace Humphreys. I know that you were sick and that sending me to live with Aunt Martha and Papa Tad was truly the best thing you could do for me." She spoke matter-of-factly and without intent to hurt Melissa. "I understand the reason you sent me away, and the reason you could not truly love me. I'm so sorry for all the hurt you have been caused."

"It's okay, Daphnia," Melissa said as she reached out to once again take Daphnia's hand. "I am so sorry for it all. Oh, Daphnia," she whispered as she fell back against the pillows. "Your father, …it was all for him, I'm afraid. I loved him too much, I guess. He was just so, how can I describe him? He was my life and when he was killed it was like I had been shot too. Sending you away was not because I didn't love or want you, it had nothing to do with Grace Humphreys, although I did hate her for taking Matthew from me, but I was sick, Daphnia. I was not just sick in my body, but my heart and soul suffered from his death. Thaddeus and Martha loved you and they were able to give you more than I ever could. Once you were gone I thought it best to just leave you be and not to torture you with coming back and forth and seeing me wither away as I have. I am glad you know. I don't know how you found out, but I am glad that we can now be honest with one another. I promised Thaddeus when he was here the last time that I would protect you and that I would not be the one to tell you the truth, I hope whomever it was who told you did so out of love and not meanness."

"It was Aunt Martha. She was all flustered and just blurted it out without thinking, but once I knew the truth we worked through everything, and honestly, I understand. Now, you look tired, lie back and rest. I will come again tomorrow." Daphnia helped Melissa to lie back on the pillows, closed the shades and left the room.

Eloise saw Daphnia coming down the hallway and without saying anything she helped her on with her coat and shawl.

"Thanks, Aunt Ella. She is resting, she knows that I know and it is okay, truly. I will be back tomorrow," Daphnia said.

As she was walking out the door she heard Melissa coughing and both she and Eloise ran into the room to see Melissa gasping for air. Daphnia ran to her bedside and kneeling against the bed she attempted to remove the covers from around her body and help her sit up. It appeared that Melissa had fainted and Daphnia was frantic when Eloise took over.

"Here, child, move away. Get those smelling salts off the bureau there, hurry." Eloise pushed Daphnia up and toward the direction of the bureau. Placing the salts beneath Melissa's nose, she saw the woman's chest again begin to rise and fall. She gently lifted Melissa's head back onto the pillow and folded her arms across her abdomen. She took Daphnia by the arm the two women walked out of the room and closed the door behind them. "She must rest now, she is real bad, Daphnia. I am afraid that she won't last much longer. Maybe on your way home you can stop at Doc James's and ask him to come by. Now, you run along and don't forget to send the doctor now will you?"

"No, I won't forget, Aunt Ella. I'll come back tomorrow. If anything happens, I mean, well, if she … please send for me."

"Of course I will, dear." Eloise spoke calmly as Daphnia left the small house and walked out into the damp morning. She ran back into the room and once again she checked Melissa for a pulse, but there was no sign of life in the frail woman. She fell to the bedside and cried into the hands of Melissa Flanders. She had been with her at the time of her birth. Melissa was always so special to Eloise. As a child, it was Eloise to whom Melissa would tell her secrets, and share her fears. All the sorrow and shame that Matthew had brought to her was poured out onto the soft shoulders of Eloise. It was Eloise who had always protected Melissa. Now she was gone, Eloise knew that and for the first time in her life she was truly alone.

Daphnia could feel the tears streaming down her face. By the time she reached Dr. James's her sides ached and her face felt raw from the cold air. "Doctor, doctor, you must come right away, it is Melissa, I believe she is, please, please hurry, doctor, Eloise asked that you come right away," she begged as she took hold of the doctor's hand and began to pull on his arm.

"Now, just a minute, child, just wait up a minute here. I can't run quite that fast and besides I just got back here myself a little while ago," he motioned toward the other room where Daniel lay silent and still. Herbert was standing next to him with his head bent and Daphnia could see his shoulders shaking. The doctor stood at the door and called into the room, "Herbert, it looks like Melissa is, well this is probably the time, I need to go right away. Will you stay here with Daniel until I get back?"

"Melissa?" Herbert asked as he turned to see Daphnia standing behind the Doctor. "Daphnia, is Melissa okay? You stay here with Daniel, I need to get to her?" Herbert started walking toward the door and then without waiting for an answer, he ran in full stride down the street toward the little house with the rock walkway.

"Stay here with Daniel, Daphnia. Try not to let him move around. He has been beaten up real bad and there are a lot of broken bones that still ain't been found. I just don't know how bad he really is. But, he can't move, do you understand? You must keep him still. I have given him some morphine and that should hold him until I get back. I need to get my bag. I'll get word to Ruth to come over here and stay with Daniel, and then you come on back to Melissa's." The doctor said as he held onto her shoulders trying to steady her. Then taking out his handkerchief he wiped away her tears. Still catching his own breath, he put on his coat, grabbed his bag and patted her arm. "Herbert, Herbert, wait up," he called as he hurried from the office.

Herbert did not wait up. He ran as fast as he could and entered the house without knocking. He ran immediately down the hallway into the dark room where Melissa lay propped up on her pillows and looking like she was sleeping comfortably. Eloise sat next to the bed with tears streaming down her face. She barely noticed when he entered the room.

He rushed to the mourning woman and kneeling down asked, "is she gone?" Eloise nodded in the affirmative and he moved her aside. He then touched Melissa's face, her hair and her neck. He leaned over and kissed her forehead and then pulled the chair next to the bed and took down a book of poems from her nightstand out of which he began to read ever so quietly. He did not hear Doctor James enter the room.

"Herbert, let me in there for just a few minutes, I'll let you come back shortly." The Doctor tugged on Herbert's arm and led him out of the room, then nodding to Eloise to follow he closed the door behind them. He went over to Melissa and removed the extra pillow from beneath her head and shoulders, checked for any sign of life and pulled the spread over her face.

Entering the parlor where Eloise and Herbert were standing he walked over to Eloise, "how're you holding up Miss Eloise?"

"She's gone, doc. That's all there is to it. She finally just gave out. She was all I had and now she isn't here no more. She was all I had, doc, all that ever meant anything to me, she was why I hung on when giving up would have been so easy, won't be no use no more, no use at all; she won't be here for me to take care of. She was all I had left, and now she's done left me here all alone. Just don't know what I'll do now, doc, just don't know." Eloise rambled on between low utterances and uncontrollable sobs.

The doctor took Eloise by the elbow and walked her to her room. He got her onto her bed and gave her a powder to calm her down and let her sleep. Then, he went back into Melissa's room where Herbert had once again sat down and resumed his reading. He had replaced the pillow that the Doctor had removed from under her head, and he had uncovered her face.

"Herbert? Herbert! You need to get hold of yourself now. Melissa put up a good fight, but she is gone now and there are things we need to do. We have to get Daphnia over here. After all, she is her daughter and she needs to be with her Mother right now. Can you come back to the office with me and stay with Daniel while I bring Daphnia over here. Maybe you should go get Ruth. I still need to finish checking Daniel out, I know that he is in a lot of pain, and there ain't nothing more that I can do here right now. I will get word to Phelps to come on over and take care of the final preparations and all. He can let the preacher know and Daphnia can be here to make the arrangements. Herbert are you hearing me?"

"She ain't her daughter, Doc. I'll meet with the preacher myself. Tell her to stop and send Ruth to your place and then for her to come on over here; that'll take care of the necessities that you need to worry about."

"What? What are you saying that Daphnia isn't Melissa's daughter? What are you talking about? I know that she wasn't the one to raise her, but blood is blood and Daphnia is the one to make the final decisions. Now I know you and Melissa had something special and I ain't never passed any judgment on that one way or the other, but you can't leave Daphnia out of the decision making at a time like this. If you want Ruth to come and stay with Daniel, well that is up to you, but you need to back away from this thing with Melissa and Daphnia. It is her responsibility and more than that it is her right – Daphnia is Melissa's daughter and she is the one that needs to be making the decisions. Now, I ain't gonna stand here and argue with you. Your boy is over in my office with most of his bones broken and no telling what all has been done to his insides, and I think you need to worry about that, Mr. Bernstein." Doctor James was more than a little confused about Herbert's words and his actions. He left the room to take one more quick look at Eloise.

"I'll be staying here, Doctor James. Melissa, after all, was more than special to me. She was my soul and the one person, before Daphnia, who could make my heart smile just by hearing the sound of her voice," Herbert yelled toward the doctor as he walked by. "Please send Daphnia to get Ruth for Daniel and tell Daphnia to come back here right away. Don't tell her what has happened. I will take care of that, after all it is like you said, blood should take care of blood." He got up from his chair by Melissa's bed and walked the doctor to the door and closed it behind him. He then returned to Melissa's bedside and resumed reading to her from her favorite book of prose.

Doctor James knew he had to go get Ruth; as much as he tried, he could barely tolerate that woman. He walked slowly down Pine Street to the yellow house. He had been expecting Melissa to pass, and he knew that when it happened Herbert would take it hard. He had known for sometime about Herbert and Melissa and their feelings for one another. He had watched each of them as they cared for the other and tried so hard to keep their love hidden. He would sometimes catch Herbert giving Melissa a brief kiss or stroking her hair away from her face and her returning the gesture in a manner that was generally reserved for a husband and a wife. He had sometimes come upon them unexpectedly to see them caught up in a passionate embrace, or overhear their laughter and teasing whispers. When Melissa told him that she had given her full power of attorney to Herbert, he was not surprised. His only question to her was whether or not Herbert should be given full privilege to her medical condition to which she answered emphatically, "YES!" She told the doctor that she herself had told Herbert everything and that there were no secrets between them. But, he knew differently. He knew that Melissa may have made full disclosure to Herbert about who she was and from where she came, but the same had not been made known to her about him. How, he wondered, would Melissa react if she knew Herbert's true connection to the untimely demise of her most revered Matthew?

As he walked along the street against the wind, he found himself remembering a cold and wet afternoon in February some nineteen or so years ago. He wasn't sure how he figured it all out or the complete connection, but he knew that Herbert had a hand in much of Melissa's misery. He thought of that day; he thought of Herbert. He could see it as if it were right before him this very minute... ... ...

... ... *"Doc, doc, open up."*

It was Herbert Bernstein standing at his door soaking wet right down to his socks. "What on earth? Herbert? Come on in here, what has happened? Is Ruth okay? Is it Daniel? Get in here and take those wet things off before you catch your death"

"I think I may be on my way, already, Doc. I'm awfully cold and just can't stop shaking. I just come in from St. Louis, and I don't think I can make it home." Herbert said as he collapsed on the floor before the doctor could catch him.

He somehow undressed Herbert and put a clean and dry nightshirt on him and then managed to get some whiskey down him before he got him into the bed. It was a fitful night for both men. Herbert's nightmares were many and usually resulted in screams that awakened the doctor. His temperature was high and Doc James felt certain that he had some sort of pneumonia at best. Just before daybreak, though, Herbert was sleeping and his breathing seemed a little better. He left him there while he went to get Ruth. It was a cold and wet morning, there was more rain than snow but not enough to call it sleet; the ice was starting to build-up along the sides of the walkway and the wind was like nothing he had felt in a long time. As he walked he thought about how he would get Herbert home to his own bed

"Why Doctor James, come in out of this weather. What on earth are you doing out on a morning like this?" Ruth asked while holding a scarf about her neck with one hand and her robe together with the other.

"Its Herbert, Mrs. Bernstein. He came in late yesterday and it appears that he has caught him a dandy of a cold. I thought maybe you and young Daniel could come up and bring him home in the buckboard. I would have brought him myself, but I just ain't quite as strong as I was once and I'm afraid had I tried to lift him myself one or both of us might end upon the floor."

"Why, I declare. He wasn't supposed to get home from Chicago until tomorrow. Wonder what happened? It is not like Herbert to change his plans and come home early — he enjoys the big city just too much, I'm afraid. Of course I don't mean to insinuate that he, well you know what I mean, Herbert is just too tight with that money belt of his to ever let a dollar of it slip away on any foolishness. Let me go and see if Daniel is awake, and we will get dressed and come right along to your place. You run on back and we'll be there directly," she dismissed the doctor by turning him around and pointing him toward the door. "You go ahead now, go on, we'll be there, you won't have to keep him too long." Closing the door behind the doctor Ruth went upstairs to get Daniel.

The rain had turned to snow, and the walkway had become slushy as he tried to avoid the temptation to dislike Ruth Bernstein. Upon entering his house he saw that Herbert had awakened and was out of bed. "What are you doing up, Herbert? Why you must have a temperature of a 104°. How'd you get so sick? You lie right back down there and tell me what's happened."

"I ain't lying down doc, I'm going home. I'll be okay. As for what has happened, I had a devil of a time in Chicago and an equally disturbing one in St. Louis. But, all said and done, I guess I've finally done what I should have done years ago. That's it. Nothing more. Nothing else needs to be said. It is over. There'll be no more women crying by the fireside waiting for his knock on the door. There'll be no more bastard children *born because of his lack of discretion. There'll be no more wives turned from their husbands because of his smooth way of talking and promises that he could never keep. There'll be no more sisters crying on the shoulders of their brothers while they wait for a child that they will never live long enough to raise. It's over. It's done. Now I need to get out of here. I have to get to the station and pick up my bag that I left there yesterday. You got some medicine for me to take or something?"*

"Yeah, and Ruth and Daniel are on their way to pick you up. Here's the medicine. Tell Ruth to come and get me if your fever doesn't break soon. And, Herbert, I don't know what you did or to whom you did it to, but whatever happened in St. Louis was between you and whomever you saw there. But, you are plenty sick, you need some rest. You will probably be fine, but just in case ... well, you know that I am here if you need me."

"I know, Doc. I'll be okay. I'll go home and get into bed and stay there, I promise. It Iooks like Ruth and Daniel haven't made it here just yet, would you mind hitching up that surrey of yours and taking me on home? I feel like I been hit by a freight train. Speaking of freight trains, we need to stop at the station first. Let's leave a note for Ruth just in case she gets here before you get me home."

"Of course, Herbert, be glad to. You just sit down and rest while I get things taken care of and I'll holler for you when I get around front."

⁓⁓⁓

That was more than nineteen years ago and the two men never spoke of that day again. Doctor James shook his head trying to remove the thoughts of what might have happened for sure, but he had surmised long ago just who and what Herbert had taken care of, but he never said a word about it. Now as he walked down that same street to the yellow house, he still had a head full of questions. Why would Herbert do anything to Matthew anyway? He remembered leaving him off at the train station and him going up to the window to collect his bag. He remembered him stopping to talk with someone, but until this very minute he didn't realize who it was. "Damn!" he said out loud. "Damn!" Now he was faced with this situation and he wondered how he would tell Ruth about young Daniel and keep these other things from clouding his decision to say anything to Herbert or Daphnia.

Walking up the stairs he took a deep breath and then paused just long enough to let it out. He knocked solidly on the massive cut glass and oak door.

"Well, good morning again Doctor. Just what on earth has happened now? I don't suppose you want to come in this time either. Well, you might as well know that Herbert has not yet returned and as for Daniel, well I don't believe he even came home last night. So, just what can I do for you? After all, I have a lot to do today and running back and forth to this door isn't one of the things I particularly enjoy. Besides, I have bread rising on the sideboard that needs attending to." Ruth said deliberately and with an air or arrogance letting the doctor know that he had intruded on her morning reverie with what she assumed to be a mere triviality.

"Well, to tell you the truth, Ruth, I don't particularly like coming to your door. However, sometimes one has to do what one must. As for Herbert and Daniel, well I know exactly where both of them are at this very minute. And, you are right; Daniel did not come home last evening. He spent last evening in a place unknown to me where he was beaten to a near corpse. He is lying unconscious over in my office. Daphnia is sitting with him at the moment, but she needs to get back to Melissa's; that's where Herbert is. Melissa took a turn for the worse this morning and it looks like she has finally died in peace. So, if you have a mind to, you might want to come on over to my office and relieve Daphnia so that she can go be with her Mother. Of course, if you would rather stay here and take care of your rising bread, then that is up to you. I plan to go back and check on Daniel and then if you aren't there to sit with him I guess I will send for that colored woman, Clarisse Hayes that he's been seeing down in the quarters, she might have a soft spot in her heart for him, although I don't for the life of me know why she would, but one never knows, now does one? Good day, Mrs. Bernstein!" He shuddered and turned before she had a chance to respond. He walked down the steps and back to his office as quickly as he could. He could hear her running behind him calling for him, trying to catch up to him but he chose to ignore her; he walked even faster trying to get as far away from her just as soon as possible. He had already said too much and much of it was not necessary, he knew that, he didn't intend to say those things when he knocked on the door, but when he saw her standing there with her nose in the air and heard her tone filled with indignation, he just couldn't help himself.

Upon arriving back at his office he could see Daphnia sitting with Daniel. She was holding his head and trying to get him to drink. It appeared that he was conscious at last, "Well, well, well. Just look at this, do I have a nurse in my presence? How's the patient, Daphnia?"

"I think he's pretty banged up, Doc, but he has managed to drink a few swallows of water and open his eyes anyway. Haven't you now Daniel?" she said as she placed his head back on the pillow and set the cup of water on the table. "How's Melissa, Doc?"

"You need to get back over there, Daphnia. Herbert is with her. She has been suffering for many years with a terrible disease, it has ravaged her body and now there is nothing left but barely a shell of the woman she once was. She used to be so beautiful and so full of life. Why, I remember when she came here with Eloise. Her mother had passed away up in Boston and it seems that there was a scandal of sorts, not involving her of course, but a scandal nonetheless. Anyway, she left your father and came here. She and Eloise opened that little gray house and went to work painting and trimming. She planted flowers and Eloise made rock walkways, and there was a little pond in the back yard that was covered with lily pads and all sorts of flowers grew around it. She would sit out there in the evenings, during the summer of course, and drink lemonade and read poems and stories to all the little children who would come around and sit still long enough. Sometimes the parents would stop by, too. She had such a soothing voice and she read so beautifully. I always thought that she should have become a schoolteacher, but she said that she didn't think she would care for a classroom with four walls. Isn't it a shame that she has spent most of her life in a bedroom with four walls instead? I guess what really puzzled me was that she loved children, but yet she sent you away, I never figured that out ……." his voice trailed off and he looked into Daphnia's eyes and almost gasped. Finally, those were not the eyes of Matthew as everyone had assumed, those eyes belonged to a much younger and happier Herbert Bernstein. "God Damn it!" he slapped his knee. "God, how stupid can one man be?" He asked of no one but himself.

"What is the matter Doctor James? You are certainly not stupid, have I said something? Is there something wrong?"

"No, no, of course you haven't said anything, it is just me and my mutterings – sometimes it takes a while for things to set in with me, it is like my mind blocks out certain things until they up and slap me right in the face. You run along now and see about Melissa, I will be there shortly. Good lord, is that Ruth standing there holding onto that lamp pole, she looks like she might faint, I shouldn't have left her running like that. You go ahead Daphnia," he opened the door and hurried out to help Ruth inside.

Daphnia put on her coat and headed back to the little gray house.

"Daphnia," called the doctor, "tell Herbert and Eloise that I will be there as soon as I can." He went over to where Ruth was standing and helped her inside the house. "Come on now, Ruth, let's get you inside, I don't intend to be taking care of you and Daniel. You are going to have to get your self together before you go in there and see him."

Ruth pushed past the doctor and ran into the room where Daniel was lying, "Oh my God, Daniel, Daniel, my baby, my boy, what has happened to you? Oh my God, Doctor will he live, is he okay, why didn't you tell me he was this bad? Oh my God!"

She ran to the door of the office and yelled to Daphnia, "Daphnia, Daphnia, you tell Herbert to get over here right now, that Harlot has had enough of his time, Daniel needs him now, you tell Herbert, do you hear me?"

Daphnia heard Ruth but chose to keep walking. She didn't care about Ruth or Daniel for that matter, all she cared about was getting to Melissa before it was too late. But once again her wish was not to come true. By the time she arrived at the little house all of the shades had been pulled and Eloise and Herbert were standing at the foot of the woman's bed holding on to each other.

"Did you bring the doctor with you, Daphnia?" Herbert asked.

"No, he said he would be along as soon as he could. Daniel has been beaten up pretty badly, and Ruth just arrived before I left. Is she gone?"

"Yes dear, she has passed," Eloise said to her as she took her into her arms and held her close. The two women stood sobbing for what seemed like a very long time before they heard the footsteps of the doctor coming down the hallway.

Doctor James walked over and once again put his hand to Melissa's forehead, her throat and patted her hands. "I have contacted the pastor, he should be here shortly. We need to make the final arrangements, Herbert. How would you like to handle this? Should you and I go talk in the other room? Eloise, is there something special that Melissa might have wanted to wear? Daphnia, I am sure that there will be some things that you will need to help Eloise with so if the two of you can give Herbert and me a few minutes ..." the doctor and Herbert turned and walked from the room.

She stood in the middle of the room watching the doctor walk away, she sighed and wondered what had happened to her life. The gray sky reminded her that winter was here and she didn't even remember autumn. Eloise had sat back down on the davenport and Daphnia once again felt the icy chill of being alone. She was not sure what she should do first, and her mind was moving so slowly. She felt almost as if her body was doing one thing and her mind was thinking something else. Taking in a deep breath, she picked up an apron from behind the door and tied it around her waist. There would be much to do. She thought of her Aunt Martha's rose garden. "No roses here," she said aloud, "no flowers at all except for a few Mums which have managed to survive in a pot of dirt on the back porch." They would have to do she thought as she went out the back door and cut the last of the few orange and yellow blooms. She tied a blue ribbon around the stems and walked down the hallway. The door was open and she could see the spread pulled over the body of Melissa. Tiptoeing into the room, she went over to the bed. She gently pulled the spread back and before she had time to think, she began to straighten Melissa up in the bed, she fluffed the pillow, smoothed her nightgown, she placed the flowers beneath Melissa's hands. She brushed her hair up and put a comb on either side holding it back away from her face. Even in death and after the illness had ravaged her so, Melissa was beautiful, Daphnia thought. She once again raised the window shade, she needed to see outside, even if seeing outside meant the gray skies of this cold wet little town. The gray dull light of Huron City's sky was better than closed up rooms with no light at all. She sat down in the chair next to the bed, "how peaceful it is sitting here," she said to no one. She could hear the raindrops softly hitting against the window, "I think it might snow before nightfall, Mother," she said only to catch her breath and once again realize that Melissa was dead, and she was not her mother. She stood and walked out of the room.

Chapter Thirty-Four

Michael knew something sinister had gone on with Daniel and he was determined to find out what it was. He walked in the direction of where the wagon had gone. He hated Daniel Bernstein and there wasn't anyone he would rather see dead, but for some reason he felt that even Daniel didn't deserve what had happened to him. He slipped through the woods and into the clearing where the wooden shacks were dark and the stench in the area was that of garbage, human waste and filth. He was looking for the wagon when he heard the voices of two men coming from around one of the houses.

"That doc should take care of him. Who would of thought that those women would have taken care of him? I hate it that Bernice got all soft over what happened. We should have locked him down there and left him, damn, do you think that colored boy had a chance to talk to him, do you think he said anything?" the smaller of the men asked of the other.

"Now, Rufus, you just worry too much. In the first place, he wasn't able to speak when we dropped him off so there was no way he could have said anything to that boy. And second, by the time that doctor fills him full of all that morphine he will be half out of his mind and with his mouth the way it is, whose gonna understand him anyways? Besides, won't nobody come down here looking for him. We'll be clearing out today and it looks like it won't take too long before this entire place will be covered with snow. Come on, let's let Joe know that we took care of everything." Henry patted Rufus on the shoulder and dropped a ring of keys into his pocket.

The hair on the back of Michael's neck was standing on end and his ears were itching; he could feel his muscles tighten and there was no doubt that there was something going on in the tumble down shanty. He crept up to one of the windows to look inside. Nobody was inside; the place was empty. He headed for home. What had they done to Bernstein he wondered? And, where were the women those two mentioned? He would come back later after he talked with his mama. She probably wouldn't let him leave again, but after supper it would be dark and he would slip out of the house without her knowing. Besides, he had plenty to do today, he had promised to go back and stock up the bar and she always had chores of some sort for him to do. Maybe he would go by the Gazette and see if Miss Daphnia needed anything done. Thinking of all that he had to do kept his mind occupied for a while, but it wasn't long before he found himself skipping and thinking of how wonderful things would be if that white assed sonofabitch was taken care of for good. Reaching down he pulled a blade of grass from where it grew against the tree trunk and holding it between his teeth he smiled.

In the doctor's office, Daniel was drifting in and out of consciousness. He dreamed that he was once again in the dark damp hole beneath the little shack and he was in more misery than he had ever known. There was no part of him that was not in pain. In his mind, he could feel the cold wet earth beneath him and smell the mold and filth on the earthen wall. He dreamed of Bernice. But, she wasn't fixing him up, she was shoving him around and slapping at him. She was hateful and nasty and the rest of the women were all coming at him jeering and laughing. He awoke in fits and moans and screamed in pain, only no one could hear his screams. It was as if he had no voice. He tried to open his eyes and adjust to the light but as his eyes opened he once again passed out. He dreamed of Konrad and Matthew. He felt like everyone was chasing him down the street and he couldn't run. He tried to sit up, but his body wouldn't cooperate.

Ruth tried to soothe him. She patted his brow with a cloth and hummed lullabies as if he were a baby, but he jerked and shook as if in spasm.

He thought he saw a woman nearby and tried to reach out to her but his arm did not move. Calling out to her was no use either; he was too weak to speak even if he were able to do so. Finally with some hint of consciousness he knew he needed some water, he was in such agony that he thought he might die. It wasn't that he was afraid of death; it was that he didn't want to die in this condition with this woman who he was certain he did not know. He was scared, too scared to cry out. Drifting back to sleep again, he heard the women in the hole, the voices faded and as he slipped back into a state of half sleep and half hallucination he thought of Michael, he was sure he had seen him, what had happened to him?

Ruth sat at Daniel's side praying and singing and talking, and begging for him not to die. She thought of how he prided himself in his appearance and always held himself with such confidence and self-assurance. The tears fell from her eyes as she looked at him now. He looked so small and undignified lying here in this bed with almost every bone in some sort of a cast and smelling of his own waste. What a difference from the way he looked last Saturday evening with his fancy ruffled shirt and his high shined boots. Who could have hated him this much, she wondered?

Unable to speak, and barely able to move, Daniel's floating in and out of consciousness was a definite aggravation to him. He could hear his mother, but wasn't always sure it was her. He knew that if it was he would be all right, but her voice kept getting mixed up with those of the women in the hole. If he could only be sure. If he could just have a little water. He managed to turn his face toward the woman and opened his eyes. The women stopped talking, and only his mother was there. She was holding his hand, and singing to him.

"Water, please give me some water." Daniel begged, only no words came out and Ruth was sitting with her eyes closed. He tried to move his hand, but it didn't move. He tried again to speak, but nothing came out. "Damn it woman, look at me," he yelled, but no sound came from him. Ruth sat quietly, praying, eyes closed.

"Please," he whispered and once again sank into unconsciousness.

Once Michael told his mama of what had happened, she immediately got dressed and left him in charge of his little sister. Coming into the doctor's office she saw Ruth sitting and singing to Daniel. The sweat beads were popping out on his forehead and he looked simply awful. She came over to the older woman and putting her arms around her she gently lifted her out of the chair and helped her to stand. "Now, you just take a break, Missus Bernstein, I am here now and I will sit with Daniel. Don't you worry, none. They are waiting for you over at the Flanders', it seems that Missus Flanders has passed away and they don't plan to wait to put her into the ground. I think you best get on over there. I'll stay here and watch over Mr. Daniel."

"You, you're that colored woman Clarice aren't you?"

"Yes mamn, I'm Clarice. I know your Daniel. He is the one who helped to bring me and my children from Morgantown. We are all grateful for him and what he has done. Now you go on ahead, I'll sit here with him now."

"You'll take care of him, won't you? I won't be gone long, I promise." Then leaning over and giving Daniel a kiss on his cheek, she took her coat and left the office.

Clarice went about cleaning him up some, changing some of the soiled linens, and re-bandaging the bandages that had come loose. She wiped his brow and helped him to drink some water. She thought of how strange life was. Here he was so beaten and broken, and it was she who was taking care of him. Her only concern was that he not die on her watch.

Daniel opened his eyes just enough to see her sitting there with him. He knew that she was the one who had cleaned him up and who had given him water. He felt better just knowing that she was there. He could feel her holding his hand, and the next time he went to sleep, he slept without the nightmares.

Chapter Thirty-Five

The wake for Melissa was small and held just before sunset on the same day of her death, December 13th, 1904. She was forty-five. In addition to the pastor, there was Herbert and Ruth ,who had left Daniel's side long enough to stand next to Herbert; she had succumbed to Doctor James's insistence and allowed Clarice to sit with Daniel after all, Tom and Brenda Saunders, Doctor James, Eloise Barnes, Mr. Thompson from the Bank, George Bentley who served as Melissa's attorney, and Daphnia. The preacher was brief and solemn in the delivery of the eulogy. There was a simple prayer, but no music and no long funeral procession. Melissa's remains were placed in a solid white casket, lined with white silk and sprinkles of dried flowers smelling of lavender. She was beautiful with a long white satin gown and her hair pinned up with pieces of the dried flowers woven through it like a crown. On either side of the casket there was a large spray of dried flowers and green pine sprigs.

Looking about the room, Daphnia was amazed. "Who on earth did all of this?" she wondered as she looked upon the woman lying in the casket. Surely not Eloise, she has spent most of the day in her own bed sleeping. There had been no one else in the house except for Herbert Bernstein and Doctor James, except for herself that is. Doctor James was not around most of the time, and Daphnia had left for a couple of hours to go home and freshen herself up a bit. Maybe it was Ruth, she thought, it had to be Ruth.

The pastor had asked a couple of the deacons of the church to come over and help with getting the casket loaded onto the wagon and then off again at the cemetery. Daphnia rode in the carriage with Eloise and the Doctor up to the small burial grounds where the fresh grave looked dark and damp. Once the casket was off loaded from the wagon and everyone was standing quietly in a semi circle, the preacher said a final prayer for the mercy of Melissa's soul; the casket was lowered into the ground. The only sounds heard were the sobs of Eloise. She was overcome with grief. Daphnia had no tears to cry, just a sinking feeling of emptiness. The small group left the gravesite without talking except for the doctor trying to calm Eloise as he helped the older woman into the carriage. Daphnia chose to walk home once the doctor reassured her that Eloise would be fine once she had some sleep.

Daphnia turned to Herbert with the intent of thanking him for all he had done when Ruth leaned toward her and spoke softly into Daphnia's ear, "You are a very special young lady, dear. The service was exactly as it should have been, and what you did with Melissa's hair and gown was remarkable. You certainly have a special knack of getting on now don't you?" Then, without giving Daphnia a chance to respond, Ruth took Herbert's arm and pushed and pulled the grieving man back to the black automobile. Daphnia stood stunned and watched the two people jostle and bump against each other as they made their way over the cobblestone walkway now slippery by the day's rain, ice and snow.

She turned back to Melissa's grave and said a prayer as the workers began to throw shovel after shovel of dirt on top of the casket. Then, she too, left the dreary little cemetery. As she walked down the hill and toward the small apartment over the newspaper office, she thought of many things and loved ones now gone. Her mind wandered back to days when life was simple and the only thing she worried about was whether or not Aunt Martha would make apple dumplings or bread pudding for dessert. She felt much older than her young years. It seemed to her that she had always just wanted to be a part of someone's life. And yet that was the one thing that had always eluded her. No matter how close she came, she never quite made it. She thought of William and how much he had meant to her; but that too seemed a long time ago. It had been weeks since she had heard from him, and she was sure that he must certainly be with someone else. His letters had become fewer and far between. His tone was less personal and certainly not that of a young lover anxious to once again hold her in his arms. She thought of Aunt Martha and Papa Tad; they had loved her surely, but she wasn't really theirs. Then of course there was Melissa who couldn't love her and Eloise Barnes whom she had always thought did love her but now she knew that it was a fondness because of Melissa. What had brought her to this place and this time, she wondered? There were no tears as she thought of Grace Humphreys and what she must have been like. Who was this woman who had loved her Father and then died before raising her only child? How much like Grace was she? As she approached the newspaper office and stepped onto the porch she shuddered, "it doesn't matter, I need no one," she said out loud feeling a tear slide down her cheek. Opening the door she looked back over the little town before stepping inside. She could feel the coldness in the air and once again there were snowflakes mixed with the icy rain.

The dampness had begun to creep into the little shack where Henry had gone back on his word, and once again the women were being held prisoners. With no heat and nothing but the shared warmth of each other to keep them from freezing, the women were beginning to worry whether or not the men were going to return and take them away, or if they were going to leave them down here to die in this hole. Henry had promised them that they would never have to come back down here again, he told them he would make things right and they would be safe. They thought of the blazing fire by which they would warm themselves, with something other than stale bread and maybe even a little whiskey to numb their aching backs and legs. It would be good to stand and stretch.

Bernice had convinced them that if the men didn't return soon they would freeze to death. She had tried to convince them to start digging a way out, but they resisted and refused to help her. She promised herself that with or without their help she was going to be free. She was tired of this place and these men. She had been brutalized and kept as a sex slave for far too long. This was not what she and Henry had agreed to when he convinced her to sign on with him back in Columbus. She told the others of her plan to escape once the men opened the trap door, and they finally agreed to go along with her. At last they had more than a plan; they had a purpose. For the first time in days, they didn't feel pain from hunger, they were smiling and even Melanie had agreed to go along this time.

As Michael sat at the supper table, he was anxious for the meal to end. He wanted to get back to the shack before it got too dark. He took some biscuits and a piece of the fried pork and wrapped them in a piece of cloth he had torn from a flour sack. He would take these things along, just in case, he thought. "What are you doing with that there food, son?" his grandfather asked the young boy. "You are as fidgety as a cat, what's going on with you? He gave young Michael a quizzical look.

"Nothing Grampa, just in a hurry, I got to get going. I'll be back soon. Tell mama not to wait up just in case I'm a little late," he said as he got up from the table and went about putting on two more shirts and what was left of an old coat his Mother had remade for him from a quilt last winter. Stuffing the food in his pocket, he grabbed his hat and hurried out the door into the cold evening. He could hear the ice and snow crunching beneath his feet as he ran down the road and back to the stand of shacks the lumber jacks had called home for the better part of the summer and fall. Once in the clearing he slowed down to barely a walk and was careful of every step.

As he neared the house from which he had seen the men leave earlier, he crept along bent over and listening for any sound or voice. He could hear nothing. He had to see inside but the window was too high. He looked around for something to stand up on. Seeing a stump, he dragged it over and leaned it against the wall of the shack. Once he got his balance on top of the stump he looked inside. There were at least half a dozen men inside drinking and laughing, he could hear the loud sounds but couldn't quite make out what they were saying. Then he saw the one called Ben. Ben went behind the bar and disappeared. Michael was afraid to even breathe. He could hear his own heart beating. Then he saw Ben again, and the women. There were three women barely dressed and dirtier than Michael had ever seen any white woman before. One of them looked bruised on her face and they were all limping as they came from behind the bar. The men began to pull at the women and tear at their clothes. It reminded Michael of the way Daniel Bernstein had treated his Mother, and he could feel his anger rising as he balanced himself on the stump while watching the men. Then more women came into the room from behind the bar, there must be at least six, thought Michael. One of the men started playing the fiddle and the men and women started dancing, some of the women drank from the same bottles as the men, and it looked like they were starting to have a good time. That's when the stump that he was standing on slipped and he fell. There was silence and his head was spinning, he could hear the men running out of the house and yelling, the women were screaming, and he saw a man as large as he had ever seen coming around the corner toward him. He managed to get to his feet and run into the woods. Spying a cluster of pines, he climbed one of the trees and sitting near the center of the tree, he watched the men and all the commotion.

"Get the wagons, let's get out of here, come on, let's get moving while we can," Rufus was yelling to the others, "Hurry, that boy will surely tell the others, let's get going, put them women in one of these wagons and let's move it. I done knew we had stayed too long when that Bernstein fella came around here the other day, and now this. We done pressed our luck just a little too far."

"Now calm down Rufus. That boy don't know anything and there ain't nobody who'd believe him anyhow. We ain't done nothing wrong and as for me, I plan to get some sleep before I pull away from here. Just calm down. You women get on back inside and get yourselves cleaned up. Maybe you can straighten the place up a bit too while you're at it. And, Rufus, I don't want no more mention of Bernstein. We done dropped him off at the doctor's in town this morning and I expect that he will be fine. He won't be talking none, either, so don't you go on about that. We'll pack up and get out of here early in the morning and nobody will be the wiser." Henry said as he took one more quick look around for Michael before going back inside and closing the door.

Once inside, Rufus would have none of Henry's insistence that they stay the night. "Henry, you do whatever you want, but as for me, I'm leaving this place tonight. What about the rest of you boys? Are you with me or are you staying to wait for the men to come in here tomorrow morning and tear this place apart and lock all of us up. That Bernstein ain't just anybody in this town. He's got money and he's got clout. He will find a way to talk, let me promise you that. So, as for me, I'm leaving. I'm leaving now." He then went about gathering a few things and stormed out of the shack and started to hitch up the horses and pile his stuff inside the wagon. The others followed doing likewise.

"Okay, okay, I'm a coming. Any of you women want to come along with me, get your rags together and come on. I'll take that wagon over there," Henry said as he pointed to one of the wagons against the barn.

"They ain't all going, Henry. And you know who I mean," Rufus said as he went over to the group of women and grabbed Bernice by the arm and took her back inside of the shack. Henry didn't try to stop him, he just hung his head and kept on with what he was doing.

Suddenly the whole place was like an ant hill with people, dogs and horses all going in different directions, bumping into one another, people yelling and things being thrown around as if there was some major calamity getting ready to take place.

Michael had watched and listened to the two men talk wondering what they were so afraid of, and he knew it had something to do with Bernstein. He sat quietly and watched the women get in the back of one of the wagons and the men piled stuff in all around them. He wondered what had happened to the one they called Rufus and the woman he took back inside, but then he saw Rufus climb up on one of the other wagons. It seemed to him that the other wagons were loaded in a matter of minutes. He couldn't tell who was in what wagon, it looked like there were more women than before, and things were starting to get loud with the men yelling, the wagons moving across the muddy yard and the horses jumping around. It was then that he saw one of the men hurl a lighted kerosene lamp into the little shack. The building exploded into flames, the wagons roared out of the lumber yard with the men whipping the horses as hard as they could and throwing lighted lanterns into every shack they passed. The entire place was ablaze. Michael couldn't believe his eyes. Scrambling down the tree he knew he had to get out of there before he was caught in the fire. The smoke was heavy and things were burning pretty fast, he could hardly breath. As he ran past one of the burning shacks he heard someone cry out for help. His ears perked up and he stopped dead in his tracks. "Sure enough there's someone in there," he said as he slapped his leg and grinned from ear to ear, "that's where Rufus done put that woman, sure enough, he put her back in that hole under that shack." Michael knew that whoever was down there was there because they were someone Rufus was afraid would say something about what happened to Bernstein. Michael was laughing, but not from meanness but happiness that he had stayed around.

"I coming, I coming, I'll get you out, hold on," Michael said to the voice as he tried to beat away the flames with his coat. He had to get inside the shack to get to the voice, but the flames were too hot and too many. "Hang on, I'll go get help. I'll be back," he promised as he ran toward town for help.

Inside the earthen prison Bernice wasn't sure if she had heard the young black boy or if she was dreaming. She knew that Rufus had thrown her back in the hole to die because he was afraid of what she might say. He knew he could handle the other women, but Bernice; well she was a different story. She was strong, and she had values. They had a respect for her that they didn't have for the other women, and she knew it. It made her sad to think that Henry would let Rufus do this to her, but she would get over it.

As she waited for the young boy to come back she tried to open the door, but she couldn't budge it. She wasn't sure if she smelled smoke or if she was just having difficulty breathing from being trapped and afraid. But it was smoke, she could see it start to come down through the floorboards, and she could feel the heat. Things started crashing and there was burning furniture and boards falling into the hold with her. "Oh Dear God," she began to pray.

Chapter Thirty-Six

The flames from the lumber yard lit up the sky behind the lumber jacks and their wagons as they high tailed it around the back of the mill and headed west as fast and hard as the horses could pull them. The women were bouncing against one another with boxes and supplies falling on them. They tried to keep calm, but it was no use. Rufus, worried that someone would hear the women pulled the wagon over. They were grateful for the stop and just as they were ready to thank him, they saw him lift one of the boxes above his head and throw it with all of his might back onto them, "now, I said shut up, I don't wanna hear no more screaming, if you break something, then you break something, we'll fix it later, but keep quiet. Then, tossing another crate on top of the first one just for good measure he turned and walked back to the front of the wagon, looked into the eyes of Henry and said, "it had to be done, they need to be quiet back there."

The women stopped crying as they realized that at least three of them had been injured, and pretty severely; they decided to remain silent. Those who could tried to gather together for consolation, warmth and comfort. They knew that they had to get out of this wagon and away from these men. And then one by one they realized that Bernice was not with them. "What did they do with Bernice?" Melanie asked of the others.

"Shut-up! I don't want to hear one word back there," Rufus said as he continued to force the horses into a full run.

The women were frightened. They knew that Bernice would be able to find a way out of this situation, but where was she? They started to look about as best they could, but they didn't see her. "We have to find a way out of here," Melanie whispered. And she began to move toward the back of the wagon; those who were able followed. "When they slow down, we will try to jump," she said to the woman next to her, "now pass it on."

As Michael reached Doctor James's he could see that the whole town was alive with people rushing in every direction. The bells were ringing and the fire wagons were racing toward the burning lumberyard. He opened the door to Doctor James's office only to see his mother sitting there next to Bernstein. "What you doing there Mama? Why not let that sonofabitch die, that's what he deserves? Where's the doc? The whole place is on fire, and them men have run away with the women, but there's one of them trapped in one of the shacks. I got to get help."

"Michael, Michael, come back here," Clarice yelled toward her son, but he just kept running.

Michael ran toward the newspaper office, there would have to be someone there he thought. Pounding on the door of the newspaper office, he was just about ready to give up when the door opened and there stood Daphnia. "What is happening, Michael?" she asked. "What is going on, how can I help you? Come on inside, its cold out there."

"You gotta help her mamn. You gotta come along with me. She going to die if we don't get her out from under that shack," he said as he pulled on Daphnia's hand and got her outside. They were running toward the lumberyard with everyone else. Daphnia was trying to put on her coat as she ran to keep up with the young boy. She could feel the snowflakes against her neck and face.

People were everywhere. There was so much confusion that Daphnia didn't know what to do or where to go. Michael held her hand tightly and pulled her in back of the crowd and around to where he had hidden in the trees. He could see the little shack was just about burned to the ground and it looked like the fire was almost out on one end. "Come on, come over here. She down there, down there somewhere," he said as he pointed to what had been the back of the shack. He could see the trap door with the padlock in place. Daphnia didn't know what to think. She followed him over to the door with the flames still burning not twenty feet away from her.

"You down there, Miss? You still there?" Michael called. "I brung help, we gonna get you out, just like I said."

"Who did you call to, Michael? Who did you say is down there?" Daphnia asked.

"I don't rightly know, Miss Daphnia, I just heard some moaning and after what they done did to that Daniel Bernstein, Lord only knows who else is there, and what they could've done to them."

"Did you see Daniel Bernstein this morning? Did you see who hurt him and dropped him at Doctor James's?"

"Yes Miss, I seen him. I seen him this morning. It was me who tried to get the doctor to come help him. I tried anyway, but them men came back and got to him first. I know there is somebody under that trap door, we have to get her out, we just have to. I promised her," Michael said crossing his heart with his fingers as he spoke.

Daphnia began to break away the padlock with a piece of wood. "Go get one of the men, hurry."

Bernice thought she heard voices, but she couldn't be sure. She started hitting her hands against the trap door. "Please help me." She whispered.

Part VI

We think they don't know
We hope they'll still care
While the silence of secrets becomes the thunder we hear

Chapter Thirty-Seven

Before she could break the lock, Daphnia felt someone take hold of her arms and lift her out of the way.

"Here, let me take care of this. Who is down there, do you know?" Tom Saunders asked while tearing at the boards and breaking away the lock.

"No. I don't know. Michael is the one who brought me here. He said he heard someone down there," she was trying to figure out how Tom got here. "Why are you here?" she asked.

"I saw that Negro boy running and calling for someone to help, and I asked where and he pointed in this direction. I told him to get the doctor. Help me clear away this wood."

Together the two of them cleared away the wood and the stench of the hole almost took their breath away. Even without the ashes and the smell of burning wood, this was obviously a dreadful place. Tom peered into the hole and saw what looked like a person lying against the dirt wall. Reaching in he grabbed the woman and began to pull her from under the building.

"She's bad. You better go see why the doctor is taking so long to get here. I'll try to get her far enough away from this place to get a breath of fresh air."

Removing her coat, Daphnia covered the woman and left running as fast as she could away from the lumber camp and toward the doctor's office only to meet him coming toward her in his buggy. "Hurry, doc, she's real bad."

The doctor arrived to find the woman breathing on her own, but barely conscious. "Who are you? What happened here? Where are all of the men?" he asked while trying to clean up her face and get a sense of what had happened to her. As far as he could tell it looked like she had been hit a few times in the face, but otherwise seemed to just need good fresh air.

Once she caught her breath, the doctor pulled out a flask of whiskey from his coat pocket and gave it to her.

Bernice gladly took the golden liquid and swallowed a large amount in just one gulp. She wiped her face with the back of her hand, and breathed in as much air as her lungs could hold. She handed the bottle back to the doctor, "Thanks."

"Okay, mamn, tell me what happened here. How did you get down there and why?" Doctor James asked as gently but firmly as he knew how. It had been a long day and he wasn't too sure that he had any patience or bedside manner left in him.

Bernice was sore from being dumped in the hole, and her face was plenty bruised, but once she regained full consciousness, she was just plain mad. "They threw me in that hole and left me to die, the bastards! After all that I did for them. I thought he cared about me, but he just went along with the others. He stood by and let Rufus just throw me down there like a piece of garbage."

"Who? Who threw you down there? Where is ever body?" Daphnia asked.

"Rufus and Henry! They left. Took out for down south I expect. They took the women with them, too. They was afraid after what happened to that Bernstein – they thought someone would figure out that they was responsible and they knew that I knew everything. I knew everything about them, their nasty habits and their meanness. I been with them a long time and always made sure that my girls showed them a good time. We never complained about how they made us live, or barely survive. Now, look where that got me – the bastards left me to burn to death without even batting an eye. They thought I would die, but I didn't and I'll show them. I'll tell the constable everything I know. I'll even tell them about up in Canada, too." She was obviously no longer worried about dying. But that didn't mean it wasn't a dangerous place to be. The buildings were cracking and popping, people were running everywhere with water buckets and the air was once again becoming thick with smoke and embers flying.

"Now, you just relax, miss, we'll be needing to get you out of here before this whole place gets blown to kingdom come," Doc James was saying as he tried to calm her down, but he was also scared. "Come over here boy, bring that buggy as close as you can get it. Here, Tom, help me get her up, we have to leave this place. Ours is not to figure out who done what to who, ours is to save this here life as well as our own, if we can."

Michael and Tom commenced to carry out the doctor's orders and Bernice was none to anxious to do anything but what she was told. She was already biting her lip and wishing she hadn't said so much about Rufus and Henry. Now she just wanted to get all of this behind her. She leaned against the men as they helped her into the buggy and then they got in behind her.

"Daphnia, come on, get up here, let's get out of here," Tom called to her.

"You go ahead, Tom, I think I will walk, it has been a difficult day," she said as she waved them on.

The snow had started coming faster and the wind was whipping the flames of the burning buildings. Small explosions were taking place farther back in the camp and Daphnia's head was spinning. She barely had time to bury Melissa before this tragedy took over for the last. What had happened to this day she wondered? When did she stop and catch her breath last let alone have a bite to eat or a moment to just sit still? She stood with her arms folded in front of her and tried to brace herself against the wind and snow as she watched the wagon pull away; she had to find a way to put things into perspective. Life and death cycles puzzled her and she never quite understood how one life could be taken hardly before having the chance to begin, or why God would allow two women to finally get to know each other and then swoop down and take one; or why a woman such as the one in the wagon could live in such squalor and survive when Melissa had been given the best of care and yet she should be the one to die. Clutching her fists to her side she raised her face toward the heaven and screamed, "its not fair!"

No one heard her or even looked her way as she cried and yelled at the invisible. There seemed to be dozens of people running toward the lumber camp. The explosions were fewer, but the chaos seemed to be escalating. The stench and ashes of the burning garbage and filth were making their way into town while the flames were casting an eerie glow in the night's sky. She walked back to the newspaper office against the stream of people going in the opposite direction. She was bumped and jostled along the way as if she were not there at all. Even in this crowd of people with a shared purpose, she was alone. As she reached the corner of the building she stood against it and cried into the rough bricks. The snow and wind whipped her skirt around her as she clung to building for support.

Tom removed his coat and placed it over her back and shoulders, and then he lifted her into his arms, "Shh, it's okay. Just lie back against my shoulder, go ahead and cry. Its okay, Daphnia, its okay."

She was too tired and too exhausted to argue. Allowing herself to lean into him, she put her arm around his neck and held on as he carried her into the newspaper office, locked the door behind him and easily made his way up the stairs to her apartment.

Chapter Thirty-Eight

There was barely any light shining through the window, but it was enough for her to see his silhouette. She watched as he sat on the windowsill; he had taken out tobacco and paper and was rolling a cigarette.

He brought her home, made her a cup of tea and then helped her to undress and tucked her under the covers of the big bed. If she had only left it at that but it had been so long, and she needed him. So, she pulled him to her, closed her eyes and melted into his arms. Their lovemaking was passionate but gentle. She allowed him to take her to the highest realm of emotion and desire, and she went willingly. He was gentle and strong; she was pleasing and pleased. There's was a balance of exhilaration and satisfaction, and as the night sky dimmed from the lumber camp's blaze, they, too, lay in the big bed of rumpled linens and covers in exhaustion. She fell asleep in his arms. But, had awakened alone with him sitting on the other side of the room.

"How long have you been sitting there?"

"Not long. Are you okay? I'm sorry for ... that is not what I intended to happen."

"I know. I'm okay. Thank you for bringing me home, and for... well, thank you. I'll see you out." She got out of bed and reached for her robe.

"No, please don't. Don't bother; I can see myself out. You have had a really tragic day. I'm sorry about your mother. You go back to bed; I'll make my way out. And, Daphnia, if you need anything, anything at all, please let me know." He leaned down and gently kissed her lips, and then he walked out of the room and out of the apartment.

She stood at the window watching him walk away and knew that her life had changed this day in more ways than she would realize for sometime. Getting back into bed, she held the pillow where he had laid his head in her arms, and she slept.

The ground was covered with ice and snow. As he walked along the street he thought of the woman they had taken from the hole under the cabin. He considered going by the Doc's but decided against it and went about his way toward home. He could see the light on in the front window and knew that his wife was still awake. He took a deep breath and slowed his pace trying to ready himself for what was surely to be waiting on the other side of the door. She would want to hear all about the fire and have him explain every little detail. She would nag about where he was and with whom he was with at this late time. Then she would start her standard rant about wanting to go home to Mobile and how much she hated this town. She would tell him that she was bored and had nothing to do all day while he was out spending time with people, talking to them, getting to know what was going on, in essence, he had a life and she didn't. She would feign an imaginary illness that the doctor's had never been able to diagnose. She would start coughing and choking, and complain that she couldn't breathe. She would blame the fact that she was pregnant for the reason he was rarely home, and before he would have an opportunity to calm her down she would go into the bedroom, close the door and tell him to sleep in the other room that she was too tired and exhausted to talk anymore. She was the most selfish woman he had ever met, and he frequently wondered why he ever fell in love with her let alone marry her.

But, that wasn't what happened this time. When he opened the door there was the midwife sitting in the rocking chair holding his newborn baby boy. "Your son, Mr. Saunders. He came about three hours ago, during one of them explosions that rocked the entire town. Mrs. Saunders didn't have too rough a time of it, this being her first and all, but she is sleeping now. I think she'll be okay. The doctor has had a pretty busy day, he stopped by once this afternoon to check on her, and then he sent word that I needed to do the best I could, but to send for him if things got worse. She actually came through better than I thought she would, but she is going to be in bed for a while, I'm afraid."

"The doctor knew that she was in labor? He didn't say one word to me when we were down at the lumber camp. We were in that buggy together and he didn't even mention it."

"Maybe he thought you knew, maybe he didn't want to worry you. Fathers are usually in the way, you know how that is, you being a newspaperman and all. He stopped by about two hours ago; I delivered this little bundle myself. He is perfect. Do you want to hold your little boy?"

Taking the baby from the woman Tom was overcome with joy, and guilt. He held the little baby close to him and made silent promises of love, protection and being a good father. As he sat down in the rocking chair he looked into the little face and closed his eyes remembering Daphnia's.

"You look like a natural at that, sir, if I do say so. Can I get you something to drink before I go home?" Mrs. Mason asked.

"No, I'll be fine. What should I do if he starts to cry?"

"Well, I suppose you will take him in to see the missus and let him get some nourishment. I will be back mid-morning, I'm sure you and Mrs. Saunders will figure things out. There is a bassinette in the bedroom, you might want to lay him down in there and see if he'll sleep awhile." Then, patting him on his shoulder she wrapped her shawl around her and left the house.

He sat in the chair with his new son and wept for all that he had been and for all that he hoped to be. He closed his eyes and said a silent prayer to be a good father and a better husband. He stroked the child's forehead lightly and thought of Daphnia. "What happened tonight won't happen again!" he promised as he felt his throat tighten and lifted his hand to his face to once again smell her sweetness.

"Tom?"

"Yes, Brenda. I'm coming. I'll be right there," he took a deep breath and walked into the bedroom where his wife was sitting on the side of the bed. "Lie down, Brenda, lie down. You did a wonderful job. I'm sorry I wasn't here, but there was a big fire down in the lumber camp and, well, they needed every hand they could get. The Doc and I pulled a woman from under a burning building. It was chaos; honestly, it is a wonder anyone got out of there alive. How are you? How are you feeling? Here, let me help you back into bed, I think this little fellow needs something to eat, he is starting to wake up and get squirmy."

"Oh, Tom, isn't he just the most wonderful little baby? He looks just like you. What should we name him? I don't want to name him Thomas; I would like to name him after my father, Robert. What do you think? We could name him Jonathan Robert after my father and yours; yes, that's it, Jonathan Robert Saunders. That way he would have both of our father's first names. Would that be okay, would you like that?"

"That would be fine, Brenda. We can call him Johnny. I'll send a wire to your parents tomorrow morning. They will be thrilled. I think I'll go over now and talk with my folks; I'm too wired to sleep anyway. What can I get you before I go? Are you okay? The mid-wife, Mrs. Mason, said you didn't have too hard of a time. You seem okay to me. Are you sure you are okay?"

"I'm fine, Tom. If you can just help me to the basin and then back into bed, I'm sure I'll be okay. I am awfully tired, though. You better move the bassinette close to the bed. And, Tom, take your things into the other room, I won't want you waking up Johnny with your snoring. Now, can you help me up?"

Helping her to the other side of the room and into the small water closet was easy enough. Thinking about her wanting him to move into the other room was another matter. "Brenda, don't you want me to stay in here with you and the baby?"

"No, Tom, I don't. Johnny and I will be just fine. After all, his crying might bother you and I am certain that your snoring and other sleeping noises will bother us, so for now it will be best that you sleep in the other room. I have the bell next to my bed if I need you during the night, I can just ring it. Help me back to bed, won't you?"

Once back into the bed, Tom put the baby into her arms and covered them. "I'll be going back out, I want to stop over and see my folks; maybe I'll sleep there tonight. I'll throw some things into a valise and come by around noon tomorrow. Mrs. Mason said she would be here tomorrow morning along with Doc James. Are you sure you will be okay?"

"I'll be fine. Don't worry about me; I'm strong. I'm tired, but I'm strong. Maybe we should get a woman to come in for a while so you won't have to take time away from the Gazette to help care for me and Johnny. I wouldn't want you to be burdened in any way. When you wire my Mother, ask her to come up for a while. I don't think she would mind, and after all, she can take a boat up the Mississippi to a port near Chicago and then take a train from there. I know it will be inconvenient, but I could use her help until Johnny gets strong enough to travel."

"What are you talking about? Until Johnny gets strong enough to travel? What are you suggesting, Brenda?"

"Come now, Tom, surely you didn't think that I would stay up here in this Godforsaken town to raise my child, did you? I am going home, Tom. And, Johnny is going with me! I have been thinking of this for some time and I don't intend to be talked out of it now. I should never have come up here to begin with. The trip was bad enough for me, but I made it once and now I can make it back. My only concern right now is Johnny and I want him to be strong enough to travel before I leave. I figure that will take at least six months and I don't intend to stay here without my mother for six months. So, go ahead. Pack your valise; pack a trunk if you want to. But, you need to be sure about one thing; my baby will not be raised here! We are going home where it is civilized and the people know how to be hospitable. You knew months ago that I didn't want to come up here to live, but as always, you managed to talk me into your way of thinking. Well, no more. No more, Tom. Now I am tired and I don't want to discuss this any longer. If you are going to see your folks, then go. But whatever you decide to do, just do it in another room because I am going to sleep now. Good night."

He knew there was no need to try and discuss this with her tonight. She was stubborn, and once she made up her mind it was usually set in stone. But, he never thought she would leave him. Deciding against going out after all, he put a pillow on the davenport and pulled an afghan from one of the chairs and slept on the too short, too lumpy and over-stuffed piece of furniture meant for sitting and not lying. Each time he heard the baby cry or Brenda walk across the floor in the room next door, he sat up, rolled another cigarette and sat in the dark until there was quiet once again.

In the bedroom where passion and love once commingled with tears and anger, Brenda tossed and turned in the big four-poster bed. She dreamt of times gone by and when awake thought of living once again in her beautiful Mobile with the wide expanse of lawn and the drooping magnolias and fields of cotton. She wanted to be home. Home to her was a bedroom filled with light from windows that spanned floor to ceiling, with balconies off each one and where she didn't have to cook or clean, but just to laugh and play croquet on the massive yard. There were servants there to help her with Johnny and her Mother to share her secrets and friends with whom to drink tea and eat biscuits in the afternoon. And, while she was at it, why not call him Robert Jonathan?

Why be reminded of Tom and his father every time she called her little boy? She got out of bed and wrote a note to the doctor:

> *Doctor James, Please be certain to show the name of my son as Robert Jonathan Saunders on his birth certificate. I will be calling him Robert and feel it will be easier for him as he grows up if the name by which he is called is his first name, the name of my father.*
>
> *Sincerely, Brenda Sue Saunders*

The streaks of sunlight awakened Tom. He shook his head and sat up; everything ached. Standing he knew what he had to do. Making his way into the small kitchen he put on a pot of water for tea and commenced making breakfast for Brenda. Once completed, he placed the plate of scrambled eggs, bacon, toast and a cup of hot tea on the bed tray along with a handwritten note declaring his undying love for her and his never ending faith in their marriage. He apologized again for not being present when little Johnny was born but promised to make it up to the both of them. Then heading toward the closed door with the tray he stopped and gently knocked before opening the door and walking over toward the bed.

"Good morning, Darling. How are you feeling this morning? I could not leave the house last evening so I slept on the davenport. I needed to be near if anything happened or if you needed me for anything. Here, have some breakfast. I have made your favorite chamomile tea and scrambled eggs just the way you like them. Here, let me help you sit." He helped her up against the pillows and placed the tray across her lap.

"Thanks, Tom. But, I have not changed my mind. I hate it here and you love it. Sometimes I think you love this place more than you love me. You didn't even try to get to know people or learn to like Mobile. I just don't want to raise our child here. This is no life for either of us. You are working all of the time, and when you aren't working you are out with that Bernstein man, or God knows who else. You aren't happy with me, and to tell the truth, I'm not happy either. I want to go home, Tom. That's just the way it is. I love you, but I'm not in love with you as I once was. Maybe some time apart will change the way I feel, but right now I just want my Mother and I just want to go home. Can you understand that?"

"Right now, let's just concentrate on you and the baby getting strong. Let's just not think of leaving or moving to another room. Let's try to make this work for little Johnny, Brenda. Let's put our own feelings aside right now and just be the best parents we can be to little Johnny."

"His name is Robert! I changed my mind. I want to name him Robert Jonathan. I want to call him by my father's name."

"That's fine, Brenda. Whatever you want is okay with me. He's my son, no matter what and I will love him whether we call him Johnny or Robert or Bubba. You decide and I will go along with it. Now, here try to eat something. You are so beautiful. It is snowing out this morning, but I am going over to get the doctor and I will be back. I'll stop by the Gazette and let Bernstein know that I need a couple of days right now. I think I should stop by and see Eloise Barnes, she might be able to come over and help out for a while until you get your strength back. You heard, or maybe not, that Mrs. Melissa Flanders passed yesterday didn't you? She had been sick for many years, but it was tragic nonetheless. Eloise Barnes is her aunt and she took care of Mrs. Flanders for a long time. I think she might be happy to have a little baby boy to care for just now. What do think? I'll go ahead and wire your folks while I am at the Gazette. Here, have some tea. Is there anything else that I can do for you before I go out?"

"Well, it sounds like you have everything worked out as usual. The davenport couldn't have been too uncomfortable. Why didn't you sleep in the back bedroom? I can't believe how refreshed and agreeable you seem this morning. And, Tom, let's get this straight, if you think you are going to sweet talk me into staying here you are wrong. I want to go home and I will go! If you want to ask Miss Barnes to come over for a while until my Mother gets here, that is fine with me, too. I will gladly welcome some help. But, be clear about this, I want my Mother! I want her here with me and when she leaves, I will be leaving with her.

I want to go home, Tom and that is what I plan to do. I do not intend to stay up here in this damp little town with its dirt roads and cobblestone walkways that make it impossible to keep one's balance with all of the rain, ice and snow. Thank you for breakfast, but, Tom, I'm going home and I'm taking Robert with me!"

"Of course, Brenda, of course you will go home. We can all go in the spring. It will be a beautiful time to travel south and Robert will be at the right age to be a joy for your Mama and Papa. Just think of how excited and proud they will be to see their grandson. It will be a wonderful adventure for all of us. Let's wait and go together; I'm only talking about four or five months from now, don't you think we can wait that long. It will be better for everyone. Your Mother won't have to travel up here and spend the winter when Eloise Barnes is right around the corner, you and Robert can have some time to get strong, and who knows, we might decide that an only child is not the best way to go. How many times have you said that you wished you had a sister or a brother, we could at least think about it, couldn't we?" He saw her smile and leaned over to kiss her, she pulled him close and he knew he had won. "I'll be back home soon, Darling."

His first stop was to that of Eloise Barnes. It did not take him long to tell her what he needed from her and to get her commitment to go over to his house later and begin helping to care for Brenda and the baby. She was happy to have the distraction, and eager to have a reason to get out of the house. Taking care of a new baby might be just the thing. They agreed that she would stay in the spare room and that he would return to the bedroom with Brenda. He promised to send a carriage for her around noon. Leaving the little gray house he smiled so wide that he thought his face would crack, "yes, things would be just fine."

He practically danced along the street to the office of Doc James. Upon entering he shook the doctor's hand and told him what a wonderful job the midwife had done and how well Brenda and young Johnny were doing. He immediately gave the doctor all of the details of the birth and signed a registry of birth for the doctor to file:

Baby Boy, Jonathan Robert Saunders,
born to Thomas J. and Brenda S. Saunders,
10:00 PM, December 13, 1904

The doctor said he would go over to check on Brenda and would let her know that everything had been taken care of. Tom told the doctor that Eloise Barnes would be coming over later to stay at the house and to help with the baby until Brenda got back on her feet. He also checked on the woman from the fire.

"How is she, doc? She looked in pretty bad shape last evening."

"She's good, Tom. It is a good thing that you and Daphnia found her when you did. Once she got cleaned up, I examined her and took care of the minor scrapes and bruises, but she wasn't hurt bad. She left here last night and said she would be going down to Chicago. That's the last I saw of her. But, she's tough. You know women like that they can take more than most of the women we know, and just about as much if not more than any man. She'll be fine. I'm more worried about Daphnia than I am about her."

"I'm worried about her too, Doc. She said she was okay last night, but I'm not so sure. I will keep an eye on her. Now with Daniel in such a state it looks like I will be spending as much time in the office as out. I don't know her very well, actually I just met her the other day, but she seems pretty strong and independent."

"Things aren't always the way the seem, Tom. Daphnia has lost so much. She came here for Melissa and now that Melissa is gone I'm not so sure she will stay. I don't even think Herbert Bernstein can talk her into staying now if she gets it in her head to leave. And, with Eloise keeping busy with your new baby and wife, there is just one more person who won't be there for her. I don't know Tom, she has lost a lot."

"I guess I didn't think of Daphnia when I asked Miss Barnes to come over and help out. But, don't you worry, Doc I'll see that she doesn't feel too alone. I'll talk to Mr. Bernstein and we'll keep her busy. But, maybe going back home to, where is it, Lansing won't be such a bad idea. She has friends there. And, didn't she teach school or something? I thought I heard that she had a fiancé where is he?"

"Oh, I guess she has a fiancé but I've never seen him. I think he is out west somewhere in the Calvary. She could probably go back to teaching at the little schoolhouse, but then she could have done that here if that was what she wanted to do. No, I think Herbert will do some fast-talking to keep her here for a while. But, thanks for offering to keep her busy; she could use a shoulder to cry on right now, she could do worse than you, that's for sure. Now, I better get over to your place. I think Mrs. Mason is on her way over there, too. She stopped by just before you got here, so let me get onto my business and you better get over to the Gazette, I don't think Herbert will be in such a good mood today."

"Thanks again, Doc. I'll be seeing you." Tom left the office and caught his breath; his next stop was to see Daphnia. He did not want her to leave and in his heart he knew why. He had held a real woman last night. He had lost himself in her and she in him. He wanted that again. But, in his mind he knew she had to leave because if she didn't he would not be able to stay away and that would jeopardize his life with Brenda and Johnny, and he wasn't willing to let that happen. He opened the door to the Gazette and closed it just as quickly without stepping inside. Instead, he turned and went back home to tell Brenda of all that he had accomplished.

Chapter Thirty-Nine

Mrs. Mason was already in the house and helping Brenda with her bath. "You stay out just now, Mr. Saunders, this ain't the time for no husband to be coming around. You can put the teapot on if you feel like you must do something, but just keep your distance from this room just now," the older woman scolded.

"Okay, can I see the baby?"

"No, the baby is sleeping, just put on the teapot. Is that the door I hear? You can answer the door."

It was Eloise Barnes with her valise and another larger case. There was a man helping her and Tom knew this was the carriage he had asked for. He went outside and paid the man and helped Eloise inside. "Come on in, I was just putting on the teapot. Mrs. Mason is inside with Brenda helping her with her bath; I haven't had a chance to tell her the good news that you had accepted the position. Come on in, let me show you your room."

Eloise followed dutifully and was happy to have such a cheerful place to live if only for a little while. "I'll put some of these things away while you get the teapot, I can use a cup of hot tea myself if you don't mind. Maybe the missus will be ready to meet me soon. You go ahead now."

Things were working out just as he had wanted. The doc arrived a mere moment or two after Eloise, and the house was full with talking, laughter and a crying baby. Brenda came out after her bath and looked radiant. Mrs. Mason was right behind her carrying Johnny and before anyone else could speak, Tom took the baby and introduced him to Eloise and Doctor James, "let me introduce you to my son, Jonathan Robert Saunders, isn't he perfect?"

Brenda caught her breath but didn't speak up. She knew that Tom would name the baby Jonathan Robert when she said she wanted it otherwise, why hadn't she held her tongue for a while. She smiled and gently took Tom's arm, "you should also know that little Johnny is my son as well."

Everyone laughed. Tom bent down and kissed her forehead, and smiled; he knew he had won. He had it all. His wife, his son, and he would have Daphnia, too. "I must get over to see my folks and I still need to check in at the paper; I'll leave all of you to the whims of my son and return as soon as I can." Giving Brenda a squeeze and a wink he left the house and whistled all the way to his parent's house on the other side of town.

Mr. and Mrs. Saunders lived in a large two-story house on what was considered a huge piece of land for these parts that abutted the lake on one side and the mill on the other. They had raised three children in this house and it was filled with plenty of love, laughter and forgiveness. They had been one of the first families to settle in Huron City and thought of it as their personal achievement. Any negativity or disappointment that fell upon the town or its people, fell equally on the shoulders of Jonathan Saunders, or so he thought. He had been the town's most respected citizen and the one to whom people often brought their grievances. He was responsible for getting the town incorporated and sat on its council since its inception. His name was his honor and he expected his children not to tarnish it. He had a reputation and he wanted them to share in its benefits and use it as a cornerstone upon which to build their own.

Jonathan was proud of all of his children, but a little disturbed by Tom's desire to work in a newspaper office rather than in the family business. But, nonetheless, he was proud just the same. He had wanted Tom to marry one of the young women from Huron City and tried to discourage him from marrying a woman of a different culture and upbringing, but Tom had done as he pleased and Jonathan and Gladys accepted Brenda, at least as much as she would allow.

"Pop, hey Pop, Mother, where is everyone? Don't you want to know about your perfect grandson?" Tom yelled as he ran up the steps and through the big house.

"Thomas, did Brenda have the baby? Oh my, I must go over right away. How is she?" his mother gushed.

"She's great Mother, the baby came last evening in the midst of all the chaos of the lumber camp burning and people running with water buckets from one end of town to the next. It's a baby boy, Jonathan Robert Saunders; we're calling him Johnny. He is just perfect. Wait until you see him. Where is Pop?"

"Your father is at the mill, Thomas. Best you go over and see him. Now that you are a real family man you might want to reconsider a real job instead of running all over who knows where for that newspaper. Lord knows there isn't enough news in this town to pay you a decent wage; at least not enough to support a new family. I'll bet Brenda would be just as happy if you worked with your father and brothers. Is she calling for her Mother?"

"Yes, she is. How did you know? I have talked her into waiting until spring at least before we do anything like that. I have brought Eloise Barnes over to help out for a while. Did you hear about Melissa Flanders? She passed yesterday, and was buried just before the fire at the camp."

"What was the rush? She died in the morning and was buried that same afternoon? Why?"

"I guess that since she really didn't have any family here except for Daphnia and Miss Barnes that there was no need to have a long drawn out wake. I guess that is the way the family thought she would have wanted it."

"Look, Ma, I have to run. I'll stop over later in the week, you come on over to the house whenever you get a chance; I know that Brenda will be happy to see you and you must be eager to see little Johnny. Tell Pop I am sorry I missed him, I will try to catch up with him later this evening," he said as he gave his mother a kiss and then left the house.

"I'll stop over today, Thomas. Thanks for coming by," she yelled back to him as she watched him half skip and half walk away.

As he walked back to the newspaper office he wondered how to handle what had happened with Daphnia. Maybe she would act as if nothing happened, and if she did so would he? Opening the door he saw her sitting at her desk behind a stack of what looked like a mountain of papers and boxes.

"What on earth are you doing?"

"I'm trying to make some sense of these old files. I thought I would sort them and then box them up so we could store them in the back room. I took them out of Daniel's office; I don't expect him to return anytime soon and thought you might want to move into his office. By the way, good morning. It is still morning isn't it?"

"Yes, Daphnia, it is still morning. Look, where is Mr. Bernstein? How is Daniel?"

"Mr. Bernstein has not come in yet today, and as for Daniel, like I said, I don't expect he will be returning anytime soon. I think he will be a long time recuperating from what those lumberjacks did to him, if he ever recuperates fully. But more importantly, how are you Tom?"

He tried to avoid her eyes and deliberately turned away from her. "I am fine, Brenda gave birth to a baby boy last evening. He is beautiful, Daphnia. We have named him Jonathan Robert Saunders – I am so excited about being a father to him. Brenda didn't have too bad a time, so she is already talking about having more children. We want a big family, the sooner the better. The only problem is that a family will be hard to support on my small salary here. I may have to go to work with my family or maybe even go back to Mobile where Brenda's family is eager to have her and Johnny under their roof." He said these things as smoothly as he could, but he knew they were not the words she wanted to hear. As he turned back toward her, she turned away.

"Congratulations! A new baby must be wonderful. You will be a good father, I am certain of it. Don't worry about leaving here right away, things change so quickly. Besides, I have been thinking about possibly returning to Lansing. That is where I grew up, I have property there and I can always go back to teaching, or even work with the newspaper there. After these past couple of days there are so many questions in my mind, I thought that I would try to stay busy this morning and let those nagging questions rest. Do you know anything about what happened down in the lumber camp? We still have to get an edition out this week, and that will surely be the lead story. With Daniel and Mr. Bernstein out don't you think you ought to get on that?"

"Yeah, I'll stop by the Bernstein's just to see how things are going and then get on it. I'll be seeing you." He turned and walked out the door without so much as a glance at her or even in her direction.

She watched him go and finally allowed the tears that were welling up in her eyes to escape and flow down her cheeks. Turning back to the stack of papers she once again concentrated on the task at hand.

He hated himself for walking away from her, but he knew it was the only way. He needed to return home to his wife and baby. He needed to make a life that was fair to them and one that would be met with honor and pride. He closed his eyes and prayed for courage and strength, and then he turned around and walked briskly back to the Gazette. Opening the door he immediately locked it, pulled the shade and placed the closed sign in the window. He didn't care if anyone was there or if she cared, actually. He practically ran across the room and swept her up into his arms and carried her upstairs.

Just as it was the night before, he became lost in her and she in him. They lay in bed and talked for hours afterwards and for the first time in either of their lives they felt truly connected. Not just by the physicality of it all, but by the mental stimulation and ease of communication they felt. When he got out of bed, she understood. When he walked out the door and out of the building, she watched knowing that he would come back, but that he would never truly be hers. She dressed and returned to her work. And, this would be the pattern that they would follow for the weeks, months and years to come.

Chapter Forty

Life was not normal for anyone in Huron City again once the lumber camp had burned. Even with the passage of time the events of that December seven years prior had taken their toll on everyone who had been a part of that tragic evening; and for Daphnia it was twice as tragic with the loss of Melissa while she was still grieving Martha and Thaddeus. And, of course her relationship with Tom Saunders had brought friction as well as satisfaction on many levels.

Shortly after the fire, Daphnia received a telegram from William's commander telling her that William had been killed in an explosion while they were trying to clear away some boulders blocking their passage through a mountainous terrain. She cried for days. She tried to contact his family back in Lansing, but got no reply. She wired Carl and asked that he go over and check on the family, but when he did so he found the house had been abandoned and there was no evidence that anyone had lived there for some time. The commander had sent her a small box of some of William's things, there was a lock of her hair tied with a blue ribbon, her letters and a button from his uniform. She felt guilt for what had happened between she and Tom Saunders; she felt sorrow for herself and asked God just how much more was she to lose. She tried to talk with Herbert, but he was in no condition to talk. She took long walks and screamed toward the heavens. She shouted out over the waters and hoped that somehow she would find someone to love her who would actually stay with her. Eventually she gathered herself and went on with the motions of life, she needed to just hold things together.

It was almost two weeks after hearing about William that she remembered the gold key. Walking into Herbert's office just before Christmas, she asked again that the trunk stored in his attic be delivered to her apartment, "Uncle Bert, I am sorry to bother you about this, but I am still waiting for the trunk that Papa Tad told me was stored in your attic to be delivered. I would like to have it delivered. I know this is a difficult time, but do you think we can get it over here today or tomorrow?"

"Certainly, Daphnia," came his reply and the trunk arrived within hours of her request. The two men brought it in and carried it up the stairs and placed it in the middle of her sitting room.

She took a lamp over to where the trunk sat and said a prayer before unlocking it. She closed her eyes as she lifted the lid and then opened her eyes and looked inside. There were blankets, ribbons, a small lace pillow and a photograph that was so faded it was hard to make out the face of a young woman sitting on a stool by a big window. On the back of the photograph was written,

"My dearest Thaddeus, please know that you will always be my one true love, you have my heart. Fondly, Sarah"

Daphnia couldn't believe what she had just read. She read it over and over again. Sarah was Matthew's Mother! She tried to make out the face in the photograph, but it was just too faded. "How could this be?" she thought. She continued to go through the things in the trunk but there was never anything else of any significance other than the photograph. She understood perfectly. Her Papa Tad, a man whom she had thought of as so perfect, so loyal, so honest was actually the father of Matthew and her very own grandfather. "Oh my God," she said out loud and then placed everything back into the trunk and locked it once again. She took the gold key and burned it in the potbellied stove.

She heard footsteps coming up the stairs and she opened the door and fell into the arms of Tom.

"Come in, please," she said as she moved away. "How long can you stay?"

"For a while. Do you have anything to drink? I think I could use some brandy tonight," he said, "Brenda is having one of her bad days and the house is not feeling very welcome just now."

She poured two glasses of brandy and motioned him to follow her into the bedroom. There was a fire in the fireplace, and they made

357

themselves comfortable in the oversized chair where they talked quietly and emptied their glasses before turning in for the night.

He left her sleeping and walked back home with the wind whipping the bottom of his coat around his boot tops and the thought of Christmas and the present he had bought for her. He had left it on her windowsill where he knew she would find it when she awakened.

The minute the door closed behind him, she awoke. She went to the window and waited to see him walk away. She could see his confident walk that was almost a swagger in her mind, she didn't have to actually watch him anymore. She had become accustomed to his arriving without warning and leaving the same way. "Like my mother, I am the other woman," she said as she traced his form with her finger. Then looking down she saw the box wrapped in red paper with a gold ribbon tied around it. She opened the box, there inside was a small hand mirror. It had a silver handle and the back of it had the impression of roses; it was beautiful. There was a note that read,

> *"So you can see how beautiful you truly are.*
> *Fondly, Tom*

She looked into the mirror and saw tears sliding down her cheeks. She had forgotten about Christmas with so much going on. How could she forget such an important holiday, she wondered. She would have to go out early tomorrow and pick something up for Eloise, Herbert and of course little Johnny. She took the mirror and the note and placed them on her dressing table, she would thank him later.

Going down to the office the next morning, she made a list of all the things she must do today. She would speak with Herbert about having young Michael spend more time at the Gazette. He could also help out around the Bernstein house and make deliveries for Ruth. Maybe Clarice could help out at the store and with Ruth at the house as well. She had to make time to pick up some Christmas gifts and she still hadn't spoken to Eloise about closing up the little gray house; maybe the two could take care of that within the next few days.

"Uncle Bert, if you have a few minutes I need to talk with you about a few things," she called to him as he entered the office.

"Sure, Daphnia. Got any coffee? Tomorrow is Christmas and I would like it if you would spend it with us over at the house."

"That would be nice, of course I will stop by, what time would you like me?"

"I believe dinner will be served around three, but you come whenever you want."

"Uncle Bert, I want to have Michael help out more around here. I think he could also help out over at your place as well. What do you think of having Clarice work a couple of hours a day in the store, and she could also spend some time over at your place to give Ruth a break. Right now is just such a busy time, and with Daniel not able to work, I think it might be a good idea to have Tom take on more responsibility around here, maybe go ahead and permanently move into Daniel's office and he really could use a raise with the new baby, if we can afford it, that is."

"Has Tom talked to you about more money, Daphnia. I know that he knows about me making you a part owner, but it isn't his place to talk to you about this."

"He hasn't said a word to me, Uncle Bert, and I haven't said a word to him. This is all my own thinking. I just see a need and I think this is the best way to fill it. These past two weeks have been difficult for both of us, and I just want to relieve you of some of the burden of making all of the decisions, that's all. I didn't mean to offend you."

"No offense taken, I'm sorry, I'm just tired, and with all of this stuff with Daniel. Why would those men do such a thing to him? It breaks my heart to see him this way. Do you know they practically cut off his tongue, they broke almost every bone in his body and his mental state will never be the same. And, for what? Do you have any idea what he was after down in the lumber yard?"

"Me! I would be the last to know what Daniel was up to. I have started cleaning out his office and in going through his things I still haven't found a clue as to what he might have been after. I still need to go through one more drawer in his desk and then the place will be ready for Tom to move in, but I have found nothing in any of his papers to indicate what he might have been looking for down there. How is he doing anyway?"

"He is doing as well as he can be, I guess. He sleeps most days and sits by the window when we can get him into his wheelchair, but he is in such pain that he can't sit for long. Ruth is taking it so hard. She has just about run herself ragged trying to keep up with everything. Go ahead and hire whomever you want for the house and the store, if you need more help here just do it, we will make do somehow. I'm leaving it up to you now, do what you think needs to be done." He went into his office and closed the door.

She went into Daniel's office and sat down at his desk. Opening the remaining drawer there was nothing in it but a journal. She was surprised since the rest of his desk and office had been so cluttered beyond belief. She opened the journal. There was very little writing in it and it looked like some of the pages had been removed. Seeing nothing of substance or importance, she packed it away with his other personal papers and mementos and readied them to be delivered over to the yellow house on Pine Street.

She went about contacting young Michael and with the permission of his mother she made more permanent arrangements to have him help sweep up, make deliveries and generally keep up with the chores around the place. She also asked that he be available to help out at the Bernstein house as well as making deliveries for the general store when needed. She believed him to be trustworthy and capable. One could often see him hanging around Doc James's house picking up, repairing shingles and just making things right. School was not an option for him, but Daphnia promised Clarice that she would teach him to read, write and use simple arithmetic.

Clarice agreed to work in the store in the mornings and then go over to the Bernstein house in the afternoons and help Ruth, or just give her some time off from dealing with Daniel.

Once Daniel's office was clean and presentable, Daphnia closed the door and locked it. She had decided to make this her special gift to Tom – she tied a red bow on the back of the chair and hung mistletoe from the ceiling. She also wrote a note telling him of his generous raise and left it folded in the middle of the desk.

The only thing left on her list of things to do was to purchase the small gifts for Christmas. She bought a box of chocolates for Brenda, a silver baby rattle for little Johnny, and a box of hand stitched handkerchiefs for Eloise, a book of poetry by Keats for Daniel, a hand painted calendar that she had seen in the diner for Herbert and she gave Ruth a jar of her Aunt Martha's apple butter that she had brought back with her from Sunshine Acres. For Tom, she bought a burgundy scarf with threads of silver silk running through it. She carefully wrapped, and tied ribbons on each gift. Then she bundled up against the cold and set off for the Saunders's house.

"Come in, Daphnia," Tom said as he opened the door for her, "you are out late, here, let me take some of those things."

"No, Tom, these are gifts. I know they are small, but I wanted to stop by this evening and see Aunt Ella and bring a gift for little Johnny. I hope I am not intruding."

"You're not intruding at all, Daphnia," Brenda said, "please sit. You don't come around often enough, and I would love to have another woman to visit with from time to time who is close to my own age."

Daphnia proceeded to hand out the gifts. Brenda said that she loved chocolates, and Eloise was delighted with her handkerchief. Little Johnny wasn't quite old enough to hold his rattle, but Tom helped him to shake it and everyone laughed. When Tom opened his gift of the burgundy scarf, Brenda immediately took it from him, "this makes two burgundy scarves you now, have, Tom. Only this one seems a little better quality than the one I knitted for you. "What is this, Daphnia, Cashmere? I saw one like this behind the glass case over in the General Store the other day. Mrs. Bernstein said she didn't have any idea who would buy it what with it so expensive," she then tossed the scarf back in Tom's lap.

Tom looked at Daphnia and shrugged, "I guess one can never have two many burgundy scarves, can one?"

"No, Tom, sometimes two of something is just what some people need." She stood, kissed little Johnny and her Aunt Ella, nodded to Brenda and Tom and put on her coat. "I had better be going, I need to stop by the Bernstein's before it gets too late, Merry Christmas," she said as she turned and walked out the door. Tom stood looking after her, and when she turned around he blew her a kiss, which she did not return.

Walking up the steps to the Bernsteins, she could see the light in the parlor, she gently tapped on the door and Herbert opened it for her. "Come in Daphnia, what do you have there and why are you out so late?"

"I want to be the first to say Merry Christmas, Uncle Bert," handing him his gift.

"What is this? A present for me? Should I open it now or wait until tomorrow?"

"You may open it whenever you wish," she said as she gave him a hug and a kiss on the cheek.

He carefully removed the ribbon and opened the box with the calendar folded inside. "Its perfect, Daphnia. Thank you."

"Where is Ruth, I have something for her also?"

"I'm right here, Daphnia, good grief I can't believe it is Christmas Eve, this was always such a happy time, and now well, did Herbert invite you for dinner tomorrow? You know, dear, we are not Christians, we are Jewish and we don't celebrate Christmas, you really shouldn't have brought gifts."

"Oh, I am so sorry. I just forgot and guess I got caught up in the spirit of Christmas and I think we all need a little happiness. Do you think you can indulge me?"

"Yes, yes, of course, come on in. Let's see what you have there," Ruth said almost motherly.

"Here, Ruth this is from Aunt Martha's own supply. It is the last of what I brought back with me from Lansing."

Ruth opened the box and saw the apple butter, tears came to her eyes and she leaned over and hugged Daphnia, "Martha was the sweetest woman I have ever known, Daphnia, I don't say this too often, but I loved her. Thank you. This is the most wonderful gift you could have given me."

"I brought something for Daniel, do you think I could take it up to him?"

"Maybe you should leave it here and give it to him tomorrow, I have already tucked him in for the night and I am sure he is asleep by now. You will be back tomorrow won't you?" Ruth asked as if she really meant it.

"Yes, Ruth, I will be back tomorrow. Good night, then."

Walking back to the Gazette and her apartment, Daphnia thought of how things had changed in her life.

❦

Christmas came and went. Daphnia had dinner with the Bernsteins, and Daniel seemed pleased with his book. It wasn't until the day after Christmas when Tom came to see Daphnia and she took him down to see his office. They would spend much time together in his office in the years to come, talking, arguing, and getting down to the business of running the Gazette. Herbert had turned over almost every responsibility for the daily operations to Daphnia, and over time he became less and less interested.

Chapter Forty-One

It seemed that the seasons and their passing happened with little or no notice. 1904 had been a tumultuous year and 1911 had started off much the same.

Michael had long ago buried his hatred for Daniel. He had not forgotten what he did to his mother, but came to realize that there was more in this life than hate. He wanted to help his mother make a good home for the two of them after his grandfather died. His sister, Ruby, had grown into a young woman with her own ideas. She had run away with a young man from Canada when she was only 13, neither Michael nor Clarice heard from her again. Michael was interested in working with Doctor James, but knew that he would never be able to be a real doctor. Just the same, he spent as much time with the old doctor as he could. He prided himself in being a fast learner and willing to do whatever was asked of him. And, that frequently included going over to the Bernstein house and sitting with Daniel while Ruth or Clarice were busy elsewhere.

❦

Even with all of the people who cared about him, Daniel was still able to show them all that he was the meanest sonofabitch that Michael had ever known. It didn't take anything more than self-pity to bring on Daniel's tirades and tantrums, he was just plain mean, and he enjoyed it.

He had been both physically and mentally damaged by the events that took place at the lumber camp. His body had been badly broken and his fractured ability to reason would never be repaired. He spent his days sitting in a wheelchair in front of the window looking out at nothing. He rarely spoke and almost never acknowledged the presence of anyone except for Ruth; and that was only when she would bring him his meals, which he insisted, on eating alone and without help. He was nasty and hateful to anyone who tried to pressure him into talking. His verbal barbs were like arrows of venom and he had the ability to aim them perfectly at the most vulnerable of those trying to be kind or to help him. He would spit and curse at strangers as they walked past his window, and throw whatever he had nearby at anyone and everyone who entered his space uninvited. He found himself wanting to speak with Herbert, or Tom, or someone with whom he could have a man-to-man conversation, but there was no one around him but Ruth, Clarice and Michael. He would wait for his father to come home hoping that he would stop and talk with him, but Herbert never did.

After Melissa's death Herbert no longer felt a need for another's companionship. He prayed nightly to be taken to the hereafter, but somehow awoke the next morning with no changes. And, as for talking with Daniel, that was the last thing he thought of doing. He had all but become a total recluse. He rarely came out into the main office except to ask for something or to get a cup of coffee, and then he would retreat into the room that once was full of life but now the one oil lamp that he kept burning barely gave him enough light to see his desk let alone read any of the newsprint. He spent his days fighting away the memories of his time with Melissa and his nights fighting his demons, which he believed were surely sent by Matthew. He could barely stand the sight of Ruth and avoided her at all costs. He would take his meals up to his room and eat alone. He might glance at Daniel sitting in his chair, but could not bring himself to go in or to talk with the man who was his only son. He had never talked with Daniel about all of his questions about Matthew, Grace and Melissa and he was glad. Now Daniel could sit in front of his window and wonder about it, no more questions, and no answers. He was ashamed of what Daniel had done to get himself in his predicament. He knew it had something to do with his inquiries into something that he had no business inquiring about. But, mostly he was angry that he was left alone, except for Daphnia. The irony of it all was that it seemed no one really noticed that he was absent from their lives. Each day was just a matter of putting one foot in front of the other.

Ruth's life was centered around taking care of Daniel. Even though Daphnia had hired Clarice to take care of the store for her, and to help her around the house whenever she could. She felt cheated out of what should be her golden years, and resented everything and everyone who had a part in what had happened. She knew the rumors that she had heard over the years about Herbert and Melissa were true, and she hated them both. She went about her days of taking care of Daniel and talking to almost no one. She allowed Daniel to do as much for himself as he could, but it seemed that he was in constant need. Although he could bathe, dress and toilet himself, he could not do so entirely without some help from her. She was a prisoner in her home. Even when she thought she could get a moment's peace or take a little nap he would call for her. Because of his dependence on her, she rarely left the house and when she did, she almost never went out for more than a very short while. She got no comfort from Herbert either, not that she wanted any; he was totally absorbed in his own personal hell. The past seven years had been pure misery for her and she often found herself angry at God for letting this happen to her.

Eloise Barnes was busy taking care of little Johnny who had a sister, Rachel within his first year and another brother, Colton by the time he was three, a second sister, Mary was born before Colton turned two, and it seemed that it was no time at all before Brenda gave birth to another girl, Sally. Eloise had not intended to stay on with the Saunders' once Brenda was able to take care of Johnny on her own, but she became pregnant again so soon that it seemed unkind of her to leave. And every time she started giving it serious thought it seemed that another baby was on the way, and Brenda would beg her to stay on. But, she was getting on in years and she longed to return to Boston once more before she died. She had promised herself that she would tell Brenda that she would need to look for someone else.

Brenda had begun to feel like a brood mare. All she did was have babies. She knew that she was taking advantage of Eloise Barnes, but she needed her. She had given up all hope of returning to her home in Mobile since her mother had passed around the time that Colton was born and her father followed soon thereafter, neither had ever seen any of their grandchildren. The family estate was heavily mortgaged and there was little left over for Brenda once all of the lawyers had finalized the filing of papers and selling of the property. She had resolved to accept what little there was and put it in a trust for the children. Tom had not argued nor had he any opinion or comment as to what he thought she should or should not do. She had given up nagging him about taking on a more responsible position with his father's business and giving up his job at the Gazette. She spent most of her time with the children and trying to keep her sanity about her as it seemed one came right after the other. She often worried about what she would do once Eloise was no longer able or willing to help her, but she dared not to share her fears with anyone else. She had not made many friends in Huron City, and therefore, rarely had guests in the house nor did she go visiting. She would, on occasion, take the children over to see her mother-in-law, but those times were rare, and the elder Saunders' only visited at her home when pressured to do so. She had learned to find her solace sitting alone in the early evenings after all the children were sleeping and before Tom came home sipping her brandy and reading. In a matter of seven years she had given birth to five babies, and another was on the way. They had long outgrown the house, and Tom had promised to find a way to add another room, but that was two years ago. The children were sleeping practically on top of one another, and there was always at least one baby in the room with her and Tom. She had given thought to putting some of the home remedies into place that would result in no more pregnancies, but didn't quite have the courage to do so; after this baby she promised herself that she would! She knew that Tom loved her, but not the way he had at one time, and she often thought that there may be another woman. She had heard rumors, and there were always those who were just too eager for her to overhear their gossip, but she chose to ignore what she hoped was not true. Besides, Tom was always so tired when he came home, and it was obvious to anyone who cared to notice that she never refused him. But, no more babies!

Tom was so busy trying to make ends meet and to keep everyone happy that he often forgot what he was doing or for what reason. He had borrowed more money than he would ever be able to repay, the Gazette was barely more than a one-page publication and the cost of producing it usually exceeded the revenue. He was in love with Daphnia and could not imagine his life without her, but he had a wife who seemed to keep him captive by having one baby after another. His father wanted him to become more involved in the family business, but the revenue there was barely enough to keep the doors open. There was a starch factory that had seen better days and was again on an upswing, but they had no use for his skills or talents. He felt trapped. Thoughts of going away to Chicago or St. Louis had entered his head and set up residence, but he knew Brenda would never leave Huron City now, and he wasn't quite sure if he could leave her and the children here, but he knew he had to do something. He could no longer go on living this life with the mother of his children and the love of his life living within walking distance of one another. He had been confronted with the gossip and had been able to successfully deny the truth of it, but he knew that the days of this double life were numbered. He would talk with Daphnia and pray that she would understand why he had to go. He would convince Brenda that their life would be better elsewhere, and he would tell his folks that Brenda had finally decided that raising the children in Huron City was not what she wanted; he knew they would all believe him. All he had to do was to convince himself that he could pull it off.

It had been seven years since the little town alongside the St. Clair River had been turned upside down. There was still a lumber camp, but the local vigilante squad was there to ensure that there would never be the type of "goings-on" that had taken place before. There was a starch factory that had been built and it seemed to be doing well, the mill was surviving, but no longer the sea of activity that it once was. Many of the old-timers had moved away and those who stayed still talked of the night of the big fire. As for Daphnia, she often thought of her Aunt Martha, Papa Tad, Melissa and William and of how much she missed them. Her few stolen days and nights with Tom Saunders were not enough for her anymore. She was in love with him and she knew that he loved her, but this was not working for her the way it once was.

Part VII

Life is but a circle
Reliving what once was
Our souls must come to a reckoning
With our silent lies
And their thunder we've ignored

Chapter Forty-Two

It was an especially cold and wintry day as Daphnia came down the stairs and into the office of the Gazette. She opened the shades and looked out at the icy walkway and rutted road where wagons, horses and automobiles had made their way through the town. She could see a streak of light coming from under Herbert Bernstein's door and she paused wondering if she should go in. It was unusual for him to be in the office this early and she wondered if he had actually slept there. Tiptoeing over to the door she gently turned the knob and pushed it open. She could see him sitting at his desk with his head down on his folded arms. He appeared to be sleeping so she pulled the door closed and went about making coffee and stoking the fire in the pot bellied stove when she heard him call out to her.

"Daphnia, Daphnia is that you? Can you come in here for a minute?

"Coming, Uncle Bert. Can I bring you some coffee?"

"No, just come on in, I want to talk to you."

"I'll be right there. Have you looked outside? We better get Michael over here today to knock down some of the icicles that are hanging from the corners of the building. It looks like the weather is not going to break for a while and I would hate to have us lose part of the roof. I think we must have gotten a foot of snow over night. You don't look so well, did you sleep here?"

"Don't worry about me, Daphnia. I am old, dear, I have seen my share and done even more. Truth be known, I am ready to meet my maker. But, I can't do that until I clear my conscience, sit down. And, Daphnia pull the shades and lock the outside door. We are closed for the day."

"Now Uncle Bert, you are worrying me. We can't just close for the day. Not that there is much going on anyway, but do you really want me to lock up?"

"Lock up Daphnia and put a sign on the door that we are closed for the day. Maybe I'll have a cup of that coffee after all."

She did as he asked and returned to his office and sat down in the chair in front of his desk. He looked tired and worn, there was no way she could sit there and not worry. "Okay, Uncle Bert, what is it?"

"You must sit still and listen. I have been thinking for years now of how I would tell you what I am about to tell you, or if I ever would for that matter, but maybe I had too much whiskey last night and I'm melancholy, or maybe I am just getting sentimental, but nonetheless there are some things that I want to get off my chest and you are the only person I trust to tell them to. Besides that, Daphnia, you are the only one to whom it will make a difference one way or another.

I've been looking at this old faded photograph, Daphnia. Do you know who these people are? Of course you don't. This is a photograph of my family, me, my sister, Mother and the older man here, he is my father. Herbert Daniel Bernstein, Esquire. He was a mean and overbearing man. He was almost as mean as Daniel, but not quite. You see he came to America with his family when it was easier for folks like us, Jews that is, to fit in. He was young and practiced law in Charleston. He was an only child and his parents gave him everything they could. Why, hell, Daphnia, they even gave him their own lives if you want to know the truth of it. He wanted to go north because he felt that he was being held back in Charleston so they gave in and moved to Boston, his mother came down with pneumonia and died six months after they arrived and his father, not being able to live without her put a shotgun to his mouth and blew his brains out. The most unfortunate part of it was that he decided to do so on the desk of dear old father with an audience of the firm's principal partner and two secretaries. Father could hardly stay on after that so he returned to Charleston, of all places and retook his old position. He took with him my mother whom he had met and married shortly after arriving in Boston; she was expecting me at the time, and she went willingly despite her own mother's begging her to stay.

Mother was the kindest and most gentle woman ever to live. She stood by him no matter how mercenary he became. She made a home for us in Charleston and soon became pregnant again with my sister, Grace."

"Oh my God! Uncle Bert are you telling me that ...."

Ignoring her interruption, he lit his pipe and sat back in his chair with his eyes toward the ceiling. He continued, "Mother wanted to return to Boston to deliver the baby where she would have help from her own mother; and Father allowed it. So, she packed me up and the two of us set off. We went by ship from Charleston to the Boston Harbor. I don't remember the trip, but I remember my grandparents making me stay in the outer room and away from her. When they finally let me see my mother I was ecstatic. In her arms was the most beautiful baby girl. Grace and I were almost inseparable. I was her big brother and promised I'd always take care of her. But I did not fulfill my promise and it haunts me to this day.

Of course, eventually we returned to Charleston, but by then I had grown up some and I had experienced what a loving family was like. I knew about laughter and acceptance. I understood that children make noise and need to play. I loved and was loved. Living in my father's house was nothing like living in the cottage in Boston. He was loud and demanding. He didn't show us love; he showed us fear. Grace grew up resenting him and hating him for all he stood for. Almost before she became of age, she met a man, Malcolm Humphreys. He was a kind man, a large man that could be intimidating when he needed to be. He was quite a bit older than Grace and he was in the business of providing passage to slaves from the south to the north. None of what Malcolm stood for sat well with Father and he vowed to disown Grace if she married him, but she married him anyway. Malcolm loved Grace and he was good to her. I always thought that she married him out of spite for Father, but I also knew that she had a high regard for him just the same. Once she married Malcolm, Father forbade Mother and me from ever speaking to her again. He sold his share of the practice and joined a firm in St. Louis. He had us packed and on our way to that Godforsaken City before we could even stop and say no. God forgive me, I helped him. I told my mother that it would be okay once he had a chance to cool off. I told Grace that we would see her again, that she needed to be strong. I was wrong in trying to make and keep the peace, I should have fought him, but I was young and just finishing law school myself. I was selfish. I was excited about a partnership in the firm of Mekelstein, Bernstein & Bernstein, I wanted to make a name for myself and I had decided that I could do it in St. Louis just as easily as I could in Charleston. I believed that I could find a way to travel to Charleston on occasion to see Grace; I was so wrong.

Even with the war ended, moving the Negroes from the south to the north was a dangerous business. Malcolm had made many enemies and finally decided to move Grace to a safer place and that meant back to Boston. She wrote to my Mother but Father intercepted the letters and neither Mother nor I saw even one. We had no idea that she was in Boston and I spent years looking for her in Charleston. She had moved into Mother's cottage unbeknownst to us. It was her cottage, of course, Mother had seen to that when she married Malcolm, but God only knows why she didn't tell me. Mother missed Grace so, and she hated St. Louis. She had begged Father to allow her to return to Boston even for a short visit, but he was steadfast and forbade her from even leaving the house without his escorting her. She did as he said even though he was gone most of the time, he had a reputation for visiting the brothel on the outskirts of town and those who should have honored and revered my mother for all that she had given up and for what she had done for the town turned their backs on her and instead of showing concern, they shamed her. I knew about his escapades, but was so wrapped up in my own glory that I had no idea of how she was suffering. I had my own apartment on the other side of town and I have to confess, I didn't go see her often enough. When I found out all that he was putting her through it was too late, she had managed to eventually give up. She died a sad and lonely woman aching for the love her children and her husband, bastard that he was. I vowed that day to find Grace and any feelings of love or honor that I had for him turned to hate and disgust.

It was not until we buried Mother that I realized what a traitor I had become to the two people whom I loved the most in this world. I left the practice and went to work for the local newspaper, the Post. I fell in love with the smell of the ink and the whirring sound of the press as I spun it around and around. I actually enjoyed ferreting out the stories about the corruption and the men that had made everyone believe that their way was the right way. I loved the newspaper business and I loved the Post. That is where I met Thaddeus.

He came in one day and when he stood in the doorway he cast a shadow all the way across the room. I looked up and saw him flash that smile of his, cock his head and hold out his hand. "Hi, I'm Thaddeus Flanders and I was wondering where a railroad bum might find a decent meal in this town. I have looked up and down this street and I don't see anything other than a few taverns and a brothel."

"Well, come with me and we will eat over at Miss Amanda's. She runs a small eatery in the back of the saloon. I think she might be able to put a steak and some potatoes on a plate for you," I told him

It was then and there that we became best friends. I think we talked until morning, and before we knew it we decided to meet up the next day and that was that. He told me about his life and I told him about mine. We drank, cussed, and whored around together from then on until we each got married. I was there when he first saw Martha, and he was the best man at my wedding to Ruth. We were inseparable except by the miles between us, but we always knew exactly what the other was thinking and we were always there for each other, no matter what.

It is strange, don't you think, how our lives as human beings travel in circles? It seems that we stay on the same plain with the same people all of our lives, they just become more or less intertwined, sometimes they may move to the fringe of things, but they are there just the same.

Well, that is how it was with Thaddeus and me. I miss him, Daphnia. I want to talk with him. I want to yell and curse my maker for taking him so soon. It has been over seven years and I still find myself wanting to sit down and pen him a letter, or send him a telegram that I will meet him in Chicago.

I remember the day he told me that he was leaving St. Louis and moving to Lansing to marry Martha. The irony of it was that I had decided to move here to Huron City and open my own newspaper office. We laughed at our decisions and each told the other that they were out of their minds, but we knew that we were following our dreams. We were happy for each other and I always knew that even though he didn't agree with my choice, he supported my decision and I supported his. We kept in touch and we managed to remain involved in major decisions affecting each other's lives. It was Thaddeus who happened upon Grace.

It was in the early spring and he had taken a trip to Boston. He was in a bank and overheard someone call for a Mrs. Humphreys, when he turned he saw a woman who looked just as I had described. He approached her and told her who he was and about our relationship. He told me that they had lunch and she gave him the many letters that she had written over the years to my Mother and to me that had been returned to her unopened. She asked to get in touch with me and he gave her my address. He wired me that afternoon that he had found her and that she wanted to see me. I will never forget the elation that I felt. I immediately made plans to leave for Boston and to see her. It was like Christmas, Daphnia. My prayers had been answered. It took me more than a week to get to her, but I did it.

When I arrived at her cottage, it was dark. She was alone and we sat and talked and shared memories and I told her of Ruth and Daniel. She was happy for me. She told me that Malcolm had died several years prior and that she had not remarried. She looked wonderful, so much like you, Daphnia ..."

"Oh, my, Uncle Bert, please don't tell me anymore, I don't think I can ..."

"Shh, you need to hear this. It had been years since I had seen her, and of course Ruth was insanely jealous of anyone with whom I might share my time, so I just never told her. I should have, I know that now, but I wanted to keep Grace to myself for just a little while before I shared her. So, other than Thaddeus, I didn't say anything to anyone. I just told Ruth that I had to go out of town on business, and she accepted that. I heard the rumors eventually, and everyone spoke of her in such a cruel manner. Even Ruth would say things that she didn't understand, but I never defended Grace, I just sat and kept my mouth shut. I am so sorry for that now.

Anyway, Ruth had become distant once Daniel was born. I tried to understand and even went out of my way to help her around the house more. I gave her whatever she said that she wanted. Even our house, why it was and still is one of the finest in all of Huron City. She could have had hired help but she always refused it. She wanted to manage the dry goods store and telegraph office, and I let her, but she didn't have to do that. Unlike now when every penny is stretched so thin that it is almost impossible to identify it as copper anymore. But, Ruth was never really happy. She married me because it was the thing her parents wanted her to do, not because she loved me."

"Uncle Bert, you mustn't continue this talk. I know that Ruth loves you. I know it has been difficult, but please, I don't think I can listen anymore. You aren't well. Why don't you let me take you home?"

"No! I am not ill. I am in full control, and I need to tell you this. It doesn't matter about Ruth right now. Yes, I know she cares, but that is habit, it isn't love. She was in love once, but not with me. She was in love with a man I came to despise; a man whose way with women was for his own gratification and any woman who gave herself to him could just curl up and die for all he cared. He took the best of her and used it up and then he sent her packing with nothing left, no more smile, no more happiness. She came home to me and couldn't even look me in the eye. I knew there had been someone else, but I didn't let her know. I acted like she had just been away and everything was fine, just as it was before she left. The only problem was that things were not fine before she left, but at least then she didn't have to deal with the guilt that he had burdened her with.

I saw him here not too long after she came home. I came into the store and he was standing there with his arm around her, she was crying but I didn't realize who he was then. She acted upset and ran over to me, and he asked if she was okay; he was so smooth, I thought he was just a customer who had happened in at the time she needed someone. She said that a mouse had run out from behind one of the shelves and frightened her; we laughed and that was the end of it. I saw him around from time to time after that but just thought he was another customer. I should have put two and two together, but I guess I just didn't see it. I knew he was Thaddeus' nephew, but he just seemed like trouble to me and he was always coming and going that I guess I just didn't bother to get involved. Thaddeus had told me about some of the trouble that he had gotten himself into, and while I would like to think that I kept an ear open for anything serious, I truly didn't pay him much mind. But, he was here nonetheless.

Eventually Ruth permanently moved out of the bedroom that we shared and I didn't bother to question her. She became more and more involved with raising Daniel and didn't seem to mind so much anymore if I went away. As a matter of fact, she had stopped even asking where I was going or when I might return. It is strange how we grew apart almost without me even noticing it until now.

I had begun to make regular trips to Boston every three or four months. Grace and I would sit and talk, and what time had passed didn't matter anymore. She was so full of love and forgiveness. We talked about Mother, and we shared memories of our childhood. But, when I asked her to come to Huron City to visit, she always resisted. She said that she never wanted to leave the cottage again. She told me that she felt secure and safe there and that she was afraid that if she left she would never return. There was such an innocence and vulnerability about her. She was trusting and giving. The town's people would come to her for flowers for the church, and she opened her gardens to them. She loved beautiful things and her yard and home were full of fresh-cut flowers, paintings and many different throws, quilts, and things that she had made. She made all of the costumes for the children to wear in the church plays; she had long since given up the practice of Judaism and had taken on the Lutheran Religion of Malcolm. She taught Sunday school, volunteered at the local hospital and worked in the soup kitchen on holidays. She was regarded as someone of prominence in Boston until 'He' came along and destroyed her reputation. He didn't care about what others thought. He only cared about himself and his own needs. They asked her to leave the church and replaced her in the Sunday school class. They stopped coming to her for flowers, costumes or anything else. She was asked to stop volunteering at the hospital and suddenly the soup kitchen didn't need her anymore. He didn't care. He told her that he would make it up to her. He made her believe that he loved her and that he could actually take care of her. But, he couldn't and he didn't. He didn't have anything to take care of her with. He was nothing but an alley cat that had somehow made it to the top of the world when he met her. He was trash, Daphnia! I tell you that he was nothing but trash! He had none of Thaddeus' moral qualities, and it didn't seem to bother him none. He had been raised on a lie thinking that he belonged to Joshua, and he was determined to be like him. It broke Thaddeus' heart, although I didn't find out until much later, but when I did, I was sick, sick, Daphnia, sicker than I had ever been. God, why wasn't he more like Thaddeus?

When I first saw him in the store I didn't think much about him. Just another customer, I thought, stay out of it, let him be. But, when I saw him keep coming around, and then I saw him with Melissa, he didn't come in so much anymore, and then he was gone. That's when the rumors started. But even then I was just too dense to put things together. Grace had wired me that there was someone who she wanted me to meet, but it was at a particular busy time and I had to postpone my trip until the following month, and then the next month and the next. It was the longest time I had gone without visiting her, but I just couldn't get away. It was either a busy time at the paper, or the mill was starting up, the lumber camp had opened for the first time and then Daniel was sick, first with the mumps, the chicken pox and before I knew it things were just building one on top of the other. I just simply couldn't get away. By then of course, he had her where he wanted her. It didn't take long before she was expecting his baby."

Daphnia had given up trying to stop him. She wanted to get up and run out of the office, and at the same time she couldn't move. She was in disbelief and shock at what she was hearing. It wasn't that this was news, she knew all of it already, but this time, it was like hearing it all over again but for the first time. She tried to open her mouth and beg him to stop talking, but she couldn't. She was finally getting answers to so many questions.

Herbert was oblivious to her discomfort, he needed to purge himself of his demons and clear his conscience and by God that is what he was going to do. He continued. "She was expecting you Daphnia. She wrote to tell me that her prayers had finally been answered, while she didn't have a husband, she was having the baby by the man she loved. She begged my forgiveness for disgracing the family, but made no apologies for being with child out of wedlock. She told me she was happy and asked that I come when time would permit. By the time I was able to get away, the doctor had already ordered her to stay in bed. She had a woman who came in to help take care of her, but the father of her child was nowhere to be found in Boston. He was right here in Huron City! The Bastard! He was right here under my very nose, shopping at my store, and if the truth be known sleeping with my wife."

Daphnia finally found her voice. "Wait! Stop! I don't want to know anymore. You must stop this. I won't listen to you tell me that my father was sleeping with Ruth, not Ruth!" Daphnia got up and started for the door, but before she could leave he had moved around the desk and stopped her.

"You must listen. I have given all that I have to give for my entire life. It is my turn now. Today I will unburden myself of all that I have known and very little of it that I have told. Sit down! You have wanted answers. You wanted the trunk! Well, what did you find? Did you find answers? No, you found out that your own grandfather raised you, not your uncle. Well, now I am going to tell you the other half of the story. So listen!

Grace died, Daphnia. She died when I should have been there with her. But, I wasn't. She died in his arms with you in a crib next to her. She died happy. And that bastard didn't even bother to let me know. I found out months later when the woman who took care of her wrote to me sending me back the letters that I had sent to her, they were unopened. All of the time that he was here making time with my wife, keeping Melissa in turmoil he was having a baby with my very own sister a thousand miles away and he didn't even have the decency to let me know she was dead.

I was able to keep the cottage out of the hands of the lawyers and managed to settle the estate. She didn't have a lot of debt, but Malcolm hadn't left her anything and most of the money she had to live on from our Mother had long since been spent. She managed to live off of what was left and with the money she made taking in sewing from the neighbors. I always gave her money when I visited her, and would send what I could along the way, but she never complained. In spite of the life she had, she died happy. I closed up the house and hired a caretaker to look after the place; it is yours now, Daphnia. Anytime you want, you can go claim it."

"Uncle Bert, you must stop this. I am beginning to think you are enjoying torturing me this way. What is it that you are after?"

"I'm after a clear conscience, Daphnia.

Ruth told me of the rumors about Matthew leaving Melissa for some woman back east, but I didn't know who she was talking about. And, truthfully, I didn't much care. I was busy wrapped up in my own set of problems. Father was ailing for so long before he died, his firm was in disarray and I was so tired from traveling back and forth between St. Louis and Chicago and Detroit then back home that when I got back I just tuned her out and let her prattle on. I didn't much care about anything or anybody during that time. But, then something rang a bell. Finally there was a connection.

Thaddeus told me that his nephew had once again taken off only this time he left behind his wife and baby girl. Hell, I didn't know about a child living in Huron City with Matthew and Melissa. It seemed like once Grace had passed away I just buried myself in my work. Father's estate was sizeable and I needed to be a part of cleaning up the loose ends. I became more interested in what Ruth had to say. I even started asking her questions. But once I became interested her jealousy flared up and she thought that I was interested in Melissa. Damn it, I didn't even know Melissa. I had seen her of course, it is a small town, but I never really noticed her so to speak. I knew Eloise Barnes, but not to talk to only to help her when she came into the store. I must have been the dumbest man in town. And then I had to return to St. Louis.

I was in Chicago and heard that Thaddeus was in town as well. I messaged him and asked if he could meet me for dinner or a drink. But it seems that he was on his way to St. Louis himself, something about his nephew being in some kind of trouble. We traveled together. I remember it as if it were yesterday. It was so damned cold and wet. I wasn't in any mood for spending another minute in St. Louis, and I swore that what didn't get settled someone else could just do this time.

The train ride was difficult for me. Thaddeus thought I was reading, but what I really needed was time to think. Things were all mixed up at home and there was some confusion over land owned by my late Father that was being held in some sort of restricted deed arrangement with the tenants. I was glad to get off the train and told Thaddeus that I needed to shake some things loose in my head. I had to get a minute to breathe. It was like all of the past memories were imploding inside my brain. As I walked down the street toward the Red Dog Saloon I decided that what I really needed was a drink and some meaningless conversation with strangers.

We went into the gaming house and once seated at the Black Jack Table I soon became lost in the game and was almost able to forget my troubles when I overheard some loud laughter and conversation going on at the bar. I was pulled into their conversation, as an unwitting eavesdropper.

I cashed out, picked up my drink and walked over to where the group of men were talking about a scoundrel who was about to meet up with the angel of death for having his way with the wife of the Sheriff while being kept by one of the town's widows. Listening to these men caused my blood to run cold, this story was too close to one I was all too familiar with; I had to know more. I ordered another drink and a round for the bar. God, the things they were saying."

Herbert's voice trailed off and he got up and looked out of the window. Then he continued.

"The icy rain had turned to snow and the wind was howling around the eves of the building. I looked up and saw Thaddeus standing in the doorway. He motioned to the bartender for a drink then sat down at a table near the fire. I saw him sitting there and he looked like he had lost his best friend. I had heard some things that night that I didn't want to believe. I was still trying to get them straight in my mind, and I must have looked like I was in a trance or something. But, Daphnia, finally everything that I knew to be true but had refused to hear was right there standing in front of me. I took my unfinished ale over and joined Thaddeus. Thaddeus lit his pipe and sat back in the chair.

He told me that he had gotten too old for St. Louis. He looked older than his years. He said that he had no more interest or desire for wild women or the black jack table. I didn't know what to say. I wanted to tell him what I had heard, but when I opened my mouth all that came out was a feeble toast to never returning to St. Louis.

I can see his face as he lifted his glass and then said probably the most profound thing that I had ever heard. He winked his eye, and said,

" *Sometimes I wonder if life doesn't just keep repeating itself until we either get it right or give up. I have come to believe that people do the same things over and over until they get their comeuppance in this world, then life just stands right up and pisses on their shoes and walks away laughing.*"

"I smiled and agreed with him and then I leaned back in my chair and let my mind race over what I had heard at the bar. It seems that one of the fellows in town had worn out his welcome and none too soon. It seems this man had run out of cash, and was once again preying on one of the widow's while keeping time with the prominent wife of the local sheriff. The men were all too willing to fill in the blanks of this guy's past, they told me of the many escapades and close calls that this fellow had been in, they were eager to share stories about how he had lived with a widow up in Boston some four or five years back and leaving her with child only to return to her when she was on her death bed. But that wasn't the boldest thing he had done, he kept time with a woman from Huron City who was married and who had left her own child and husband to stay in St. Louis for months just to be with him, what a meal ticket she was. He had bragged that while she was no looker, she had money to spend and she was eager to spend it. She carried him for months paying his gambling debts and bar tabs, then he up and left her stranded when he met an empty headed beauty back east. Word had it according to the men that he had at least one bastard girl child born to the Boston Widow and Lord only knew of how many more strewn around the country. Now, he was in over his head with the wife of the local Sheriff as well as being deeply indebted to one or two of the men with whom he played poker.

I felt my blood turn to ice as I listened to the men. I wanted to engage them in conversation. I finally got up the nerve to ask one of the men about him.

"Just who is this guy, and where does he live?"

"Aw, he sleeps bout anywhere, but I thank he's up at the Fairmont, why? Your missus one of them that's keeping him company?"

"No, no, not my wife, of course not. I am just here on business. I just came into town this evening and will leave tomorrow. Just curious, boys, just curious. Does this Casanova have a name?"

"Well, bub, I guess Casanova is good enough, most of the ladies just call him Mat but the men in town have added their own version, they refer to him as Mat the Cad" but if you see him, you'll know him, he's to proud to be humble. But, don't worry, I don't expect him to be out tonight, not with the Sheriff looking for him, if you know what I mean. And, I don't think he'll open the door to that shabby little room of his for just anybody. At least not to nobody without a feminine voice, that is."

The men at the bar howled at this last remark. I couldn't listen anymore; I had to walk away. It was then that I saw Thaddeus enter the saloon. I was sitting there at the table with him in a state of confusion like I have never known. The voices of the men were still loud and their frequent eruptions of laughter were almost more than I could bear. I told Thaddeus that I had promised myself every time I came to this hellhole that I would never return again, and this time I meant it. I told him that I had some things to take care of and that I would see him back at the motel. He didn't seem to mind, and actually looked relieved to be able to sit alone.

He told me that he found his nephew at the Fairmont, but that he didn't expect that he would still be there tomorrow. He said that Matthew had promised to leave town immediately, but had just one stop to make. Thaddeus was angry that Matthew was still flirting at the dangerous thought of seeing the Sheriff's wife just one more time.

I left the bar and walked out into the night. I knew just about the path that one would have to take to get from the Fairmont to the sheriff's house in the dead of night. I knew the alleyways and back roads of St. Louis as well as anyone, and I traced his path. I didn't have to go far before I saw him. I replay our conversation to this day in my mind. I'll never forget his face or his arrogance.

He didn't see me at first, but then I came out of the shadow... ... ... *"Matthew Flanders?"*

"Yes, that's right whose asking?"

"Well, I'm the husband of Ruth Bernstein, does that ring a bell?"

"Hmmm, Ruth Bernstein? Yeah, I seem to remember that name. Doesn't she run some little store back in Huron City? Is that your wife? Well, gee, buster, I'm sorry about that. What can I do for you?"

"How about Grace Humphreys? Do you remember her?"

"Now, look, mister. I don't know what you want, but I got no business with you. Whatever Ruth told you is between the two of you. But you keep Grace out of this."

"You know something, Matthew Flanders. Sometimes bad luck is just plain bad luck. Don't worry, though, it's all you'll ever know. You have managed to skate around from town to town and woman to woman without too much bad luck, but now it is here and I'm the man to see that you get your share."
... ...

He backed away from me. I thought he might try to run for a minute, but he decided to try to talk me into my senses. It didn't work. I already had my pistol out and I aimed and pulled the trigger. I saw him fall. It was like watching someone go down in slow motion. It took a long time but his face hit the ground first. I saw the mud fly up and land on the cuffs of my trousers. And then, I just turned and walked away. I slept that night better than I have slept since.

The next day I finished up my father's business and returned to Huron City two days later. That is when I saw you and Melissa. I had gotten in the afternoon before and I was sick. It had rained the entire time I was in St. Louis and I had managed to come down with a bad case of pneumonia. Well, anyway, I got into Huron City and went directly over to Doc James' I was in a bad way. It wasn't until the next morning that I was able to get myself together enough to go back to the station and pick up my bags. That was the moment of truth for me, so to speak. I saw you there with Melissa and Eloise Barnes.

It all became crystal clear. I realized who you were and that I had just killed your father. I had to make things right, but I didn't know how, not then anyway."

Daphnia jumped up from her chair and ran over to the older man. Grabbing him by his shoulders and shaking him she yelled and screamed. She cried and finally collapsed against him. "My God, My God! How could you? You killed my father and you are proud of it! How did you get away with it? Oh my God." She sobbed.

Herbert moved her back to her chair. "Sit down, Daphnia. I never said that I was proud of anything. I said that I made some things right and I did it in a wrong way maybe, but I made them right nevertheless. I'm not so sure that I ever got away with anything. I have suffered, and so has everyone who knew and loved Matthew Flanders.

News finally got around that Matthew was dead and everyone assumed that it was the Sheriff or one of the other men of the town. Thaddeus and I never talked about that night but I always suspected that he knew the truth. It took a while but the two of us finally came to terms with how intertwined our lives had become and we agreed that we would protect you from the truth until you were old enough to understand. I guess you are old enough now.

I made it my business to set up a trust for you and to set aside a monthly stipend for Melissa. I became a friend to her and, yes, Daphnia, eventually we fell in love. Ruth never asked about her or about where I went or what I did. I was discreet and there probably aren't more than the three of us now who even know about it. I think Thaddeus figured it out before he died, but other than Eloise Barnes, Melissa and myself you are the only other person to know the truth about Melissa and me. Please don't hate me." He got up from his chair and put on his coat and hat."

"Where are you going? Don't hate you? You have just told me that you killed my father. What am I supposed to feel? You can't just unburden your conscience and then expect me to deal with it. You can't just leave …"

"I can and I am. I love you Daphnia. I loved your mother, I loved Melissa, and I despised your father. He cheated three women that I cared about out of a life of happiness; he deserved to die and I'm not sorry that I was the one who sent him to hell. Before I leave I have just one piece of advice, stop the cycle! Tom Saunders has a family, let them live it in peace. I know you love him and he loves you, but he made a choice long before he ever met you to marry Brenda. I'm sorry that young man you were engaged to didn't make it, but you have some thinking to do, Daphnia. Good night."

He walked out of the building into what appeared to be a solid wall of falling snow. For the last time Herbert Bernstein walked from the newspaper office that he had given his life to and home toward the yellow house on Pine Street.

Daphnia was dazed from what she had heard. Walking into the main room of the Gazette, she looked about but wasn't quite sure what she was looking for. She checked the lock and cross bar on the front door and then turned toward the stairs leading to her apartment. Looking up she saw what looked like beams of light shining through the cracks around the door. She could hear the voices of her Uncle Thaddeus, Aunt Martha and William Johnston; they were laughing and calling out to her. She felt tired and older than her years. As she ascended the steps toward their beckoning voices she ignored the knocking at the door behind her and Tom's calls for her to open up.

The End.

Breinigsville, PA USA
15 October 2009
225858BV00001B/4/P